To Nicole
  We are so ~
of our lives. It is ~~ you~~ ~ ~~~ ~m
as part of our family.
    Enjoy the book. I really loved writing
it. And the CD, its a little bit of the
musical ones in the family.
    When are you coming to see us in our
new home.

The World
United

love, Peter.

peterdrfama@icloud.com

The World
United

PETER FAMA

LiFi PUBLICATIONS PVT. LTD.
NEW DELHI

Published by:
LiFi Publications Pvt. Ltd.
211, 2nd Floor, Gagandeep
12, Rajendra Place, New Delhi–110 008, India
Phone : (011) 2574 1000
E-mail : info@lifipublications.com
Web : www.lifipublications.com

ISBN 13: 978-93-82536-32-1   ISBN 10: 93-82536-32-9

Copyright © Peter Fama 2015

Peter Fama asserts the moral right to be identified as the author of this work.

First published in 2015

Cataloging in Publication Data—DK
[Courtesy: D.K. Agencies (P) Ltd. <docinfo@dkagencies.com>]

Fama, Peter, 1964– **author.**
    The world united / Peter Fama.
      pages   cm
    Novel.
    ISBN 9789382536321

    I. Title.

    DDC 823   23

Printed in India by D.K. Fine Art Press (P) Ltd., Delhi–52

To
Salvatoré 'Samuel' Famā,
from whose seed I am,
and to
Maria Pauline Emelia 'Peggy' Fama
who bore and reared me

Preface

This book was written over a period of two years, in three countries, part of which, was while traveling in Thailand in the cold season of 2004. Some in the Republic of Korea, and the beginning in rural Ontario. Several people have asked – "Why did you write this book?" And I must answer with a question, "Why does a man climb a mountain?" And the answer – because it's there. I wrote it because it was always there. There in my dreams, there in my travels, there in conversation, and there in my mind.

When one writes a book, or a song, a play, or any form of art for that matter, there are certain necessary ingredients that must be present. For each form, the right components are essential. You have to have a plot because it is the kernel of the story. You must have the setting in just the right place, or places. The characters are developed according to the needs and shape of the story. If you are an author, or an artist, or an entrepreneur for that matter, you will understand these qualities and the inclusion and arrangement of them to the success, or failure of the product. In the right measures, in the right way, it will mean beauty and satisfaction, for the listeners, the readers, and all the recipients of your final creation.

Is it a true story? No, but it is set in the future, and anything that is forward looking could someday become. The future is not yet made. Yet, the things that already are cannot be unmade. Therefore, we will look to the future. The past is gone. Let us dream then, and in the following pages and chapters, as the story unfolds, may you see the picture of what was intended, of what was painted, and woven and that which developed and grew…like a tree stretching out in all directions, with roots that go down deep, and fruit borne at just the right time in its own way.

Enough of these cryptic sayings, let us delve into the clarity and the plain language of words, for that is all we have to communicate with, in whatever tongue you are familiar with. It is words that you are going to read, or perhaps have already read, and words that you have purchased to discover what this story is all about. And we certainly want you to get your money's worth. Yet, technically speaking it was not the words themselves to be exact, but the ink, the paper, the binding, and possibly the shipping. Now we are mixing words and I do not want to do that, but to be clear.

This is a story about hope; it is a story of peace. It is a story of dreams, and of love; and also of a quest: a search for truth. It is a story of war, and of peace; of good, and of evil; of travel and adventure, world diplomacy and international intrigue. Now that I record these words after the novel has been finished, I do see that you certainly did get what you paid for. Writing a book on the one hand is not that hard to do. And then on the other hand, it is no small task. It is easy, in that, it is only words. Just words from your heart or head, whichever the case may be, put down on paper (usually anyways; although these days you'd be surprised at how many recorded words never make it to paper). The harder part is that it requires breadth, and scope, and timing, and dedication, and consistency, and discipline, and passion, and creativity, and sacrifice, and after it's written… wisdom and decisions and strategies and co-operation and gas and trees and stamps and credit cards and people. People who finally absorb and mentally ingest the words on the pages, and either are entertained or enlightened, or simply appreciate the art for its own sake, I do not know which. It is up to the receiver what their own personal response is.

I want to thank those who assisted in the making of this book. All those professors at Handong Global University who engaged in meaningful (or possibly what might be considered trivial) conversations, and that includes those who actually are real professors, (thanks Dr D.G. Sasser). Thank you to all, whether knowingly, or unbeknownst to them, you passed on information, trivia, or words that helped shape the story into what it is now. Thanks to those who provided the reality all along the way, which was then turned into fiction by way of creative freedom and poetic license. Those who may be in the story, or it may seem like they are there because the name is similar or there is some resemblance in some way shape or form, this was unintentional and all was generated out of the natural flow of the story. But I want to thank all who had some dealing with myself and so in some way influenced my experience, whether it be for good or ill, only God knows, and in fact in the great scheme of things will nevertheless use it in the end, ultimately for the Greater Good, and all will be made right again, perfected, purified, complete.

I also thank my large family, my mother, and all our brothers and sisters for their affiliation and love and support.

And without question, my companion and friend, my wife Joanna, thank you for all that you are. To Joanna's family, the Schlatter's, especially her father and mother, thanks for their service and love. Thanks also to the Kanta family for their love and hospitality. And on this first edition of the book, thanks to Fred and Judy Fama, and Peggy Fama, and thanks to Mary Anne Stockdale, all of them for their revision consulting work. And to Rico Fame for his marketing connections and for *I Shall Be Free No. 10*. Thanks to Rose Belfry for her good suggestions and the borrowed foam. Thanks to Tess Fama for her emails and her art. Thanks to Tony Fama and Linda Morton for those times at Tim Hortons and for advice. Thanks to Mike Fama for sharing music and life. Thanks to Linda Williams for talks on the phone and secret meetings at the German Embassy. Thanks to our eldest, Doreen Bligdon for her seemingly endless optimism and enthusiasm. Thanks to all of our friends that we have in Peterborough, Canada. Thanks to all my friends at Bangkok University. And also at Nakhonpathom Rajapat University, Udonthani Rajapat University, and King Mongkut's University of Technology North Bangkok. Thanks to D.K. Agencies' new arm, LiFi Publications and to the staff.

And anyone else I didn't mention, but you think I should've – *thanks*.

Even though I am not acquainted with him personally, Mr R Dylan deserves my gratitude.

Thanks,
P DR FAMA

1

There were seven billion other people on this planet, and he was only one. Dalee opened his eyes to another day in his home. Slowly he got himself ready, performing his morning rituals. After having breakfast he made his way out to the street, the public, the cruel world. He dreamt of a Utopian society again last night. But he couldn't think of that right now. He must shake off the cobwebs and press on to this new day. To the responsibilities that lay before him. To the people who expected him and that depended on him.

In Washington there were few jobs that he could do or really even wanted. But the nation's capital had held a certain allure for him, a certain inexplicable fascination. He didn't know what it was, but there he was, with his wife, living and working in Washington DC, in the United States of America. The most powerful nation in the world, and there he was, right in the center of it.

Dalee sometimes thought about the past, about former empires and their height. He liked to compare them with today's current situation. 'What was the difference?' he thought. Those nations had their pinnacle. They had their great achievements, in technology, in war. They rose to a certain peak...and then they all declined. That's right; they all had a period when they began to decline. Egypt, Babylon, Rome. In fact, great as they were, none of them are present today. Sure, there are vestiges of them, but those nations as superpowers, are now nothing but a yellowed page in a history book. A crumbling artifact in an archaeology exhibit. A tourist site for someone on a vacation to look upon for a few seconds and then move on. So, how can a country keep its place? How can America, number one in our world today, maintain its power? He didn't know the answer, and in fact he had a silent, gnawing sense, that he did not think there was a way.

On he went, past other citizens, rushing to make it to work on time. Hurrying across busy intersections, jammed with the traffic of the morning rush. He wondered sometimes, if anyone else thought about these things. But the looks on their faces, the conversations with them over lunch, and the content of the media gave him the answer. 'Avoid it. Run away. Fill your head and your life, with things, with noise, with distractions, so you'll have no consideration of where we're headed.'

Dalee had a 9.30 appointment with Penny to go over the travel schedule for Sam Delainie's trip. When he got into the office she quickly told him that she'd be there in just a few minutes. That gave him enough time to check his email, gather together all the necessary notes for Mr Delainie's itinerary, and to catch his breath and compose himself. Preparing for the travel arrangements for all the officials in his department was part of his job. Foreign Affairs, it had such an international sound to it, but at his level there wasn't much foreign involvement. Most of his work was done by communications using various internet technologies, and he didn't need to actually go to any foreign land, which was fine by him, in some cases, because of the serious risk involved in certain regions. But sometimes he would like to get to experience it first hand.

Penny was late as usual. They exchanged their small talk for a few seconds and got down to the schedule. "Okay, what time is he arriving in Cairo?" she asked as she gulped her coffee to wash down a bite of doughnut.

"6.32 a.m. Cairo time. Dr Hassad will meet him at the airport. He will be there for only three days. After that it's on to Jerusalem. He arrives there at 4.18 a.m. their time. We thought it would be a safer time given the situation there."

"What kind of security have we got this time?" she asked.

"The usual one," he answered, but Dalee had never got used to the elaborate measures the American government used for security purposes. There would be an eighteen-person team accompanying Mr Delainie throughout the entire trip. But the firearms were really the incredible part. It was enough to start, and win, a small war. When it came to protection, they didn't take any chances.

Once they had formalized the information and had it stored on the computer, Dalee could go over it, scrutinizing every detail until it was flawless. Then and only then could he submit it to his superior. It took 55 minutes but when he was finished, it was ready and it was perfect. Once his boss saw it, it would be sent directly to Delainie's laptop where he could access it. Paperless society, this was the latest trend and politically correct buzz word. It came right after – cashless society.

Submitting it to his boss simply meant emailing it to him.

But then he did have to follow up with a phone call. "Stan? Ya, it's done."

"Can you come in?" was the quick reply.

"Ya, sure. I'll be right there. What's up?" But he had already heard his answer and cut out. It took only three minutes to walk to Stan's office, but it was long enough to wonder what he wanted. It was obviously something else since he had only just sent that morning's work. Was it something good or bad? He didn't have a clue.

His boss merely looked up at Dalee as a form of greeting and then began. "We've noticed your work." Okay, could be bad. "And your drive," he continued. Uh-huh, sounds good. "We want to send you out with Mr Delainie this time Dalee. It would be like a trial for you. To see how you make out." He was a little surprised, and relieved that it had indeed turned out to be something apparently good. "But that's only a week away now, do we have time to…"

"We've already included you officially in the trip," his superior reassured him. "You have clearance at every stage. We just need your acknowledgement." Normally he enjoyed a little time to think about things, to not make rash decisions quickly under pressure. But in this case he knew the answer was yes.

"Of course I'll go."

Finally, he thought, a chance to see it for myself. Sure it was a sensitive area, but he'd take that risk. With their firepower it really wasn't much of a gamble anyway, so why not go for it. He'd have to break it to Janvieve. That could be a problem. But eventually she'd understand.

Okay, he had to think. What personal preparations did he have to make? He considered this on the subway ride home.

He saw some Middle Eastern passengers get on the next car and it was a vivid reminder of where he was going. He couldn't help but feel a twinge of fear for the first time since it made him think of the danger involved. Brushing it off, he tried to think of his plans, and what this could mean if he did well on this assignment. Cairo, and then Jerusalem. He looked forward to it. To the cultural colorfulness of it. But mostly to the being in the center of it. Yes, Washington was the center of the United States, but this was the center of the action, the intensity, of the international community. All eyes were on this place wondering what will happen next. What does the future hold? For them, and also for us all.

✦ ✦ ✦

2

The plane bumped onto the runway. The trip over the ocean had been uneventful. He didn't sit with Delainie but was told that he would be briefed when they arrived. The security team was a serious bunch, not talking much; they were concentrating on memos they were given to go over beforehand. He liked being in on one of these Foreign Affairs deals, and this time on foreign land. The objective had been simple as he'd understood it. Meet with the government representatives; discuss the conflict in Israel, and possible economic repercussions. Then in Jerusalem, discuss possible sanctions, and try to leave on a positive note, if possible. He didn't actually know what his mission was there. He was told to observe.

The air was stifling. He could hardly breathe, but the aides were swift and efficient and they were quickly brought to the limousine. Here, he was permitted to accompany Mr Delainie. "How did you find the trip, Dalee?"

"Fine sir, fine. And you?"

"Typical," he commented. He knew he flew often so it must become routine no matter where you go. The waiting in the airport, boarding, take-off, a long mundane flight with the usual punctuations of activity of travel companions, descent, and then the arrival. Modern travel was incredible and yet it could become so generic. The sights at their destination were anything but boring though. Bustling activity on both sides of the street. Vendors everywhere selling chapattis and fruits, strips of various meats roasted over crude barbeques. Bright colored jewelry glistening in the blinding Mediterranean sun. Racks and tables full of clothing of all styles and colors. Carpets, kitchenware, garden tools, religious icons, trinkets, live animals, toys, magazines. If you could think of it, you could find it there. It was a new experience for Dalee. It seemed so uncivilized and chaotic to him, and yet at the same time it had its own kind of rhythm. This society had its own style of civilization, its own brand of order in the midst of chaos. He didn't understand it, but there it was: moving, alive, almost fluid, on both sides of the road as they wound their way through to the heart of the city.

"Alright, here's what we're in for," Mr Delainie began. "We'll meet with two representatives, one of the Egyptian government, and the other of the Arab League of Nations." That much he knew. "We need to go out of there, with them, convinced that we are not condoning what the Prime Minister of Israel is doing militarily. Any hint of the opposite of this, and we've lost them. Do you understand, Dalee? This is extremely important." He assured him that he did. And he knew that 'lost them' was in reference to the oil trade agreement the United States had with several Middle Eastern countries, and he was also aware of the ongoing tension between the West and the Middle East over the massive terrorist attacks which took place on the American soil. Something, before though unheard of, but now had become a distasteful, unexpected reality.

"How's your dental and DNA records?"

"Sir?" he asked, puzzled at this change of topic.

Then with a grim smile Delainie explained, "You never know out here when someone might need to look them up to identify your remains." He didn't like his implication or his sense of humor.

The briefing lasted about fifteen minutes and the drive was about an hour. But he also gave him more information to digest in the form of recent communiqués between the Arab League and the Vice President. The messages were brief but there was definitely some underlying hostility in the carefully selected words.

When they arrived at the estate, they were escorted to the guest house by three lovely Egyptian women, dressed in traditional costumes fitting for Cleopatra's court. After getting settled in they were called down to an elaborate breakfast buffet in an airy sunlit dining hall in the main building of the estate. Egyptians, from what he was seeing so far, certainly made an effort for a good first impression; in spite of the tensions. As far as he was concerned, traveling was hard work, and this was the first decent food in many hours, so he was more than willing to oblige. There were all the American favorites of course, and then some more exotic foods, that you might not normally eat for breakfast. Fried bananas, some type of waffle filled with a colored whipped cream, every kind of fruit you could think of, and then ones you had never seen, like rambutan, cactus fruit, jackfruit, and some strange kind of grapes. Eating whatever he thought looked safe, and afterward washing it all down with a very small cup of extremely syrupy coffee, they turned their attention to the matters of the morning.

Dr Hassad had motioned to the dark complexioned gentleman on his right, indicating he was the official representing the Prime Minister's cabinet. They rose with him and bowed slightly as he gestured with his hand. "It is an honor to have you with us today. We look forward to working together on an acceptable bilateral agreement." He sounded civil enough, Dalee thought. They certainly picked the right one in his case. The other one, introduced next, however, seemed to have an air of indignation about him. He was dressed in an all-white, cotton, long-style shirt, that went down to his knees, and had an intricate embroidered design all over it. His head was covered by a small rounded cap made of the same material. Below the cap was the face of a man, who had lived through conflict, listened to and had been a mediator in a long-troubled region. And the eyes. Dark and serious, and sharp, but somehow intelligent, and could show a complacent diplomacy.

"We are pleased that you have arrived safely gentlemen," he said, his accent thick but his English good.

There was some small talk and then they moved to a conference room where Delainie professionally navigated his way through the issues of their trade agreement with them, the present situation in Israel, and diplomatically responded to comments about the terrorist attack in America. By lunchtime they were beginning to feel the effects of the time change and the jet lag, so Dalee was relieved to hear that their sessions were recessed until three in the afternoon. He took that opportunity to go back to his suite, check his email, go over his notes…and to doze off….

A loud knock on the door awoke him, but not quite fully. He was still in a drowsy state of mind when an aide entered the room to inform him that it was time to go. The afternoon, and then the evening, were basically going over the same ground, but just in more detail; and then documented for reports on both sides. During those meetings, and ones the following day, he was beginning to see how Delainie tactfully used diplomacy to reassure their hosts of disapproval of the current position of the Israeli Prime Minister. He kept to his priority in spite of accusations of, too harsh, and possible misdirected retaliation to the terrorist attack.

The third day in Cairo was mainly a wrap up and then a prep time for the main leg of their trip, in Jerusalem. He felt the past few days were just the preliminaries and the real business of their journey was about to begin. Although this was Dalee's first trip to this part of the world, he had seen a lot of the rest of it in previous travels. He'd always wanted to go, he just could never bring himself to take the plunge. But now he was going. Technically it was the next morning, but really it was the middle of the night as far as he was concerned. The flight was at 3.10 a.m. It seemed a lot easier on paper when he was scheduling it for someone else, but now that it was him going he thought it was an odd time to be flying. However, he remembered the security concern, and bit the bullet.

✦ ✦ ✦

3

Once these preliminaries were out of the way Delainie and Dalee were able to sit down and go over the plan for the last part of the trip. Late in the afternoon in the guest suite of Dalee's superior, they sat side by side with Delainie's laptop in front of them. The security team was in the next room going over their layouts, schedules, maps and various drills in the event of an unpleasant incident. This kind of incident in this region meant highly trained manoeuvres which require quick reflexes and split second decisions. Dalee was glad he was in his room and not theirs.

"As you know Dalee, we will meet with Ambassador Philip Carnagie, and General Gandenberg, the military leader of Israel's army, on the first day in Jerusalem. I know Ambassador Carnagie personally, so this helps to break the ice."

"Why is it that they are sending the military leader to discuss this with us?" Dalee asked.

"I know. It's not something I'm looking forward to," Delainie responded. "I see it as an attempt to heavy hand us. They mean business. But regardless, we must maintain our position with the Muslim side. And not only that, I cannot also allow myself to be dissuaded from seeing their opponents the following day. Chairman Assad is expecting us and we owe

that to the Palestinians. We simply cannot afford to see only his
and their side of things. Not only because of economics, but
also because of our alliances." Dalee understood clearly.

They had ordered a light supper brought to the room,
and worked right through. After wrapping up, Delainie
commented, "I don't suppose we'll sleep much tonight." It was
then after nine in the evening, and they would need to prepare
to get their flight in a matter of hours. Dalee considered that
he probably wouldn't sleep, because of the odd time of the
flight, and also because of his anticipation toward arriving in
Jerusalem. When they both retired to their respective bedrooms,
Delainie opened his laptop again to make a few notes, but Dalee
flicked on the television to try catching some bit of recent news
that may shed some light on the crisis. GNCN's coverage of
flooding in Qinghai province in China was the last thing he
remembered…. And then a loud knock abruptly awoke him
from his slumber. "Half hour till departure," the voice said. He
sat up quickly and rubbed his hands over his face. "Better get
ready," he groggily mumbled to himself.

The time passed quickly, and suddenly the short flight was
over. They landed at the main airport of the embattled land
in the thick darkness over an hour before dawn. Even at this
early hour there was still activity starting to develop in the
streets and open markets. They were escorted to, what looked
to Dalee like a palace. The people of this part of the world
certainly had a style and cultural richness that the West lacked.
They were all shown to their private quarters, and the two
American government officials were informed that the first
meeting would be at 8 a.m., right after breakfast. They moved
into a type of conference room after they had eaten. A large

decorative mahogany table sat in the center of the room, with ornate elaborate seating surrounding it. The room itself was graced with the presence of various paintings, sculptures, and religious artifacts.

Delainie strode across the room and firmly shook the Ambassador's hand. "Phil," he said smiling. "Good to see you again. How are you keeping?"

"Well, I am personally all right," Mr Carnagie replied. "It's just the circumstances that we're in presently, as I'm sure you understand."

"Of course. And we're going to do everything possible while we're here, I assure you."

"Gentlemen," a voice authoritatively announced. "If we could all be seated, we can get started." Slowly the table filled with the occupants of the room.

"All right, let us begin with the first order of business. General Gandenberg, do you foresee the possibility of a mutual ceasefire in the near future?" Delainie queried.

The General looked directly at him and said, "How am I supposed to mutually agree on anything with a terrorist organization? It is not a nation we are dealing with, but a band of rebels. You, Mr Delainie of all people, as an American, should understand this above all others." And everyone present understood his reference.

"Surely, we can separate a 'band of rebels' as you call them, from the good people of Palestine," the Ambassador joined in.

"Mr Ambassador, my people have gone over this ground before with you. We have no more patience with these senseless killings of civilians by way of suicide bomb attacks. You've seen the statistics. Anyone can turn on the news and see it. You don't have to be military or diplomatic personnel to see what's happening. No my American friends, we have taken too much for too long. For a year and a half now we have tolerated senseless violence at the hands of the Palestine people which you call good. Now is the time for my army to retaliate. It is crush or be crushed. There is no other alternative."

"General, we have got to consider the Palestinian people, and more importantly their allies. If only for your own sake and for your own people's security. Think of the broader implications. The Americans want to help you in every way possible, but we have our alliances too," Delainie explained.

"I understand that your people are not under the heavy attack that Israel is right now, and has been for many months." Sam Delainie nodded his head in sad agreement. "But we are here, and we must fight to survive," the General added.

And with a look of disappointment, Delainie replied, "Then you leave me no choice General Gandenberg."

"And you leave me none either Mr Delainie," he said, returning his gaze with one of equal potency.

They had feared that it might come to this, but Delainie was still optimistic. There would be other sessions. But he had to admit that the General's position was understandable. In his position he would have done the same, sooner in fact. However, he was not in his position, and he had his own priorities and objectives to fulfill. Dalee was thinking to himself: It certainly did not look possible with a beginning like this. What was next? What diplomatic manoeuvres did Sam Delainie have in mind for the coming sessions? The idea of sanctions was clearly in the cards because of the apparently firm Israeli position which had just been presented to them.

Outside photographers flashed, video cameras rolled, and microphones and lines were tangled together in an attempt to get a comment, a word. Some clue as to the course of events which had been set in motion. "Mr Delainie, could you give us an indication of the outcome of the meetings today?" the first question thrown out at him. "Nothing concrete yet I'm afraid," he remarked placidly. Two more were hurled at him immediately after, "Do you think there is hope for a ceasefire? Does General Gandenberg plan to declare war on Palestine?" He ignored them and got into the limousine. Dalee was left alone for a few seconds. Several questions were fired at him simultaneously, to which he had no time to respond. He simply assured them that the press conference would cover everything on their return to Jerusalem tomorrow. He ducked into the car and it slowly began to move away, through crowded streets, a sea of faces etched with concern and strain. On and on through the city, to their next destination. To the camp and headquarters of Chairman Assad and the PLO. The sworn enemy of Israel, and the ally and friends of the Muslim world.

✢ ✢ ✢

4

The compound of the Palestinians was somewhat primitive compared to the previous places they had visited, but it was no less ornate, and the inhabitants were just as hospitable. With much fanfare, the Americans were met as they emerged from their vehicle, and then ushered through the waiting crowds, to the compound of Chairman Assad. All the while however, the security detail kept their bodies close to the two officials. Assad met them inside in his greeting room surrounded by his closest aides and advisors. He approached Mr Delainie and kissed him on both cheeks. Then shaking his hand, he gestured to a comfortable looking sofa behind him desiring for them to make themselves at home. After sitting down, Delainie introduced Dalee. With a clap of his hands, various fruits and other refreshments were brought for Assad, and distributed to his guests.

"You must be tired, my friends," he said with his characteristic gesturing of the hands. "Our sun, I'm afraid spares no one or nothing." They thanked him and appreciatively took the drinks. After exchanging some small talk of their journey so far, their host announced, "We will not weary you any further, my friends." And after clapping his hands again, he spoke in Arabic to two aides who had appeared. "These men," he continued with a smile, "will show you where your rooms are. Please let them know if there is anything you require." And with that they were escorted out of the welcoming room. Due to the lateness of the hour, they would begin their business the next morning.

The next day Assad informed his guests that he regretted he had to join his military leader in the war room, but that he would join them as soon as possible. His closest advisor would take his place until his return. Mr Sahad greeted them in the welcome room, and apologized for this rescheduling. "Chairman Assad has some very pressing matters which have just come up. He must deal with them immediately."

Delainie replied, "We quite understand. Can we begin then?"

"Certainly. Please follow me."

Mr Sahad led them into a room off the main hall. They were shown their seats and offered coffee, and some Arab-style pastries: walnut and raisin cakes, biscuits with sesame seeds, and various sponge cakes. "How did your meeting with the Israelis go?" he began, wanting to get right to the point.

"Not very well I'm afraid," Delainie replied, glancing over at Dalee. "General Gandenberg is quite firm on his position. A ceasefire seems really out of the question at this juncture, unfortunately. However, on our return we will see him again, the day of our departure from Jerusalem. I plan to make at least one last effort before we leave."

"Good, good. You know we are very grateful for all that you and the American government are doing on our behalf. All these terrorist attacks, I'm afraid, are putting us in bad relations with the Jews. They don't seem to understand that it is beyond our control," the advisor explained. "The group responsible is very secretive and difficult to communicate with."

"Yes, we have been briefed on these matters, Mr Sahad," Delainie assured him. "We are here to reassure you that you have our backing, and our alliance, with you and certain Arab nations in this region. We want to do everything in our power to prevent a war from taking place. We, and our government, urge you and your military to restrain yourselves as long as you can, from formally retaliating against Israel. There still may be a small possibility yet, for them to withdraw. With the imposing of sanctions on selected and essential commodities, they may quickly change their minds."

"Let us hope so," Sahad replied.

In the afternoon, they only had time to say goodbye to the Chairman of the PLO. He explained that matters beyond his control were taking place on the military front. "I trust that Mr Sahad covered everything you desired. He's very good. Like a brother to me," Asaad said, putting his hand on his comrade's shoulder.

"Yes, we have covered everything," Delainie replied. "Now we must be going. We are expected in Jerusalem this afternoon. Thank you for your time and hospitality. We will be in touch, Chairman Asaad." Delainie was in a hurry in order to have the chance to speak with the General for the last time before they returned to the States.

As their limo pulled out Asaad retreated to his office. Speaking to an anonymous caller, now in his native tongue on his personal phone, he said "I wouldn't advise it, this is not a good time my friends. But I thank you for the tip." And somewhere outside of Jerusalem in a makeshift secret militia headquarters, in the basement of a newly acquired member of Hadaas' home, a young woman with about 3 kilos of explosives hidden beneath her chador, left the building prepared to receive salvation for the act she was about to perform.

They arrived in Jerusalem, relieved that the trip was almost over, but Delainie was still expectant that Gandenberg might move on his previous stance. As they pulled in to the palatial structure where they had been just the day before, they heard a loud noise that sounded like a rumble, and then faint screams. They entered their building and found the place buzzing with activity. They dodged the reporters there for the press conference as they pushed their way past them and frantically disappeared down the steps in the front of the building. Inside the hall, an aide met them and brought them into a receiving room. The security team was on full alert and they were on their cell phones and personal communication devices speaking quickly to their partners at the limousine and their other stations.

As things started to quiet down, General Gandenberg's assistant entered the room and informed the Americans that the General would be able to see them briefly. They were briskly ushered into an office, and Gandenberg was just hanging up the phone. He stood to greet them, his face tense. "Mr Delainie you will have to release me from my previous promise to meet with you. An emergency has come up."

"I feared the worst when we heard the explosion," Delainie offered sympathetically.

Then more firmly, "Mr Delainie, 18 people are dead from the most recent suicide bomb attack, three blocks away." The statement itself fell like a bomb into the already tense mood in the room.

"I'm sorry," was all he could say.

"Now if you'll excuse me, we have troops to deploy."

"But General...." But his assistant had already stood between them, and the General had picked up the phone again. Leaving the room Delainie was informed, to his relief, that the press conference had been canceled for lack of reporters and obvious reasons.

"Well sir, could that be considered the good note we were to leave on?" Dalee commented. Neither smiled but the attempt was appreciated.

"Let's get the hell out of here."

The rigorous schedule up to that point, and now the drone of the plane began to make Dalee drowsy, but he wanted to catch the GNCN coverage of the bomb attack. After about ten minutes of various news spots, there it was. A short clip of the debris and bloodied bodies being carried away. It had been in a shopping mall this time. A black and white picture was flashed for two seconds; it was an image of a haggard looking but not unattractive, young Arab woman, who was possibly in her twenties. No one suspected her, made up to look as if she was pregnant. Some really were pregnant. These zealots, moving away from expected methods now seemed to use anything that would give them an advantage. Religious celebrations, children, the elderly, the disabled. It was reported that they purposely timed the attack to coincide with the American's visit, to give them a message and to show their displeasure of their alliance with Israel. Dalee was thankful to have left unharmed, even alive for that matter.

The Mid-East segment was wrapped up with pictures

of Israeli forces in the form of tanks, helicopters and ground troops moving through Palestinian towns. The scene following was one in Europe and Dalee was about to turn it off, but when the announcer said, "In Rome today, former Advisor to the Director of the United Nations Peacekeepers, Joseph Cazara announced the forming of a new global alliance," he thought to himself, what now?

The reporter continued, "He plans to lead the merging of all the commonwealth countries, European Union, and the Federation of Communist Nations." The picture changed to an olive complected, dignified man. "Yes, I am in the process of speaking with the leaders of these organizations today. We want to move things along as swiftly as possible. We see the need for peace more now than ever. And what we need," Mr Cazara explained, "is an alliance of not only these, but all nations of the Earth. Today they all fall into six major groupings on our planet. By the end of this week I believe we will have achieved the merger which will successfully join three. By next month, the other three will join also. Do you intend to invite the Arab League of Nations into this alliance? Peace, is our main focus," he looked directly into the camera, "and only with all nations' cooperation, will it be achieved. For too long has mankind endured racial hatred and religious discrimination, and the negative societal by-product or disease we call – war. And with this new collective and co-operative union, we will finally put an end to the madness." And then with great feeling he concluded with, "You have my solemn pledge that I will personally see this through."

"What the…? Who is this character?" Dalee found himself saying out loud, as the scene changed to one in Asia. Minutes later just before he fell asleep, the phone rang.

"Honey…" It was Janvieve. "Will you be back on schedule?"

"Ya," he responded. "I'll see you at the airport. Thanks for coming so late."

"Okay, love ya."

"Love you too, bye now."

✦ ✦ ✦

5

He was both relieved and excited to return home. Home. Home was where his wife was. His privacy. His yard. And home was where he could buy a newspaper, drive his own car, speak his own language. Dalee enjoyed the trip to the Mid-East, but he was also quite happy to arrive back home. Janvieve was there for him at the passenger exit just like she was always there. He could count on her. On the ride home, he groggily and at the same time excitedly gave her the highlights of the trip.

They pulled into the driveway and he walked to the back of the house. It was dark but he knew what was there. His home. His space. Pausing for a few minutes he rested. In his space. His place. Going inside he looked at the familiar furniture and rooms, and then went outside to get the rest of his bags. The night was quiet in their neat suburban neighborhood. That's the way they liked it. Them, and their safe neighbors.

Inside, after getting ready for bed, they, after such a long absence, their bodies yearned for each other, and they found one another in the cool darkness of their bedroom. Sharing their most intimate physical and spiritual moments they spiraled upward and inward into ecstasy. And then softly drifting down, down, back to Earth, and level ground. After a quick shower they lay ready to sleep and dream into the night.

But before Dalee slept, he revealed once again in the place they called home. Beside his side of the bed he could easily reach his nightstand. In the dark, with his eyes closed he could touch the undersurface of the shelf with the flat of his fingertip. It was the feeling of rough unfinished wood. He knew it well. His mind went back to his bed as a child. He recalled the touch of the cool steel of the frame of his fold-up cot. The cold metal that gave some relief to the heat of the night there in his room at that time. For a moment his mind briefly traveled back to that time. And then he slept a dreamless sleep.

The next morning they were awoken by the phone. What time was it? He was in that in-between state of sleep and consciousness. The sound startled him.

Now preparing for the caller he reached for the receiver and picked it up. It was Delainie. They spoke briefly and then Dalee hung up the phone. He had just returned to the familiarity of his home, and he was being asked to leave it again. But he had just arrived. If there was one thing he hated, it was this. Not so much that he had to go, but rather, that an unexpected expectation was required of him.

Dressing slowly he found his things and proceeded downstairs. No time for his usual rites, just a drink and he was gone. Things were slightly less harried at this hour but still the masses were beginning to move. The machine was starting to turn. On the subway he began to wake up as he sat in his space on the smooth plastic seat. Delainie wanted him there early to prepare for yet another trip. Where was he going this time? Being the Secretary of State took him, at times, to various parts of the world. For the most part Mr Delainie worked out of DC. Oh well, at least Dalee would only have to work out his arrangements, not actually go this time around. His compartment was propelled along under the ground, closer and closer to the center, making its fixed stops every 2 to 3 minutes.

At his stop the human traffic was much heavier. Making his way to the State Department Building he was surprised to see Penny there before him. In order for her to be on time during regular hours great feats had to be executed. Something must be semi-serious. Delainie greeted and briefed him and he started to work. His superior would be going to Europe this time. To Rome. The ancient capital of the ancient world.

After checking and rechecking and re-rechecking, he finally gave it the once over, and so the Secretary of State's itinerary was fully complete. Dalee sent it to Stan for his customary approval and he started walking the moment he sent it. When he reached Stan's door his superior was picking up his phone to call Dalee. On catching sight of him he began, "Mr Delainie tells me you did fine on the assignment." Dalee took the nearest chair against the wall and waited. "So fine we want you on the current one too."

"It doesn't sound like you're asking."

"Sarras will brief you on the details. Your schedule will follow the one you just sent me." Then, looking at his watch he added, "You have till 3 p.m. I gotta go." And he picked up his jacket as he made his exit.

Sitting there alone in Stan's office, Dalee had his first moment to put together all that had occurred since his introduction to the present project. He knew very little but from what he did know he got the impression that it was a mission of particular significance. Joseph Cazara was an important component, and from what he gathered his role was a pivotal one.

He decided to go straight to Sarras and get the whole picture. Sarras was a fifty-ish tanned man with little concern for his clothes other than that they covered him. His wavy black hair wouldn't stay flat regardless of the amount of gel he applied in the morning. And he didn't really mind, except that it might make him appear unable to manage something. His voice was clear but so soft that you had to lean in, a bit too close, in order to hear everything. Being so close one couldn't help but catch the scent of his gel, and also the vaguely familiar smell of some cleaning agent, mixed with tobacco.

Sarras welcomed him into his office somewhat too formally for his liking. He then proceeded to download all the necessary information to Dalee. It turned out that this Mr Cazara was requesting the presence of several world leaders in order to lay out his proposed plan for the 'merger of all mergers', the one Dalee had heard him refer to on GNCN. Apparently, Cazara had a dominant role in certain circles in Europe, the Middle East, and to some extent in Africa. He had worked independently but was quite influential and was now emerging as a public figure.

The logistical details of the trip were transferred verbally from one man to the other. Dalee acknowledged and departed.

On the way back to his office he checked his mailbox. There was usually very little in it anymore. Society at this point was such that paper was almost obsolete. There was only one solitary piece in his box. It looked like a slip of paper but when he picked it up it was of a heavier quality. More like a light cardboard. It was folded and perforated for easier opening. He slipped it in his shirt pocket for later.

14 hours later he was in Southern Europe. The sun was about to rise on Rome. Samuel Delainie, Dalee Delliv, and the rest of the American delegation, along with extensive security, disembarked from their aircraft. This trip wasn't to be a long one but there was an unusual anticipation attached to it. What did this Cazara have in mind exactly? Mr Delainie had spoken with Dalee on the plane this time. He had told him of Cazara's plan to unify the major organizations of the world. And how at this point the United States' interest was involved and how it interconnected with the Arab League of Nations. America, as well as Israel, was at a critical stage in their relations with the Arab world. This also involved several terrorist groups which almost daily launched vicious attacks in various parts of the world. Their role was to first of all, with the other nations' co-operation, determine the legitimacy of the merger and this man. Then second, to ensure the United States a prominent and leading role in this new organization. And finally but most importantly, to initiate a peace treaty with the Arab League and the people they have been attacking, which was essentially the rest of the world, but specifically Western nations and Israel. And Delainie and Dalee were to achieve this final objective with or without Cazara or his new organization.

The delegates and the entire entourage were escorted to their accommodations. They were being housed at the Marriot Place Casa de Roma, a colossal structure in the center of the capital. Dalee was mesmerized by the beauty and the richness of the architecture and the artistic decor. The Italians had more than a flare for style. The oversized paintings with their ornately engraved frames, along with the sculpture, the fountains, the lighting, aesthetically blended with the existing architecture all created a sense of awe and reverence. In this majestic setting Dalee left the front desk and was about to ascend the plushly carpeted spiral staircase, but stopped at the bottom and turning to the lobby decided to relish this moment a little longer.

He walked to a table near a lot of large feathery ferns and with a view of the street in front of the hotel. He was admiring and enjoying this moment, being suspended from the hurried pace of his party. After some time he noticed seated at a nearby table, a bearded, bespectacled, black-suited, elderly Jewish man, topped with a black hat. He was reading, but would from time to time pause to look at his surroundings. Finally at one of his pauses he observed Dalee, and said in a voice just loud enough for him to hear, "Vivaldi I believe. But the orchestra is not European. I would place it as recorded somewhere in the early 1960s." He got up and walked over to Dalee's table. Extending his hand to him he introduced himself, "Dr David Ben-zoheth."

His open countenance and kindly voice made it difficult not to trust a stranger. Reaching out his own hand Dalee returned the customary greeting and responded "My name is Dalee."

Beginning again with his original commentary he continued, "The types of instruments they used and the treatments of certain parts of this particular piece by Vivaldi show a more American style in the performance. May I sit down?" Dalee gestured to a chair. "Forgive me for intruding. You didn't look particularly occupied."

"Well, at the moment I am not."

"I'm here on a holiday." And glancing around he confidentially added. "But I'm not really staying at this hotel.

You won't turn me in will you?"

"You can count on me."

"Good. With my common attire sometimes it is a passport to places that I had not expected."

"It is common to you doctor, but I don't think it is to those who regard you. Particularly for the first time."

"Do you like music? I am an art lover of all forms."

"I do appreciate art."

"If you have any free time I would highly recommend the Vatican's museum."

"Yes. It must be beautiful."

"Would you like to go with me then? Let's say tomorrow at nine in the morning? I can have the transportation arranged…"

"Actually I do have a lot to do. The meetings I'm attending begin tomorrow at 2 p.m., and…"

"You have the morning free then."

"Yes, but I had a long flight from Washington and…"

"So you are American then. I thought you were East Indian."

"That is my heritage, but yes I am an American. And you?"

"I was born in Dakar, but my parents moved to South Africa. I studied in England and then did my graduate studies in Jerusalem. And I have been there since that time. I wanted to live with my people in the City of God. Would you like to return to your people?"

"Where are my people, doctor? My family actually emigrated from Pakistan many years ago, but they came from Nagaland before that. My mother was born Afghan, and my father in Mumbai. Much of them followed later to the USA, and some are in Toronto. But there are those who would not leave their villages for fear of the West and all that they had heard." Why was he telling all this to a stranger?

But the old Jewish man had a pleasant kindliness about him. And slowly nodding his head he smiled in a knowing kind of way, while with his hands he softly patted the edge of the table in front of him in double time to coincide with his nodding.

"Now that we know each other, you will accompany me to the museum tomorrow?"

"As I said…." But his warmth and hospitality were not to be refused. "Sure. Where should we meet?"

Smiling he said, "How about in the lobby at 8 o'clock?"

"Okay."

✦

The next morning Dalee came down rested, but not quite feeling himself. He greeted Dr Ben-zoheth when he met him in approximately the same place they had their conversation the day before.

"Have you had your breakfast?" inquired the Jewish man.

"Actually, no."

"Good. I know a place. Have you tried the Italian coffee? Let's go then."

In the street they saw the vendors selling their various wares, and people exchanging their bon journos. The morning traffic was at its peak so they were wary and mindful of the infamous Roman drivers while getting their taxi. The doctor seemed to be fairly experienced at this.

"This isn't your first trip to Rome doctor?"

"My second actually. And you?"

"It's my first time here. You just seemed to manage the taxi almost well enough to be a regular."

"Experience my friend. When you've traveled as often and as widely as I have, some things come quite natural after a while."

As the cab wound its way through the maze of morning traffic and the driver aggressively pushed and swerved, taking space whenever and however he could, Dalee blankly stared out of the rear passenger window. He absently watched as the other drivers attempted the same feats to get to their own destinations all with the same gusto and apparent irritation. Some of it was feigned and some genuine, but it all flowed together somehow in the surging, pulsing movement something akin to the blood coursing through the arteries and capillaries in all of us.

"No offence, but what exactly are you a doctor of, doctor?"

"My studies centerd around the Jewish holy scriptures, so my speciality is Theology. Of course as I'm sure you've gathered, that was quite some time ago now. However, I do continue in my studies at the synagogue. It is just not the quantity that I used to do. When one is preparing and defending one's thesis, as you may know, a student is much more motivated at that most critical time. I assure you that the qualitative aspect of my work is at the forefront in my golden years." And with this, added a mild chuckle as his arms returned to his sides, after making quotation marks with his fingers.

Without comment, Dalee simply gave an obligatory smile and returned his attention to the window. The view had changed then to some architecture worth noting. They then crossed the river and his companion announced they were almost to the Vatican. Dalee was getting a little hungry now and returned his thoughts to breakfast.

Speaking to the driver, Dr Ben-zoheth handed him some Euros and then the driver pulled over. Trying to reimburse him on Dalee's part only produced protests and then refusal. "No, no, no. You are my guest today. Please allow me. It is already taken care of. Come, we are here."

He discovered they were actually a few blocks from Vatican City. Then his guide led him into a small café not far from where they got out of the taxi. "Bon Journo" the patron sang out as they entered his domain. They stood at the bar and two shots of cappuccino were ordered. They took them and each carried his own to a booth near a window.

They ordered their respective breakfasts and resumed conversation.

"And what is it exactly that brings you to Roma." The last word was attempted with his best Italian accent.

"I'm on business."

"Top secret, is it? You Americans are so private about your affairs."

"I can tell you that there will be high level multilateral talks, and my role is that of assisting the Secretary of State."

"So you are the assistant to him? I have seen this man on the news reports."

"My most recent unofficial title is 'Diplomatic Attaché to the Secretary'."

"Well, of your meetings you have told me nothing more than I might learn through the media."

"And that is how it must be."

"Well, you may keep your confidentiality. I am only an

inquisitive layman in regard to American politics, not a spy. You needn't be concerned about me."

"It's not like that. It is merely a standard procedure in this work. And your vocation, how do you like it?"

"My vocation is my vacation at the moment I'm afraid, so we have both chosen rather poorly for our conversation."

As they finished their breakfast Dalee turned his wrist to look at his watch. "I really don't have a lot of time. Would it be alright if we just saw the highlights? What would that involve?"

"Without question the Sistine Chapel is the singularly most significant exhibit at the Vatican Museum."

"All right, we will see it then. Lead on good doctor."

"Only God is good. But I will do my best," the Rabbi stood as he spoke. They paid their bill and exited the café.

The walk was short but brisk and it was covered in the span of a few minutes. The forecourt of the Holy See was bustling with the usual population of tourists and citizens and pilgrims. Dr Ben-zoheth began threading his way through the crowd but passed the front gate and proceeded to the right of the entrance.

"Wait!" Dalee called out. "You've missed the entrance!"

Turning and speaking over his shoulder he shouted, "It is this way. Come, you will see."

Having no other choice Dalee continued to follow until they got a little further where he could get alongside of his companion. "I thought we were going to the Vatican Museum. Don't you think we should go to the Vatican then?"

"Yes, Master Dalee. But the Italians have not arranged things quite so conveniently as we might have anticipated. You see the entrance... is here." And with those last two words the rabbi made his last two steps to the front doors of a building marked as the museum of Vatican City, and halted. With some surprise and confusion on Dalee's part, the two men walked through the doors and entered the museum. They both regarded their surroundings, once fully inside, with care and interest. After a few moments of walking slowly Dalee mentioned to the rabbi that he really should move a little faster in order to go directly to the Sistine Chapel in order to have the maximum time to appreciate its beauty. Having agreed, the two quickened their pace.

They passed through several rooms and halls and scores of art pieces when suddenly Dr Ben-zoheth approached a door, opened it and passed through it. Dalee being close behind him, followed quickly. They ascended two or three flights of stairs and emerged again into yet another room filled with more art pieces. They were moving fairly swiftly now and Dalee was surprised at how fast this old man could move. They continued in this manner for 5 or 10 minutes more, with much of the same surroundings and passageways. Halls and stairwells, rooms of paintings and sculptures and other art pieces. And periodically there would be a very small sign with a tiny arrow with the words written in magic marker: 'SISTINE CHAPEL.' Dalee did not think he would have noticed them if not for his alert, agile tour guide. They were ascending a set of stairs and the sound of the clattering was echoing off the walls of the confined space, when all of a sudden he stopped.

Pausing a few seconds, they could hear their own breathing. And then he stated, "I believe we are being followed." Puzzled and concerned Dalee looked behind and all around them but couldn't see or hear anything. When his guide started again, he continued to follow. Then they entered a larger room and Dalee glanced at his watch starting to worry about the time. Passing as quickly as possible through about five more large rooms with wide corridors, and then they finally saw it. They both entered a crowded, hushed, large space which wouldn't be mistaken for anything but Michelangelo's Sistine Chapel. So much of the surface was covered with extraordinary artwork, one couldn't look anywhere and not see some magnificent portion of his painting.

For some time, Dalee and the rabbi seemed suspended in time, staring up at the ceiling, gazing at the walls, even examining the corners. Finally the guide spoke up, "I remember the first time I saw it…. What is your impression?"

"I can see why they go to such lengths to preserve it." And then looking around the room he added, "The detail, the color, the precision. And you can see that he thoroughly understood anatomy. There's no question in my mind that this is the work of an artistic master." Then after a pause, "But I do have one question unrelated to art." The rabbi waited. "Wasn't Michelangelo a homosexual? How can you, being a religious man, accept such a person or his art knowing this? Isn't that morally wrong?"

"That is more than one question," he remarked, and then continued with a smile. "It is true, we disagree with that kind of lifestyle. But God loves his own creation. He wouldn't just abandon mankind, over one issue would he? And those who do things that we don't agree with can still produce, accomplish, and also create things. Sometimes magnificent things. Does this mean that we should dismiss, or that we could simply obliterate their work?" Dalee had to agree with this reasoning and acknowledged it by his expression.

"I really need to go. Thank you for your expertise today, doctor."

"You're welcome...." He paused and then, "...and you needn't call me doctor all the time. I realize my name is a little hard for English speakers to pronounce. It's actually pronounced '*Ben-zo-khayth*'. But I prefer that you use my first name anyway."

"Yes of course. What was it again...? Daniel?"

"David," corrected Ben-zoheth. "Daniel was in the lion's den. And I haven't been even near one of those.... Well, not since my South Africa days anyways. Should we go then?"

"That's quite alright, doc...I mean, David. I can make it back myself. Thanks again for your time."

"Thank you for coming. It was good to meet you. Perhaps we will meet again."

"Yes, perhaps," he repeated. And with that the two travelers shook hands and parted company.

✦ ✦ ✦

6

The scene was set. The leaders of the world's major organizations were present. In addition to them, some other leaders from a few other countries were represented. The heavy wooden table could have easily seated thirty, and there were at least that many there in the conference room that day. Jean Saché, the Head of the European Union, Roosten Gladskopf for the Federation of Communist Nations, King Edwin I for the Commonwealth, and then there was Abdula Yosaf Khadahar, the leader of Arab League of Nations; the Director of the World Council of Churches, Stanley Panteen was present, as was Bakka Telatach the Secretary General for the UN. Along with these were Samuel E. Delainie, the Secretary of State for the USA, and also Chala Calaandra representing South Africa. Each of these dignitaries of course had at least one of their senior aides accompanying them. The table was filled. The seats against the walls were also full.

There was a general buzz of talking among the attendees. The chairman of this meeting had not yet arrived. There was one empty seat at the head of the long table. Suddenly four men briskly entered the room; all were dressed in black suits.

Behind them entered a distinguished man in his late forties, bustling as he walked rapidly the distance from the door to his chair. He stood for a brief moment, nodding once to ceremonially acknowledge his audience. He sat and began, "If you will all please take your seats we will now get started." There was some rustling and murmuring from this small crowd with representatives from all over the globe, as they found their seats.

"I am Joseph Cazara. And with some of you present here today I have spoken directly, and others I have spoken with your assistants. If there is any question as to why we are here today I will first clear that up." His voice was crisp, and strong. His presence commanding. He had eyes that penetrate, and that had seen much of the world. Serious, deliberate, engaging.

"You know why we are here today. You know the many and recurring problems of our world today. You know that we have entered this new millennium of which the first century is very close to half over, and still these global scale headaches do not go away. When are we going to solve them? And if not us, then who?" The last word was spoken with greater force than the others of his introductory remarks. He had created an air of anticipation and urgency in just a few minutes.

"This is all very fine, I assure you Mr Cazara, but we understood that this gathering was intended to discuss the possible merging of the organizations represented here." His voice was also crisp and his British accent enhanced his perfect diction as he spoke.

"Ahhh, and that is the point King Edwin. If in fact we do succeed in such a merger, it will follow that we can succeed at eliminating some, if not all of these perpetual problems of our planet. War, disease, poverty. Let us begin with war. Or more specifically our most recent enemy: terrorism." With this last word, spoken carefully, and slowly, Abdula Khadahar imperceptibly but acutely gave his full attention to the words about to follow. "Terrorism," Cazara repeated, "is in fact a focal point for us all today," pausing for increased attention of all his listeners, "since it has gone on for decades…unchecked, unchallenged, and unresolved." He stabbed these three words in to the air of the conference room, almost spitting them out at the leaders in front of him. Rage was rising in the dark skinned man's eyes. No one had yet noticed a change in Khadahar for they were all looking in the same direction. But the chairman was aware of it, though he made no move to respond, nor gave no acknowledgement to this change. Khadahar had seen this type of political man before so he would wait, and carefully watch him before any rash words were exchanged.

"What can be done?…" Cazara then lightly threw out to his listeners. Silence for a moment. "To begin with…these men… are our brothers." With this protests came from every corner of the room. Everyone speaking at once, chaos reigned for a moment. Only the chairman and the small Middle Eastern man with the embroidered cap were not alarmed. Khadahar, whose muscles had stiffened but were now relaxing slowly, began to open his hands under the table which had been clenched into fists.

Next, Sam Delainie spoke up, and this immediately quieted the room. "Mr Cazara. Although we appreciate your concern for this, and other quintessential world problems, we need to see your connection with a governing body, a nation, some ruling power. I am aware of your former involvement and appointment with the UN, but your other work in the Mid-East, from our research, has shown it to be unknown to the worldwide international community, and largely independent."

"Mr Secretary," He addressed him in such a congenial and benevolent fashion that the listeners were immediately disarmed. But Delainie held his ground, facing his opponent, with chin slightly lifted, and awaited his response. "The UN will give you all the endorsement that you require. And as far as my independent work here in Europe, in Africa, and in the Mid-East, I assure you it has not been independent to those recipients of the benefits of my work. But let us..."

"...Yes but why are we not aware of such benefits?" he broke in.

"...Let us return to the issue of the hour." And then more firmly, looking directly at Delainie, "Ms. Saché, I am certain, would be happy to assure you of some of my independent work, at the very least, here in the European states."

With that Saché stood. She was in her fifties but looked like forty or younger, wearing a dark blue business suit well-fitted to her trim form, with the skirt cut exactly at the knees. On her head was perched a pair of narrow tinted glasses, which she fitted perfectly on top of her ears and face before she spoke. She was staring straight ahead as she addressed the group. She spoke as if accustomed to speaking to officials and rulers; and she spoke as if reciting a rehearsed speech. Her voice was soft, her accent faint. Her vocabulary and tone, that of the highly educated and carefully groomed.

"We of the EU are largely familiar with Joseph Cazara's independent work." She adjusted her designer glasses as she spoke, holding the right arm between the thumb and index finger, pressing them closer to her face. "I assure you that his work is both legitimate and extremely beneficial. Though he has chosen to avoid the public eye, it in no way, diminishes his credibility or the exceptional quality and value of it. He is an independent, no question, but remains a magnanimous philanthropist, if you wish. We of the EU unequivocally approve. Not only of the man, but of his causes." And with that she almost silently returned to her sitting position.

There was a brief lull in the conversation, before the UN Secretary-General spoke, "We too, know very well of Mr Cazara's many peacekeeping missions which he spearheaded through his many years with us." His voice calm. His words evenly spaced and pronounced slowly, almost rhythmically. His gaze level. Cazara gave a nod of appreciation in the direction of his former chief.

Gathering himself and now with even more confidence than before, he began again, "It is without question that my efforts for peace and stability in our world go before me. They speak for themselves, they are my credentials…." And then turning to the American, "…Mr Delainie." Another pause, and then, "Can we proceed then…" The words were spoken softly, but annunciated clearer than necessary, and showing some disdain and impatience. "For too long have the Muslims and our Arab brothers been ostracized, and treated as outcasts. My fellow citizens of Earth, we do not need to attack this fellow people group. We need to make a peace treaty with them."

The Americans were insulted. The Arabs were suspicious. The religious representatives were hopeful. The Communists were suspecting some ulterior motive or hidden agenda.

The Brits were cautious and were the first to speak. "Mr Cazara," Edwin the First began after consulting with one of his attendants, "this conflict which you speak of, has been the expressed interest and focus of many nations of our Realm, in addition to several alliances; none of these efforts, I might add, have you been a part of." His accent alone was condescending, but the King added his own intentional tone to make the remark hit home.

Ignoring his highness' caustic comment, Cazara continued resolutely. "We find the focal point or points of these international terrorist networks, which will be their top men, and we broker a solid deal with them. There will be your end of terrorism. Only there will peace on Earth become a reality." Then, with no verbal response given, he went on. "We begin here. We begin today. Is this not all of our concerns? Is this not the foremost issue of us all today? We cannot allow this injustice to perpetuate this way. We…"

"And what could you have to offer the Muslims," a low voice with a thick accent cut in, speaking slowly but intensely. "You who side with our enemies, and give them your weapons. You who ravage our countries and demolish our holy temples. Who take from us our honored leaders, and treat them like criminals. Who are you?"

In his softest voice yet, Cazara graciously continued his interrupted monologue. "As I have stated, the Arab peoples, all over the world, are our brothers, my brothers. With all due respect, Mr Khadahar, I have done none of those things mentioned. Do not judge me, by the brutal and foolish actions of others. I am a new voice. We, my council and I, are a fresh face in this seemingly perpetual problem." Khadahar turned his face aside at this point to conceal his disbelief and disgust.

"We can and will do it. And it will take some time. Not years, but only months. I give you my promise, my solemn pledge, that I will see it done." His hand was on his heart, his expression unwavering. "But we must begin here; we must have your support as the leader of the Arab nations. And also the support of those in this room today. Together we can do this thing." And walking to the man he had been addressing, standing over him he watched for his response. But he held his position. Nothing for...but in the seconds passing, nothing against Cazara's comments. He simply sat, expressionless, numb, staring down at the blank table in front of him.

With no response, Cazara again continued. "We need not resolve that problem today. But I assure you, we indeed will get to it. But as was mentioned earlier, the intent of this session was the merger of all mergers. And yet, I am afraid I have not been completely honest with you." A change of direction was taken as a result of this question of what was coming next. Enjoying the mystery which he had now created, he watched. And then, "I do desire a merger, let there be no mistake. But a merger even above this one is in the works, even as we speak. A merger of the whole Earth, of all the nations, under one governing power. Never in history has this ever been successfully achieved. Oh, it has been attempted, but not accomplished. I am convinced that now is the time to do this. It is now that we have the ability, the technology, the co-operation, the openness, the willingness, the freedom, the opportunity." Some of those present were captivated, some skeptical, some curious, and some interested. "What I, with your help, hope to accomplish today in this room, is to garner the support of those that you influence. Your allies, your trading partners, your neighbors which share your borders. The hour has come my friends to unify all peoples, not only those warring factions we discussed earlier. To unify all nations of the Earth, in peace."

"I believe this speech has been made before," finally came one response from the otherwise silent group. His strong Russian accent and slow style of speech gave his words a mysterious air of dignity, and the flare of a monarch.

"Yes...so it has," was spoken softly, with the finals of his yes trailing, and Cazara pausing and pensively gazing into the air. As if somehow looking into the past, summoning up history, recalling the Napoleons, the Genghis Khans, Czars, Pharaohs, and the Caesars. The Kings of ancient times, who all tried in one way or another to create a universal Empire.

Turning back to his audience, and clearer now, "Yes...it has, Mr Gladskopf. But as you know, and as I have stated, there has never been a time like this in history." Collecting himself, and returning briskly to his place at the head, the chairman of the meeting now gave full force to his words. "I today propose to you present here in this conference room, that a council be formed next month. One that will comprised a single individual, for each continent or region of the world. That individual will be the ruler or King if you wish, for his portion of Earth." With that he signaled to one of his assistants who pressing a remote, lowered a screen at the front of the room. The control was handed to Cazara. He pressed a sequence of buttons releasing the visual technology with his security code. Then from his jacket pocket producing a handheld device, which after pressing another button produced a glow on the white screen. He stood back a little but directly in front of the large screen at the head of the room. Finally, pressing a last button an image of a map appeared. He stood and aimed his device for a few seconds and the image remained, illuminated in an iridescent light, as if somehow burned into the white background. Standing back now, he spoke in a clear, passionate voice.

"Ladies and gentlemen, this is…The United Society of Earth." The spectators were studying this new version of their familiar world, puzzled, somewhat curious, and to some extent in awe of both the marvel of Cazara's technology and this colorful display of the major regions of their world. "As you can clearly see there are seven main regions of the Earth on this map before us. North and South America, Africa, Australia, Asia, Europe, and Russia. For purposes of organization all territories in the Northern Arctic Circle as can be observed by the color white, are included with Russia, and Australia is associated together with the Antarctic continent, and certain islands of the Pacific, as indicated by their blue color. All other continents as you can see by their respective colors, are straightforward. A short geography lesson is necessary for the transition into the subject of what I will call 'admino-politica', that is, administrative politics." The lights had been gradually dimmed at this point. Some of the attendees were becoming uneasy with the presentation before them.

Delainie spoke for all of them and released some of their tensions when he said, "What are you basing such imagine-ary geo-political regions on?…John Lennon's 1970s peace song?" Some low laughter followed and Dalee congratulated Delainie, who smiled and chuckled to himself.

"If you will bear with me, Mr Secretary, you will soon see.

And after this present segment I believe we are near due for a break." His assistant checked his watch and confirmed his employer's suspicion with a quick nod. "Each region, as you can see, includes all the countries of that area. For example, the Asia Region will include Japan, Korea, China, and so forth. This in some ways is no different than what you now know to be true." He stalled a few seconds, but in the darkness no one could view his visible signs of eagerness, his excitement. Controlling his voice and continuing in the same tone, "The difference will be, we will soon have a leader, a ruler for each of these regions." The words entered the dark room but there was no apparent reaction. Cazara pressed on. "Continuing with the Asia example, this ruler will govern over the entire region, including the countries mentioned earlier as well as all of the other nations you see highlighted, in this example, by the yellow color." Allowing his audience to study the map, Cazara sipped his water and then placed the glass on a small table beside him. "Delaying the details of each individual region for a time, allow me to give the whole picture first." He cleared his throat. "As logic would naturally allow you to surmise what would follow, there would be a total of seven rulers, only seven, for the whole Earth. And these rulers would be connected to and responsible to the central unit of my administrative government. I won't venture to outline my council or cabinet here, but suffice it to say that it will be comprised of the top people, the world's best, in areas such as Commerce, Military, and others; and this I will unveil to you all in its entirety as the afternoon progresses."

Then the lights went on.

Blinking eyes stared around the room as the brightness of

the lights filled its space. The door flung open and the staff, dressed in crisp and stylish uniforms whisked trays and trolleys into the conference room. The attendees sipped their choice of coffees and teas from fine ornate china. Some walked out for fresh air or to inhale the smoky air of their cigarettes inside the smoking room. There was much talk, much conjecture, and general buzzing of what they had just witnessed. Their chairman was nowhere to be found and couldn't be reached for questioning of this bold and revolutionary presentation which he was in the midst of.

For the remainder of the afternoon, Mr Cazara outlined his plan, with surprising tact given its content and exceptional breadth, essentially on how he intended to rule the entire Earth from his hand-picked central 'admino-politica' governing body. He had continued where he left off before the break, and explained further the different aspects of his own council. There would be a Minister of Commerce, a minister of all military matters, and then another minister would be in charge of the areas of Science and Technology, and another of Entertainment/Arts. There would also be the Minister of Health, and the Minister of Transportation, and one of Education, and then finally of Communication. Each of these ministers, it was explained, would manage and maintain his area of responsibility. Again, for the whole Earth. For example, the Minister of Commerce would handle all matters of business and finance, but the scope would not be limited to a single nation, or even just one region, but for the entire Earth. Never before had this been legitimately attempted, Cazara explained, and never before had there been the opportunity, the possibility. With similar such words of conviction and persuasiveness, and near preaching, the Chairman presented this new vision of a new world, a new society which would spring from the ashes of the aftermath of hatred and prejudice, of war and fear and mistrust, of the years of terrorism which had made the citizens of planet Earth groan and cry out, for a solution – A Savior.

✦ ✦ ✦

7

Dalee walked out into the morning sun and surveyed the grounds of the luxury hotel. It was large and spacious, with lawns meticulously landscaped and carefully tended. The large fanning plants and brightly colored flowers were alternated along the walkway, and periodically plaster statuary, of heroes of modern Italy and the Roman world, could be seen throughout the extensive gardens. Pope Paschal I, Saint Peter, Frank Sinatra, Billy Joel, Robert Deniro, Leonardo da Vinci, Galileo, Julius Caesar. Also, there were large gazebo-like structures which dotted the landscape, and within some of them, small crowds had gathered to watch concert performances of violinists, cello players and other musicians as they serenaded the guests.

He found a table in a patio and sat down on a cushioned chair. He still hadn't opened his piece of mail he'd collected from his box back in Washington two days ago. Removing it from his leather folder on his lap he examined it. It was postmarked Shanghai. His friend Xieng Lee lived there, but it looked more like a government voting notice than a letter. Pulling up with his finger he tore open the perforated edge. He unfolded the document to find a handwritten note, in small but stylish English script.

Xieng Lee had his own mini empire of a chain of

convenience stores. He was an unusual blend of the modern and the old fashioned, of technology and the human factor. Or as Alvin Toffler put it – 'high tech and high touch.' Lee accepted only those aspects of technology which would benefit him, then adapted them to serve him and his business needs. But he refused to give up entirely the human component and so he would add the human touch to his small corporation. The letter Dalee had opened being a perfect example. His publishing room, which consisted of at present four working machines, and two non-working, was where all his advertising and other paper documents were produced. They could be automatically addressed, stamped, even mailed. And of course whatever message desired could be printed out on the paper. But somehow he managed to do all of the other steps, but insisted on writing by hand, the actual message.

If he had wanted to, Lee could've by this time have expanded much larger and gone beyond his region of Southeast China. But for some reason he refused to go nationwide. He could have even expanded globally, his tactics and skill in business so successful and his product popular. He liked his life small, his fortune manageable. Maybe it was the big fish-small pond scenario and the small fish in the larger pond was unappealing to him. Or maybe he had the ability above his realm but only the capacity to work in the little China pond that he found himself in.

The letter read as follows:

Dear Dalee,

I wish you are fine. I am good too. Thanks for your mail and I appreciate for your praise.

And I took your called, I am stayed in the factory cause that year end report when I late say hello! congratulation on your trip to Middle East after that my grandmother has inviting through to me. She's name Lee (family name), sook yhe. She loves you and Jan. And say hello to Jana, because she present my wife that a herb plant. The day and that time's our stores had many customer. My wife doesn't say a return courtesy.

Sorry and see you sometime!

Lee Xieng

After reading it Dalee chided himself for not helping him more with his English while he was there in China some years ago. He remembered that year in Asia with some fondness. They had made some friends, experienced another culture, and probably most fascinating saw the expansion of that area into a new hotspot for business and trade. Shanghai, at the time they were there, was on the threshold of developing into a world-class city. With its new mass transit system, skyscrapers, mega malls, and latest nouveaux Dutch architecture, they watched as the city was transformed.

His mind went back to the noisy streets, the limousines and bicycles jockeying for position on the highways, the steamed dumplings fresh from the vendors in front of the glittering bank office towers. He could hear the bells clanging, and the voice of the merchant calling out in his dialect, how good and fresh his product was. He could smell the pastries as he walked by one corner, and the pungent exhaust garbage odors on another.

But the most memorable thing he could look back upon was their ferry trip to the Korean Peninsula. Being present at that historic moment when North and South were finally reunited as one nation was a great honor. In the year 2020, Mr Yom Song Won led the Unification Movement to its final fruition when the DMZ came down. It was not a simple crumbling and breaking affair as was the tearing down of the Berlin wall so many years before that. No, this one required the services of some heavy-duty equipment. Heavily reinforced chain link fence segments were bulldozed over and pulled up from the ground. From the leftover débris the spectators were permitted to collect any souvenirs that they wanted. Janvieve had come prepared with a tool to cut wire with for just such an occasion. And so, Dalee got his memento to represent in physical form the peace between the two nations, and North and South Koreans exchanged their Truce for a Peace Treaty, their flag flying proudly in the land once again.

Dalee had only read of the Berlin wall in the history books, but to actually be there during the making of history was certainly exciting. At that moment, during his reminiscing of the time in Korea, Dalee incredulously stared as a huge passenger aircraft angled its way from the sky strangely in the direction of the hotel. Standing up and moving away from the building as others were beginning to do, the plane moved closer, and the sound of its engines louder and louder. Suddenly the plane right before their eyes, hurled itself directly into the main building of the hotel and exploding into huge clouds of fire! The bystanders could feel the heat of the fires which at this point were engulfing the central and tallest portion of the structure, and spreading quickly to the other parts of the compound. The first impact and the ensuing explosion now over, the guests then watched in shock and horror as the fire began to consume what remained of the hotel complex.

By the time Dalee had collected himself and was watching from a safe distance away the sound of sirens could be heard wailing faintly at first, but then growing more and more, until several ambulances, fire trucks, police cars and some other emergency vehicles arrived on the chaotic scene.

In the pell-mell of the aftermath Dalee went through a barrage of questions – who was in there at the time of the explosion?...Who would have done this?...What had he left in the hotel roo...ring-ring, ring-ring. He fumbled, searching his pockets.

"Hello?" he answered, dazed and confused.

"Honey it's me, I heard the explosion, are you alright, I'm so glad..."

"Janvieve?...Where are you? What are you talking about?"

"Oh, dear, please don't be angry, I was so worried about this trip. I followed you here to Rome."

"What?!" What are you talking about? What are you doing?"

Emergency crews were engaged upon rescuing whoever they possibly could find from the wreckage. Firefighters shot 20 meter streams of water into the fires now blazing out of control.

"Janvieve," he finally managed, "where are you right now?"

"I'm at the Quando Piazza Hotel about 10 minutes from your hotel."

"I can't believe you came here. You know..."

"I know, but I just felt so afraid this time, that something might happen."

Dalee looked up at the wreckage, the flames, and the chaotic scene in front of him.

"It did," he whispered. Still in a kind of shock he was trying to digest the events that had occurred in the last few minutes.

"We followed you yesterday at the museum and…"

"That was you! We thought we might have been in danger. Who are we?"

"I brought my friend Tasha with me."

"Who could have done this?" he thought out loud.

"I know. Are you sure you're alright?"

"Yes I'm fine. I was outside of the building when it happened."

"What building?!"

"The hotel."

"What?!!!"

"Yes, the plane hit our hotel!"

"What?!!! It was a plane!!!"

"Yes," he was speaking more firmly now, restraining his excitement and anxiety in the chaos. "It was a plane, and it crashed into our hotel. Well, I do not think it was a crash. I can assure you it was intentional."

"I have to meet you. Can I come there now?"

"No, wait. The security is going to keep us under tight wraps for a while. You really need to go back. It's not safe for you to be here."

Then quickly, "…And what about you! Is it safe for you?!"

"You need to go back, Janvieve, I'm sorry."

"I actually have a ticket that stops in Paris for a few days."

"Oh, really? Are you going to see your uncle?"

"Ya, I already contacted him."

"Okay."

"What about you?"

"I know. I need to get out of here too. Look I've gotta go now." Part of the security team along with emergency aid workers were finally getting to those on the hotel grounds and waving them over to a safety zone set up for survivors and the wounded. "I'll meet you in Paris. Wait for me there. I'll call you as soon as I can. Goodbye." And he was gone.

More questions. 'Where was Delainie? And the others?' And then he considered the unthinkable, What if he personally had been in the hotel during the explosion? Shuddering, he forced himself back to the present, and the fact that he was still alive. A disaster had just occurred. The Secretary of State of the USA may be injured or possibly dead…. He hailed one of the security officers who was on his two way trying apparently to locate Delainie and any others in their party. The security man looked distressed. How could this possibly have happened? Dalee questioned the man on the walkie-talkie first about Delainie. He replied that so far that they had been unable to locate him. This was not good.

Emergency workers were then checking Dalee's vital signs and questioning him about his health. He assured them all that he was perfectly fine and that he had not sustained any injuries whatsoever. All around him there were so many kinds of people: Italian police looking for interpreters, American security were trying to locate those who they were responsible for, the military had been called out trying to protect from any further attacks. Dalee was recovering from the initial shock and was now growing fatigued. Thoughts began to pass through his mind now that he had a moment to himself to think. He thought of Janvieve and how she had come to Rome...the day before with the Jewish rabbi...the lives that were almost definitely lost in the present crisis...and a final question which he couldn't help but wonder about – what would his new role be if in fact Mr Delainie didn't survive? Would the baton then pass to him?

The survivors were then loaded up and transferred to the best hospital in that part of the city. The security detail divided themselves up between Dalee, along with the other staff from his party, and the scene of the attack, in hope to recover the lost and to protect from any further onslaught. During the ambulance ride, other than hanging on for dear life, he took stock of his losses in his hotel room. There were two sets of clothing, which could be replaced, a few papers from the session the day before, some miscellaneous items in his suitcase, and the suitcase itself. And unfortunately his laptop and case, which were not fireproof, but which actually could be replaced. And fortunately, Dalee made it a practice to keep a handy drive backup and daily copy all files on to it. He also had insurance on the hardware itself, but he didn't like to lose his own PC which he over time had gotten used to.

At the hospital there was a buzz of activity surrounding the arrival of all the new patients. Once they got through the preliminaries of registration, and the passing on of all their information at the emergency department reception desk (and this entirely done using interpreters), they were brought in for more testing. Some were severely wounded, brought in on stretchers on wheels, and some could walk in. Dalee went with the latter crowd and was taken to a certain ward with about thirty beds and many divider curtains and they were checked over once again. A security man had accompanied him and once the nurse was near finished with him, informed Dalee that they would be having a debriefing at one of the hospital's administration rooms. The nurse, who couldn't have been more than twenty, had dark eyes and thick dark hair. Her movements were brisk, and with little or no makeup she had a raw beauty about her. She pulled the Velcro from the aging blood pressure gauge and wrapped it around Dalee's arm, and then recorded the numbers on a keyboard beside the hospital cot he was sitting on.

Feeling a little bewildered, he was left alone for a few minutes. He had been given a small slip of paper with the location of the hospital room where they would be having their meeting at 1.30. He looked at his watch and was surprised at how early it was. It seemed like a lifetime had passed since he walked out of the hotel that morning.

The nurse returned and in broken English but with a shy smile told him he could go. Her name tag read, 'Theresa' and some other Italian words which he could not read. She had gone and was attending another person from the hotel. He sat alone for a few more minutes. He looked at the paper in his hand. It read, *Sinacore Wing, fifth floor, Stella Room.* Shouldn't be too hard to find. And he was on his way. But it was the elevator that was difficult to locate. He ended up asking about seven or eight people, orderlies, nurses, limping patients, none of who spoke English. Finally with the elevator nowhere to be found, Dalee walked the four flights, having begun on the first floor, being the ground floor to Americans, but which is called first in certain European and Asian countries.

Having no numbers on the doors he had to wander

around a little bit before he came upon the Stella conference room. When he walked in, he recognized some of the people but others were from the hospital. Orderlies had brought in refreshments and a lunch was in the process of being served. Just what he needed – hospital food. The Italian staff were speaking to one another in their own language quickly and with a generous amount of gesticulating as they came and went. Dalee noticed he was one of the last to arrive and when he took his place at the long rectangular table the team leader called the meeting to order. He first informed his small group that those present with the exception of Dan Kechum, were the only survivors of the American delegation. Dalee knew instantly that Delainie was dead. Shock settled in, but he then quickly looked around the room at those present, conscious of those people who had traveled with him on this trip but were now absent. Swallowing down hard the seriousness of the situation, he again sat further back in his chair and braced himself for more chilling information.

The security team leader was then passing around a rare single sheet of a document. Paper was rarely used, and was usually destroyed afterward. When it reached Dalee he examined it and saw that it was a list of names; those deceased as a result of the events which had transpired that very morning. They were being asked to give any further information regarding these individuals. He stared at the name, *Samuel Emmery Delainie – deceased*. He was alive just a few hours ago. How could he be dead? Where is he now? He looked at the total at the bottom of the page. It read 17. He blankly stared ahead and then passed the page to the next person.

The only survivor outside of the Stella Room, it turned

out, was another security officer who had been at the hotel entrance at the time of the crash. He had sustained second degree burns and some glass fragments had struck the back of his head as well. He had a chance of surviving but was counted as critical. The leader then went on to explain what they then knew of that morning's events at the Casa de Roma hotel. It was confirmed to be the work of a Muslim extremist terrorist group, but yet unnamed. The sophistication of their methods would, when later released to the public, astonish even the worst critic of the terrorists. They had somehow hacked into the airline's computer system, assumed remote control of the plane, and directed it into the target of their choice; which unfortunately for the delegates and the guests, was their hotel. The exact reason had yet to be determined, but top intelligence people were working on that. They did have some idea that it was something related to blocking Cazara's effort, particularly in relation to the treaty which he had mentioned at the first session. The terrorists, but also who they represented, wanted to make sure that a peace treaty with their enemies like the previous one in '45 didn't take place again. The memories were still fresh and the devastation still felt.

Any further meetings were suspended but it was added that the leader was required to inform the team that Mr Cazara had requested a rescheduling of the meeting which had been in progress at the time of the crisis. No one was very eager to attend but the point was noted by all the staff present. The team leader collected the solitary document and handed it to his attendant to be destroyed. The final point covered at the meeting was that of their dispersal. Their return flight would be at 6.00 and they would be transported directly from the hospital to the airport. Four staff members would remain to see to it that the bodies or remains were properly taken care of. Dalee thought of Delainie again and grimly remembered his dental records comment on their last trip. As people were getting up to leave, Dalee approached Jarvis, the security lead, and informed him that he would be going on to Paris from Rome. They exchanged uncomfortable condolences concerning the late Secretary of State, and the others lost. Jarvis told Dalee that it was necessary for him to pass on all the information regarding that morning and anything that might help in their investigation, which he did, en route to the airport.

At Fiumicino, Dalee was thankful that he had followed the traveler's rule of keeping your passport on your person when visiting a foreign country. He found a seat on Thai Airways, bound for Paris, at 5.14 p.m. TG 413 left from Gate 19. He managed to get through immigration without incident. Being completely void of luggage would normally have been unusual. But European travelers moved about frequently between their neighboring countries and it was business as usual to carry little, and at times, nothing. Customs, therefore, was a breeze. He made his way to Gate 19 and found the expected arrangement of airline staff, generic furniture, huge plate glass windows, muted television monitors, subdued colors, and weary and sometimes rumpled in-transit passengers.

The moment he sat down, as if on cue, the little device in his pocket sang out its jingle. He quickly checked the small screen and found the number blocked. I don't know anyone who does that. Somewhat suspiciously he answered.

"Hello?"

"Mr Dalee Delliv?"

"Who is this?"

"Forgive me. We are being additionally cautious after today's events in Roma. This is Gávrá Tuldiá. I am Mr Cazara's executive secretary. You saw me at the meeting yesterday afternoon."

"Okay," Dalee impatiently awaited further information.

"We deeply regret the loss of the Secretary of State. You were his primary aide. We are sorry." He pressed on, "As early as this may seem, we anticipate that you may be replacing him and so require your cooperation. And very possibly an opportunity for you."

"I am on my way to Paris at the moment," he managed, changing his tone a little. So, is it possible…but how would they know before I did? Dalee quickly considered the new role. He also wondered what he meant by opportunity."I haven't really had time to consider it," he responded.

"Would you be willing to meet with our superior?"

"I don't know how long I'll be in France. Can I contact you from there?"

"As soon as possible. We know the United States government may have other options."

"Yes of course."

"I'll give you a number where you can reach us."

The man at the other end of the line passed on 11 digits and he pressed the buttons on his handphone accordingly.

"Thank you for your time." And he was gone.

Dalee found the number for Stan at the State Department and pushed the automatic dial button. The conversation that followed informed Dalee that he indeed was being asked to at least be the Acting Secretary. The current Deputy Secretary of State had just been removed due to a personal scandal. He told his supervisor that he was fine and he would be spending a few days in France. He needed some down time which seemed to satisfy the normally insatiable appetite for work of Stan Walden. Must have been the shock effect, thought Dalee. During the conversation he noticed a vaguely familiar figure cross his path of vision, as he was facing the wide corridor just outside the waiting area at Gate 19. A thin man, with an upright posture, bearded, and wearing the customary black hat of the rabbis. Standing up, while continuing the conversation with Stan, he walked away from the lounge area. Upon recognition of Dr Ben-zoheth, he informed Stan that he had to go, and then called out to the Jewish man walking at a steady pace already past the lounge. Unexpectedly hearing his name, diverted the good doctor's attention from the task he was engaged upon, and he turned his head suddenly. Catching sight of the familiar face surprise turned to pleasure as he realized who it was that had hailed him.

"Well, we meet again Master Dalee."

"What a coincidence that you should be here at the same time."

"Ah! but there are no surprises with God. Are you leaving already?"

Dalee proceeded to update the rabbi on the account of the disaster at the hotel. Responding with shock and concern, he asked if there was anything he could do. Ben-zoheth was returning to Jerusalem at 4.20 by way of Tel Aviv on EL AL Airlines. For some reason Dalee decided to go and wait with him in his lounge. It was only a short distance away at Gate 23. He had arrived quite early for his flight and the doctor left first. Dalee looked at his watch 3.30. Plenty of time. It would give him someone to talk to. So he walked quickly alongside the aging Jewish clergyman.

Finding his gate he checked in and then left his carry on bags with the attendant at the counter asking her to hold them just a few minutes. He and Dalee stepped out into the main hallway and sat down in the colorful cushioned seating provided there.

They talked of the tragedy and the rest of the elder man's trip. Dalee told him that it was his wife and her friend who had been following them in the Vatican Museum. To which, the doctor responded with teasing Dalee for having such a gallivanting spouse of which he had not been aware of her whereabouts. They even discussed a little of the meeting which Dalee had attended. Dr Ben-zoheth finally insisted that Dalee call him David. David admitted he had never heard of this Cazara but commented that his ambition surpassed that of your average political proponent.

After Dalee relayed some of the more general subject matter of the meeting at the hotel, but nothing more than what one might derive from a GNCN news broadcast, David became pensive for a moment. He then proceeded to, in the final ten minutes before his boarding call, give his would-be student a brief, impromptu compare/contrast lecture on the views of Judaism and Christianity regarding a powerful individual who may one day rule the whole world.

The Jews, he explained, were expecting a Savior who would rescue their nation and destroy their enemies. He would set up his rule in Jerusalem and govern not just Israel, but all the nations of the Earth from there. This Messiah would restore for

Israel all that they had lost and endured as a race throughout all of history. Their enemies would finally be paid back for all the atrocities committed against them.

"The Christian view, I have to admit," continued Benzoheth, "is certainly more colorful, at the very least. Have you ever read *Revelation*, Dalee? The last book of the Christian Bible," to which his listener replied in the negative. "A very imaginative piece of work…full of symbolism and allegory. You simply must read it sometime, really." He didn't seem to Dalee like someone waiting for his final call for a flight. He seemed more to be on the verge of waxing philosophical, theological, anything but in a hurry. So Dalee listened on. "Where was I? Oh, yes…. It is in this final book of the Christian Bible where this character is found. There are other references to him in other places as well. He is known as the Beast, the Son of Hell, or the Son of Perdition, the Antichrist. He will somehow convince all the people of the Earth to become unified. He will also rule like the Jewish Messiah I mentioned earlier, over all the nations of the Earth. He will have powers too, above that of a normal man. Supernatural powers which will amaze and persuade the citizens of Earth. There is no mention of a personal name, but his number is given as six-six-six."

This started to sound familiar to Dalee and he told the rabbi so. "Yes, your Hollywood has glamorized, embellished upon, and capitalized on and profited from this whole phenomenon. However it should be known that it was not always an accurate depiction. Yes, the horror genre of the film industry loves to play on this particular theme." Dalee recalled some gruesome movies which he had seen as a child and made the triple six connection. He looked at his watch again, 'his flight must be delayed a little.'

"You may or not remember a certain man in the '20s who had attempted something not in the fantasy world of the movies, but originating in a country close to your own origins Dalee?" Short pause, then, "India...do you remember Sleeva Sadari? In 2023 he unsuccessfully attempted a unification similar to what you have told me this Cazara is presently attempting."

"I was born in 2019. Too young to remember."

"Well, I was a young man then and distinctly remember the events which took place that year. Sleeva Sadari was one of those super gurus out of Mumbai. Only he wasn't satisfied with his hundreds of millions of followers in India and the Muslim world. Nor was it enough to claim the devotion of the Hindus or even the Buddhists throughout all of Asia. His lust for power was unquenchable and when he attempted to gain popularity and support in the West, everyone thought he had gone too far. He started no wars like Hitler of the 20th century did. That was not his style. He went on a religious-political campaign. At that time period people were hungry...numb, is a better word, in regard to...spirituality?...no, something to believe in, no, not even that. Just a void, that's the only way I can explain it. Similar in this respect to Hitler's social-political environment. Well, not his environment but the zeitgeist present during his era. Are you getting all of this?" Dalee replied that he was.

"You don't remember, I know. But in fact history is somewhat selective in what it chooses to remember, and how it or man rather decides to record it. The whole affair was surprisingly short-lived actually. Wouldn't take up much space on a historical time line, probably just a dot. And who wants to remember a cult figure anyway, such that managed to deceive and influence so many when all he had in mind was his own fame and fortune. Now, he did do it well. A very charismatic personality, persuasive, good looking, charming. But what country would go out of their way to put them in their history? India? He was a failure. And a greedy one at that. Would America remember him? I didn't tell you how he met his ultimate demise. He had only just embarked upon his North American campaign. His fame had indeed spread there and to some extent popularity too. But at one of his first massive rallies in Los Angeles, California, Daniel Sanjay Clarke snuffed out his life with a couple of well aimed bullets from an extremely high powered rifle, while suspended in mid air, in a helicopter over 2 kilometers away."

"Now boarding, Flight 313 El Al Air at Gate 23..." the echoing voice with an Italian accent came.

"That's my call."

"Have a good trip."

"Thank you. Perhaps our paths will cross again sometime."

"You said that the last time we parted company."

"And they did."

They exchanged business cards and Ben-zoheth started toward the waiting lounge counter to reclaim his carry ons. Closing the distance between David's gate and his own, his mind rehashing some of the things from the moments before, Dalee smiled a little at the fantastical story he had just heard. Shaking his head he returned to the waiting area and took out his phone. He dialed his wife's hand phone number and gave her the details of his flight. He then remembered that he hadn't checked his email, since he always did so using his *late* laptop. He had never used the function on his phone which allowed you to do this. After about five minutes of manipulating the appropriate buttons, he managed to get a connection to the internet. Then another two or three minutes of finding the right codes and sections and subsectors, he could view the new messages in his inbox. There were eleven.

Once he weeded out the unnecessary ones with the delete key which he deftly and more swiftly carried out than his previous more technical efforts, there were four. One from Russia. One from Cazara's executive secretary. Another from GNCN, a reply to an earlier inquiry he had made. And one from Stan Walden. The second and last he was aware of already. The third, when he managed to open it, presented an opportunity for a tertiary level position with the world's largest news agency. Looking at the clock on the screen, time was running out, and just as he opened the Russian message, his last call came. Standing and skimming quickly the final message, which was somewhat cryptic, he got the impression that Gladskopf, whom he had met briefly at the meeting, was offering him some kind of secret service job. Staring at the screen, but forced to close it, Dalee shuffled through the line, strode through the jet way with the other passengers, and boarded the plane bound for Paris, France.

✦ ✦ ✦

8

Ah, Paris in the springtime,
Now that's the place for me.
But it's lovely still in autumn,
Now wouldn't you agree?....

He drank deeply from his can of Singha beer. Thai was a bit more expensive but the service was the best. The clock on the screen indicated '1.23 for Time to Destination'. Just a little over an hour until they reached Paris. Reclining his seat back a few inches further, Dalee glanced out the small window to his right. Just stars. And clouds. He didn't accept the things David had told him in the final minutes before his departure, but he found himself mulling it over when his mind was free. What did he mean, supernatural powers? And could the person he encountered at the now demolished hotel in Rome be another Sleeva Sadari?

Again he shook his head, brushing it all off as ridiculous. He couldn't bring himself to make a connection with the fanciful stories Ben-zoheth had passed on to him, and the Mr Cazara of the present. And yet something still bothered him about the historical points he made. That much he had to believe, didn't he? He planned when he had some time in France to look it up on the web. And also, to do a little research on Cazara as well. What was that date again?...It was 2023, he recalled. Dalee pulled the name card from his shirt pocket. With English on one side and Hebrew on the reverse, he studied the strange script for a moment and then turned it over. It read:

Dr D. Ben-zoheth
Bethelzoe Synagogue
1231 Jarious Road
Jerusalem, Israel

Then it gave various contact numbers and an email, <elzoe@dabranet.is>. There was a star of David at the top of the card, centered and printed in blue and white. He wrote, '2023 Sleeva Sadari' in a space in the corner. He looked at the name he had just written. He didn't believe in numerology but he had to admit that the name he had just written had six letters in both first and last. He didn't know his middle name so he couldn't check that one. Then, fiddling around with names he had heard associated with this kind of thing, he wrote Hitler's full name and this time saw a full three sixes. Well, that makes sense. Evil dictator, guilty of genocide. He deserves to be a devil. Then slowly he wrote out Cazara's full name as he had seen it once on a memo. 'Joseph Sargan Cazara'. He was surprised at himself for believing such childish nonsense, but for a moment he found himself wondering what that might mean; if it had any meaning at all. He didn't know. But there were three sixes in that man's name. All those movies, he thought, I've really watched way too many movies.

He put the card away and considered his present options

for employment. His watch told him he had 38 minutes to arrival. He carefully began to go over all the possibilities. The Secretary of State. This one was without question the most prestigious. That was, depending on that other possibility that Cazara's executive assistant seemed interested in him for. How could he know if that one was even going to work out? Then there was the position at GNCN. This one he liked the best. But what did it pay? And would it require a lot of travel? Finally, there was the mysterious Soviet position. Sounded thrilling. But excitement had its risks. He wanted to live as long a life as possible. After doing a few calculations with as many numbers as he had, Dalee lay back into his seat as far as he could go and closed his eyes.

About five minutes later, the aircraft began its descent. He felt the familiar thrust of the engines, heard the sound of the landing gear being released, and knew there was still a bit of a wait yet to come. So he settled in for a much needed rest. Once the plane touched down, and then some ten minutes later the seatbelt light was switched off, many passengers in a flurry of activity rushed to grab their bags from the overhead compartments. Dalee waited, still with eyes closed, but listening for his auditory cue that it was time to make a move. Finally, when the sounds began to subside, the forty something Indian-American man, weary from the days events, the travel, and his own sometimes perplexing thoughts, pulled himself from his seat, safely at France's de Gaulle Airport.

Dalee was met by Janvieve and her middle aged, middle height, middle looks cousin, with a generous midsection. After a kiss and a long embrace with his lover, he next was welcomed to France by Chanté. She spoke a single word, 'quatre' while leaning in to give him the traditional French greeting, speaking the number of kisses which one is about to give before planting them. Left, right, left, right. She must have been pleased to see him having bestowed more than the necessary pecks. They then, having no luggage to bother about, proceeded directly to the car.

His French was very limited so his conversations with his wife's extended family were brief.

"Comment *ça va?*" the driver asked him in the antique Smart car as she skilfully manoeuvred her way out of the short term parking.

"*Ça va bien. Et toi?*"

And she began on a monologue which his partner didn't bother to translate because of the rapidity of her robust cousin's speech. After Dalee passed on the shock and some of the trauma of the recent tragedy, which now seemed so far way, he stared at the landscape as their vehicle left the capital city and began the relatively short land journey to Angér. Angér was where most of his wife's relatives resided. The chateaus were beautiful in that region, and Dalee enjoyed his excursions thoroughly every time he traveled there. It was dark by then but he could still make out the hills and the countryside which had become familiar to him as an aid and a tonic to help him put any troubles behind. He decided to save the job news for another day.

The days ahead provided more than enough restoration for him, with the rolling hills of the rural French villages, the extensive vineyards, and the quaint cobblestone streets. The people seemed to forget time there and the lunches were long and with plenty of local wine. There was wine, women and the song was in his heart. His mind relaxed and his troubles forgotten, time was suspended as the days went on there in his wife's family's country chateau. Another of the fringe benefits of having a spouse of French descent was that their zest for life and romantic passion made them lovers extraordinaire; and Dalee and Janvieve took their fair share of this passionate love in the *bleu boudoir*.

The time passed by slowly and pleasantly as their string of idyllic days were unbroken upon during the stay in the country. Then one day Uncle Camas with his twenty-ish daughter Michelle came to visit. While the others were in the summer kitchen having coffee, the young woman was sitting quietly in the sunroom. Through some stroke of bad fortune she happened to overhear something on the radio that triggered an attack of some kind. She had been troubled by a mental illness since her early teens and the doctors had never been able to treat it successfully.

"Mary! Mary! Mary is coming back to save us all!!!" she screamed hysterically.

Her father seemed quite used to this behavior, calmly but quickly was at her side trying to settle her down.

"She's coming!!! She's coming!!! We have to get the cross! The one on the fireplace!"

"It's alright Michelle," came Camas' soothing familiar voice.

Dalee stood at the archway from the living room and watched, somewhat puzzled.

"She's coming! The people are coming! And Mary too! I want her to come! To save us!" She was on the floor now trying to wriggle free at this point. "Won't she come father?"

Breathing heavily and crying softly, she called over and over, "Mary! Oh, where is Mary?!"

"We must find Mary…" And her voice trailed off to other mumblings and incoherent rambling. Her father helped her to her feet and half walking, stumbling, and dragging, directed her to a guest bedroom where she could lie down.

Back in the summer kitchen they resumed their conversation, Dalee a little unsteady. They gave him a glass of red wine to help compensate and told him she would be alright now and that the attack was over. Once the episode was quite over and he was sure that there would be no relapse, Dalee asked a few more questions, more out of politeness or nervousness, he wasn't really sure which.

He did know that Michelle had acquired this state some years ago, but hadn't actually been present during one of her fits. They talked on about how sad it was and each gave their theory as to what was the source of her perplexing condition. Then as good armchair clinicians they each in turn gave their recommendations as to what might be best for her. There were more or less scientific solutions ranging from the more uptodate medication to proper very specific laser brain surgery. Then there were the more holistic solutions and while Dalee was mid sentence explaining something he had read that a spiritual naturopath once gave as a prognosis in a similar such case, the two objects of their conversation reentered the scene.

"We tried all of those," Camas offered as he stood in the doorway, stroking his daughter's thick sandy hair which almost reached her shoulders. She seemed quite content and certainly fully recovered and was distracted by a small puzzle on a LED screen which she held in her hands. "Doctors don't understand our problems. We believe there are deeper things than what medical science can comprehend." He whispered something to Michelle and without looking up she backed out of the room through the doorway, went around to the back of the chateau, and sat on the patio where she continued to play with her puzzle.

Camas walked up to the table and stood. He was a tall man and ruddy. His salt and pepper hair was wiry and bushy. He bent just slightly when he walked, and his back was hunched a little when he was standing over them at the table at that moment. He spoke softly and slowly, and not without regret. His dark almost black eyes moistened but were steady. "My wife, Colette," he continued, "none of us could understand her dark moods. The antidepressants the doctor recommended only seemed to make things worse." The others around the small table seemed to understand and had apparently heard previously at least that far of the present story. "Of course we understood the mental effects of a debilitating illness, cancer, has on a person. She didn't want to suffer. And she certainly didn't want any of her loved ones to suffer…

"She loved to pray to Mary. She was our patron saint, bless her forever. But when she was only 29, she went to the hills one night…and took her life. It wasn't a terrible sight, she looked so peaceful, like she was finally happy. She was beautiful in life, she seemed even more beautiful in death. But it was Michelle who found her." He spoke haltingly now. "She was haunted by her image of her body on the grass; pale and cold she was." And his voice trailed off.

Chanté stood and put her short arms around as far as she could reach up to him. Then with tears in his eyes, "She just used the doctor's medicine, but just too much of it." Then clearing his throat, "Euthanasia is allowed in the hospitals, why can't we use it at home?" He sniffed a little, and reached for his green handkerchief.

Traveling to Paris by car enabled the couple to talk privately. They discussed the different job choices, when they might leave, any dangers that they might be facing. Dalee had replied to his vocational suitors by email upon arrival to Angér.

The more he talked about it, the farther he got from the lesser choice of the spy job. Where would it take him? All that suspiciousness. No, that was clearly not the job for him.

Now the possibility of the Cazara job held more of an interest for him. That one seemed like it was going somewhere. Like he would end up in a very good position. But the problem was that it only seemed. What if this was a big flop? How could he be sure where this was going? Sure they had a very high profile face on the whole thing, but how far was it going to go? Seemed pretty risky overall. In addition, they appeared to have some very angry enemies. How long was that going to keep up? What could Cazara do to protect himself against that unseen enemy which has been terrorizing globally for decades? He liked the outfit, but there were too many unknowns. Little did Dalee realize just how much he had not known, and the breadth and the depth of this solitary organization, this entity, which would evolve and encompass humankind in the coming months and years.

The job he currently held had many benefits and the pay was good too. He understood it, and was familiar with the role, with its duties. It had that going for it too, the familiarity factor. He knew the territory, both geographically and socially. And he knew the office politics, and the political aspect of the work, as in a political science sense. And just the work itself. He had accompanied Delainie on a number of trips, and he certainly knew his every move. He was the one who planned it for him. He understood it all too well.

The question in this particular case was, did he really want it? It was one thing to back the Secretary of State of the USA, but it was an entirely different thing to take his place. As well, what about the possibility that it may be short-lived. They very well might keep him until they find a more suitable replacement. He talked with Janvieve until she grew tired of the various options and possibilities. She pulled into a gas station and they refueled.

Once back on the road again, Dalee first thought it through before speaking out loud. His final option was the one which he was most fond of. He enjoyed and appreciated the media. His passion was once reporting/writing/the collection of the news and he had once done so at the conglomerate which now sought him. But now he had aged a little and his interests had evolved and certain skills and abilities had been honed, so that he desired to be on the administrative end of things. He thought that it would be good if he could have a hand in the orchestration of the presentation of the product rather than the production itself. Yes he thought he would like that very much.

And so at last he spoke out loud, "I think I should like to conduct the orchestra."

Janvieve was puzzled a moment and expressed that this was not one of the options. In fact she said that she thought that *he* was crazy, but at the same time, she knew her man and understood that there was some other translation of what he meant by this last statement.

And then when he gave no further response, she coaxed him, "…Ah yes, the symphony. And what kind of a baton will you use?"

"I think I should like a pen as a baton. But what kind. That is the question."

"Ball point, felt tip, quilled?"

"And should it be depressor, or twist-opening style?

"Or perhaps one with a cap?"

"No, not a cap. They inevitably get lost. And certainly not one of those fat little clickables."

"No I think it should be a twister, and a ball point. A quill is too ancient. And metallic, not plastic; something of a variegated texture on its surface."

"What about a clip?"

"To clip, or not to clip!…"

"I would say clip." And then in a louder voice, "Clip on! Clip on to the distant future! To distant lands, where no one has ever heard the voice of the media and a news broadcast. Pierce the darkness, shatter illiteracy and ignorance. Blaze a torch through pitch black dark caverns…"

"Speaking of black, what about the color? We must have a color? What shall be the color?"

"Yes, a color…of what color shall this baton be, this beacon of light, this tower of knowledge? Red, green, blue, or black?"

"Or something unconventional like white or pale; or mustard or khaki."

"I think blue. Blue is like the ocean. Vast and unknown. Deep and yet peaceful. The Pacific. *Pacífico*, as Magellan first named it. The way he first saw it. Peaceful. And calm. Serene.

Yes that's the word. Serene. I like that word."

"In Middle English pacífico would be *pacifique*."

"Ye…es and in Latin, *pacificus*."

With the sound of pages rustling, a dictionary was brought from the glove box, and he added slowly, in a dry aristocratic voice, "Middle English, from Middle French, from Latin *pactum*, from neuter of *pactus*, past participle of *pacisci*…" Then clearing his throat and raising the volume three notches, he announced ceremoniously, "…To agree, contract; akin to Old English *fon* to seize, Latin *pax* peace, *pangere* to fix, fasten, also Greek *pEgnynai*."

"And the clip. You didn't mention the clip."

"Without the clip there's no stability, but with it, the surface is interrupted."

"Oh let's have the clip then. One must be practical at times."

Paris was just ahead in the distance. There was a shimmering light, of the sun reflecting off the skyline.

"Serene. That's what it will be. And it will be gold on the surface and maybe bits of mirrors.

"Dream on!…dream of your baton, and it will guide you, lead you on!"

The City became closer and larger in their view.

"Yes I would like to conduct the symphony with my pen of gold with its variegated surface of shiny little mirrors."

They traversed the final kilo meters and then crossed the streets that intersected the city, until they reached the Seine. Which was also a sign, that it was time to turn. And then wound their way along the river until they reached their favorite places. They saw the Louvre, with its countless priceless paintings, and wings and luring corridors of endless history. They wandered streets and window shopped. They took their time and drank lime pop. Then lingered in cafes, and watched the Parisians pass their day with living and walking; and wrapping up their work, as the sun began to sink in a clouded swirling smoky sky.

"Do we have to go back?" she listlessly asked, playing with the handle of her teacup, at a small table by the window of a street side espresso shop. "I mean to the real world."

"I'm afraid so," offered Dalee, drinking the last of his cup. "Our time has come."

"If you get the GNCN job, I haven't asked you yet, is it out of Washington?"

"They have one office there, but other ones all over the world."

"I don't want to move again Dilly."

"I know. We'll see where my position would be. We may not have to after all."

The maître d' came and they settled their cheque. Slowly they rose and gathered their collection of various prints and books and ladies apparel and accessories. Finding their vehicle they coaxed its engine to life, grinded its gears for forward propulsion, and headed back to the country in the west. The ride home was considerably less wordy. It seemed to fly too quickly by, and it wasn't long after they had crossed the city limits that they were stowing their automobile safely away in its rounded, wooden storage shed.

The home was dark except a light left on for their visitors. Late was the hour of their arrival so they quietly as possible found the way to their boudoir and climbed into bed by the aid of a yellow moon. But ere he closed his eyes, the remembrance of the bright flames in Rome burned before his mind. And not frightened, but curious about a holy man and his theories. What did they mean? Could there be some validity to them? In the pale moonlight, west of Paris, and east of home, he pondered things he'd never known to be true but that might have some bearing on his future; and just may direct the course of history and the fate of all. He closed his eyes and sleep pulled him into the subconscious world.

The next day he contacted Steven Iswald of GNCN and an interview was arranged. They would meet in London on the 17th of November, 2049. Dalee did not know this man but he was recommended to him by the news room skipper at their headquarters in Virginia, where Dalee had once been employed. He took down the details of the office building, the suite number, and the part of town it was in. He was to meet Mr Iswald at precisely 9.15 a.m. Dalee planned to arrive the day before, stay overnight, and possibly travel using the ferry. He enjoyed the sea air and sailing on a ship now and then. It enabled him to slow life down a notch, and feel the turn of the tide.

He spent the afternoon in the library collecting all his necessary documents, updating his resume, and putting together a portfolio of his journalistic and literary efforts suitable to his prospective employer. He had purchased a new laptop while in Paris the previous day charging it to a credit card, with the insurance money pending. Normally he waited for the completed credit transaction to his bank account, but with the interview only a few days away it was essential he had the necessary tools to get the job done right. It was a Toshiba XT, with voice recognition, biocybernetic interface, and haptic synthesis override. It could do everything else and possibly even had a kitchen sink function. Even the most basic factory standards were equipped with the highest capacity and the smallest components with a sleek and light design. International computer competition had been such that it became the norm to include the same machine and offer basically the same options, with a few minor variations.

By the end of afternoon he had gotten almost everything done, although he only got a start on the portfolio. He was attempting to assemble appropriate samples of his writing which he thought might persuade Mr Iswald and his associates that Dalee was indeed the right person for the opening. Looking through all his writings which he had successfully uploaded onto the new Toshiba, he chose three or four, of what he considered his best of the journalistic genre. The breadth of his writing repertoire was impressive to say the least, with pieces ranging from academic to scientific in fields from medicine to entertainment. He selected a historically significant editorial piece pertaining to the turn of the millennium. His eyes scanned until they reached portions he wished to read for relevance. They fell on these words.

"Freeze that moment in time, take a look at the area of Arts and Entertainment, and what would you see? To begin with, what kinds of music are popular now. Without question, there are some very talented artists in the field of music, but what about the styles and content of some of the current popular musical pieces in the world today? If you compare some of the classical works of Mozart or Bach, to some of the most recent songs which are considered great, you will see stark contrasts. One obvious difference would be the timelessness of the former. Of course, one cannot seriously compare classical music of previous centuries with the music of today because they are of entirely different eras. But perhaps that is the point. Maybe the music of the previous centuries, was representative of that time, and so what we see today is a product of our time now. Take the emergence of a style of music called noise. After listening to a few samples of this style, one would quickly conclude that it was a very fitting name for it. For that is exactly what it is: noise. From the time rock music began, in the 1950s, several schisms branched off of that main trunk of musical style. One of which was known as psychedelic rock, and another called punk rock. And then alternative rock later came from punk. And later still, noise has evolved, (or rather should we say that it is devolution).

We see that music has diversified into many new styles. In addition to this, there also has emerged a kind of international pop. The pop music from many countries, from East to West, all seem to have a distinct similarity, even though they come from extremely different cultures. One could relate this to the emergence of a kind of international culture. This type of phenomenon was initially seen in places like Europe, where much of the youth generation became a blending of the cultures of several different neighboring countries. On a larger scale, the same could be said of the pop music all around the world. The similarities are obvious and it has a common style regardless of what country it came from. Much more could be said about the topic of music: about the icons many musicians have become, about the extreme popularity of the music industry today, and about some of the unchanging elements of this art form which, still today, keeps music lovers satisfied. However, we will now turn to the art of film making.

Because the art of film making has only been in existence since the turn of the twentieth century, one cannot compare it to earlier times as with the arts of music or painting. But we can observe the types of movies watched by millions and millions of people. There are definitely those movies which were classics, but they many times came out of the early period. The classics, *It's a Wonderful Life*, with Jimmy Stewart, and *Twelve Angry Men* starring Henry Fonda and several others, are perfect examples. Also classics such as *Black Beauty*, *The Sound of Music, Casablanca, and My Fair Lady*.

There were also those which were produced out of the years that followed, ones like *Schindler's List*, or *Dead Poet's Society*, or *The Lord of the Rings* series. To be sure there are some which could be counted among the great productions of all time, but it seemed that there were less and less good quality movies produced at the turn of the millennium, than that earliest period of film history. Like the area of music, these newer expressions seem to lack the quality that the earlier classics possessed. Quality in acting, quality in development of plot, in characters, interesting story lines. Not to imply that there were no bad movies in say, the 1940s or 50s, but they were just more present in the latter half of that century. And that may be due to the explosion of the industry during that period. Movies during that middle period, seemed to concentrate more on special effects, audio quality, and more often than not on violence, fear, sex, and things like anger and revenge. Not to say that all of these things are necessarily wrong, but the artists, the producers and directors of these films, tended to concentrate on the latter qualities, rather than the former ones just mentioned. They should have perfected the latter while concentrating on the former, such as acting ability.

Of course in later years this art was even further developed to surpass our predecessors, and the result has been phenomenal in the past ten to twenty years. Films such as *Trade Secrets,* and *A Night in the Park,* and of course, *Tanzania,* by Dalford Werdman. Impeccable works of art! As a final note about the film industry, one can easily observe that it has become something that our society gives a large part of their leisure time to. You can easily verify this by the number of hits to downloadable movie web sites, and even now movie theatres are still visited and used quite frequently. These evidences prove that the viewing of films is a form of entertainment which is still highly favored.

Another important type of art is that of literature. There isn't sufficient time or space here to go into detail in this area. We'll just mention some of the classics and other significant works in this written art form here. These are the stories which have been read avidly by hundreds of millions all over the world: *The Adventures of Sherlock Holmes, The Lord of the Rings* trilogy, *Oliver Twist, Frankenstein.* And we must also include here the writings of Confucius, Socrates, and Homer. And then there are the authors of the 20th century and onward, people like, Tom Wolfe, John Grisham, Agatha Christie, Danielle Steele, Stephen King, Tom Clancy, Gainer Thompson, Dan Stowes, just to mention a few. The writings of these and other people are what are filling the libraries and the minds of people everywhere in our world today.

The final art form to consider is that of painting. One can see that art is no longer confined to only painting, but like the area of music, it has fragmented into new more advanced art forms. In earlier times painting was a common medium of expression. Today painting still remains a central form of art. However, some modern artists use some variation of this at times, for example computer image mosaics. This involves taking hundreds of images and creating one picture in the form of a mosaic. This was made popular in the beginning by the advertisement for the movie *The Truman Show*. Another branch is that of *installation art*. In this type of art the artist goes into a museum or some other place, and installs their art piece. Some examples of these are: an old car sawn in half with a chainsaw and then filled with grease. Another exhibit in a museum was a pile of individually wrapped candy in a corner of a room. Nothing more. It must have been the simplicity of it that the artist was trying to express. You may read into it what you like, but that was the modern art piece: maybe somewhere between fifty and a hundred candies, piled into a small heap on the floor. And this made national television at that time in both the USA and Canada.

With the turn of the new millennium many new and different art forms have emerged. The artists have stretched the limits of their creativity, art teachers are encouraging their students to push out into new areas, and to explore and try almost anything at all. This allows the merging of several different mediums into one. The possibilities are endless. We have seen that many have evolved over recent years.

Certain examples of art forms have been mentioned in this part of this article, but it does not mean they are the best. They are simply used as a reference point. There are others just as great which were not able to be mentioned here. But the ones noted are recognized as great, and the world salutes them, and all artists, and art. Thank you artists, and art lovers alike, the world over."

Yes, that should do the trick, he thought. He was about to peruse the other two selections of writing when the dinner bell sounded. He hadn't realized how late it had gotten. It was broad beans and bacon. After dinner he packed all that he needed in his newly acquired suitcase and retired early for a fresh start the next day.

On those nights before you travel, and particularly before an important rendezvous one doesn't always get that ideal sleep which is required. This was the case with Dalee, and when the alarm summoned him from the deep recesses of the dream world he felt as if he had just laid down a few minutes. In spite of his apparent lack of sleep and the mood which often accompanies it, he pressed on and prepared himself for the day. He was partially pacified by the fact that he had a day and a night between that morning of his inevitable professional grilling. And with his faithful navigator at the helm they ventured forth to the dock of the Channel Ferry along the northernmost edge of the French Republic. Some 80 minutes later and the seconds it takes to kiss and get out of the Smart car when the boat you seek is on the verge of shoving off, Dalee walked onto the plank and boarded the ferry. A few moments later the seaworthy ship was sailing from the shores of France soon to land on the coast of England. Dalee stood at the railing on the deck with sun and wind in his face.

He stared out across the waters separating the two nations and whispered, "The white cliffs of Dover."

✦ ✦ ✦

9

As it commonly does, the rain was falling on London when he entered that city. He passed Regent's Park in his cab and watched pedestrians huddle together under umbrellas, and pull higher collars on trench coats and pull hats lower over ears and foreheads to somehow escape or at least shield from the cold and drizzling November rain. Lifting his eyes higher, to the sky, he searched for a word. The right word. The cold grey skies, the icy rain coming down, and the bare leafless, lifeless trees in the park…"Bleak," he spoke the word into the rear passenger window as he was looking upwards. That's what it looked like to him. The driver, in a tweed jacket and cabby's cap pulled in quickly to a free space he had spotted and announced, "Ere we ah." The meter read 34.50 Euros. Reaching into his pocket and leafing through the paper currency in his wallet he considered the attitude and driving of the cabby. He then handed him two twenties and a quick gesture indicating that he was to keep the change. "Thank ya kindly, guv," was his response, and with that Dalee grasped the handle on his travel bag and exited the vehicle.

With the cold rain pelting his felt hat he stared up at the twenty something story building where he was to stay that night. Checking in he found his room satisfactory and lay down to rest a few minutes. After a while he got up and started again on the remaining choices of his written pieces for the interview the next day. He also put on the finishing touches to his portfolio. When all was up to standard, his standards, he saved it all on a small disc and safely put the package away. After a short survey of British television, he ordered up his supper through the room service. He had a grilled cheese and ham sandwich with some chicken noodle soup. Perfect, for a cold and rainy night in England, he thought.

The next morning the sun was trying to peak through the ever present cloud cover. He thought this a weak, but nevertheless good omen for his meeting in just over an hour from then. His taxi took him to 131 Baker Street, and he got out in front of the Echo Tower building. He paused just a moment to admire the building's unique structure. He passed the concierge and found the elevators, pressed the necessary buttons and waited. When it arrived he touched the button for the 33rd floor and the device swiftly carried Dalee and several other finely dressed businesspeople to their desired levels. Stepping off, he was met by a burly security guard with a large GNCN logo behind him. He asked his business, to which he replied he was to see Mr Iswald. The guard directed him to the reception desk where a young Indian, could've been Pakistani woman took it from there. In her fine British accent she politely asked him to wait and that Mr Iswald would be right with him. Somewhat mystified by her striking looks, he sat and picked up a nearby magazine, considering her warmth may have come from a camaraderie she must have felt toward Dalee looking as if they may have shared the same national heritage.

Seconds later a man walked softly out of a door joined

to the receptionist's counter and extended a pink manicured hand. "Good morning, Mr Delliv. I'm Steven Iswald. Pleased to meet you." Dalee returned the greeting and the two men went through the same door. They continued to walk down another hall and finally Mr Iswald led them into a door with his nameplate on it. It was a spacious office, tastefully decorated with various art pieces on shelves and walls, and a few framed degrees proudly displayed over his desk. He looked as if he was in the middle of something with books, magazines, a laptop, and his desk monitor with screen saver spinning and asking for his password.

"Let's go over to the coffee table, shall we?" and he took a file from his cluttered desk and sat down across from where Dalee was still standing, waiting for his host to be seated first. Once seated across from one another, he opened his file and the questioning began.

He asked all the routine questions to which Dalee had all the rehearsed answers. Once the interviewer was satisfied with this phase's completion, he asked for Dalee's portfolio which he pulled from his shirt pocket and handed it over to him in its envelope. Fetching his laptop he inserted the disc and began to scan its contents. Some three quarters of an hour later, after Dalee had his turn at the questioning, the process was almost complete and the conversation turned to more informal chit-chat. At close to ten o'clock, interviewee and media manager shook hands and the former was escorted as far as the reception desk, where he bade a fond farewell to his sister of the near east. Riding the elevator down to Earth again Dalee summarized and estimated what had just transpired, and felt optimistic about his chances of working there at Global News

Communications Network.

Hailing another cabbie in front of Echo Tower, he got in and gave the driver the name and address of his hotel. On the ride back he telephoned his wife and told her how the interview went. He also gave her the details of the trip he was informed he would need to make to Geneva. The United Nations meeting was on Friday going until Sunday, and Cazara would be giving an address. Dalee would be going in his then-current position as Acting Secretary of State. His possible new employer at GNCN would make their decision following that very weekend. And they were both happy to hear that, should he get the job, he could continue to operate out of Washington. He would periodically need to make trips overseas but that was fine with him too.

Back at his modest but comfortable hotel room he regrouped. The day seemed to pass quickly and that evening he had time to check the Net for news. He found various items of politics and economics, terrorism and other war related spots. He didn't actually read a lot on the web but preferred a newspaper for reading. He scanned some of the articles that interested him, then came across a statement released giving condolences to those dignitaries who had lost their lives in the Rome hotel attack. Cazara had published it and the various news agencies had picked it up. Among the usual words of sympathy there was a pledge, stronger than ever not to pay back, but to once and for all end the madness of the ongoing terror problem. Contemplating Cazara and his lofty ideals for a moment, he found himself just for an instant believing that it just might be doable. Then he went back to news.

He liked surveying a variety of sources and then comparing

them for content, by geography, style of writing, photo shots and their quality, and overall layout. His thoughts shifted and he considered the many news agencies and their products. The minutes slipped by and he found himself musing on the acceptability and the plausibility of a single media agency to deliver news to all the people in the world. One web site, one TV network, one main newspaper. But what about free speech. What would keep such an agency in check? And what if those who held the strings of power chose to manipulate, subliminally or otherwise, for their own personal interests? How could it be ever regulated to prevent such problems. But then there could be a board, accountable to the government. And it would be an equal board with all members having the same amount of say. That might work.

His screen went dark and the solar system appeared in front of him. Slowly drifting past all the planets beginning with the closest, past all of them with all their moons, further and further past Neptune and then finally Pluto. Passing the outer limits of our system, the view then turning to the Milky Way up ahead in the distance. The lights were shimmering and twinkling in the black dark void of space. Other galaxies the viewer now past, faster and faster until the stars ahead and in the periphery were suddenly streaked; and time stood still for a moment…. Then the view was one of drifting stars, and then the planets. Dalee was almost in a trance-like state, looking as if he might be pulled into the void, until he shook his head and looked up from the screen in front of him. His favorite screen saver.

Space. It was so vast. Where did it begin, and where did it end? Where did it come from? He always thought that its endlessness alone must indicate some kind of Superpower beyond what man could ever dream up. It was far too great, too intricate, too complex, with systems of amazing perfection, such beauty in design. Like Orion or Pleiades. Celestial symphonies engineered with precision and artistic style beyond the human scope or even comprehension. Superhuman, supernatural, superseding and surpassing beyond our reach. Where did it come from?

He didn't know. But he thought of the rabbi and all his words. And he contemplated the recent events and how the world was turning and changing, and of someone who seemed to be shaping the fortunes of us all. Then he thought of the UN meeting in Geneva he needed to prepare for and get to. He knew what these were like. Interesting, fascinating, and yet always a bit confusing and he usually left feeling a little muddled. So many people of so many different nationalities and different cultures and languages. It was good to be there and nice to meet them all, but it was just too much variety. Sort of like a dinner with every kind of food for you to eat in just one sitting: Indian, Italian, Thai, Chinese, Japanese, Mexican, Russian, African, Australian, and American. They simply cannot be appreciated individually because of the sheer volume of different styles. They say it's a small world, and in some ways it is true. But regardless of how small our global village becomes it remains that there are cultures that are worlds apart.

On the plane he settled in for his little flight. He watched the clouds, as they rose above the blanket that looked like wool and stared into the void that they were flying below. On the edge of the world, just at the limits of the atmosphere. Was it the edge of time too? Was space the void where time did not exist?, he wondered. When would time cease? Or would it ever end? He had to think about such things. He needed to discover. Looking up at black space for real, it was more quiet than the artificial one on his man made machine. It was silent. Was it inviting? It was peaceful. And peace is always inviting.

He fell asleep and there was yet another world. A different world, where the wars had stopped. The weapons were gone and energies and abilities were directed to more productive ends. All the time and money and manpower that once occupied the world in the business of destruction, were put towards advancing and progressing knowledge and science and medicine and technology and modern agricultural efforts. The results were astronomical. Humankind grew in leaps and bounds and more progress was made in twenty years than in any other age that had come before then. Because hatred had been put away. Because jealousy was gone. And racism was eradicated. A few small changes and it made the world of difference.

This was his recurring Utopian dream. He didn't usually dream it during the day like that. Must have been all the travel. He awoke groggy and to a dimly lit cabin with most people sleeping or resting. The indicator on the screen in front of him showed about forty minutes to destination. He collected himself and also some of his things and sat back to read one of the magazines in the pouch on the seat before his. And he waited.

At the assembly Dalee registered and found his accommodations. He met up with his assistants and US colleagues, and also was introduced to his acting aide to the

Secretary. Mr Derryl Smithers, an Austrian-looking young man bustling with energy and ready to aid in every way possible and in ways that Dalee wished that he would just leave alone. He was so overly conscientious that he eventually had to tell him plainly to back off a little, which in the end made the event a whole lot more enjoyable.

After all of the usual preliminaries of meeting the dignitaries and eating and drinking and the exchanging of pleasantries, and some of the plenary sessions were over, on day two Mr Joseph Cazara was introduced. He began with many gracious thanks and various acknowledgements to certain VIPs, and then proceeded to outline basically the same thing Dalee had heard at his previous encounter with him in Rome. It was similar in content but the style and presentation were quite different. This time it was tailored for his present audience, and given with more force, even vehemence, than before. And although there were some questions, or requests, in the speech, it was less asking and more telling this time. One got the impression that this was one who knew what he wanted and also, was going to get it. He finished with a strong plug for the peace treaty between the current warring factions of the Muslim nations and their foes.

"There can be no peace, without a Peace Treaty," Cazara continued, "no resolution without our mutual intervention. The time has come to stop the killing, to cease the violence, the senseless slaughter." And pointing to certain relevant delegations before him in the assembly he exclaimed, "You know what I'm talking about. Your people have taken the losses." Then after pausing appropriately, he added frustratedly. "When will we settle this madness!…if not now." The last three words with such deliberation and confidence it would've convinced the most reluctant skeptic. This was the characteristic speech of this man, and the signature style of which he would later on become so well known, even loved by the world for. His words continued on in persuasion and finally conclusion. He then asked the UN representatives of the following nations to meet with him and his colleagues afterward for a brief pre-meeting planning council before an agreement could be made as to formal peace talks at The Hague the very next month: The New Iraq, Saudi Arabia, Iran, Palestine, Indonesia, Malaysia, Thailand, and then Israel, Britain, USA, Canada, Australia.

They all filed into a smaller board room and once they had all entered, it was filled to capacity. The layout was such that the desks encircled the circumference of the room in a U shape, and then the head table in the front of the room. Because of this arrangement the reps of the Muslim countries lined up on one side of the room, and those of the other nations filled in the other side. Cazara began graciously, affably, and humbly.

"Please let me begin by congratulating you on this gesture, in that at the very least, you all have come thus far," he said gesturing at them with a free hand. "You are all to be commended," he then added louder, and began to clap vigorously. Some in surprise, some seemingly pleased, but all one by one began to clap as well. Dalee was clapping too. There was nothing else to be done. And when Smithers saw him clapping, he wholeheartedly joined in with his superior. Once this display was over, and Cazara was satisfied in succeeding at reducing some of the electrically charged tension in the room, he continued.

"My plan for this informal yet immensely significant

session is simple. We will, each UN rep, in this room take turns in voicing your reason why you desire peace for your country. It will be necessary to limit the length to give equal time to each person, for each nation involved in this matter. My assistant will give the signal when the time is completed." At this he gestured to a sharply dressed African man on his left with meticulously groomed hair, who stood briefly at that moment and gave a brief nod/bow to the group. "I would like your interpreter to speak out loud for you rather than using the headset provided at the desks. On my left, we will begin with Saudi Arabia. Thank you." And he quickly sat down and all eyes were on the Saudi man first in line.

With colorful robe and the headdress of that of the wealthy in his country, he began slowly in Arabic, with his translator following up in English. His interpretation came out something like this, "Our country means no harm to those nations who have suffered at the hands of terrorist organizations. We ourselves have a high number of casualties annually, of both foreigners and our own people. We do not condone the actions of the small band of extremists who terrorized the United States on that fateful day in history at the turn of the millennium, and then later again there, and then in other lands in our more recent time. If we could, we would make them stop. But their zeal is too great my friends. You do not know all consuming passion until you have met some of their representatives or heard their pleas. So, for us, for me, the reason we wish for peace is to make these extremists to see, to understand that it is in vain, it is futility, to use their methods. They suffer, we suffer, and the victims and their families, their friends, and their countries suffer. No good can come out of it. Nothing. Of course to stop the killing of innocent people..." The African man timekeeper was looking at his timepiece when the Saudi rep said this last statement. And when he began on his next sentence, he raised his arm extended in front of him and showed his palm flat to the assembly, and then turning it over indicating the time was up.

The first man wrapped up, Cazara thanked him, and they went on to the next. They each in turn went through the same procedure until the last UN rep had finished. They each had their own stories to tell and reasons to give, some were more personal than others, and more emotional, but there was a common theme, and a common desire to stop the ongoing war. A war that wasn't in any particular geographical location, and was extremely unpredictable. A war that no one ever knew when or where its next battle was going to take place, or what weapons were going to be used. Each spoke of their losses, each told of their desire for the end. And it was this which Cazara capitalized on.

"My friends, my brothers, it is as you can see, the wish of us all, to resolve this ongoing problem. And as you all know, we are not the ones who are doing the killing. But you are the ones who can make contact with their people, their organizations. We cannot do this today, but this is the beginning. The beginning of the end. The end of the erratic violence that frightens innocent citizens of your peaceful nations. This is where it starts. Right here. Right now. Today." And he looked at his watch. "At 5.38 on a Saturday evening in Geneva, Switzerland," he said smiling. "We will now take this beginning, and go back to our countries, and find those people who are the driving forces of these loosely connected terrorist networks, and we will revisit this issue, and make peace, in Holland, next month, at the Peace Palace in The Hague." He spoke his sentence in small segments because there was some applause and cheering from his audience. "Thank you for your contribution. Thank you for your work for peace." And with other well chosen words of assurance, and with his charisma, he won them over. They believed it could be done, they believed in themselves, and they found someone they could finally believe in to work on their behalf to make peace and do something about a problem they never dreamed would go away. But that night, they really thought that it could.

✛ ✛ ✛

10

Drifting aimlessly was a stray cloud just below what looked like snow that their aircraft was just about to plunge through. As they pierced the cloud cover, the plane became drenched with moisture. One more flight and he'd be home. He'd had enough of flying. He wanted to get back. Back to DC. Back to English again spoken in public, on the streets and in the shops. His Euro tour was over. There was danger, challenge, romance, international intrigue, and high society. What more could one ask for? Now he was awaiting his call from GNCN in London. It was Monday afternoon.

It was a relatively long flight, and the first meal just being served, he decided to kick back and enjoy the in-flight entertainment. It was a new movie he hadn't seen before. With bright new aspiring actors. The first five minutes held his attention so he kept on. Four friends had signed up for the military together. One to the Navy, one to the Army, and the others to the Air Force. They kept in touch through email regularly, and in this way could share their individual experiences with each other. The army guy got stationed in Korea, the navy one was sent to patrol the shores off of Northern Africa.

The two Air Force buddies were pilots and used to like to

race when they had a chance. As Dalee watched he began to wonder, as the story continued and built, where this would go. Will there be some kind of romantic betrayal, a murder perhaps? Or maybe a deal with the enemy to work covertly in an espionage role? A good story needed a hook, something to keep the viewer interested. It turned out that one of the pilots was a sleeper, planted years before, and at a very early age. He had gained the trust of his friends, and then the military, and even had a good reputation. Once he, Kaagan was his name, had secured his position in the Air Force, he was free to communicate on a secure channel to his superiors in another country. Dalee had partly guessed right. Kaagan was a spy, of sorts, but only for a time, until it had outlived its purpose. He then turned to the real business he was trained for, sent for, bred for. But his friends suspected something when his communications to them slowed and then stopped. After many attempts, the other one in the Air Force, who was in another squadron, went to Kaagan in person. The sleeper, once discovered, tried to convince his friend to join him, and then he was caught between the loyalty of his friendships and the cause and his country.

Dalee saw the Traveler Companion go by with the trolley, and he asked for white wine, and chocolate. When he had received them and was engaging himself on both, and continuing with his movie, there was a struggle between Kaagan and his good friend. They fought, not unlike they had fought as teenagers just for fun, but this time they both had weapons on their persons. Neither wanted to use them, but the conflict seemed irresolvable. They were then called on an impromptu mission together and were sent on a carrier plane where they had to parachute from it to a targeted location. But the plane was unexpectedly attacked and it went down.

Only the two friends survived of course, and they managed to get to an island in the vastness of the center of the Pacific. The remainder of the story turned out rather unexpected. They, after some time and struggle, discovered the island was inhabited after all, and by primitive peoples too. They were primitive and yet not savage, nor were they hostile toward the two visitors. The conflict between them, for the time being, was forgotten and survival and ultimately rescue became their immediate priorities. After many weeks passed and the small band of natives showed no sign of harm or threat to them, though they neither showed any sign of ability to make contact with the outside world, Kaagan and his companion resigned themselves to their fate, for the time being anyway.

In the last five minutes of the film they did actually by some freak coincidence or act of God, get rescued, but not before learning something from the islanders. In a bizarre reversal of roles, or what's more commonly known as the 'ol-switch-a-roo', the primitive people showed the civilized, the basic human and humane concepts: of forgiveness, acceptance, and trust. It was only while separated and removed from their troubled environment in civilization that they could see clearly, and have a chance to put away their destructive differences. It was a happy ending. Dalee liked happy endings, so it left him feeling satisfied. He then lay back in his seat and rested.

Forgiveness. What a simple concept. Sometimes greater countries forgave the debts of lesser countries. But what about the wrongs of other nations? Could those ever be forgiven? He thought of certain scenes as he lay there, and replayed them in his mind as he often did after watching a movie. He critiqued and analyzed. How well was it acted, produced? How was the setting, the props, the costumes? And then the story behind the story. Why would a person create such a story, with a plot like this one? He pondered it and concluded that he must have had some underlying benevolent motive to send a message to the viewer. The writer of the original story must have wanted to let the audience see that it was possible for man to resolve differences with his fellow man. Now how much of this was intentional he didn't know. Who knows? The writer may have just been working out a small scale disagreement with a relative that went off the scale. Sometimes that's what these artists were doing. Working out some personal crisis either of the past or present. Dalee decided to leave that for the psycho-socio spin masters. His field of interest and expertise was more along the lines of form. Let the modern day mind witchdoctors do the analyzes.

He looked at the TTD. He had miles and miles to go and plenty of time to fill. Nothing but the deep blue ocean below and the black emptiness of space above. And there he was, suspended between the heavens and the Earth. Like a small cloud that didn't know where to go. Drifting not on the waters nor in the universe but in the firmament. In that great expanse between Earth and sky. It may be that time did stop here. Where there were no fences, no borders, or government. These coordinates where there was void and yet there was life. Oceans and oceans of it.

The actors were new and fresh and they did have talent. But paramount to a good production, the director knew what he was doing. If there was one thing that Dalee despised it was when there was all the right ingredients and the director couldn't hold the reigns. If that person couldn't put it all together it was nothing but a unpalatable sloppy goulash, and with no taste! Now where's that at?!

The phone rang. He lifted it from the cradle it was resting in on the wide armrest beside him. "Hello."

"Mr Delliv. This is Steven Iswald. How are you?"

"I'm fine," he blurted out, just remembering he was expecting the call.

"I called to tell you that we are prepared to offer you the position at GNCN."

"Great. I'm glad to hear that Mr Iswald."

"I take it then that you accept."

"Yes, of course. It's like I mentioned at the interview, this job is who I am not so much as what I do."

Laughing Iswald replied, "Well then, I look forward to working with you. And please call me Steve."

"Alright then Steve."

"We'll be in touch with the details once you get back to the US. I just wanted to ring you to let you know the good news."

"Well thank you. Will that be all then?"

"Yes. We'll be in touch with you Dalee. Have a safe trip." And with that he was gone.

This was good news indeed. But he wanted to get back to his thoughts from before the phone call.

No, a good story that translated into the cinema had certain ingredients which were necessity. There was cinematography. The camera angles, the shots. Also the setting. For certain films it is mandatory, such as *Tanzania* by Werdman; and of course the very old classic *The Lord of the Rings*. One simply must have the right location for the right story. And this one did. So as far as Dalee was concerned, they executed that one right. Then there was the character development. The introduction of the cast, who's who, what they look like and what they are like, where they came from and where they're going. This was well done in this story too, however as far as he was concerned they might have spent more time on the development of the companions' characters, leaving a kind of blank of Kaagan's background. This would highlight it in much the same way a dot is placed on an otherwise empty page. One could either focus on the dot, or see the alternative: the negative space. This was Kofi Annan's philosophy. It can speak loud and clear if used carefully, and it has, many times in paintings, music, advertising, and other media. Sometimes what we do not see or hear can make us search for that thing, miss its presence, cause a question to arise in our minds. This is a very effective tool and is often overlooked in good productions.

Yes the form was where his interests lay. How was it packaged? How was it presented? How would the viewer perceive it or receive the story? Then there was the question of the music. This wasn't a major concern, but it could accent the story to make it a poor, good, or great production. It could tip the scales for a mediocre film to become a great one, or even a good one to exceptional. The right score in the right place can make a huge difference in a given scene, most notably the opening one and sometimes the ending. Soundtracks can make a difference. And finally there is plot. A good story has a good plot, a followable plot, and at an appropriate pace. Sometimes believable. Sometimes unbelievable, but this type would belong to another category and of a different genre. But the plot is the kernel, it *is* the story, it is the frame from which the whole thing is built. There are good stories and then there are the greats. A great story, or in the case of a film, a good story turned into a great production happens once in a long stretch. There were few of these and they only came along perhaps once in a generation. Greatness is that difference between the good and the exceptional, that which is set apart from even the best quality. Dalee had seen it in all of art, but particularly in literature and movies. He had seen the whole spectrum in all mediums. But he wondered, there in the sky, suspended there in no man's land, floating like a cloud on the air: could that be applied to a person as well? Could such greatness be in an individual? Could a human being be separate from the rest in quality and ability, in both integrity and inner strength? He had seen so many corrupt individuals, encountered the morally bankrupt, and daily met people void of consideration and without any shred of concern for others. Was it possible that there could exist, a great person?, who would care for the needs of mankind? Was Dalee thinking of Mr Cazara? Such were the thoughts that crossed his mind that day, as he and the other travelers crossed the Atlantic on their flight from Geneva to Washington. He was growing tired and his mind cluttered with all of these ideas so he decided to leave this for a time.

Upon arrival in the capital he found his sphere much as he had left it. He joined the race once again in the same routines as he had had before he left for Europe. His acting role as Secretary had not actually officially been passed on to him yet. And in fact shortly after his return it was time for him to take his scheduled vacation of three weeks. They had planned to go to their favorite place in Florida – Miami Beach. This was non-negotiable and their schedule was fixed. They looked forward to this all year and new job or nuclear war, they were still going to go. They also chose to drive rather than fly, and enjoy the gradual change of landscape and, more importantly, of climate as their vehicle made its way along the vanilla coast to the gold coast.

The day arrived, the car was packed, and the couple embarked on a journey of blessed freedom from the imprisonment of time and schedules and endless appointments and deadlines. All this they would leave behind in the City of politics and the center of the modern Western world. They left it behind that morning and headed south on highway A1A.

Meandering down the East Coast at a leisurely pace they saw the little towns along the way, ate at homey restaurants and stopped and slept when they got tired. The first stop was a mom-and-pop inn called 'Stop-a-While'. And they did just that on a clear but cold last day of November afternoon.

Dalee sang as he brushed the snow from the car window. He made up his own words to a tune that he used to hear his father play when he was a child in their home in West Virginia. It was a pleasant melody and the words were fitting because it was indeed the first of December, and it really was covered with snow, just like in *Sweet Baby James*. It was that soft feathery kind that swirls and blows like dust in the wind.

Driving along the coast that December morning, they felt as if their troubles had been left behind, and the more miles they put between their origin and their car as they drove, the farther away their present but diminishing-into-the-past problems seemed to be. Time passed and scenes changed from winter to that of spring, and then summer as they entered into the subtropical zones of the south. Finally on the third day they arrived at their destination, checked in to their accommodations, and promptly changed into swim suits and walked out onto the sandy sunny beach to soak it all in.

After some time of drinking in the warmth of the sun, Dalee commented, "This secretary's job isn't near as hard as I thought it was going to be." Janvieve gave him a wry smile and got up to take a dip in the Atlantic. At that point there was no concern of being recognized the way the former Secretary was. It was difficult to have a normal life when one had global fame. It was particularly noticeable and annoying while on vacation. With little to concern them, the first day passed without incident and they retired to the condo on the beach. They were far enough from the noise and busyness that it was quiet at night. But they were close enough that should they desire some nightlife it was within reasonable walking distance.

Several days passed and the effect of the great ocean they were settled upon and its sea breezes began to work their magic. The calm, the peace, the restoration on the soul began to settle into place. On the fifth day they decided one evening to walk to the hub of excitement and dance at one of the clubs. The Latino beat could be heard long before the strip was in sight. Trumpets, drums, guitars all playing together that symphony of rhythm that makes dancing a necessity rather than an option. Moving to the music even as they entered the area on the beach where the party was evolving they made their way to the makeshift dance floor. Moving to that fast-paced cadence while on the sand was harder than one might think and took some skill. When the number was finished the next began almost immediately and so they continued. The second seemed, if it was possible, faster than the previous, and when that one finished and yet another started, they decided to go for a drink. They had walked some distance and were thirsty even before they joined in with the music. Flushed but exhilarated they sat down at a small table a short distance away from the action.

"Are we having fun yet?!" she shouted. To which Dalee gave his partner a wink and a nod of the head. They drained their glasses and ordered two more as soon as they could find a waiter in the tangled mass of people surrounding the bar. As the evening wore on and the crowd grew even larger, there was no sign of slowing and if anything the energy seemed to accelerate. After more dancing they had enough and began on the walk home.

However, they enjoyed the time there so much they decided to go back again to the same spot the following evening. Everything was as they had left it, but with just as many new faces as there were the night before. Janvieve took a break to the restroom and Dalee approached the bar for a drink. After ordering his choice, a man next to him who he hadn't noticed before turned slightly and said, "Dalee Delliv?" Surprised that his name was spoken he was startled for a moment.

The man discretely revealed a badge within his jacket and quietly said: "Agent Berarros, Secret Service." He had square shoulders and a square haircut but his race and his clothes blended him into the background.

"This is Agent Knowles," he spoke with the same discretion without looking at either of the men. Collecting his things at the bar, he spoke while he stood, "We were assigned surveillance duty." And with that he walked into the dance floor. Knowles, a thirty-ish African-American, remained nursing his made-to-look-like vodka.

"Is nothing sacred anymore?" Dalee finally managed after taking in the situation. Knowles made no acknowledgement but continued with his prop on the stage of his assumed role and stared straight ahead. When Gen returned he guided her back towards the general direction of their condo. She thought it still a little early yet until he explained what he had just encountered.

"Does this mean you're in some kind of danger?" she asked slowing down since they had gotten far enough from the dance club.

"No, it's just a precaution. There's nothing to worry about."

"Nothing to worry about? You now have goons shadowing you and you tell me not to worry? There's got to be a reason!"

She was growing excited and he knew where this was going. "It's just standard for my new position."

"But you haven't even started it yet, and they're starting to invade our personal lives? I don't think so. We're on vacation for God's sake." Her eyes flashed when she became angry. She had a couple of drinks as well which didn't help matters.

"I will accept the necessary procedures of my position when they are warranted. I'm not ready to give up everything I've worked for because of a small loss of privacy."

"But you don't even need this anymore! You've got the other job."

"Yes, that's true. But I don't want to close any doors that I may need later."

She turned away and walked ahead. He followed at a safe distance to watch, and in a few minutes she turned into the entrance to their place. When she was inside Dalee walked on a little further, and glancing behind saw two figures in the distance, almost certainly Mr Berrarros and his sidekick Knowles.

They had discussed the double job situation when he first returned to Washington. Since he wouldn't be starting the media management position until into the new year, he waited to speak to Stan about it until after his vacation. He desired to maintain his connections to the State Department and to work in some capacity there even though he had accepted a position elsewhere. And working out of DC would allow him to do this. He turned around and began to walk back. He passed the secret service men and they asked him if everything was alright. He told them it was so they continued on and then kept watch from a strategic location.

Standing outside he watched the waves for a while. The sound was soothing, rhythmic. His mind went back to the tragedy in Rome just a few weeks earlier. The intelligence had shown terrorist networks working like they did in countless other attacks. It also had been discovered that Cazara did in fact have some opposition, and that he had made some enemies along the way in his crusade for peace with the Muslims. So much hate. Would it ever end? He began to think of history and all those who had tried to achieve peace and revolution. Mahatma Gandhi, Ché Gavera, Denny Castellano, Mother Theresa, Martin Luther King, Jr., Gautama Buddha, and Jesus of Nazareth. What did they do? What was the final outcome of their efforts? And what became of each of them.

Gandhi was most assuredly a man of peace. His work involved the reconciling of two extremely different belief systems, and others as well. Dalee considered the Muslims of Gandhi's time and their hatred for the efforts that he was putting forth to accept and embrace the Hindus. He didn't care what religion they were. They were just people to him, and his brothers too. If the Muslims wouldn't accept the Hindus then, and those were their own countrymen, how were they going to agree to a treaty with Christians and Jews. Unheard of! Impossible. Look what they finally did to him in the end. A zealous Indian Hindu shot and killed him in public. No, Dalee did not think Cazara could succeed. Not in a world of such hate. But he seemed to think he could pull it off. That was what seemed to gain his popularity, propel his momentum. Where did he get his optimism? Was it legitimate or was it feigned? Whatever the case it was working so far. He wondered how it would go at that summit held in the Netherlands. It had been scheduled on, of all days, December 25th. Cazara's statement had said that this was the day that "peace would reign on Earth. Finally, and with finality." He also made reference to the significance of the day, that neither Jews nor Muslims recognized the 25th so they would definitely be free at that time. It was sort of a historical celestial joke. Imagine, world peace, achieved on the Christian holy day. Peace between the warring factions in the Middle East, and also simultaneously, they were projecting anyway, to put an end to the world wide violence which has terrorized so many nations for seemingly countless years. Now that would be a grand act, a shining moment in history.

What about the Buddha? There were hundreds, perhaps thousands of gods, and religions at his time and in his region. He had a great following. Well, at least he did later after his death, and definitely did in the present time. What was his strategy? Was it a strategy to unify religions? Or people? What was on the Buddha's agenda? Whatever the case, in the end, well the long run, he succeeded. The diversity of religions of that time period was brought together somehow through this one man's efforts. Not that there was anything wrong with diversity. But there was also chaos and without the unity, the cohesiveness which was lacking, the region would never have had the later successes they achieved. This was attempted economically in the 2020s, however, without success. Whoever had attempted it, Dalee couldn't remember, did not have the same staying power, the same quality that Gautama Buddha had in that time thousands of years before. Perhaps it was the time period. It was a different era then, as they say. Or perhaps it was the tool which he used to change the society which he lived in at that time. Religion in that day was something that people valued. And lived by. The economic effort so many centuries later was indeed with something that people valued, that everyone valued money. But of course this was a different kind of valuing.

Perhaps this was the difference; that the subject of the matter, the tool which was used in attempting to achieve the unity, the cohesiveness, was valuable, and yet was not genuinely valued. He was thinking of the difference between religion and money, in the eyes of the people. Now, of course one must take into account the different time periods, and to the people of the 2500s BC, religion was a way of life and the glue which held society together. As opposed to the society in the modern era in the years of the 2020s, where money was used to unify the same region some four and a half millennia in the future.

Although the people were the same, Asians, the time period and the tool were different. And though money is valued, it is not valued in the same way as religion is, at the core of people's lives. As well, the initiator of this economic revolution, for lack of a better word, Dalee believed did not have in mind the same things the Buddha did at the time of his revolution. Unity may have been one of the beneficial results of the Asian Currency campaign, but it was not the sole motivator for the initiator. His agenda was more along the lines of financial and political benefits.

And then there was Mr Denny Castellano. In 2035 at the age of 44 he single-handedly took on the task of joining the then European Union of 25 nations, to the then African Nation which consisted of almost all of the countries of that continent. It would have worked too if it hadn't have been for the famine. Just wasn't the right timing, he supposed. But Castellano's efforts centerd around the unity of cultures, and it drew upon the success of the EU up to that point. He, being part Italian-American and part African no doubt aided in his efforts. The Mid-East issue was also a factor. It was an underlying thought that in the unification of the European and African peoples would somehow give wings to the hope of peace in the Middle East. It was a peripheral hope, and a by-product of the primary vision of a man who wished for his differing peoples to join together in a union which would be mutually beneficial. But the bi-lateral talks broke down when a very real and pressing need came to the forefront and the whole multi nation, dual continental project was stalled indefinitely. Dalee thought that it was quite possible that the two entities joining together could very well have had a positive effect on the instability in that region between the two. It being a natural phenomenon which dislodged Castellano's efforts made Dalee, and many others as well he was sure, give some measure of optimism to the notion of a solution to the endless violence and the hopelessness of the regional dilemma which became a global problem.

He picked up a shell on the shore of the beach and examined its intricacies and its unique form. All these great men couldn't achieve such a small thing really. Peace itself was right here in front of him, wasn't it? The Earth itself had its own systems and cycles which depended upon one another. And they worked together in harmony. The tides, the seasons, the winds and the waves, the fish and the birds, the plants and the trees. Somehow this worked; and seemingly without any help too; without a director or conductor? How did it work? Was there a Creator to all of this? If peace could be achieved in nature why couldn't it be achieved among the lord of creation, humanity...? Then there was the universe. And he looked to the heavens that silently shone above him. The countless stars and suns and galaxies and the endless black space, and space, and space.... What of this natural occurrence of a peaceful existence? The planets turned on their axes, the planets revolved around their suns, the solar systems were the delicate pieces of their galaxies, and the galaxies turned in their motions, and so it went on and on. All were parts in a larger scene, in a greater picture, where the sum of all the parts, do make a whole and it all does make sense. The big picture; that's what he needed to look at. He would see what would happen at this summit on Christmas Day in the Netherlands. This may be just the time for such a grand achievement. At a time such as this peace may just be possible. All the others couldn't achieve it, but it just may be that the hour had come. The shining moment in history when wars would actually cease, and the terrorism problem which had for so many decades plagued the whole Earth, would be resolved. Why couldn't it be now? Why shouldn't it be doable. If Nature could do it, then so could we. If plants and creatures and hydrogen and oxygen and stars and moons could operate in harmony in our common dimension, the micro and the macro, seen and unseen, then we can too. Mankind can too.

It was on Christmas day that one was born into the world that brought that very message – Peace on Earth. If he could do it, then why can't we on that same day carry out that order. Though it is seemingly impossible in our world today, but very credible when one looks at the actual Earth and not the world? He put down the shell and turned around to go back to his vacation home. Back inside to make peace with his partner. It wasn't so hard. It just took understanding. It just took some faith.

The next morning they drove to Cypress Gardens to experience the poinsettias in all their glory. The bright red flowers cheered them and put a lighter tone on the situation compared to the previous evening. Then later at the Epcott Center they viewed all the different countries' cultures and saw the splendor of the various nations at all the exhibits.

They heard their music, and then later on tasted various foods at an international dinner. There had Indian food, yellow curries and red curries, chapattis and special kinds of pancakes to eat the main dishes with. There was English food, bubble and squeak, Cornish hen, broad beans and bacon, and *Yorkshire* pudding. And there was also Belgian waffles, Spanish rice, cabbage rolls, Pirogues, *sour kraut*, kuchen, black forest cake, baklava, Swedish meatballs, and Welsh rabbit.

Then there was Korean food, *bokambap*, bulgogi, *kalbitang*, *samgyupsal*, *kimbap*, and Korean pizza. Italian food, lasagna, alfredo fettuccine, *pasta facule*, and Sicilian wine. Thai food, *tdome yum gung*, *pat grapow*, *pat thai*, *mussamun*, *gaeng gali guy*, *pballo*, *khay yat saey*, *kanom jeen*, and so many of their desserts as well, *rotee*, *ruam mit*, *kluay buachee*, *sang khayaa*. The foods of the Middle East, Africa, China, Indonesia, and on to the countries of the Americas, the foods of Chile, Argentina, Venezuela, Columbia and Ecuador, Guatemala, Costa Rica, Mexico, the United States and Canada. The Caribbean, Australia, New Zealand and to the far reaches of the globe. Every nation, every people were represented in room after room of samples of exquisite culinary delights. Of course they could only try certain ones and were limited to some of the rooms. It was just too grand to see in one day let alone in one meal. So they had to be satisfied with as much as they could take in a few helpings.

Dalee, as he observed the different foods from so many different places his thoughts went back to the evening before, standing at the shore of the Atlantic. He thought again that it could be possible for even enemies to live in peace. If there had never been a war, or in this case, ongoing terrorist attacks from an unseen enemy, then it would surely be possible. Of course if there had never been any hostility between the different sides, this would make it so much easier. This was in fact the neutral state of nature. Of course there was survival, but not the malicious killing the way only the humans could do it. But if the natural world could live harmoniously, then so could we. The myriads of food types displayed in front of him were a visible reminder of this fact.

They returned to their vacation base very full of foods, but also a sense of optimism. The air in their condo took on a rosy tinge and so did the days that followed. The weeks passed and the rest they had so much needed from the daily grind of life restored and recuperated them – body and soul. They had their fill, in those three weeks, of sun and sand, of sea and sky. Also of the music and clubs, of drinks and dance, and long leisurely, or passionate, nights as they so willed. The drive back seemed shorter and the winter season seemed to come too quickly. But so it did, and they watched as they progressed northward and the scene changed from sand to snow, and they returned to the world of the conventional, the more traditional, expected landscape for the Christmas season.

Back at work Dalee continued in his usual routines and responsibilities, but the new role he was asked to take on had its own obligations. However, he adapted to these and made the necessary adjustments. There were ones he had expected, but others he had no idea that Mr Delainie had to take care of. It took some juggling but he was managing it for the time. It in fact was only going to be temporary, and the time came when Dalee had to discuss his new job at the media corporation with his current boss.

"Stan, you got a minute?" he asked half leaning into the doorway of his office.

"Ya, but just that," he responded, with a quick glance up from his laptop.

Dalee slipped in and sat in a chair near his supervisor's desk. His face was a little sad and this was supposed to be the intro to his brief but poignant speech. He decided that with Stan the man, he had better go with the more direct approach.

He didn't like lead-ins or bush beatings.

"I took another job with GNCN that begins early next year." There it was – brief, concise, and to the point. The only vague-ery or wiggle room he included was the 'early next year' part, intentionally given as a courtesy for his benefit.

"We will have to use Grahmer to replace you," he responded while pushing his portable PC to the right. There was just the slightest, almost imperceptible, yet still present, sense of loss. It was the sentiment that a man of his position was permitted to show; it had to be of the barest minimum quantity, and with just the right acceptable quality, in order that the recipient and/or observers would perceive enough to satisfy their required need, but at the same time prevent jeopardizing or compromising his authority. Such was the circumstance of people of power of that day in America, and particularly in the Capital.

They further discussed the Secretary's responsibilities. Stan liked to cut to the heart of a matter, and then once that was out of the way, to work steadily on the present problem. They worked out an arrangement where Dalee would continue some of his responsibilities at the State Department, and of course remain on the payroll, and begin his new job in February. He hadn't told Stan until that point that his position would officially begin on February 14th, 2050, which happened to fall on a Monday that year. Until he started his new job he would continue in a limited capacity with his old one. So for the remainder of '49, and January and half of February of the next year he would still be employed officially with the United States government. Dalee agreed to the arrangement and once they had settled that end of things, they sorted out the logistics of his schedule at GNCN and to what extent it would be possible for him to work on a periodic basis with some degree of consistency. Finally they discussed the summit in The Hague. He would attend as the Acting Secretary of State. But he would later discover that he would also have an additional role there, more in the interests of the media. And he also did not realize the weighty matters which in fact would be decided, and the course that would be set in motion which would turn the tides of all who live on Earth.

Christmas was celebrated early by the Delliv family that year. They usually celebrated on their own first at their home: exchanged their gifts, had their traditional meal, even sang a few carols, of both the old and the new. Then there was the drive from DC to Maryland where his wife's relatives were. They spent some time visiting and socializing, and catching up on the old and the new. The French had their own traditions, and quite different from what Dalee had been accustomed to, but he was used to them, and some he even enjoyed. However some they missed because of the earliness of their visit. Janvieve would remain there for the actual day of Christmas, but first they made their pilgrimage to Dalee's family's home in West Virginia.

The mountains were beautiful that time of year, and during the drive there, they were covered with the fresh snow of the previous day. The Blue Ridge wasn't so blue as it was white the way they saw it that crisp December afternoon. The Delliv estate was decorated elaborately as they typically did at that time of year, with many strings of colored and flashing lights on the trees along the paved driveway. And then on the building itself there was much shimmering of garlands and bands of yellow and gold and red and green. Also very large lettering fixed to the front of the house, just over the third floor windows: **"Season's Greetings, Happy Christmas and a Safe New Year's to all."** They pulled up their vehicle to the garage at the side. They only had a small travel bag, and of course the gifts.

At the door his Dad greeted them with his sing-song accent of rising and falling tones that East Indians were famous for, "We are so happy to see you. Come in, come in. Let me take your things. Here you can put them here." There was a lot of commotion in the front hall, with stamping of feet and removal of coats, and finally they were ushered into the living room where Dalee's mother greeted them both and bade them sit down and rest while she got them drinks. She had the traditional red mark centerd on her forehead, and her eyes were soft and kind, her face compassionate with a beautiful permanent tan.

The receivers and the received reminisced and caught up, and then the party moved into the dining room. The food was of course Indian and no turkey was in sight. You can take the Mumbian out of Mumbai, but you can't take the Mumbai out of the Mumbian. He had to have his traditional food. Christmas, New Year's, Ramadan, or Fourth of July, it had to be Indian. Later they opened their gifts and much paper was piled on the living room floor. Dalee particularly took note of his mother's thoughtful gift to his spouse that year. It was a very modern jeweled bracelet. Nothing tacky or remotely resembling anything of previous years. It was tasteful and very much appreciated by the recipient. Janvieve tried in vain to hide her surprise of such a well chosen present. She did however succeed in openly showing her appreciation with appropriate French affection.

When all was done and they were sitting by the fire on the night before Christmas eve, they sat and chatted while they sipped their favorite seasonal drinks. This was one Western food tradition which found its way into this Indian home. Dalee drank his eggnog, seasoned just the way he liked it, and the others nibbled their chocolates and other sweets and treats. His flight was the following day to Holland. He made it up to his partner by promising a New Year's Eve party that would equal what was lost by his missing Christmas. Now what exactly that meant he had yet to discover and devise.

As they discussed the past and then the plans for the coming times ahead, Mrs. Delliv made an observation which rung true for Dalee. "You know, I sometimes think of you two and how different you were at first. But now you've seemed to grow together into one." She sipped her tea. "If someone of French heritage and another of Indian heritage can get along the way you do, I think there must be hope for the world."

Dalee stood, and sat beside his aging mother. And putting his arm around her, looking into her face, he responded warmly, "There might be yet, Mom. There just may be."

✦ ✦ ✦

11

"What do other people call it." It was a question, but spoken without the intonation of an inquiry. He was speaking to one of the Dutch delegates at the Summit of Peaceful Nations. The man was in his early thirties, slightly taller than Dalee, and thin. Hair and eyes, were blonde and blue, with a face of angular shapes that seemed somehow softer when it talked.

"Some have called it 'the hag'," he was saying, his English very good, but his accent unmistakable. "Others will say 'the hog' if you can imagine; or 'the hack'. Still, even others, from certain parts of Asia will pronounce it 'the haguu', or 'haygooeey' depending on which part. It all depends on the part of the world. There can be so many different pronunciations and variations of the very same thing you know."

"Oh, I know," Dalee agreed, with only the slightest hint of mock sincerity. He'd found this person shuffling through name tags when he had arrived at the beginning. He'd flown in to Amsterdam at 4.15 p.m. the previous day, had a brief and frequently interrupted sleep, and was becoming somewhat annoyed at this conversation he had somehow unwillingly become engaged in.

"Of course the correct way to pronounce it is, the Haag, with the long 'a' and the hard 'g'. Which is more like a 'k' for you I think, in the American manner of speaking." His accent became even more pronounced upon the emphasizing of this word in question.

Becoming irritated with a national of the host country of a global peace conference, not a very good way to start the Summit. However Dalee made his way to the appropriate hall, found his seat with his name and position indicated, and settled in for the first session of the morning. Of course Daryll Smithers was right there by his side, prepared for every and any possible situation.

He was also aware that there would be no mistake this time around as far as security was concerned. Armed guards were stationed at strategic locations, including a heavily equipped unit on all four corners of the roof of the structure in which the conference was held in. Anti-aircraft, anti-tank, and anti-anti-aircraft guns were the order of the day, and the roof was full of them. It was a wonder it didn't cave in with all that heavy artillery up there. The front, back and every other location of possible point of entry were heavily guarded and carefully monitored with elaborate and complex coded, decoded and recoded checking systems. They were working together with a Special Forces unit that Dalee didn't even know existed until he was asked to have a hand in its administrative end of things. That was one of his responsibilities in the time leading up to the Summit before the trip. It was that week in between Miami Beach and the West Virginia Christmas. Of course Smithers had his hand in it as well. Both of them actually, and feet, arms, legs. Basically he just plunged right in, what ever he did. He did all of Dalee's excess paperwork, itineraries, arrangement of errands, certain correspondences, and other communications of routine nature. Sometimes he'd wished he could do those things himself like he used to do. But he supposed letting go of certain tasks came with the territory.

The Summit of Peaceful Nations was as high profile as you could get. Advertised on the two major networks, having its own official very slick highest tech website www. summitofpeace. com. No expense was spared in this elaborate endeavour which those powers that be had arranged. And they also took great care in inviting only the top, the most, and the best. These were those key players, the ones who made the difference, and most importantly those who had the ear of those who pulled the strings of the terrorist networks of the world. It was possible that some of the very kingpins of both the major and minor international terrorist groups were even present themselves. If not, there were certainly representatives, official or unofficial no one was really certain, but the Chairman wanted them there anyway, whether overtly or even if they were under cover. The special security/military unit was especially trained not to attack or detain certain individuals and how to behave and respond in situations that could go either way. Based on subtle cues they were to make quick decisions and strictly stay to their trained manoeuvers or the refraining of certain "operations" as was required by their expert judgments. These people were good. The best. And nothing was going to jeopardize this mission.

Much attention was paid to the environment in which the actual sessions were to occur. The ambiance, the tone, the setting was very important. Certain rooms had specific framed prints, even select original paintings brought in. Specially made maps of appropriate regions were diplomatically and tastefully placed in just the right places. Preselected music was played on cue out of the best imported sound systems. Tropical plants, art pieces, and other things of beauty were also placed prominently or in the background as experts had so decided beforehand. Even walls had been repainted colors to match, blend, and to soften the viewers' moods. All orchestrated to work together in the grand scheme of things for the theme of the Summit – *to foster peace*.

The advertising, on all fronts, and in every medium, leading up to the event; the security to protect from anti-peace demonstrations or an attack of any kind whatsoever; the physical environment and atmosphere of the facilities, all worked together for this one purpose, towards this one end. And that was: to ensure the success of this effort and to bring an end to the unrest that troubled the people attending, those they came to represent, and the remainder of the citizens of Earth. And very effective it was. The attendees were impressed even as they filed in one by one, or by twos, or in groups, each finding their own places in the large room where the opening session was to begin.

There was the PLO Chairman, the Presidents and their Vice-Presidents of some of the Muslim nations, and at the very least the second in command in the form of the deputy minister or the vice president alone, for the remainder of the world's Islamic countries, and of course the Prime Minister of Israel. Then there was Mr Khadahar himself for the Arab League of Nations, the Acting Secretary of State for the United States, the Prime Ministers of Britain, Canada, and Australia. All of these were accompanied by each of their own entourages, and their own security personnel; such that the main meeting room was becoming so overcrowded that certain secondary and even some tertiary level delegates had to be asked to take part in the adjacent room and get wired in via video and audio feed. The individuals of the latter category of attendees just mentioned had to be plied with additional executive accoutrements until they were finally satisfactorily pacified and were given new appropriate places of honor befitting of their positions. There were also other heads of state of other countries, sent as a courtesy even though they were not directly related to this attempted peace treaty.

The media was certainly present, but only somewhat visible. Specific regulations were kept in accordance with the Summit's committee. There were plenty of reporters with their digital cameras, web feed micro video recorders, burning audio onto paper clip sized MC3 chips, or just sending various clips to live television and radio, these were all outside of the main event. Only select prescreened preapproved media people were permitted into the area where the meetings would be held. Inside, behind the closed doors of the conference, those who were allowed into the sessions themselves, were required to adhere to certain guidelines concerning their dress, behavior, and speech. If they were with any media agency of any kind or in any capacity, their actions and appearance had to be such that they were inconspicuous, if not invisible. As one could deduce, this type of situation would effectively reduce these ultra extreme adventuring news hunters of the free world to the role of mere chroniclers, or simply observers. In the inner courts of this session there would be no messy, noisy, tangled mass of the usual scenario of a media frenzy. There would be no series of successive flashes that blind the victims of the paparazzi, no barrage of questions they so often unleash at a typical press conference. No, the reporters of this carefully managed occasion would blend in, even help motion forward the great cause of peace, if that were possible. The Acting Secretary certainly looked his part, and no one would even have known that he worked under the auspices of the greatest media corporation on the globe.

The beginning was actually fairly predictable, Dalee thought, from what he knew of the Chairman of all this, Mr Cazara. With just the right amount of fanfare and not too much levity in opening remarks to be careful to not be trite in light of the gravity and the caliber of the subject, but just enough to put the listeners at ease…the Christmas Day 2049 peace summit at the Peace Palace was underway. Once the preliminaries were out of the way, four or five individuals gave graphic accounts of their personal losses as a result of the terrorist attacks, from various parts of the world…. All very recent. Then a brief summary of the history of war throughout the world but restricted only to the past 14 years, and the horrors and atrocities associated with those wars. The mood became tense, the multicultural audience began to be uncomfortable with the other sides which they were keenly aware were also present in that same room with them. Great care was taken in the seating arrangements of various dignitaries and the different nations represented so as not to make anyone uncomfortable in that regard. While the first two segments were intended to make the viewers more than just squirm, they were not obviously, to cause such a stirring that might lead to physical altercations between co-conferees. Therefore, a short clip was introduced at the optimal moment, and Dalee had to commend them on this one, that it was right on the money, in both its timing and the content.

Short and sweet. An excellent production with a consummate performance. It was both simple and direct. "Warm and sincere" was what the media was already calling it. Two friends, not much dialogue because they were both of different languages, therefore expressions and gestures had to speak clearly. This is where good acting is essential, and it must be natural. The casting was perfect. Simply put, it portrayed these two people who would be enemies, who were enemies in the real world, but in that room that morning, it presented them as comfortable, natural, at ease with one another, talking, eating, and working together on some small but common project. They succeeded at this task and completed a common goal. The whole thing couldn't have been longer than ten minutes, but was for some reason very powerful in that room, on that day. Maybe it was the lead-in and the emotionally charged previous parts, maybe it was the ambiance they had worked so hard to achieve, or maybe it was some greater reason, such as the time in history was right, the people; they were fed up, and just tired of the killing. Both sides had had enough. They were sick of it, and they were numb.

The film was followed by a very short break and then the Chairman was introduced. Listing his credentials, and his involvements both in the past and presently, and then his achievements dwelling chiefly on his large scale successes in multilateral arbitration on three continents, and once he was fully recognized, he came out to greet the guests.

"Honored guests, Heads of State, and Officials from so many parts of our common world, we thank you for your graciousness, and your goodness for being so kind to join us here at the Summit of Peaceful Nations on the 25th of December, 2049. I personally thank you all." Applause but only enough that would be necessary. Some were feeling a little uneasy, but most were at least neutralized, which was exactly what was intended. He spoke on the need of the hour and the theme of the conference, which had already, before any of this even started, been saturated nonverbally into the minds of everyone there, carefully and intentionally. The speech wasn't all that long and he had wanted simply to introduce the summit, clearly, and concisely, and to put it in words for his listeners so that clarity would peal like bells, so that it would be crystal clear what they were after there, that day. He welcomed them all, assured them repeatedly of his and his colleagues' design for the Summit, and verbalized what had been given to them prior to his speech. Lunch was then served.

It was an international dinner of course, which had been prepared by chefs flown in for the occasion. Most of the guests stayed with their own people; however there was some mingling within the cosmopolitan crowd. And so as to adhere to the wishes and customs of the nations which normally had an afternoon siesta they broke immediately after lunch to reconvene at 3.45 p.m. Many were jet lagged from the flight, and the Western guests had given up their most important holiday so it was important for them to at least videophone to their loved ones, in spite of the time difference.

After the extended afternoon break, the conferees were ready to get started again, and the first session was a multi-level forum like set up. It wasn't exactly like a public debate for fear this would turn into something unpleasant. It was a discussion, but it was stacked. Stacked in the sense that there were a variety of different levels involved, but also in the sense that to some extent the participants were prearranged. There were several of these groups which were meeting simultaneously in about 20 different rooms. The result was better than expected in most rooms, while in others there were some heated debates that went on. The planted individuals were people from nations that were predominant in a particular group, so that in any given room there was at least one familiar accepted person, but who sided with 'the greater cause' of the day. These people were paid well and had tremendous skill in arbitration, diplomacy, and an education in international law. In the group that Dalee was with, he was not informed of who it might be, but was aware that there was a covert individual or individuals present.

It was held at a round table with approximately fifteen people seated there. Each room was different but there were somewhere between fifteen and twenty in each different place. Many kinds of drinks were served from Turkish coffee to jasmine and green tea, and also pop. The subject in Dalee's session was: "War criminals and their proposed disposal." Now disposal in this case was not supposed to mean to discard as in waste or other unwanted material, but this was actually an amusing point of discussion at the outset of their debate. The subject was originally written in the English language, but when it was read by the moderator, some of the interpreters misunderstood the last word to be deposed. And then when it was translated, the official members of the discussion group got a different message. Then when they tried to give a response the hearers got something confusing to them, not quite what they expected and so they were puzzled. A very small difference but when you are dealing with interpreters and at least four different languages, it could turn into a fiasco. After some minutes of this, all was in confusion; Dalce received a call on his hand phone and had to excuse himself.

He saw by the number that it was Mr Iswald. Pressing the button, he answered. They discussed the conference, and Dalee asked how his Christmas was going. Dalee was to oversee the GNCN crew for the Summit and Iswald was just checking in on him to make sure his hot story was staying hot enough. Dalee assured him this was the case, wished him a very Merry Christmas and got back to his round table, by which time they were advocating deposing all war criminals after all!

They delved back into history and discussed appropriate internationally known figures beginning with Hitler, which all seemed to be in agreement on, most likely because he had been dead so long. Then went on to others such as Slobodan Milosevic, General Pinochet, Pol Pot, and some very early ones as well. Some debated the point whether Genghis Khan, or some of the Roman Caesars could be condemned for their actions, those for them, citing their military responsibilities and legitimate aspirations for their home countries and their own people. Then, more recent offenders were introduced, but carefully so not to include certain individuals which would cause not only a little dissension, but would surely be disastrous.

Rizard Lznydak was one. They discussed his crimes, which were without question the most horrendous of this category. Between the years 2043 and 2045 he, and his band of rebels, assaulted Chechnya, the city of Kiev, and the United Koreas in random attacks from secret strategic military bases. Most of them were in China, and he paid off the Chinese government handsomely to look the other way. The slaughters were merciless and men, women, and children alike were murdered by the thousands. And the total in the end reached in the millions. He was bent on conquest and had his own personal agenda of war. He would later also capture and torture many. Their weapons of destruction included both biological and chemical. He was a perfect example of a war criminal, and so could be discussed as to his appropriate disposal, or to some in the group, his disposal. Some thought he should be executed, though no one could decide who would be the right nation to do it. Others thought he should be made to serve society using his skills to help the side of good in military matters. Still others thought exile would be right, with all privileges cut off. Some even thought prolonged torture would be most appropriate. And using many of his own techniques on him, and his top officials as well.

One common theme, the moderator pointed out after some time, was that many of these people never did receive justice and their cases were ongoing. This was largely due to not having the proper international laws in place, the absence of an appropriate governing body with a legitimate globally recognized power to deal with the case, and also there was the fear of possible retaliation, and then there was the issue of evidence as well. It was pointed out by some that Joseph Cazara had a plan to create such a body, and a strong stable one. In fact he had one already. This was only mentioned and then discussed for a moment, but Dalee took note of it and made some notes on the details. He would later use this for his second function at the conference's responsibilities that would enable them to piece together a story, along with other information, which would be world news in a matter of hours.

By 5.15 they were wrapping things up and going back to the main hall. This segment was intended to persuade and convince those present that peace was not only desirable but inevitable and from the Chairman's perspective: a necessity. He gave another address at 5.30 sharp, which included references to many if not all of the round table discussion topics ranging from war crimes and their perpetrators and victims, to religions and their similarities, with much weight placed on the sanctity of culture. At his highest and at his best Cazara would implore, exhort, even cajole, and castigate. His words, his tone and his manner all focused upon persuasion of the audience.

These people were not easily convinced however, and particularly not by an "infidel" as he was to some. But he was aware of this, and came prepared. In part of his speech he revealed that he had practised Islam beginning some ten years prior, while he was working among the Africans. He believed strongly in the five pillars and commended all of his "brothers" in the faith at the conference. This seemed to win a lot of support, and softened his audience considerably. He assured them as well that he had in mind what was best for both sides and not only one or the other. "There must be an end to the senseless, the needless killing of your family members. Your brothers, your sisters, your uncles and cousins and friends. And we are the ones to do it. If not now, when…" He was the right person and it was the right time, Dalee thought. "Your country's safety, stability, and security depend on it," he continued. "Your future. Without reconciliation there can be no more future. For Palestine, for Israel, for the Middle East, for the World…we are brothers, don't you see!? The Jews and the Muslims. We have some different traditions, cultural traditions, but some are the same. And the religions are very similar, I'm sure you noticed that in our smaller sessions earlier this afternoon." A native of Palestine was translating for him on the stage, all others received interpretations via headset at their tables.

Cazara went on to very carefully and most delicately outline the proposal of his associates, as he explained, of both Islamic and Jewish religious experts and Christian as well, of a combining, and a coexistence, of the two religions. The word merger was never used. It was crucial for him to not appear in any way to be trying to persuade either side to give up any of their religious beliefs. He then described his plan of religious tolerance. Religious coexistence he called it, and the way he presented it, and how it came across in the translation seemed to strike a chord with both camps at the conference.

The hour grew later and they were given a ninety minute supper period, but they were to reconvene at 8.00 p.m. for the final session. It was explained to the attendees, that the Chairman and his colleagues would stay as long as it took, and that they had no intention of closing the Summit until there was a mutually agreed upon solution to this seemingly never ending dilemma. The food was ordered and brought in, right where the delegates sat. Finally the time to begin the last session arrived.

✦ ✦ ✦

12

Cazara reviewed his coexistence idea again, and this time called upon some of his experts he had mentioned earlier. There was a Jewish rabbi, and two Muslim religious scholars. They each in turn proceeded to discourse on their religions and present the major tenets of both. Then the third person went on to point out the similarities and where the two overlapped. These were actually obvious to the listeners by this time because of the way the first two speakers had chosen to present the points, one of these being the reliance on the Pentateuch in both religions, also the common belief in a monotheistic deity. Their views were also very similar in that both sides had such similar cultures and customs. When those three had completed all that they were to say, a fourth individual appeared and this time a Christian theologian, who would present his case but from a Christian's world view.

By this time it was getting on into the evening, but they had been forewarned that they would go long that night. Some were growing a little tired. But others whose customs were such that they became even more alert and attentive due to the lateness of the hour, were just getting warmed up. The final official presentation was about begin. But after that, there were still other essential and practical aspects of the Summit that the committee had included at the close of the Day, namely the signing of the official, legally binding, documents to seal the peace deal. These had all been prepared beforehand, in English, Hebrew, Russian, Chinese, and several different Arabic dialects. They were drawn up with the assistance of lawyers, religious scholars of both the Bible and the Koran, selected politicians, and high ranking diplomats from the UN and around the world.

The final session was designed to specifically deal with the geographic end of things. Most specifically of the area which was surrounded by the greatest amount of controversy: Israel, and her neighbors. And particularly, Palestine.

A map of the region was displayed and illuminated where everyone could see. It glowed in a soft light and many of the viewers present saw their countries before them, side by side in the Middle East. Then maps of other selected parts of the world were visible but to the sides, smaller, and not as bright. The Mid-East map was central, displayed with bright colors, and each nation was illuminated with a different color. The peripheral maps were colored as well, but with not as much brightness as the main one. A finely dressed professor entered the center stage.

He was introduced as a Near Eastern historian and geographical world expert. An elderly man of at least seventy, but age was difficult to tell sometimes of an Asian. Dalee thought he was an Indian and he at least got the location of his research and life's work correct, the University of Delhi. But his origins were actually in Afghanistan as he could tell when his name was finally mentioned.

The distinguished gentleman below the maps proceeded to

inform his audience of the basics of the present geographical situation in the Mid-East, the recent past, and then in earlier times as well. He went on to highlight the gradual changes over the years, decades, and centuries. The maps above him changed to the appropriate image at the right moment of his lecture. He then invited Mr Joesph Cazara to join him. Light applause accompanied his entrance. They had seen him throughout the conference, and a few were even growing tired of him.

However, he came out, with just as much enthusiasm, perhaps even more buoyancy than before and shook hands with the professor, kissing him on both cheeks. He then changed the map to that of present day Israel, and a very large one. As he spoke, he held a device in his hand and the image changed slightly in accordance with the words he was saying. He was outlining a proposal of a shared nation and the boundary lines were drawn to give part of the country to the Jewish people and partly to the Palestinians. It was not much different to the viewers than what they were presently familiar with. But as he spoke, very slowly and by degrees, the map changed. The Jewish people grew uncomfortable and Cazara was aware of this. He stopped his changing map and began to ask questions of the historian present with him on the stage. But the map continued to change in steps. He asked a series of questions about boundaries, national property rights, border crossings, and historical questions of particular significance to the topic.

He then turned to the crowd and specifically addressed Israel and Palestine and their officials and representatives. He implored them to see that a more generous share of the nation known as Israel had to be given to the Palestinian people. He very forcefully insisted that the alternative was the continued blood of the people of Israel, and that of others, and that this would never change. It had been seen historically, and no hope in the present was seen, and absolutely none in the future could be seen. There was no choice but to agree. The background changed to that of lists, side by side, in Arabic and Hebrew, against the white screen, simply of names. It was the names of the casualties of their mutual, ongoing war. It went fairly quickly, but it never seemed to end. The font size was quite large so that even those with the poorest eyesight could read it. When the more recent names were displayed, some in the audience even recognized people they knew, and some, even relatives. The names scrolled on and on, by this time in silence.

Finally after a long pause without any speaking, music, or even murmuring in the audience a voice spoke from the side of the stage. "Yes we know that the land of Israel was given by God first to the Israelites." Pause again, and then Cazara spoke further. "And we also know that our brothers are entitled to some land for their children to grow up, for their livestock to graze and roam freely, to carry on business, and to worship the same god that you both believe in with all your hearts and souls…" He walked slowly out of the shadows. "The time has come my brothers, to put aside all of our prejudices, both religious and national; both from the old and the modern times." The translator was continuing with his interpretation, and the listeners were getting the clear intention of the words.

"If we don't do this deed now, then tomorrow, and we're not just talking about the near future, but it will be then as well; tomorrow there is only more, and more, of the same in store; of the needless loss of the lives of people just like the people here tonight; perhaps those sitting next to you, in the very next seat!

We don't want to see that happen! None of us do. And it's not just your future. It's the future of your neighboring countries in the region, and it's the future of the world; our world." The scene on the screen had now changed to pleasant landscape scenes of the Mid-East accompanied by soft music.

"People...we need to make a change tonight. Today on this December 25th. With the world watching, let's show them that we can do it. That we're people not animals. Civilized men and women, not barbarians. Isn't that right?!" Some were nodding; some were rumbling sounds of at least half-hearted approval. Others were still numb. And still others remained unconvinced. Some opposed. But Cazara knew his target peoples. He had done his homework. He pushed on. "At the tables to your left," and most people looked in that direction, "there are assistants waiting to offer you the peace treaty of the century, of millennia, perhaps the greatest in the history of humanity. Let us do it today. Let's agree to peace. Let us usher in a new era like you've never known before. I promise you I'll see it done. I will personally assure its authenticity. And I personally will stand by it and carry it through to its finest details. When you get back to your home countries, when all the fanfare and hype of this conference and all the glitter and the glamor that the media creates, dims and dies. I solemnly pledge to you, that I will see it done!" These last few words were pounded out and struck the air with great force, and they reverberated off the walls of the meeting hall that evening. It was 11.38 p.m.

People were weary but wide awake. Cazara stepped down off the stage and made his way to the tables. He stopped at the regal looking ornate table on his right and picked up a pen and just held it up, in front of his chest, waiting. And he watched. And he waited. Finally Abdula Yosaf Khadahar, the director of the Arab League of Nations stood up, and two or three others stood with him. He slowly began to walk over to the area where Cazara was standing. Someone shouted some kind of protest in Arabic, but he was quickly silenced. He came face to face with Mr Cazara and with a steady gaze made his stand. "I will need to read it thoroughly," his face softened a little, "if we are to sign it." And he sat down with his assistants in a large velvet, upholstered chair. Meanwhile, the Chairman of the PLO and the PM of Israel had met while they were both on their way. As they spoke, standing together, there was a sense that this Summit would very possibly be a success.

Word was somehow sent to those media people who were outside the doors and a high speed race of global proportions had begun, through airwaves, via satellite, over cell phones, and all at once. The messages were different variations of the same thing. Perhaps they were a bit premature. However they would later that night or, rather, early the next morning discover that it would turn out to be true. But at this juncture it was conjecture: that a peace deal was underway with these long time enemies, an end was in sight to this long standing feud, this Arab-Israeli stalemate which for so long a solution was beyond anyone's grasp, that on that night, it might possibly happen. And that part of the world that was awake, held their breath. And the part that had not yet seen the dawn of the new day, slept.

The time passed and the two heads of state earlier in conversation, actually made their way toward the direction of the tables. Their cortèges followed. All eyes watched as they pored over the pages of the treaties. Much discussion ensued, aides and legal experts were asked specific questions on particular points. Cazara called in the historian-geographer who was up earlier. More discussion, debate, and more debate, and then finally after some give and take, some promises of certain concessions, they moved to sign their names.

The people were astonished! The change had come. The agreement was being made. They were actually going through with it. At this point a few designated photographers were signaled to capture the moment pictorially, digitally, for history, and then they signed.

The Chairman of the peace summit stood by and watched. His microphone was reconnected and he spoke. "Ladies and gentlemen…people of the Free World…tonight we have begun to make our planet a better place." Then there was applause; it was stronger this time, and without reservation. "My friends… this is not simply a truce we are entering into today. But rather, this is a *Peace Treaty*, an agreement that will change the futures of us all. Not simply for the region, but the rest of the world." More applause. "This is the beginning, and I know it's late, but we do have one more thing to do tonight." And they waited.

"There is the matter yet to be settled, once and for all, regarding the terrorism question." Silence. "The Western world, but not restricted to just that because many others have suffered great losses, but particularly the Western peoples, await resolution to this problem." Cazara then went briefly into a similar progression which he had earlier presented, but more brief and to the point. Other people came to the stage and gave their segment in a session aimed at those who could influence the terrorist networks. There were people from Afghanistan, in so that there was an avalanche effect. The leaders of th Western nations near the end of the line, had approached the tables more cautiously. The prime minister of the UK along with his aides, carefully read every page. Reread actually, for they had had their own copy sent to them beforehand so that they could mull it over and make sure it met their complete approval. The PM of Canada had his own copy translated into French since that was his first language. Dalee, as the US representative, sat and carefully reread his copy to ensure that it said nothing different than the previous version he had seen earlier. The American President having been unable to attend due to pressing matters, had given full and complete authority to accept or to reject the terms as the Secretary of State so determined appropriate.

In the end the total came to 37 signatures. When the last person had signed and it was realized that there wasn't anyone else, cheering began, small at first, but then it began to grow. It was almost as if there was a disbelief of the actual possibility that peace on a global scale as they apparently had achieved, could be genuine. The joyful response of these heads of state seemed quite irregular, but in light of this unprecedented move and unexpected success, there was acceptance of the cheers and the noise, and then the exuberance grew. Cazara was found and as old fashioned and simplistic as it may sound, was lifted to the crowd's shoulders and the cheers become even louder. Those outside heard the commotion and eventually made their way into the main hall but were met by the surging crowd with their hero lifted up above them. The procession moved forward into the outer area and the camera people started recording. The ecstatic moment was caught on camera and transmitted

to television stations all over the world, and to the World
Wide Web. Hundreds of millions, even billions, witnessed it
and it appeared to them a scene of great jubilation, with the
excitement of a national election win, the end of a long war,
and a great international sports victory all rolled into one.

The clamor eventually died down after it reached its peak,
at which time their now beloved Chairman addressed the
crowd. He simply made a few closing remarks. He wanted
the moment to stand on its own and speak for itself. Which
of course it did. And this was important to those contained
within the compound at 'The Peace Palace', but also important
to Mr Cazara and his world audience. They both would matter
critically later on in his campaign which was soon to follow.
People milled around a little for a while after things settled
down. Then one by one the different groups began to leave,
and each nation and people group represented made their
exit. They made their way out just as the first light of the new
day began to show itself. The dawn was arriving on Europe,
but also a greater dawn, on the world. And the agreements
that were made on that site in The Haag, Holland would send
out waves of influence that would reverberate the sounds and
the seeds of a revolution the likes that modern nor ancient nor
prehistoric man had ever seen. All through the Dark Ages, the
Age of Reason, the Middle Ages, to Modern History. Beyond
the Industrial Revolution, the Space Age, the Computer Age,
the Information Age, right up to the Digital Revolution.
Nothing could compare since it would be the culmination, the
great crescendo, the finale. And it had just begun.

✝ ✝ ✝

13

Echo Tower was one of the tallest buildings in London. It was even taller than the new JD Sumadi Building, but not near as mysterious as Stone Henge. The design was intended to attempt to modernize the ancient wonder of the world, and bring it architecturally and technologically into the 21st century. Alfred D. Thompson, the great designer of the time, spent months on drawings and computer simulations at the actual site of the original structure which he was modeling his new building after. He painstakingly ensured that the original concept of the structure was preserved, while at the same time it was transformed into a modern office tower. It was the only one of its kind. No one had ever been bold enough to attempt such a difficult and challenging merger of the ancient and the nouveaux but Thompson. He succeeded physically, but somehow the timelessness, the unexplainable, the metaphysical characteristics could not be recreated. These were Dalee's thoughts as he paused in front of the building. It was some months after his first visit there, and this time under somewhat different circumstances. He was going for business matters again, but this time as a full-time employee; an executive director/producer in fact.

He had been asked to spend a little time at the London

office of Global News Communications Network in the initial
stages of his appointment. This was his first week and people,
facilities, and the responsibilities were still new to him. He
would become familiar with the international operations out
of the main headquarters there, and then he would return to
Washington and be based out of there as per request.

Past the concierge, up the mirrored lift, past the friendly
receptionist, and down the hall to his assigned temporary
office. He hung up his coat and put his umbrella in the
stand. He hadn't sat down yet when the phone rang. It was
their Moscow office requesting clearance for funds regarding
a breaking story there. Part of his job was to manage the
approvals for projects abroad. This was one of his many new
roles, and it seemed to Dalee that he was getting more than
what he bargained for. His predecessor seemed to enjoy going
beyond the confines of what his job description outlined, and
as far as his subordinates were concerned this was one of the
many carry-overs which were non-negotiable.

The story of the *Christmas Peace Treaty* broke the evening
of Christmas Day in North and South America. The Eastern
Hemisphere had gotten it during the middle of the night or
very early the morning of the following day, and of course
Europe and Africa received news of the great pact at more or
less the same time of day that it occurred in the Netherlands.
Whenever it had reached its listeners, the reaction was always
the same: one of joyful disbelief. This may sound something of
an oxymoron, but the disbelief was only a temporary reaction.
Once confirmed there was then extended exultation on the
part of the recipients, joyous exuberance unequalled, which
erupted into spontaneous parties as a result of the great relief

of the citizens of Earth. If this report that they were receiving was true, gone was the fear they had experienced for so many years, the terror of random attacks which had been the norm rather than unusual, if one could get used to brutal murders. If the news was true, no more would they have to travel in fear of a hijack or an attack on their hotel or tourist site they would like to visit. Suddenly it was all gone.

There were also those who remained skeptical in the weeks that followed, but when months passed and the events that followed confirmed the authenticity of the treaty and the practical results, no one could deny it as a reality. The terrorism stopped completely. There was not one major attack having the earmarks of one of the large terrorist organizations. It very much created an atmosphere of peace. And then there was the complete and utter ceasefire on both sides of the Israeli war. This had all the experts stumped. No one could understand how this could possibly be, for starters; nor could they fathom simply the indisputable fact that it actually did happen. And that there was no sign of anything to resume the fighting again. It was East and West Germany. It was North and South Korea. It was the joining of two parts, the two halves to make a whole. Only this time it was not the two sides of a nation, but they would end up sharing the same land. And that would be part of the unifying effect. It was also the merging or the coexisting of the two religions into one. In theory it was one, but for practical purposes it was more like one and a half where both kept their own sides and they overlapped at certain basic similarities. This was all outlined in the reports put out by GNCN which Dalee had the pleasure of producing and overseeing. One was even entitled, *The New Order of Israel*, with the subheading – *One and One=1.5*. This went on to explain this merging of the two and where they agreed to compromise. It looked something like this on the Net version.

THE NEW ORDER OF ISRAEL
December 28, 2049
The Hague
Gertrude Vanderleywith reporting by Domonique de Graaf

Two days ago, in the political center of the seemingly insignificant little nation of Holland, but also the seat of the Cour internationale de Justice, the Peace Treaty of the century was signed. The Prime Minister of Israel entered into an agreement with the Chairman of the Palestine Liberation Organization to cease all and any military activity within the borders of Israel and in the surrounding districts. The treaty involved the division and distribution of land so outlined within a mutually agreed very specific contract drafted by Mr J. Cazara, international philanthropist, and independent politician.

The treaty also included certain stipulations regarding the coexisting of Israel's and the Palestinians' religions, that of Judaism and Islam. Coexisting, as defined by the contractual agreement, is the tolerance of the contrasting differences, while joining at the points of similarities. The definition gives several such points, all of which are clearly defined. They included the worship of the 'One True God, the sacredness of holy sites, and the use of repeated daily prayers', sources revealed. These and other points are now in the process of being practically installed as regular new forms of worship for both parties' religious traditions. Their developments are under the supervision and direction of Mr Cazara's Committee for Religious Affairs. The partial amalgamation is unprecedented since the two nations have been at war for decades, and the two religions, for centuries.

Mr Cazara could not be reached for comment but his council issued the following official statement. "Only now can we begin the rebuilding of our broken relations with the Middle East. My staff and I will work relentlessly along side of the Jewish and Palestinian people to ensure that peace remains our mandate throughout the duration of this transitional period. Personnel at all levels will be monitored and assisted professionally every step of the way in this new day for Israel, the Muslim people, and indeed for all of Mankind."

Various other media had their own spin on the same or related stories. The following is a smattering of what was published.

"This is a milestone on the roadmap to peace."
Washington Post

"The world stands amazed at this landmark of religious tolerance."
International Herald Tribune

"Cazara is the miracle worker!"
The London Times

"Three cheers for the hero who made peace between age-old enemies."
The Bangkok Post

"A remarkable victory for peace, a boost for the tolerance of different religions, and a Sign from God."
New York Times

"Two nations become one? Unthinkable for the parties involved, but Mr Cazara has done it."
The China Morning Post

"The 'Prince of Peace' has saved the day."
Time Magazine

The GNCN story of the new order of Israel had been drafted, edited and then was sent to Dalee upon his request for final approval. The word coexisting had replaced merger since merger was not accurate. He also had wanted to put a name on Cazara's committee but in fact there was not one in existence at that time. Dalee phoned Gávrá Tuldiá, one of his aides, and the title was created on the spot. Referring to Cazara as an independent politician was not mentioned in the phone call, and later it was looked on distastefully by his camp. Dalee had considered changing it when he initially read the article but decided that it was the media's job to report the news from an outside perspective. He didn't want to be party to becoming a channel to disseminate any kind of propaganda. Propaganda was not his business, news was, and as unbiased and as clear as humanly possible.

These were some of the new Producer's basic priorities – news without bias or particular influences, clarity, precision, and the global citizen in mind.

He had developed these not in the time he was in his

present office, but over time, in the years which he had observed life in general, the news, people, politics, and as strange as it may sound, Hollywood. But Hollywood in the sense of productions, stories, drama, etc. Not the cheap, cheesy and sleazy glamor of the entertainment, but the quality and also the artistic component, even the beauty. He observed the news in all its forms, on TV, via radio, and the internet. And also the printed word in the magazines, e-zines, newspapers, newsletters. He became fascinated by it all at an early age and over time developed interests, honed skills, and studied hard. And he watched, and he read, and he thought. Years passed and now Dalee was ripening and mature. Now, in the GNCN position he was in his element. Perhaps he had found his niche. He had only just begun, to live, and explore that which held his highest interests. 'We shall see,' he thought as he sat at his desk, looking through the window and at the city of London down below, 'we shall see.'

He had enough of politics and all the jockeying for position, personality cults, jealousies, back stabbing, mud slinging, and ruthless cutthroat competition. Not that the media business was a picnic, but it just wasn't the same as the political games, in the arena where presumably 'all is fair....' Yes, he had his fill and he was ready to move on to a new direction. But this was more than just that. He was in a place that he loved. A situation where he could expand and blossom in this new arena, this space, his own space that could be developed and designed the way he liked it. The way it was supposed to turn out. To create a picture with all the colors in the right place, and perspective aligned correctly, the proportions right, and choosing the right subject. And let's not forget negative space.

To develop a production with plot and characters, and scenery and technology, and budgets and wardrobe and music, and an audience. It was a place where he could incorporate all this, and more. And it was time.

The media was a medium for Dalee that allowed him to express himself, and what was more, to use his talents and gifts to create. In his position at this corporation he would be responsible for the ultimate and final product of the presentation of the news as it would be broadcast all over the world. He must see to it that it was delivered professionally, in the best quality, and with the right timing. Timing could be crucial in this game. Dalee's job was confined to news programmes. Others would handle the entertainment division. He would handle all forms through, Internet, television, print media, and what little was still used in radio broadcasting. He would then have people in charge of each of these departments.

It was 9.14 a.m. and he was just beginning the day. He worked on the layouts, some planning for the next week's programming schedules. He also spent some time on a new pilot project they were working on. Lunch would be 'in' that day. Then in the afternoon it was catching up on some correspondence and making some telephone calls. It seemed as if he had hit the ground running. It was a good thing he had taken Phys Ed in his freshman year in secondary school. High school had been an influential and formative time for him. Some have said that everything that is needed to learn can be learned in Kindergarten. Psychologists say that we are in a sense completed in the years between 0–5, and our personalities are formed at that time as well. Dalee considered his first year of high school as an especially influential time for him. West Virginia was a nice place to grow up in. Sometimes he recalled those days of carefree recklessness with fondness. But at the moment he must direct his energies and focus his concentration on the present task at hand, and his new job.

Some of the people he had met already, some he would meet later on. Some would stay there in London, whereas others would leave and work in DC with Dalee when he returned. One such individual was Ted Bestard. He was 48, a graduate of MIT, in fact wanted to work in the technology field, but like so many others found the market saturated by the late 2020s so turned to a related field. He was in charge of the e-magazine for GNCN International.

When he had met him he distinctly remembered his face because he resembled a fish. His lips were a bit large and reddish in color, and even slightly puckered. His eyes were large and he had an intense look in them as well. When he was at work it aided him in at least appearing to work industriously. Whether he was or not in fact hard at work Dalee had yet to determine. He only met him a few times. He was heavy set and had thick wavy sandy-grey hair. He did not wear glasses, which Dalee was thankful for, for if he did, the fishbowl effect in addition to his fish like appearance would simply have been too much to bear. He seemed to have a matter-of-fact, almost nondescript personality. Work seemed to be his life, which was fine by the Producer. It meant greater concentration on his duties and better quality work. He was even married to his work. The type who never married and didn't care much for a social life. Basically, he made his workplace his home, and when he was at home, because of the nature of his job, he could work out of his home office too. In fact, with the portability of computers, the advancement of microtechnology, and the ability to tap in to the internet virtually anywhere, anytime, the director of the GNCNI E-zine could work any place, anywhere, and round the clock if so desired or so required.

The name they had chosen was *The Atrium*. It was laid out in several different sections just like a traditional magazine, but with all the conveniences of web-based hypertext technology. There was the world news by continent, and then in subsections the different categories for each of the regions. And it was all laid out so user friendly on the home page that it made finding what you were looking for quick and easy provided your server was good. For example, if one wanted to look at the economic situation in Taiwan, from the home page you would click Asia, Taiwan, and then Financial News. Then you would have a choice of a variety of choices by topic, like Stock Quotes, Currency Exchange, Mergers, and various industries' news. There weren't many photos, except a few small ones included for a break in text. This was intended for people who were interested predominantly in reading the news, and that without interruption. The text size, font and even color was varied according to theme.

Then there was Salem Degras in charge of Net Advertising. Advertising meaning which companies to sell spots to on the GNCN web site. Another department took care of all advertising for the corporation. The latter was outside of Dalee's realm of responsibility. Advertising for GNCN required hundreds of staff, and millions of dollars. Salem was 35 with large brown eyes, medium length fuzzy dark brown hair, and a round face. She would often tilt her head to one side or the other when talking. One couldn't tell if it was a nervous habit, she was growing tired, or she was hard of hearing, because she didn't do it every time. She liked gold jewelry and often wore it. But not in the same place. One day it would all be on her fingers, and a lot of it, and the next time it would be a large link chain around her neck, then another time big hoop earrings from her ears. She would wear them separately, on different days, never all at once. But it would always be gold, and always salient. She spoke with an Iraqi accent and her voice a little low for a woman.

She would be the one who decided which advertisements stayed and which were left out. She also oversaw the layout of which ones went where in relation to the news stories. They were mostly in the form of banners, and the sizes were strictly regulated by company policy. Pop ups were frowned upon and so she tried her best to keep them at bay, but sometimes paying advertisers won the battle since he who holds the gold calls the shots. Salem was passionate about her work and took it seriously.

The person responsible for the radio broadcasting portion was in his mid-fifties. He had a Scottish accent and in addition had a wheezy kind of whistling quality in his voice. He was only five foot six, and his name was Carter, Cecil B.Carter. He was a smallish man who had the gift of the gab. If you were in a hurry you shouldn't initiate or accept an invitation to a conversation with Cecil Carter. He loved to talk, about work, his current projects, past projects, his history, his opinions, your family, his family, the news, the old days, the endless possibilities of the future, literature, anything, and everything. One time Dalee was in a hurry and he bumped into him in the lobby at Echo Tower. He was interested to know a little more about Dalee, but it was Dalee who ended up learning about him. Almost everything you could possibly know about the life and times of Mr Cecil Carter. His early beginnings in Scotland, and even some of his family's history in the late twentieth century. Then how he traveled to America and lived in Ohio where he got his education. The following years were spent in broadcasting itself where he had eventually won some prestigious awards. His talent paid off. Unfortunately for Dalee he was very tired and wished to get home to a hot bath and the same kind of supper. Cee-Cee, which he insisted on being called, also insisted that he bought the new boss a drink. Being too courteous to say no, he accepted and the dialogue turned monologue began in a pub nearby.

Such were the beginnings of Dalee Delliv's experience as a media manager. His first impressions with the company were good, and there was a spirit of camaraderie, at the London office anyway. This being the world headquarters for the corporation was a good sign, and he expected the American branch in Washington to have a similar atmosphere, professional ethic, and high caliber people. Also the fact that he would be on his own turf would help too. Staying in the UK was a nice change for him, but the British were different. They spoke English and that was his language. But sometimes the accent was hard to follow. At work he was alright because there was such a multicultural staff there, but outside of that was where he would sometimes run into trouble. The language for the most part was the same but the customs, the approaches, even the humor were quite different. Yes he enjoyed his time there, but he would be glad to get back to familiar things again. Not just his home, family and personal things, but the sights, the sounds, the landscape, and the familiar culture, the customs: much of which one takes for granted, until you are denied all of these for a time. Yes, it would be good to get home. In the mean time, he was there with Big Ben, Buckingham Palace, the Thames and the Times, and the echoing vestiges of Stone Henge as he entered the lobby of Echo Tower every morning, through the fog and the mists of London Town.

✦ ✦ ✦

14

The air was fresher, the sun was brighter, the water cleaner. Time had stopped. Nature and architecture seemed to blend harmoniously. And there was a sound. It was small at first, but it seemed to grow. It was music, singing in fact. Soft voices singing words...*Yahnuu So-yay, Yahnuu So-yay, People singing on this Day. Yahnuu So-yay, Mahnuu So-nay, What we live we also say.*

The song was without instruments and the voices from people unseen. There were all kinds of people living in peace in villages along a river, a river that flowed gently, and wound its way through village after village of one people group, and then a space, and then another different people group, and on and on and on. There were Brazilians, and Russians, and Chinese and Indonesian people, Nigerians and Namibians, Australians and Koreans. There were Thai and Burmese, Indians and Kazaks, the Swiss and the Dutch, the French and the Fins, Inuit, Canadians, Americans, Iraqis, Israelis, and Turks. Living as neighbors without strife and without wars. Traveling and trading and fishing and dreaming. They had their own cultures and they had their own customs. They had their own languages, they had their own colors. They each had a flag. But there was also another flag.

There was a common flag that linked their common

ground. It was a white background and it had a picture of the Earth on it. It was a photograph, a lifelike likeness of their world. Green and blue with spots of white and grey and some swirls of clouds. And no borders. And it flew in every village. In the morning with its banners flying high caught in the sunshine and the early breezes, each village proudly displayed their common theme. It was the Earth just as it was. It was not a perfect circle. Its shape was its true shape as it was suspended in space in its place.

There was rain and there was sun; there was summer and then the winter. And the trees grew tall and the fruits and flowers they blossomed. Apples and oranges, and mangos and bananas, cherries and jack fruit, and peaches and figs. The leaves were green and then in the autumn they turned colors. Colors of yellow and red and brown, of gold and of silver and white. And the cottonwoods rained, and it snowed the white cotton in its time. All of them gave their fruits and seeds in their times.

There were animals to care for and the people took care of them. The horses and carriages carried the loads, of people, and fruits, and vegetables, and tools, and clothes, and blankets, and books filled with words. There was no pollution and the environment was green. And everyone could read. The young and the old and the wealthy and the middle class. And poverty was nonexistent. There was no memory of it.

There were no hospitals or doctors or nurses of any kind. Health care was unnecessary, because no one got sick. They would eat and sleep and work and laugh and live their lives, without fear, without hate, without war. The song had stopped now and there was silence. The world was turning and the seasons changing. The moon was spinning around the Earth.

There were more words and they were in other languages. And the tempo changed, and the instruments. Each village took up the anthem, but in their own tongue, with their own rhythm, and their own style. The tune remained the same. The song remains the same. But each people had their own way of singing it. They each beat their drums to the sound of a different drummer. They were all distinct and unique.

And there was technology. A new technology that incorporated the human factor. Man and machine, harmoniously coexisting. Machines recognized speech for what it was, and not 'wreck a nice beach'. It was Alvin Toffler's 'High Touch with High Tech' concept realized. And there was no future shock. The internet was finally the information Superhighway instead of the 'world wide wait'. Any data from any place on any subject could be accessed any where. The globe was connected and information flowed freely. The Global Village had the common connection of the internet. All trading, banking, communication, images, files, music, sights and sounds, could freely be sent and exchanged without limit. It was a very broad band, a wide berth. And it ranged from Pole to Pole and from East to West. It indeed made the world a smaller place. It was finally a small world after all.

Friends in Mongolia could see friends in the Maldives. Family in Sumatra could view family in Siberia. Staff in the Netherlands could conference with staff in Nigeria. People in Columbia could communicate with Canada. Without interference, without interruption, and with clarity. The images were as clear as the highest definition known to man the sound like you were in the next room or closer, the quality couldn't get any better. And the music played on.

The sky was bluer and the grass was green. As green as green can be. The Oceans were blue, and the wind was pure. The tides would rise and the tides would fall. The breezes would blow over land and sea. The seas were vast and the oceans were full. And the skies were clear and bright, and at night they went on and on forever. The stars and the planets, and the galaxies. In space, the endless place. And time would stop. There would be no time, or clocks. No dates or months or years or measurement of them. No sand to slip the minutes by. The sand had stopped slipping through the pinched glass hole in the hourglass. It stopped dripping, it stopped ticking, it stopped moving. It was the end of time. Timelessness. World without end. Time without end. The love of life was all that was left.

The music stopped and the lights were on. The sun had risen in London, and the pale light edged its way through a crack in the curtains. He was groggy. It was morning. It had been Dalee's dream. It was Utopia.

He sat up and rubbed his eyes and stared blankly at the window of his apartment. After a few minutes he reached over to the nightstand and took up pen and paper and wrote down these words:

Morning.
7:00.
Open those windows and smell that fresh air.
Open those curtains and look at that sun.
Shiny.

It was a poem. Albeit a short one, and he was tired. But he wrote it down anyway. He put down the pen and the paper, found his slippers and his dressing gown, and went to the window. He opened the curtains, but it was not sunny. And the air was not fresh. Not in downtown London. But they were on that paper on the nightstand by the bed. They were in those words. They were in his dream. They were in his heart. There was hope for the world yet, he thought. There must be some hope.

✦ ✦ ✦

15

The meeting would be held in Jerusalem this time. Many representatives, ambassadors, presidents, prime ministers, and even kings from almost every country would attend. This was the meeting of the rulers of the world. Joseph Cazara was the Chairman and he was the initiator and founder of the whole project. It was the follow-up meeting to the one in Rome a few months before. It was planned out and organized weeks before the conference date. In fact it was actually in the making long before, during the time of Cazara's years in Africa, assisting certain nations in creating and maintaining their political stability. The date was February 27, 2050. These leaders had gathered to hear Mr Cazara's plan for Global unity. This great miracle worker who had brought about genuine and lasting peace to the troubled region surrounding Israel, and what was more, single handedly ended the global terrorism problem. These rulers and representatives of these many nations, the whole world in fact, had stopped to take note, and listen what this now, great man had to say. And say it he would in the next few days at the International Conference for Globalization, him and his distinguished colleagues and his Council.

The security was handled by the same outfit as last time. They were prepared in the event of any sort of attack, nuclear, biological, chemical, and from any side, whether it be land, air, sea, even technological. The troops were employed and deployed, and were ready for action. The roof of course was covered, the front and the back entrances of the building, and there was a unit stationed at the only gate to the compound. They were armed similarly to the last meeting at The Hague, and had an elaborate communication system to keep in instant touch with one another, and their base. The meeting was held at the Jerusalem International Cultural Center. It was the only one in the city that was appropriate for this kind of gathering.

Outside of the gate, and even some distance from the fences surrounding the compound, chanted protesters. The anarchists that defied globalization, that hated the unifying of all countries for fear that the rich would rule and the little guy would be squashed. They had signs and banners with slogans like: SAVE YOURSELF FROM EVIL DICTATORS, THE END IS NEAR, CAZARA IS THE DEVIL. They had fires and some were singing. Most had come from foreign countries, some from as far away as New Zealand. They tried to hand out propaganda leaflets at the gate but the soldiers squelched their efforts. The papers explained that if we allowed ourselves to be ruled by the few rich and powerful individuals of the world, all freedom would be lost; big brother would take over, and what little that we have would be taken from us.

Inside, things were gearing up for the great conference that would defy those defiant rebels that were against the unifying of humanity. This was the moment Cazara had been waiting for. He had begun to sow the seeds for this endevor at the Rome meeting; however radical militant Muslims had something else in mind. In spite of their efforts, he would not be thwarted and he would continue as per schedule, terrorist attacks or not. The peace deal worked in beautifully with his plan and now at this conference most were ready to listen to the hero of the hour. In Rome, before the attack, he had requested the gathering of as many nations as possible to discuss his admino-politica model. And that was just what they were going to do that weekend. He would attempt to persuade the people, present his model, and if they bought it, begin implementation right away and the installation of his existing Council, and the rulers of the seven regions as soon as they were chosen.

Jerusalem was a fitting place for this spectacular moment in history, he thought. It was geographically the center of the Earth. It was the place where East met West. It was also the center of his most recent triumph, his greatest achievement to date, and he felt, an excellent location for this event. Religiously, some people believed, it was the coordinates for Heaven on Earth. Cazara even considered setting up his headquarters there. He would wait and see. There may be better possibilities. One step at a time. He had a whole world to manage, and the first phase was securing his position as CEO. But a CEO was only the head of a company. Perhaps president would be a better title. But that was only for one country, and this appointment was for every country on the Earth. King had a nice ring to it, but seemed rather archaic. Lord also was outdated. Executive something or other would be right, he thought. He would finish that later when the time came.

The conferees were all accounted for, checked-in to their lavish accommodations, and settling in for the first session. The first segment was intended to greet and recognize the host's honored guests. And that's just what he did. With great fanfare each head of state was honored with a flattering announcement, a gift presentation, and escorted to their seats by beautiful women from all over the world. The Chairman had spared no expense and was not going to take any chances in this opportune moment to convince his audience at this strategic moment. A banquet also welcomed them on their first evening together. And after the meal even a little light entertainment.

The next day Cazara reiterated some of the same things that Dalee had heard at the earlier session four months prior in the Italian capital. He described his plan for a unified world, of the reorganization of how the nations are governed, of the seven regions with their seven rulers. He again explained his council and the functions each member would have, and that was about as far as they had gotten before the attack the last time. The mood this time was very much different from the last session. Dalee was keenly aware that the tone of the audience this time had changed dramatically from one of suspicion, to one of relief, even festive. There was a sense of excitement in the air, an anticipation, an expectation of what might happen next.

At one point, the Chairman displayed an appropriate very large map outlining the new organization of his Regions, and announced solemnly and authoritatively, "Ladies and Gentlemen, I give you…the United Society of Earth!" And this time in keeping with the new tone, there were cheers and bursts of applause from some sections. With pride and dignity he held his head up high and surveyed these great and powerful ones seated before him. These were the powers that be, the ones who pulled the strings, that held the reigns. Contained within that room, were the most influential people politically in the world. From here he could seize the reigns and branch out; he would reach out and spread his influence to all.

In one of the sessions, Cazara explained how some of his Council had already been selected and others were yet to be arranged. He reviewed how he intended for seven rulers to rule more or less seven continents; and then he announced with much personal excitement and in an anticipatory sort of way, the names of the ones that had already been chosen. There was Mr Chung Wang Lee for Asia. He had for many years conducted business throughout Asia with his own very successful corporation, then while still in his thirties started into politics. He worked out of Hong Kong, but traveled all over China, and to Taiwan, Korea, Thailand, and Vietnam, where he promoted unity among these and other Asian nations. He also attempted to take concrete steps to develop a single Asian currency, like the Euro, but it never got off the ground. Nevertheless his track record and his influences and his popularity among many of the Asian people in general was such that it won him the title and the position over the Asia Region.

Next was Mr Dalugani Tsabi from the Bantu Tribe for Africa. From his humble beginnings he was branded a leader and destined for greatness at a very early age. He was ahead of his class and went to university early in Johannesburg where he excelled and also where he became a leader among his people, a political activist, and humanitarian. He believed strongly in the equality of all tribes and all Africans, and fought strongly and consistently for this over a period of several years. He was officially appointed by the United Nations as an Ambassador of the Tribal Bands of Africa. In time this became accepted by many of the nations on the Continent, and so this was the most obvious and logical choice for Africa.

For the Western Hemisphere it wouldn't turn out to be quite so simple. It would later be a long process to find their Regional leader. After much debate and elections and meetings and summits and conferences and more debate and more elections the North Americans had it narrowed down to the 100 most influential people of the continent. Their area included USA, Canada, and Mexico. There were 45 from America, 38 from Mexico, and 17 from Canada. Finally it was narrowed down to the top ten. Further scrutiny and elections and research and campaigning and they finally decided on one person. And that was Charles E. Dargon. His credentials, background, beliefs, cultural sensitivity, and intellectual capability proved him to be the best choice over all the others. He was a career politician with a clean track record. He was surpassed by none. He was the one.

Some were still to be decided, but the ones present there that day, were presented, introduced, and paraded for all the leaders there to see, meet, and become familiar with. Cazara wanted these kings to be accepted, and he wanted them to be popular. He intended for these presidents and prime ministers and all the others to go back to their home countries with confidence that their particular Region was in good, stable, and capable hands. And that's just what they did.

It was explained that the leaders of the other Regions were to be selected and elected in the next few months. In fact, upon the approval of those present, it was intended that the projected date for completion of the Seven Regions of the United Society of Earth was the first of July of that year. Some of the sessions were multilateral talks, dialogues with the heads of state present at the conference, designed to persuade and convince them that this was the best, the only, road to take for the future, for peace, for prosperity, and for progress.

On the third day of the conference, which was March the first, the Chairman began the process of introducing his distinguished and long anticipated Council. The proposed Council of U.S.E.... With great fanfare and pomp, the first council member was presented. The Minister of Science and Technology, Rajiv Palotangaradi.

He was a leading expert in the world, in general in the area of science, but more specifically on Information Systems, but much of his cutting edge research was done in a variety of disciplines: genetics, biotechnology, and engineering. The responsibilities involved in this position would encompass all sciences: the life sciences, applied sciences, and all and any technological issues. His office and department were responsible in these matters for all of the Seven Regions. He would also have people in his department which handled various other areas in the broad spectrum of the parts of this category.

For clarity, a scenario was given as to how, functionally, this would work, since this type of administrative, political set up had never been done before. The Chairman thought it necessary to spell it out for his audience under these unique circumstances. He had explained already how the regions were to be governed, and how each Regional Ruler would manage the affairs of an entire continent. No small matter but he tried to be as brief as possible in this short conference. The Council operated by its own policies. The policies that governed the whole world were to be the same with certain variations due to cultural differences. The Internet for example was managed by Mr Palotangaradi. It was his responsibility to ensure that the global network of information moved smoothly over the face of the entire Earth. It was his department that made certain that the World Wide Web was always available and ready to be used. He was also responsible for new technology, the development of the internet and working on improving and refining it. His teams must always be on the cutting edge of the newest and the best of not only the Net, but also anything related to the science or the technology fields.

Supreme Commander Halloway Draik was introduced next. And he was responsible for military matters and all related affairs. Other areas he was assigned to were security, emergency preparedness plans, and major disaster relief. All the armies, militia, air force, navy of all the seven Regions were under his command. Every top general, admiral, and other military leaders were to report to Draik. In the event of rebellion, or the recurrence of terrorism, the military was to join forces to combat the opposition and eradicate the enemy. All security for major events was channeled and managed through the Supreme Commander.

These Ministers were scrutinized, and selected with the greatest of care by Cazara and his colleagues. They were sought out from among the greatest and the best, the top in the world in their fields. These managers were the best of the best. They were chosen, but they also came through recommendations; the recommendation of the local area they came from, or where they had carried out their work. They had to meet stringent criteria that very few could possibly measure up to, not just regionally but worldwide. So these people were literally and unequivocally the crème de la crème.

The Minister of Commerce was Thaddeus D. Cromwell III, multi-billionaire, financier, freelance philanthropist, business tycoon, former president of the World Bank, and CEO of one of the most successful multinational corporations that ever was. He was also an inventor, visionary, and it was his dabbling, or meddling as some of his opponents would put it, that probably sealed the deal for his newly acquired appointment. The outcry against him as choice for Finance Minister of United Society of Earth, indeed of the world, was mainly due to the fact that people thought that his great wealth would obviously influence him, and his shrewd business sense and practices throughout his long and celebrated history. He simply lacked, they felt, the tempered quality that they expected in such an influential and powerful position of authority with such a broad scope. He was no Alan Greenspan, or so they thought.

This person was to be responsible for each and every type of issue in matters of finance. He and his office would handle all the banking systems, currencies, stocks, bonds, all trading, percentage rates for all financial matters and products. They would also lead the way in research and new developments in the field of economics. In fact, at the very conference where he was introduced, Chairman Cromwell introduced his latest and perhaps greatest invention, or innovation, to his credit to date. At that point it was only a model, but he was certain and confident that it would soon become a reality.

"With hard work," the visionary explained, "this dream will become a reality." He had actually worked on this project for years, and behind the scenes for perhaps most of his life. It was his personal and pet project, but it was no less professional, (and of the highest caliber), than the rest of the branches of his work he had dedicated himself to for the whole of his life. It was: the introduction of the concept of a single currency for the whole world. It was at this point in the conceptual stage, and it was still merely a model, but certainly well thought out, planned and designed. Cromwell planned on a release date shortly after Mr Cazara's first of July time frame, although they hadn't decided on a name for the currency yet.

Of course, the entire council would be answerable to Mr Joseph Cazara, since he would be the leader. He was the founder and president of the whole operation. Then the rulers of the Seven Regions would report to the Council, much the way a company has managers and they have to report to a board of directors. So, as simplistic as it may appear, the rulers/presidents/'kings' of the world were like the presidents or CEOs of regional offices of a single multinational corporation, and the way that such leaders would be under a board of directors for the corporation, the Seven Rulers would be under the Council comprised of Cazara's ministers. They all felt that given the magnitude of the operation, it was best to keep the concept as simple as possible. This would enable the whole thing to be managed more efficiently and effectively, administratively, hence the admino-politica model. It had been likened to the way the city state nation of Singapore was run. It was similar, but of course on a much more grandiose scale. The comparison broke down because in this case it applied to the running of a group of nations, or in this case, in fact it was the whole Earth. But it was the same in the sense that a government was ran like a large business.

Dalee attended the conference but this time in quite a different capacity. He was representing his media corporation. He sat with the media VIP's this time rather than those politically representing their countries. His country was there of course, and this time it was the president himself who attended. Times have changed, Dalee thought. Fifty years ago our president would be leading the way in this kind of endevor, however now we are just one of the nations in an international community. It was a different era.

He knew this was a big story. The peace deal was big, and this was even bigger. They had several excellent reporters at this conference, but Dalee wanted to personally be there. In fact he was invited, because of both his positions: Executive Producer, and former Acting Secretary, (the latter being an emeritus type role). Even though he was former, he still held responsibilities there at the State Department, and still had the ear of some influential people; and the USE Council, and Cazara, knew it. It was advantageous for them at this juncture to have as many people, and from as many places as possible, and from various strata of the higher echelons that swayed the powerful people of the world, on their side.

Nearing the end of the third day, they were to begin their *talks*. This would involve the dialogueing between the various nations present and would have taken days if not weeks had they not incorporated a system. It was a system by which the delegates were rotated, in order that as many, or all if possible, had an opportunity to communicate with one another, and that no one nation was excluded. Of the 243 nations of the Earth, 229 were present in some form or another. Of the ones unable to attend, ten more were hooked up by satellite so they were at least to some extent represented, and made aware of the events of the conference as they took place. The remaining four countries either boycotted the developments of Cazara's plans, or were in the midst of political unrest or some other national crisis.

After many talks, and changing of many levels of their multilateral group there at the International Conference for Globalization, they were ready for a survey/vote. What this involved was, at each of their monitors at their stations, there were touch screen surveys as to what they thought of the proposal of the concept of this USE, the Council and its Chairmen, and the Seven Regions with their respective rulers. There was so much to decide upon that they thought it best to put the vote into the form of a survey. And what better format than by computer, and the simplest and the fastest way was through touch screen technology. This was Chairman Palotangaradi's doing and it made an excellent first impression on the delegates because of the simplicity of it all, and the swiftness and the efficiency with which the results were formulated and published.

The first survey/vote was completed and showed an overwhelming acceptance of the models under consideration. But it was not unanimous, and it was not yet a genuine endorsement from the relevant authorities. The fact that it was not across the board was not a problem. That could be remedied easily enough. The pending endorsement was what Mr Cazara was after. And so he continued.

There were few in the end that resisted, and the ICG ended on a successful note. The majority approved. Those who didn't, did accept the concepts in theory if not in practice, and wanted to see how it functioned before they joined this global EU. Many European countries were convinced that a union of nations had worked extremely successfully with their countries, so they felt this was the way to go, the next step in the progress of the human race. There was overwhelming support from this part of the world. There were others who were optimistic and yet more cautious. Africa had benefited so generously from Cazara's former campaigns there that they wholeheartedly agreed. The other regions and nations to one degree or another agreed to the idea of it, and wished at the very least to put it on trial and observe its progress and success over a set period of time.

Dalee had a hand in that, and he monitored the dissemination of the words and images as they spread out everywhere. He watched as the reports of the news filled every corner of the map on his still new laptop. Every crack and crevice, every nook and cranny, would be informed of the latest developments of this grand scheme which would affect every citizen. The words traveled through fibre optic lines, through airwaves, sped through space, and bounced off satellites. They flashed at the speed of light, were converted into digital bits and bytes, and translated into characters of hundreds of languages, onto millions of computer screens, to millions even billions of people. To computers, and televisions, and radios, and telephones. In the day and through the night. These words couldn't be stopped. They were the present. They were history in the making. They were the future. This was Dalee's job now. It was his destiny.

+ + +

16

It was 4.15 a.m. EST when he woke up in Washington, DC, at his home in the suburbs. Back to America. Back to normal life. The new job required some adjustments, and he'd been waking up too early in the mornings. He'd had a lot on his mind. So he would get up and write down a few ideas, look over some of the projects they'd been working on there in the DC office, and then do some exercise. When the sun rose he actually started to feel tired again. "Go to sleep when the sun comes up," he thought groggily as he made his way downstairs to have breakfast with Janvieve.

"Good morning. You must have got a lot of worms, Mr early bird."

"Ya. I haven't been sleeping very good the last couple of days."

"I noticed."

They consumed their French toast, which was not French at all. So Jan had illuminated Dalee some years before. The syrup was what made it good, so Dalee thought. He had to have something sweet in mornings. French toast, a hot drink, and seasonal fruit. Today it was fresh strawberries shipped in from California or someplace. By the time they had eaten it was time for him to go. He got in the car and began to drive. It was a fair distance away and the metro didn't reach all the way to his GNCN office, so he drove.

The sun was trying to shine that day. It was March 11th, 2050, Friday; TGIF. Thank God it was Friday. 'What was going to happen?' he thought, as he drove along the neat suburban streets, with carefully groomed lawns, and beautifully landscaped backyards. "What will happen to all of this? All that we've known. Where is this all going to take us?" He was thinking about the fruit and the repercussions of the conference he had recently returned from. He found himself feeling a bit like when he was a kid. It was a fear, mixed with a kind of excitement. Especially when there was a bit of danger in there with it all. But this time it was more like when he was supposed to do something new, and it was sort of scary, and there was some responsibility involved. But he was excited because it was different, because it was new. And it was because he didn't understand it, and that fascinated him. It was a challenge. It was something to be conquered. That must be in all humans, he imagined, to one degree or another.

In this present scenario, he didn't understand it. But he knew something big was about to happen. The biggest thing in his lifetime. A change was about to take place. A huge one. The likes as none had ever seen. How was this going to pan out? How was it going to look on the field? It was one thing to see it on paper, theoretically, but it was a whole 'nother thing to see it in the real world. You could have a plan in a playbook, or even drawn as a formation on a whiteboard for sensational players to view. But it could be a whole different scenario when put to the test. What about other factors? What about the other team? The weather, physical and mental health of each member of the team, the many possible distractions, team morale, coach team rapport, the physical playing field, use or misuse of substances, location (i.e. home or away), the team's present standing, the time in the season, even the time of day. All these things affected what the outcome would be. If that was the case in a sports game, then how would it be in a mammoth undertaking such as this one?

USE. It all sounded good to Dalee. And yet he felt a little uneasy about it. He was one of those who liked the concept of it, but wanted to see how it would work, practically speaking, in the real world. The Council of ministers, the rulers of the major regions of the world. And Cazara. What about him? He seemed to have the best interests of all in mind. But he was human, and Dalee had seen enough of how human beings can behave in a variety of situations. He knew what people could be like, and what they could become. Not only in his personal experience, but through things he'd read, of people present and past. In fact the historical record didn't tally up very many points on the "good" side of the ledger. However there were those few that he had been thinking of that night watching the waves on the Gold Coast some months before.

He switched on the car radio to get the news. He listened to music for a few minutes before he actually got it, which was fine with him. Music calms the savage beast, so they say. He wasn't sure who they were but they were probably right. It calmed him a little, and he wasn't very savage. The news was about to begin.

The first item shocked and surprised him. A giant Tsunami caused by an earthquake somewhere in the ocean had killed tens of thousands. It must have just happened moments before.

He was incredulous how so many could be dead in so short a time. They gave the few details that they currently had, but it was enough to send waves of shock through the whole world. The devastation to homes, ships, vehicles, and various buildings all along the coasts of at least five countries was great. The earthquake had been so large that it created tidal waves far beyond what anyone had ever seen.

Dalee recalled a similar situation that happened the day after Christmas back in 2004. He remembered studying it when he was in high school in West Virginia. The death toll reached almost 2,50,000 people. At the time he couldn't imagine that many people dying so quickly. But there it was in his history book in black and white. And then now, while he was driving to work, these words across the airwaves and through the radio to tell him of another disaster equally devastating, and in the same fashion. The previous one had been in the Indian Ocean off the coast of Indonesia, but this one occurred in the Pacific, not far from Taiwan. Taiwan at least was to a certain extent ready. They had special instruments that seismologists had designed and set up off of their eastern coastline and when they were triggered they knew something big was on its way. But they had to act quickly because it was only minutes before the tsunami would reach their shores.

As he drove, Dalee listened on, trying to concentrate on both his driving and intently focused on the breaking story. Yes, it had occurred some distance off the Southeast coast of China in the Ocean there. Of course it hit those island countries nearest, the hardest. The Philippines, and Taiwan, even down to the eastern part of Malaysia at the island of Borneo, and then Papua New Guinea. In the North Japan and the United

Koreas, were also affected, but the damage wasn't as severe. But the waves did hit their coasts as well, and the flooding was severe. All along the eastern coasts of China and also Vietnam there was much damage and in all of these places a state of emergency was declared.

Much to the dismay of so many international businesses, Hong Kong, the financial capital of the region, was hit quite hard. This may have been a setback for many, but relatively speaking it was small in comparison to the loss of lives. The number was approaching the 1,50,000 mark even at such an early stage. If this was going to be anything like the one in '04, with reports coming in over the days following, it could very easily be doubled. As Dalee was listening, some of the initial shock began to wear off, but none of the amazement as to all that was happening so fast. Even in the midst of it all, he knew that he would have his job to do. And when he arrived at the office it would be like a beehive in there. He and the staff were directly affected by this whole thing, in the sense that it was their job to get the news out as accurately and as swiftly as possible. He would also think about its presentation as well. Crises or election, catastrophe or business merger, it was Dalee's nature to arrange the production. It had to look good; it had to be done right. He paid attention to detail. It was part of who he was. He was concerned about those people, and the relatives, and those nations affected. There would be those who would help them, bring them aid, assist them in the initial needs in the wake of the disaster. And his duty in the midst of it all was to send the messages in the best possible way. Communication. Words.

For the next 10 plus hours, that's just what he did. It *was* a buzzing hub of activity when he arrived, and it hadn't subsided much by the time he left. There were calls to make, emails to send, people to make contact with in that part of the world. Stories to piece together, images to edit, and interviews to arrange. And there were many decisions to make. It all seemed like a blur when you were in the middle of it. When he was finally finished at the end of the day, he got in the car and closed the door. It was silent at last. He looked up at the building, and there were people hustling still even at that hour. The world never sleeps, he knew. It was always moving, and turning, and buying and selling, and changing. He looked down at the car radio. He wouldn't turn it on just now. Then he turned off his hand phone. The calls could wait.

When he arrived at home there was still a light on in the living room. He walked to the doorway and went inside.

"So this is the way the world ends… Is it the way the world ends?" he commented listlessly and solemnly, upon catching sight of his wife at the TV.

She looked careworn from all the information she must have digested throughout the day. He sat heavily on the couch beside her. "T.S. must have stood for 'That Serious Eliot'," he commented as he looked at the screen filled with images of the same things he had seen all that day.

"How did it go?" she inquired.

"The London office was even busier than ours if that was possible," he answered rubbing his head. Then looking up, "Fine. And how about your day?" he asked with a tired smile.

And they talked and they watched and they reviewed some of the day's events. And the TV got turned off and the supper was started, and a rather late one it was. The food was refreshing and the conversation light. The cares and the troubles began to get left behind. It was Friday and he would not work the next day. It was busy but it was all taken care of. There were capable and reliable professionals at the helm, so Dalee did not concern himself. He had to leave it behind, to let it go and have a private life too.

He went to the study and found a book. It was quiet, all but for the hum of the technology to provide a comfortable room temperature. And he sat comfortably in an armchair and read. The lamp beside him illuminated the pages in a soft white light. He read something about a boy playing on the beach, making a sandcastle. It was nothing really. Just an account of a seemingly insignificant event. It was in Reader's Digest. A pleasant little two, or three page story. Then it started him to thinking about the Chaos Theory. How the beating of a butterfly's wings on one side of the world months, even years before, could later on cause a gigantic tidal wave on the other side of the planet. And he began to wonder where the winds came from, and how hurricanes and typhoons were initiated. He never studied meteorology. He did know a little about the tides and the moon. He was becoming groggy. Low tide, and high tide. But what of the earthquakes, on land and under the sea. What could have caused the quake that started that tsunami on the Pacific today?

For the Chaos Theory to work, minor, seemingly insignificant random events, and seemingly unrelated, must cause major significant events far, far away. How could you prove that the first, caused the second, being so far in time and also physically from the original event. He supposed that that was why it was only a theory. A good conspiracy theory didn't usually have any proof did it? But what if it was chaos that ruled in our world. That everything just randomly happened and then randomly affected everything else. What if it was true that chaos reigned on Earth and that was the only driving force behind everything in the world, and all matter in the universe. Wasn't that where our scientific authorities had concluded that life and all matter came from. Order from chaos? A big bang? And that was how Darwinian thinking originated and evolved to what it was today. And how it permeated every corner of our educational systems and every strata of society.

But how could order come from chaos. How could it be that random events were running the great timeline of human history, and that of the whole universe? Did the planets align themselves perfectly, and the galaxies? Was it a random chance that a morning dove's physiology is such that it can coo softly in the morning, making a sound so specific so unique, that it is the only creature that has a song like that? How about the atoms and how they are arranged, with their protons and electrons and the nucleus? And how that the number of each of those simple little particles determines whether something is water (H_2O) or something as complex as $C_6H_5 \bullet SO_2 \bullet NH$-. Or the fact that all of the elements can be ordered perfectly within the Periodic Table. And what about the genetic codes of the human body. The 1000s of combinations in one DNA strand of one individual person from the sea of humanity from the beginning of time until the present, the code that makes that person unique, different from all the rest, the only one of his or her kind. The way no two snowflakes are alike, but much more complex than just a snowflake, as fascinating as that is. And then the marvel that this is true for one individual is enough, but the same is true for the millions and billions who were ever born into existence, who ever took a breath of air, whose heart ever started beating and their mind became conscious. To be. To live.

Was that the result of a random chance?

And he fell asleep from exhaustion.

✦

The waves in the Northeastern Atlantic were high as the sun rose. The gulls were crying as the waves were crashing onto the coast. The waves didn't know it but they were halting on the shores near to where great things were happening. Great in the sense that they were large, and also in the sense that they were historical. Future history that is.

Joseph Cazara was there at his office in London with his council members, and the regional rulers which had been appointed so far, just beginning their day. They were perfecting their ultimate administration, ironing out the minor changes, and arranging the major divisions of the New World Order. The time had finally come. When the world would be governed from one place. From a place of organization, from a place of authority. From a central unit that managed the affairs of all the Regions. A centralized office of power, with a Council, and chosen rulers for each continent. And one ruler over them all. That man was Mr Joseph S. Cazara.

The tsunami disaster that shook the countries in, or on the shores of, the westernmost part of the Pacific Ocean the day before, was being handled by Supreme Commander Draik. He had mobilized troops and organized rescue teams to work alongside local governments, and bring the help they needed as swiftly and as efficiently as possible. The immediate needs were the physical order of their devastated towns and cities, the clean up of massive debris. Aid had to be brought to those in need, in the form of food, clothing, shelter, and other basic needs. The emergency medical needs were phenomenal as can be imagined. The hospitals quickly overcrowded and overflowed beyond capacity. The injured needed caring for, the sick needed doctors. The dead needed tending to, and there were tens of thousands. The toll reached over 2,10,000 by the second day. Search and Rescue teams were sent out to find the missing, predominantly deceased.

The basic infrastructure had to be restored at the very least, on a temporary level, and then of course later, rebuilt again. This was where Chairman Palotangaradi was called upon. He ensured that those countries in dire need got what they needed, quickly, at least on a superficial level. There were massive power outages, and so 1000s needed electricity. Businesses needed to make millions of transactions and computers needed to be online. The technology was such that many things required an internet connection, so servers and hosts had to be quickly restored. Transportation was another problem to be overcome so arrangements had to be made for shuttles to begin to those stranded in flooded areas. There was some overlap between the technological, and the military responsibilities during the aid and rescue efforts. The UN was also involved, as well as several other non profit NGOs which came to meet the countless needs of the affected nations.

Much energy was put towards and much attention was paid to the need of the hour. But in London that morning, as the sun was rising, the new leaders of a new world, were preparing and planning and organizing and executing. A new day was dawning, and the waves on the shores of the Atlantic not far away continued to beat against the sands on the borders of Europe, on that line between land and sea, on the coastal lands near the white cliffs. Unknowing, innocent, unaware of the doings and the deeds of men, in an office in the Capital, near the river Thames. The winds were high on that day in the United Kingdom. And the ever-present clouds were there covering the nation, shrouding it in a mist, in a fog, hiding it from the sun. Or was the sun hiding from it.

✦ ✦ ✦

17

The Prime Minister of Israel, and the Chairman of the PLO sat side by side with one another at the large table, examining the documents, charts, and maps. And also drinking, and eating some light refreshments which had been graciously provided by their host. The host was provided by Cazara and his colleagues. The venue as well. It was on neutral ground, too. Well, as neutral as could be. They, and their aides and many assistants and advisors, were dealing land. They were negotiating as to where the boundaries would lay, what the borders were going to be, in this new agreement. These were the fruits of the glorious peace deal that had just been brokered. This was the follow-up, the practical outcome of the Summit of Peaceful Nations just a few short months before.

There they sat together, as the red dawn rose over the reddish Earth of that land. They had been at it all the day before as well, and now they were starting early again. There were some initial disagreements and the arbitrator/broker had to earn his pay for that week. He had his work cut out for him. It was a lot of give and take. The Israeli side didn't want to give up such and such a part of land, and the Palestinians thought they should have a different area than what had been assigned to them. And so they went, back and forth, for long hours, talking, deciding, compromising, undeciding, redeciding, agreeing, disagreeing. Both sides had very strong opinions about what they thought was right, the way they thought it should be. Which was where the mediator came in; and mediate he did. It seemed that every point was an issue. Every square meter of land was fought over. But the arbitrator was the best that money could afford. Coming from the USE administration's pool, he was top.

Mr Khadahar himself of the Arab League, along with his companions, were there too. He was present to ensure that the Palestinians were treated fairly as Muslims. They would intervene and give their side as often and as passionately as they saw fit, and this made the arbitration all the more challenging due to the lively nature of the participants.

At one point, a debate concerning religious matters developed, and this with an even more heated discussion than what had taken place previously. The Jews wanted to keep a certain tradition, where Isaac the son of Abraham was recognized, but the Muslims insistently asserted that they all must honor Father Abraham's other son Ishmael. The mediator being versed in some of the two sides' religions, and also having some experts in both sides' beliefs accompanying him, gave him the tools to do his duty there at that table, with these in some ways, two opposite poles, to execute his duties expertly, keenly, and intelligently. The two sides were also quite similar in some ways too. They were very similar in their cultures in particular. Because they both resided in the same geographical region, their foods, their arts, their clothing, and even their languages had similarities. This became very useful in the bilateral talks throughout the process. And the mediator made excellent use of each and every one.

He even found one song which they had in common. Somehow one of the Jewish songs had at some point in history, when it was unclear, found its way into Palestinian culture, and it was added to their musical repertoire. It made sense; they were much alike in some respects. They used some of the very same instruments, and the time and the cadence were similar as well in the piece. With the linguistic and religious differences their composers were going to write different lyrics obviously, so in that respect they were different. But the mediator found this commonality and used it to the max, to the hilt.

The Palestinians of course insisted that it was the other way around, that their song was used by the Jews, and that they were the ones who had originally created it. After some surprise and reluctant admission of the fact, somehow they both got to singing it. It wasn't clear which side started it but they sang through the whole song. And more than once too. The Israeli camp sang it in Hebrew, and the Muslims sang in Arabic. And each side tried to outdo one another in volume, and in spirit, and then facial expressions, and gestures and gesticulations. It became so loud that some of the attendants had to leave the room.

But it was the same song; the very same melody and tune, and this enabled them to have some sort of bond, a place to connect, a bridge to start building from. The mediator used this, and other things he discovered, and they made some headway. Then the land issue came up again. And again the religious beliefs came into play. The Israelis were certain that God had given them specific pieces of land. And again the Muslims thought it was exactly the same, but in their favor. They went back and forth and back and forth on the same point until it had been beaten to death, the issue that is. The arbitrator at some point in the melee asserted, "We're flogging a dead horse here!" The participants in the session on both sides quieted down a little, and then when the translation was given into their respective languages, there were different responses. Some thought it was extremely humorous, others were very puzzled because the idiom had made no sense at all to them. Others were insulted because the translation into their language came out rude and profane. And still others were angry.

For some time chaos reigned at the negotiation table, and it took extended effort and time on the part of the negotiator and his cohorts to resume some semblance of order again. More drinks were brought in, and some of both sides' favorite foods, and some time afterward they were finally pacified. The mediator in all his training had neglected an extremely vital precept in cross-cultural arbitrations. But after that incident of clamor, and pandemonium, and rancor that echoed still in his ears, he had learned his lesson, and from that time on applied the maxim: Never use an idiom in a multiple culture situation. It just didn't translate very well, as he discovered that day.

They had actually been meeting in the neighboring unbiased nation of Syria. Much controversy had come about over the location of the sessions. First it was going to be in Israel, because everyone thought that was the best. Then they couldn't decide on the city, but even when they reluctantly agreed to one, then trouble started all over again concerning the venue within the city itself. Then they considered a Palestinian location, but this didn't last very long. Some of the Jews objected on the grounds *of* the grounds. The place just wasn't appropriate for the magnitude and kinds of decisions they were making.

Finally they sent out word to various surrounding countries that they were in search of a place to hold historic land deals that would alter the course of the near and long range futures, and there would be a note of honorable mention and also a show of gratitude toward the hosting nation, in the form of generous remuneration. This brought about several interested suitors, and so the responsible administrative personnel were quite busy in the days that followed. After all the inappropriate ones were weeded out it had been narrowed down to four; and then those were scrutinized. Finally it was between two: Kuwait City and Syria.

Both sides ended up miraculously agreeing on a place in Syria. And so it was that they had the meetings there, much to the delight of the Syrian peoples, but also to the people working diligently on finding an acceptable spot for their delicate purposes.

By the afternoon of their fifth day together, they had amazingly and successfully assigned and distributed about 75 percent of the land, and that to some degree of mutual agreement and presumed fairness on the part of both parties involved. It was nearing the end, that things began to get a little more heated up, if that were possible. But the mediator knew his man (men, in this case). Though he was certain he would never use that idiom in this session, nor any other in the foreseeable future, or for the rest of his natural life, whichever came first.

The final distributions and divisions of portions of land seemed to be the most contested as well. It was almost as if his clients had saved the best for last. There were certain parts of Hazafon, and then one other portion by the Mediterranean

Sea. And last but not least was the capital itself, the Beautiful City, the City of Peace, Jeru Salem. They got through the former pieces, by the sixth day, then they haggled over, bargained over, struggled together over the latter, on the seventh. With great difficulty, vexation and near exhaustion, their leader finally convinced them that the only way to resolve this part was a sectored off capital. Similar to the way the Old City was sectioned off, but applied to the whole city. One section would belong to the Israelis, and another would be the Palestinians. It was the only way it could be done. And by the end of that long week neither side was showing any signs of giving in, in spite of the fact that all had grown very weary of the whole thing.

With smiles of relief they exited the building with their respective entourages, greeted by starry-eyed story-crazy paparazzi and other media people from various local and international companies. The deal had been done, the land divided up. But it was in those divisions, that arose the unity which would create the lasting peace in the Mid-East that had for so long been sought after by so many and with such energies and collective efforts. They had finally succeeded, and the headlines shouted it, the media trumpeted this fact from LA to Seoul, from Siberia to Libya to Chile, they all got the message: the Muslims and the Jews were no longer at war, the enemies had made peace. For all intensive purposes it was true, and the world rejoiced. What was ahead no one could foresee. There was a hush and a moment of silence as the new day began, a new dawn was upon them, and those responsible knew it, and they would use it.

✦ ✦ ✦

18

Back in London, at the present office of the headquarters of the newly established United Society of Earth, the news was met with shouts of victory, with cheers and hugs, and handshakes. The celebration lasted until it was lunch hour and then they went out to take their brief midday break. Upon returning to the building which housed their multiple offices, it was business as usual. By that it is meant that they were bustling once again to as soon as possible have the entire organization in place, up and running, and in operation; in order to manage the affairs of planet Earth. This was the center where all aspects of all the nations of the world would be controlled, and where all the people on Earth would be ruled. *Center* as in focal point, as in hub of central activity. This was where it was all originating from, this was the source.

But the *physical* center was about to change. The geographical location was about to shift. Mr Cazara felt that his original office in the UK was not the proper place for the world headquarters of the USE. He and his council were considering a few different options for their appropriate relocation. One was Russia; St. Petersburg, or possibly Moscow. Another was Shanghai, China. Another was Jerusalem, Israel. And there were still others such as Tokyo, or possibly Chicago, USA.

They had many things to consider. One thing was that it was important for it to be a well known, world class, urban center. For it to be trusted and accepted by all was very important. But it should also be close in proximity to everywhere, which obviously posed another problem. And it should be a very modern city. Of course where the city resided was going to be within the borders of a particular nation, and this could not be helped, but they were also concerned that this might result in possible fire raising of some other nations. So the choice must be made carefully. This was a difficult decision and all criteria for the ideal place could not be met, but it must be weighed carefully and then decided upon.

Mr Cazara had a preference toward Jerusalem, since its location was so central, and it had other advantages as well. But there were some concerns about it too. The recent, and even current, negotiations regarding the land was a factor; and it was thought that it might be unstable there even after the peace treaty. Israel had a very long history of political instability and some didn't want to take such a risk for what, in effect, would be the capital of the World. And they wanted to delay a move for the moment and observe the outcome of the treaty which had just been made. Chicago was another possibility and it had some good qualities about it, but many thought it too Western and would most definitely be distasteful for too great a portion of the world. And they simply could not be unpopular with the majority in a circumstance of such magnitude and decision of such gravity.

Shanghai was also a good choice, and had its plusses. It had become a very modern city with some of the most nouveau structures and architecture. It was a coastal city, which had its advantages. It was in Asia which also gave it other advantages. At the moment, parts of it were actually in the process of being renovated, the city being partially affected by the recent tsunami disaster. Some of the great buildings near the shore sustained significant damage, and the electrical and transportation systems were under construction. But many of her great buildings further inland were still intact and life there went on undisturbed. Many of the nearby cities and countries in that region were also being reconstructed.

The USE had issued a statement conveying deepest sympathy for those people who were lost, and that they were diligently working to restore the urban and rural regions which were affected. Part of the statement that was aired/published by GNCN went like this:

"Rest assured, that we will rebuild and repair your towns and your cities. No one can bring back those relatives and friends, and for them we deeply mourn. We must work together to reconstruct, to restore, and also to revitalize, to make better, to rekindle our faith in mankind, to help one another...We have fittingly named this project: Urban and Coastal Renewal (UCR)..."

It went on with much of the same, and to explain their plan of reconstruction of those places that were destroyed. And also some details of how they would even improve the cities, their infrastructures, and even their quality of life. The status of their country would improve, the standard of living, and society as a whole (on Earth in general) would become better and better and better. With such promises and pledges and words of optimistic encouragement, the council and their Executive Director, (Cazara was currently calling himself), conveyed to his citizens his proposals in the statement. Within the article was GNCN's spin on it, and Dalee had a hand in it.

Mr Delliv, Global Network's Producer gave his approval for this statement and the article in which it was included, to ensure the most unbiased, impartial presentation of the information as possible. And comparing it with several others one could see that the influence of the Administration went far beyond their call of duty. The other news media were clearly showing the signs of either third party tertiary level pressures, or monetary benefits, and that in sizeable donations. Based on a broad cross-sectional sample of the various news companies and government run media organizations, one might come to the conclusion that the whole world was accepting and buying into the propaganda like stories which were being published and broadcast. But that was just the information, the presentation, and also the words themselves, and Dalee knew that the output has a source, and that may be different from the receiver. In other words, the producers may say one thing, but the reader or listener may come to his or her own conclusion. And then on the other hand, he also knew the power and sway of the media. And how a story given often enough, and in an excellent package and presentation, will not only spread like wildfire, but would also be believed.

Because the office of Joseph Cazara was about to relocate, the whole thing was in a state of flux. They were all in transition, even while they went about their highest profile business. They had the setup of their new government to contend with, and all the political and administrative obligations involved. Then there was the choosing of the remainder of the council. About half had been selected, and they were in the process of choosing the other Chairmen. Then there was also the other Regional Rulers that had to be decided upon. Only three of the seven were in place. This would require screening, short listing, consulting of the proper national authorities of dozens of countries, and democratic elections. Democratic in this case was their own brand of democracy. One in name, but in practice, was a mixture of socialism, capitalism, some new form of communism. There was definitely some dictatorship influences with Cazara involved. But in fact it seemed more like a monarchy than the dealings of any dictator anyone could say they had seen from history. It was a blend of all of these and seemed to have a dynamic all its own. It was growing, evolving, changing to adapt and be accepted by a new breed of people. It encompassed all the political ideologies and all the societal models to give birth to a new and broadly accepted form of government that could be assimilated into cultures from East to West, in all hemispheres, and in every city and town, and on every street, and in every home. The new leading experts on this entirely new grande subject were describing this whole phenomenon as the *Barnum Effect* in their essays and reviews, implying that the USE administration were trying to appeal to, and therefore please, everyone.

Then finally on top of all these large scale responsibilities, there was the relocation. Several options were being entertained, and several others would continue to be offered since the word was out that the USE world government sought a location for their office. It would require buildings that would house all of their executives and officials, departments and ministries. The Regional Rulers would also have their central offices there on the compound. The architecture would need to surpass that of any other structures. And they felt it should have a name, just as other important government houses and other notable places have had, the Kremlin, the Blue House, Red Square, Hero's Square, the White House, Nathan Philip's Square. One such name they were entertaining was Green Eden Place. This was a working name of their center of the Earth, just as a book might have a working title.

The task of selecting the remaining members of the Council was a daunting one. The Minister of Entertainment and the Arts, for example, had to fully understand the needs of all the different cultures. This person would have to be schooled in the art of the arts, must be versed in the versatility of the intricate weavings of the fabric in each individual region's and country's culture. Therefore Anthropology, Theatre, Sociology, Psychology, as well as Marketing, a good sense of business, and also fashion and trends, and globally at that. This individual would need to be multi-talented, and to be multi-lingual would be an asset, enjoy travel, and would also preferably have some background and experience in performance on a professional level. The advertisement-slash-job-description included all of these requirements and more.

The appointment of one such person was being entertained by the Committee for Human Services. This committee was now employed by USE and was used in the selection process of all high level positions in their government. These individuals also worked in conjunction with an executive board, of which none other than Joseph Cazara was the Executive Director. The one being considered at the moment was James Tuscan, art connoisseur, novelist, movie critic, painter, musician/conductor, member of the board of directors for EU Arts and

Entertainment Committee, and former actor/producer of some 25 top grossing films in the past five years. In fact, he had sought them out and desired this position as soon as he heard of its creation. His portfolio and his controlled exuberance and extreme passion and motivation for the newly created role caught the Committee for HR's attention from the beginning. There were other good possibilities, but James E Tuscan was the current front runner in this arena.

The selection of the Australian Regional ruler had been completed without too much difficulty, and he had begun his duty that very week. It was Carvel Dustene, long time political proponent, and popular environmental activist. He had a deep respect and genuine love for the region he fondly referred to as Down Under, and the satellite and surrounding islands and island nations as well. His responsibilities included New Zealand, and PNG, and many Pacific and Indian Ocean islands up to a distance of 1000 kilometers.

For the South American continent it was Dalingeste Cecamante. He had risen to the top after much vigorous campaigning, and conventions, and festivals. He had won by a landslide, and was continuing with great energy and stamina. He was intending to show his people that he was without a doubt the right one for the office. He was Brazilian and had been competing with several others, just as energetic, but it was his determination that set him apart from the rest.

It was the Asian Region that was proving to be the complicated part of the whole process. The larger machine was moving, the plan was proceeding as they had indented it to. All was going as per schedule, all accept for Asia that is; and specifically Central Asia and its western neighbors, the Mid-

East. The Middle Eastern nations, along with a few Central Asian countries, would not have a Chinese Regional Ruler govern over them. There was much controversy, protesting, and lobbying, until finally there was no other choice but to allow for a dual-governing for the Asian Region. There, the two rulers would be counted as Asia's leadership. Chairman Lee would rule over the entire eastern portion of Asia, and another was chosen for the mid-east. But it was still considered as part of the Asian continent. So now there would be a total of eight Rulers for the seven regions. The Arab leader had yet to be decided upon, but a rigorous search was being made.

For the remaining two areas, Europe and Russia, Donald C. Carleighs, and Ryzard Lazniek were chosen and assigned respectively. Much was to be done yet as to their installations and inaugurations, but the groundwork had been done. The framework for this grand organization was near completion. And the world waited in anticipation as to how it would pan out. The future was awaiting its rebirth and renewing into a new and glorious day. It was the dawn of a new era, the Age of Aquarius, and the beginning of a finally realized empire. An Empire long sought out by heroes and dictators and czars, by Caesars and Kaisers and Kings, by pharaohs, by generals, by tyrants. People like Napoleon, and Attila the Hun, like Julius Caesar, and Hitler, and Osama bin Laden, like the Pope of the 21st century, and like Sleeva Sadari. The future was here and the United Society of Earth was shaping it.

✦ ✦ ✦

19

Dalee was browsing in a new book store he found on Florida St. in the Northwest corner of the city. He went through the philosophy and psychology sections, he leafed through the magazines, he'd even checked out the children's books. But still he didn't see what he was looking for. He actually wasn't really looking for anything at all. First he just wanted to feel out what this new bookshop was like, and secondly he just enjoyed being in a book store. There was something about them that fascinated him. Maybe that they were becoming obsolete, or that one could find something written on any imaginable subject. Or perhaps it was that they contained words, and this was definitely one of his favorite preoccupations. Words, language, communication. It was something beautiful, it was art. It was the way to truth. Words could give life, or they could take it away. It was simplest thing in the world that we use and take for granted daily, or it could be the most complex concepts, or could win the Nobel Peace Prize, or change the course of the future forever.

He was browsing in the sociology/anthropology/psychology/physiology/endocrinology section, as if there could be such a hybrid but in fact that's what it was. And he stumbled upon a book by an author that he thought looked strangely familiar. It was by a Dr Ben-zoheth, so it read on the cover. He looked at the back, nothing more about the author. On the inside sleeve though, there was the same man he'd met in Rome, David Ben-zoheth. There was a small picture of him, but no mistake, it was him. He had never mentioned anything about being an author to Dalee. After looking over the various summaries and endorsements, Dalee perused the inner pages and tried a few samples.

After some minutes, one particular thought caught his attention. It read:

"We must never think that we have the right, to do wrong, in the face of seemingly unjustly dealt suffering. We must do everything within our power to change the situation, but we must accept it during the interim period, as from God's own hand."

That's right, Dalee thought. That's progress. That's what separates us from the animals. He was impressed and he read a few more excerpts. His writing style wasn't as good as others he'd read, but the concepts and his insights were impressive. How much? He checked the price, $55.99. These hardcover prices are so ridiculous. He browsed a little more through the book and then put it down. Couldn't bring himself to pay that much for a book.

Dalee looked around a little more, bought a paper and exited the shop. On the way back to the car he decided that he would locate the card David had given him. He would send him an email. He would ask him a few questions about the subject of that book. But first he would ask why he hadn't mentioned that he was a famous author. He'd probably say something about not wanting to blow his own horn. Not in those words, but the idea would be the same. He maneuvered his way out of the stacked up parking lot, and navigated his way to his home in suburbia.

The card was in his stack of other name cards people had given him over the years. He kept them all. Well almost all of them. His rule of thumb was that if the owner of the card was neutral on up, he generally kept it. In fact, unless the giver was far below the middle ground level he would keep it. The person, who's name was on the card, would have to be a bottom-dweller, the lowest of the low, or a barbaric inconsiderate primeval primordial primitive savage who had the sense of someone from the stone age for Dalee not to keep it. This was generally where Dalee drew the line, and he discarded ones from people that he had met, from the category just described.

The email on the card was different from the one given on the sleeve of the hardcover book he had just seen about an hour before. He studied it while he lifted the lid on his laptop. '| | | | | | | | | | | | | | | | | | | | | | | | | | | | | | | | | | | | |', his computer said as it warmed up to his touch. <elzoe@dabranet.is> was David's email. Elzoe, he wasn't sure what that meant, but Dabranet, something looked familiar about that. Dabranet. What was that? He puzzled and scratched, and he studied as he sat. He separated the net and got *dabra* and net. Now he knew he had seen that before, but it still didn't make sense. So he left it and started his message.

To Dr David Ben-zoheth, World-traveler, Cappuccino Connoisseur, Art Critic and Lover; Taxi Rider, People Person, Theologian, Lecturer, and Book Writer.

Dalee had wanted to italicize the book writer to highlight it, but on second thought changed his mind. He considered that the words may be altered upon Dr Ben-zoheth's receipt of the message, and he may not even see the words at all, and that was the most important part of the whole introductory line. That was the problem with people using a such a wide variety of different software. He thought that someone should deal with this problem, the way the hardware situation had been resolved, and now everything was standardized. It just made so much sense. So he removed the italics for practicality's sake and reluctantly yielded his tool of emphasis. There was always the old standby: capitalization. But it was universally accepted and understood that giving a word or words in capital letters in an email was the equivalent to shouting!!! So he changed it to plain old vanilla text and left it at that. And so he continued.

Greetings from the center of the United States of America, the home of French Fries and Football, Democracy and Freedom, Capitalism and the American Dream. I'm in Washington, in the District of Columbia, nestled in a little village (or AKA, a gated community) just on the political capital's outskirts, which we fondly refer to as Suburbia, or simply, the Burbs.

How are you doing these days? You must remember me by my name beside the email address at the top of the message. If not, I am Dalee Delliv, your tourist partner at the Vatican Museum in the City of Roma some six months ago. To the day I believe, now that I think about it.

I was in a bookstore today, and I came across a rather interesting book. The author had the same name as you doctor. And lo and behold, there was a photograph, and I had a positive ID with the very same Dr D. Ben-zoheth that I had met in Italy six months previously. So. Why didn't you didn't tell me you were an author, and such a famous one at that?

Regardless of your reasons, I read a little of your writings, doctor and I found some of your findings quite interesting. The part about not doing wrong when we are in the midst of some kind of suffering in particular. Where did you get such an idea? What was your source? I felt that this was the advancement that we need to move forward and change the way people think in order to make progress. This kind of outlook would propel us forward out of primitive thinking, and so therefore our actions, and into more advanced, superior beings. We all suffer in one way or another. It is how we deal with it that makes the difference.

Well, that's all for now. If you have some time, I would like to hear from you.

Take care, have a good day,

Dalee

He read the message over, making little changes to his liking, and then sent it. After checking his new messages and doing a little e-maintenance, he closed the top. It wasn't until two days later that he reopened his personal e-account again, and checked for new messages. And there was a new one, as indicated by the blue flag. One from an address that had never been in his box before. It was indeed from the doctor, and this is what it said.

Greetings in the Great and Gracious Name of…YHWH

Dear Dalee,

(Aside Note: The rabbi's message took quite some time for him to write it, not because of its length, but for the way he wrote God's name. When he wrote the ancient transliterated form of the name of the Hebrew God, also known as the Tetragrammaton, 'YHWH', he performed sacred rituals which he required of himself. Before the typing of each letter, he must wash his hands thoroughly, dry them, then go back to the keyboard, kiss the character he is about to type, and then he could touch that letter. And he would do the same for all four letters. The more devoted and reverent among rabbi's would do this out of respect for their God. This name was also translated in some Bibles as 'Yahweh', and still in others as 'Jehovah'. But Dr Ben-zoheth insisted on using the direct-from-Hebrew translation of YHWH. He also ensured that the name itself was set apart, spaced away from any other word or even punctuation. This was a further attempt to honor God's name. It was all very small, he felt, in comparison to the greatness of God. It was also in order that people viewing it would see that like the name in the piece of writing, *God* is set apart. David also answered Dalee's question regarding not 'blowing your own horn', though he did not use that expression. Rather, he used another kind of saying, a proverb, as his reason.)

"It was so very good to hear from you. It was so good of you

to write to me. How are you? How is your wife you told me about? How is that new job that you have now? Is the pay better after all? I hope in the Lord that all is well with you and your family and your extended family.

As to an answer to your many complex, and multi-faceted questions, which is just like you, never asking just a simple single question, but a series of serious inquiries; but then that is likely how you got to where you are today; in answer to why I didn't tell you, the Proverbs, as written by someone known as the Teacher, the Preacher, Jedidiah, or more commonly King Solomon, the son of David, have the answer. There is one in particular and it reads, 'Let another praise you, and not your own mouth; someone else, and not your own lips.' The author or creator, as a human being should not tell others how skilled or good one is, but we should let others do the praising if it is indeed good quality workmanship.

As to where I found the ideas, and as to what was my source, the answer to the former will be different from the latter, therefore I will deal with them separately, though they are not all together different, as you will see what I mean, I think, as I try to explain using the simplest means as I know how.

Firstly, the source. The source of all life and matter and everything that exists, whether in concrete or even abstract terms, is the Creator, and the Sustainer of all things, and we bless his Great Name, and his Name is…YHWH.

There is no other besides him, and there is no other that can reach him. He is the beginning and the end. He always was and always will be, and that is why we call him the Eternal

God, the Everlasting Father. He is everywhere at all times and that is why he is Omnipresent. He is all knowing and all seeing and he possesses all wisdom, he is the great keeper of information of every kind for all time, and that is why he is Omniscient. His name is also Jealous for he will not share our devotion with another. His name is also Provider because day after day through all of time he gives from his hand all that is required for the Earth and the universe to continue. His name is Justice because he deals out what is fair and right to the good and to the evil. His name is Love because of his great compassion for all that he has made. And this is my original source, as is all that exists in all of the realms, including our own limited sphere that we call the Universe.

Perhaps that is more than you bargained for my friend, but you'll have to forgive an old theologian for expressing the best known subject to his old heart. Now secondly, as to where I found the ideas you read in my book. To be specific, there is a book in the Jewish Bible called the Book of Job. (The O in Job is an o as in your words: snow, or hope.) It is within the Book of Job, the character of that same name is found. Job had a very good life; in fact he had it all. And he was a good man. Then, to make a long story short, everything was taken from him, bit by bit. Until finally his health went, and as we say, that was the last straw, which has broken the back of the camel.

At this point Dalee took a little break from reading and looked away from the screen. He rubbed his eyes and then stood up. He was surprised that the rabbi knew the idiom about the last straw. But then he remembered it was about camels, so…. He wasn't expecting these kinds of replies to his inquiry, and he didn't know much of this subject. In fact, the bit about Job kind of stumped him. It was good he explained how to pronounce it or he would have thought it was job, as in get a job. And Dalee didn't know there was a Book of Job, let alone who he was. In fact, the only Job he knew was a character in a Stephen King short story called *The Lawnmower Man*, which actually is a lot better than the name sounds. So this was the only Job that he knew and he had a feeling that it wasn't the same one. He went back to the table, sat down on the chair and began again to read.

That part I just explained was just the beginning of this fairly long book, as Bible books go. It has 42 chapters. And did you know that men once asked the most powerful and sophisticated supercomputer what the answer to the universe was, to which it replied: 42. That was just a little trivia for you, at no extra cost. The remainder of the book, actually the next forty chapters more or less, is a conversation, which goes on between Job, his three friends, and I use that term loosely here, and God himself. What I'm going to do here, is give you selected portions of the original story, in English of course. It is in fact the final chapters. If I give you references of chapter and verse I'm afraid it won't mean a thing to you and therefore will be a fruitless exercise for both you and me. The part I'm giving you is the ending and it is God's response to the earlier conversations. Incidentally it is written in poetic style, therefore it is presented, much of it anyway, in verse. Now lest you think that I spent a lot of time typing these parts which you will find below, I assure you I didn't. I simply found them on a web site, and copied and pasted. I realize that it may seem extensive, but these words are unlike any other. Be patient my friend and savour verse and line, as all good poetry is meant to be enjoyed.

One last thing – bear in mind that the questions asked are mostly things that are beyond man's scope. Okay, here it is.

38. 1 Then the LORD answered Job out of the storm. He said:

2. Who is this that darkens my counsel with words without knowledge?

3. Brace yourself like a man; I will question you, and you shall answer me.

4. Where were you when I laid the Earth's foundation? Tell me, if you understand.

5. Who marked off its dimensions? Surely you know! Who stretched a measuring line across it?

6. On what were its footings set, or who laid its cornerstone.

7. While the morning stars sang together and all the angels shouted for joy?

8. Who shut up the sea behind doors when it burst forth from the womb.

9. When I made the clouds its garment and wrapped it in thick darkness.

10. When I fixed limits for it and set its doors and bars in place.

11. When I said, 'This far you may come and no farther; here is where your proud waves halt'?

12. Have you ever given orders to the morning, or shown the dawn its place.

13. That it might take the Earth by the edges and shake the wicked out of it?

14. The Earth takes shape like clay under a seal; its features stand out like those of a garment.

15. The wicked are denied their light, and their upraised arm is broken.

16. Have you journeyed to the springs of the sea or walked in the recesses of the deep?

17. Have the gates of death been shown to you? Have you seen the gates of the shadow of death?

18. Have you comprehended the vast expanses of the Earth? Tell me, if you know all this.

19. What is the way to the abode of light? And where does darkness reside?

20. Can you take them to their places? Do you know the paths to their dwellings?

21. Surely you know, for you were already born! You have lived so many years!...

39. 1 Do you know when the mountain goats give birth? Do you watch when the doe bears her fawn?

2. Do you count the months until they bear? Do you know the time they give birth?

3. They crouch down and bring forth their young; their labor pains are ended.

4. Their young thrive and grow strong in the wilds; they leave and do not return...

40. 1 The LORD said to Job:

2. Will the one who contends with the Almighty correct him? Let him who accuses God answer him!"

3. Then Job answered the LORD.

4. I am unworthy how can I reply to you? I put my hand over my mouth.

5. I spoke once, but I have no answer twice, but I will say no more.

6. Then the LORD spoke to Job out of the storm.

7. Brace yourself like a man; I will question you, and you shall answer me.

8. Would you discredit my justice? Would you condemn me to justify yourself?

9. Do you have an arm like God's, and can your voice thunder like his?

10. Then adorn yourself with glory and splendour, and cloth yourself in honor and majesty.

11. Unleash the fury of your wrath, look at every proud man and bring him low.

12. Look at every proud man and humble him, crush the wicked where they stand.

13. Bury them all in the dust together; shroud their faces in the grave.

14. Then I myself will admit to you that your own right hand can save you...

42. 1 Then Job replied to the LORD:

2. I know that you can do all things; no plan of yours can be thwarted.

3. You asked, 'Who is this that obscures my counsel without knowledge?' Surely I spoke of things I did not understand, things too wonderful for me to know.

4. You said, 'Listen now, and I will speak; I will question you, and you shall answer me.'

5. My ears had heard of you but now my eyes have seen you.

6. Therefore I despise myself and repent in dust and ashes.

7, 8. After the LORD had said these things to Job, he said to Eliphaz the Temanite, 'I am angry with you and your two friends, because you have not spoken of me what is right, as my servant job has. So now take seven bulls and seven rams and go to my servant Job and sacrifice a burnt offering for yourselves. My servant Job will pray for you, and I will accept his prayer and not deal with you according to your folly. You have not spoken of me what is right, as my servant Job has.'

9. So Eliphaz the Temanite, Bildad the Shuhite and Zophar the Naamathite did what the LORD told them; and the LORD accepted Job's prayer.

10. After Job had prayed for his friends, the LORD made him prosperous again and gave him twice as much as he had before.

11. All his brothers and sisters and everyone who had known him before came and ate with him in his house. They comforted and consoled him over all the trouble the LORD had brought upon him, and each one gave him a piece of silver and a gold ring.

12. The LORD blessed the latter part of Job's life more than the first. He had fourteen thousand sheep, six thousand camels, a thousand yoke of oxen and a thousand donkeys.

13. And he also had seven sons and three daughters.

14. The first daughter he named Jemimah, the second Keziah and the third Keren-Happuch.

15. Nowhere in all the land were there found women as beautiful as Job's daughters, and their father granted them an inheritance along with their brothers.

16. After this, Job lived a hundred and forty years; he saw his children and their children to the fourth generation.

17. And so he died, old and full of years.

There you have it Mr Delliv. I do trust that this gives you some kind of answer to the questions you asked me. You should also know that I like to travel long distances, and read broadly. These also are my sources. This ensures me that I have covered the length and the breadth of experience and knowledge. Both are good teachers. So are Job, and Solomon, and our great and glorious God.

Now I must go, and it has been good to be back in touch with you Master Dalee.

In the Name of…YHWH…I say goodbye.

Shalom,

David.

✦ ✦ ✦

20

It was only the three of them – The Executive Director of the USE Council, Joseph Cazara; the Minister of Commerce, Thadeus D. Cromwell; and the Minister of Science and Technology, Rajiv Palotangaradi. The Commerce Minister was presenting, then they were discussing, and finally the three were putting their ideas together and they were devising. Asking the question: How could this be done? Chairman Cromwell had given them everything he had developed from his research and on his plans for the one world currency. This was an important meeting and all calls were held, and all interruptions were diverted. Cazara wanted to make certain that this product, this newest innovation-slash-technology-slash-creation would be ready to be released on the July 1st deadline. Not only unveiled, but he wanted it functional, a task that seemed almost humanly impossible. But this was the type of challenge that these kinds of men lived for. They breathed success. They exuded it. And they craved conquest of the most challenging and most daunting of tasks.

There was one thing though, that they had agreed upon in the early stages of their meeting, and that was to refer to the Minister of Science and Technology, exclusively as Chairman Rajiv. No one could pronounce or remember his family name so it was mutually and unanimously agreed upon, that from that time forth he would be referred to by all as Chairman Rajiv. This was to include all staff at USE and the media as well, much to their great relief. This was in fact a common practice in certain parts of his native India, so it was actually following the custom of his culture.

In order to have a single currency, it must first of all require the cooperation of all banks and financial institutions of all countries. The unification of the nations under each of their respective Regions, and so Regional Rulers made this step easier for the 'Big Three' as they were being referred to recently. The World Bank was contacted and communications between Chairman Cromwell and its president had been very productive. Then some of the major banks of the world were included in the dialogues, the Bank of Tokyo, Deutsche Bank, Citigroup, Bank of America, and several others. The possibility had to be discussed, and then the security issue, and then the technology of how it would function internationally, and finally what unit it would come in.

Much discussion and general buzz took place among and between these superbanks as some were referred to. Some had merged with other very large banks making one extremely large international bank, thus the term superbank was born. Others swallowed up smaller banks and so contributing to the eventual disappearance of local banks. Finally it was happening, as some had rightly guessed, that the wave of the future was to unify all banks into one bank. This actually sounds more complicated than it was, and also more simplistic than in reality. It sounds simple because of the fact that it was only one bank to be used by the whole world. One might think that would simplify life tremendously, and so it does, once it was complete. The process in arriving at that point, though it didn't take, relatively speaking, very long, was in fact anything but simple. The USE Council, and particularly Chairman Cromwell, was bent on achieving this by the July 1st cutoff date in 2050. The process was a complex one because it required, not only the cooperation of the banks involved, but the permission of the nations where these banks resided, and that meant the governments, the people, and much more.

Even with approval of simply the concept, this was just the passing of a law, an idea, the acceptance of the model of a single currency. Then there was the practical aspect of things, and that was where Chairman Rajiv came in. He would handle all the technical aspects of how this whole project would work. Cromwell gave him and Rajiv's people all the information that they needed to get the job done to spec. They were handed over the basic framework of what the currency might look like, how it should function, and what Cromwell thought it should do. The functional aspect of this project was long in the workings in the years of the early part of this third millennium, as well as the latter part of the previous century.

With the advent of a global information highway, and then the logical continuation and extension of this technology in its use in financial matters, the prospect and use of a *world bank* and a world currency was simply the next step. (World Bank is used here in the sense of a one World Bank, and not in reference or any relation to The World Bank.) Once the mega banks agreed, and the government permission was granted, Chairman Rajiv and his super techies set to work immediately. And he had the best in town. These were the ones who had surpassed all the others, from where they originated, in their countries, and then internationally. No one could do this job better than his team. Nobody knew computers, inside and out, hardware and soft, as well as them. They were the programmers, technical people, AI people, internet security, and bio-technology people par excellence. That final category would become one of the most important since this new currency would evolve and later become a hybrid, a fusion of the living and the digital.

The security also had to be the best. It would involve the highest level of protection from internet theft, identity theft, and any other kind of breech of sensitive digitally stored information. The funds of every person in the world would be stored in these files. The assets of the great corporations, governments, organizations, and even royalty. Everyone who existed on the face of the Earth, both high status and the lowest, would have their wealth, whether great or small, stored in this new innovative, highest-technology-to-date, system.

The unit of currency was a problem to be tackled to be sure. There were teams who worked on this round the clock. National currencies around the world were researched, experts were consulted, models were developed. But only one could be chosen, only one would be accepted. One that all countries and all people could accept and use with ease and freedom. The various currencies were considered. The Euro of course was carefully looked at and mulled over. The idea of a currency that covered many nations was perfect. But it was distinctly European, and the new one had to be global, and all encompassing. It had to bear the mark of every nation, every Region, and every culture. It must not in any way be biased, or one sided, or multi-sided for that matter, swaying in any one direction, showing the favoritism of any country or grouping of countries. It must not either, have the trademark of any corporation or any organization or person. It had to be a symbol for all people, for the unity of all mankind.

It was also decided that it was to be a completely internal currency, and no physical funds would ever be seen. This simplified matters, and also cut costs. There would be no printing costs, nor ink or paper required. This seemingly small detail saved countries millions of dollars in labor, management, administrative costs, and machinery, and others, and all those in addition to ink and paper. It would be a cashless society. Yes, it was the way of the future. It was the future, and it had arrived. Or it was arriving and Chairman Rajiv and his workers, Chairman Cromwell and his research and models, and Executive Director Cazara were taking us there.

The idea of using the dollar was considered since it was so well known. But after some time, thought, and testing, it was discovered that it was largely unpopular in certain nations and was eventually rejected as a possibility. The idea of simply using credits was also entertained. But many thought it was simple, too simple in fact. From the surveys and consultations of the teams working on the project, the results were unanimous: something more personal had to be developed. Something more appropriate for the needs of all involved needed to be sought out.

Other currencies were examined, studied, and researched. The ruble of Russia, the yen of Japan, even former currencies before they merged with the EU, the Deutsche Mark, the British pound, and then the various dollar currencies around the globe. Each one was carefully scrutinized; each country where they all originated from was researched. Financial institutions and their staffs were consulted; the best economic professors of each nation were sought out. There were even attempts of various hybrids of several different currencies combined into one. For example, the yen with the pound and the dollar, taking the best of all three and blending them together. The first letters of all the currencies were pooled and they tried creating an acronym. Then various combinations were attempted.

Finally in the most unlikely place, it seemed, the Minister of Entertainment offered some timely advice and the teams considered it. They compared the suggestion to all their other possible choices. Tests were done, surveys were given. Time was passing. The deadline drew closer, and they, in spite of all their efforts seemed no closer than they were in the beginning of the project. James E. Tuscan in fact hadn't even formally been accepted as the new Entertainment Minister, as there were others vying for that position even at that very time. But it was that suggestion, Mr Tuscan's bold and unique idea, that tipped the scales for him in the days that followed due to the overwhelming success of his discovery. He gave the name of the new single currency for the entire world, and him in the entertainment business. Well, (so people later thought), if former actors could become the most powerful president in the world, and one was also a foreigner, then an artist/politician could come up with the name for the world's currency system. It would from then on be called: the *Khoda*, by all.

✦ ✦ ✦

21

The new currency was called the Khoda, and it would be capitalized since there would be only one. The abbreviation would be simply that of an upper case 'K'. So for a price of a new car, as a common example of a high volume product, it would be read, 23,995 K, meaning Khoda. Although K was used in other abbreviations, it would become solely the symbol of the new currency. Kilometer, as in a 50K race was usually understood from the context, but it was eventually replaced by kilometer. And sizes of files as in 400K, or 600K were rare since files were generally much larger anyway and referred to in M for megabytes. But when smaller files were used they still were measured in fractions of an M, as in 0.4M or 0.6M respectively. Finally the symbol for potassium was replaced and accepted by K followed by a period, so it was 'K'. This was widely used in most academic and scientific circles and the transition was made more or less complete by around the mid 2050s.

The monetary unit was announced as a currency prior to the deadline in an attempt to prepare the world for its practical use when they became online with the grand unveiling of the new global government in July. This would involve not only the introduction of the world to its new currency, the Khoda, but to a completely new, efficient, global, administrative and political system. The teams responsible, and Mr Cromwell himself, decided it would be most beneficial to all to have a preemptive announcement before the actual using of the Khoda in the seven Regions of the world. First there would be the revealing of the unit as a new concept, and then on the first of July, the world would be free to use it in all transactions, in trading, in buying and selling, in all financial dealings in all and every nation.

Then there was a phasing out period for the former currencies. The guideline that was followed was similar to the procedure when the Euro was about to be introduced and many of the European currencies were going to become obsolete. The citizens of the United Society, this time, were the ones who were going to bring their fading currencies to their local branches of the One World Bank, and have them exchanged for the new *world wide* currency. But in fact there was no physical exchange, due to the fact that there was no hard currency. The people would bring their old currencies of their respective countries, and the banks would credit their accounts for the equivalent, in accordance with the current exchange rate at that moment. It was a true cashless society.

People brought in their green dollars, with their former presidents stamped on it. They brought their reds and their blues, their browns and their greys. And on them were the faces of their presidents. But also their queens and their kings, their generals and their heroes, their prime ministers and their dictators. There were the ones and the twos, and the fives and the five hundreds. The ten thousands and some people brought in millions and millions of old currency units, to be changed into Khoda. And there were also coins. From the very small, to the large and shiny, the loose change of the world kept pouring in, from Brazil to Botswana, from Nunavut to Nakohn Sawan. The chink of coin was passed from customer to teller for hours upon hours as the days passed by. Until every lepton, every satang, every cent, every half penny. Every pence, every kyat, every peso, every birr, was exchanged for their equivalent in Khoda. It was automatically deposited into their accounts, and displayed onto a screen and shown to each customer as soon as the transaction was completed.

There were no bank books, no passbooks; there weren't even any bank machine slips of paper for receipts. And there would no longer be any plastic either. The ATM card, even the credit card, along with the debit card, the smart card, holo cards; all cards would go the way of the dodo. Extinct, obsolete, fading to black and nothingness. To be replaced by a new and paperless, and much more efficient and streamlined system. The barcode system would become the new way of the future. The barcode would now apply to people. The digital and the technological would be fused together with human and the organic. The connection to the currency and the banks would be in the form of a small black point on a person's hand. It would appear as nothing more than a dot to the human eye.

When completing any transaction of any kind whatsoever this identification number would be the point of reference for every person on Earth. Whether it be buying a banana or a boat, renting an apartment and doing a credit check in Ohio, or trading stocks on the FTSE, the individual personalized numerical sequence, in the form of a barcode, would be used, every time. It could be scanned just like a product purchased in a department store. It would be similar to the barcodes we see on merchandise that people buy every day; everyday items like shampoo, CDs, shoes, or drinking glasses. Only the barcode that would be on people's hands would be much smaller. So small in fact, with modern technology, that it was almost unseen. It would be an extremely small code in the form of the barcode used on products, and it would be readable by a scanner. Once read, transactions could be made.

The ID number would also be stamped onto the back of the hand, the right hand. It would be printed in permanent ink, of the finest quality, and digitally readable. This number would instantly enable the bearer to access their bank account for whatever reason. It could also be read at an ATM machine anywhere in the world. The number could be imprinted on the right hand, or in the event for some reason that was not possible, it would be imprinted on the forehead of the person. Each person would have a number, and each person must have it secured on their bodies. And there could be no exceptions. Without it, no one could function in the new society about to be unveiled.

The ID would be like a barcode on a product. It was also likened to the number on each and every book, called the ISBN, or ISSN. This number would allow a person to locate and identify a book of any kind, any that was ever made and registered, anywhere in the world. The ISBN (International Standard Book Number) is the ID of each and every book that exists. Now with the new USE system, each person would have this advantage. Human beings could be recorded and organized in the most efficient way known to man. But it was not only going to be in the field of finances that this technology would be used.

During the research process, Chairman Rajiv received inquiries and advices from various other leading world experts on the possibility of using the ID number for various other purposes. It only made sense, and in the end it was decided that personal digital code would be used for *all* information for *every* person in the world. And this would be assigned at birth. The information associated with each individual would be included in the code. In addition to finances, there would also be: hospital records, driver's licenses, even passports and visas. There was no longer any need to carry a passport when one traveled. There were also memberships to all businesses, and social organizations, criminal records, education records, library cards, fishing licenses, work permits, any other kind of national identification numbers, any kind of records or information that ever existed about the individual was referenced by *this* code.

It was meant to revolutionize how we lived. No longer would there be any need for cards to identify people for various purposes. They could never be lost again, and they would never have to be issued again. The ID number imprinted on each person would quickly access all information about that individual, and only the information necessary would be accessed at the port of scanning. For example, if the person was going through immigration at the border between China and Russia, the code would be read and the scanner that read it would only have access to the pertinent data. The info would be determined by the port and the scanning equipment. Any breech of this would be considered identity theft, and the penalty would be severe and the retribution swift. Or, if a person wished to make an inquiry of their balance of their current bank account in England while traveling in the United States, they could simply let any ATM read their code from their hand, and indicate that they wanted to see the balance. The machine would read the miniature barcode and solely process that person's financial information. The other data would be irrelevant in this case. So it would be at every port of reading. The information relevant would be determined at the point, and so the machine, where the code was read.

Of course the implementation of this system was a long process, but to those in charge it seemed a small price to pay in return for 'the best system known to man' the periodicals were calling it. Relatively, in terms of time, compared to the long range if not permanent benefits of the system, it was just a drop in the ocean. The entire process in total took six weeks. But that was working round the clock, at every possible station in every country. They came in droves from every city, every village, every town and community, every ghetto, every settlement, every trailer park, every campsite, every mountain, every canyon, every boathouse, every desert, every port, and every arctic substation. From every shack and tent, and every castle and mansion, the populace came and took their turn in line, they waited for the time to come up as the queue moved along, one by one, person by person. Until the days stretched into weeks, and the world had been organized; they all had been signed with a tiny little mark that would from then on, reference every bit of information about them, for the rest of their lives. Every person in the world, every man, woman, and child, at the end of it all, each had their coded ID permanently fixed on their right hands, or on their foreheads.

This in fact was the practical, the functional signal, or

symbol of the beginning of the dominion of the USE. It was
the ushering in of a new day. It was the dawn of the age of
peace and the new order. The New World Order that had long
been talked about, theorized, and dreamt about by so many,
had finally arrived. And to the anarchists, the protestors, the
anti-globalists, and even the Greenpeace people, and other
similar anti-corporate America people and anti-establishment
types, it was the realization of their worst fears, and their
worst nightmare come true. And yet true it was, and it was
implemented as the world's international system. It had
become a reality, and the dream of a united society of peace
and prosperity on Earth was finally realized. The general
public accepted it, the masses adhered to it, and the rulers and
founders rejoiced in it.

The July 2050 Day of Genesis introduced the new system
and it passed with flying colors. The transformation took place
and the whole world, every nation, every people, every tribe,
and every clan, all accepted it as their own. They had kept their
national identities, but at the same time became part of each
of their Regions, and also had joined the bigger greater society
for the whole planet: the USE. The metamorphosis had taken
place, and the face of the Earth had changed, not geographically,
and not the landscape or the physical terrain of terra firma.
But in a societal sense, organizationally, and internationally.
The individual cultures would remain the same, such as the
customs in the country of Uganda or Paraguay for example, but
the system and the network would be joined together. There
was only one financial system, operated by the One World
Bank, and Chairman Cromwell was the steward. There was
one technological system that held everything together, from

banks to hospitals, and schools to department stores, libraries in Pakistan to fisheries in Ireland, embassies in Africa to zoos in Australia. They were all connected by the international network, and Chairman Rajiv was the gatekeeper.

Each country could retain its own culture while simultaneously being an integral part of the larger system for the greater good. There actually had been emerging a new brand of global people, who travel the world frequently, who come from many places, and who were an eclectic mix of many races. There had been an international culture in the making for several years beginning at the turn of the millennium. In fact it had actually begun even before, throughout the 1900s with the industrial revolution and the space age and other of the many breakthroughs during that unique and magical century. The music and fashions and many other trends that knew no borders, and crossed cultures and became part of the fabric of the global tapestry, all contributed to its development and acceptance. Until the culmination and the merging of that culture, with this new society for all of mankind.

Other leaders had been chosen for the other ministries and smaller departments, like the Department of Transportation, and the Department of Education. Then there was the Department of Health and the Department of Communication. The chairman for the Transportation Department was Bandell Dristard, of the Department of Education, Estanni Svorg, and for the Health Department, Treshton Tillton became the minister. Finally the D of C selected Dr Thanu Mitconta as their leader.

Everything and everyone had found their place. The pieces and the players were all there, and the game was in play, the machine was in motion. This was the beginning of the greatest enterprise ever formed, the greatest accomplishment ever achieved. On July the first, 2050 history was made. And the future lay ahead, everyone's future. But in all the greatness and all the glory, there were those who wondered, where will it lead? Or, where will we go?. Where can one go from up, from the top. Time was going to reveal the answers to these, and other questions.

✦ ✦ ✦

22

Dalee arrived after eight as he had been doing as of late due to the strenuous demands of his new job, had his dinner and was looking through some documents in search of a form he had once used when traveling quite a few years earlier, when he came upon an old travelogue of his. He had told a certain story so many times that his relatives and friends urged him to put it down in writing. He, and his then traveling companion Janvieve Dozois, had been doing their round-the-world tour; sort of a grand scale Grand Tour which the wealthy, educated aristocracy once did so long ago on the European continent. But this was on a larger scale, with many pit stops and even work stops along the way. It therefore took a lot longer than any euro grand tour, or even regular around-the-world tour.

It was in their young and crazy days, wild days, when they were in a kind of carefree reckless stage of life. They had visited several other countries, did the European stint, and were just beginning the Asian leg of their wild and woolly world tour. They had planned to spend a little time teaching English in Korea because their funds had diminished to just a few hundred dollars. Things didn't go quite as planned there, and they only spent one month in that country instead of the six as they had intended to, and so then it was off to Bangkok. They would use it as a base to see Thailand and the surrounding nations in the Southeast Asia region. But before they left Korea they arranged the purchase of their ticket with a friend of a friend. He ended up paying for the airfare with his credit card, (the friend-of-the-friend's name was 'Q'), which started them on an obstacle course through several Asian cities, and led to what later developed into the tale that Dalee would tell and retell so many times after that adventure.

He had been leafing through some papers when he came across one with the title:

The Legend of the Replacement Credit Card

He smiled at the memory. Then he skipped the introduction and looking down, began about half-way into page one. And then he started to read…

I phoned Q and asked if he knew any deals on flights to BKK. He responded unusually quickly, but at that moment it was helpful to me since our time was running short and we were required to be vacated from our accommodations the next day. He phoned me back with good news! He got a reasonable deal on a flight, so we proceeded with the arrangements. I mentioned that I had wanted to use my credit card but somehow by the end of our conversation he didn't have it. He hung up without getting my information and we later discovered that he had used his own Visa credit card to pay for the tickets.

A small point this may seem, but it would later turn into the stuff that legends are sprung from. I figured that I would simply reimburse him when we saw him in Seoul. He owned his own business and had an office there. I thought that he would have some kind of setup where I could use my credit card to pay him back. This was a fatal miscalculation. In fact we would later find out, that there was no setup or means of repaying him with our card, and we would need to use cash to pay him back. Now this was the one thing we did not have.

It turned out that there was no other way, but to pay with the cash advance portion of the credit card. Which would have been fine under normal circumstances, but this wasn't your regular everyday situation. We were traveling, in unknown foreign countries. We were in fact on our way to a small country that mainly used cash to pay for services and purchases. And this depleting of a full half of our cash resource would inhibit and limit us considerably. And so, having little or no other choice we proceeded to the Korean bank to withdraw 50% of our cash which we desperately needed to live on.

I still remember entering the comfortable and muted atmosphere of the plush interior of the bank. We approached a special desk, only for other transactions, not the plain old withdrawals or deposits. Mr Q spoke his native tongue to the finely dressed bank representative. I was presented offering my credit card and passport. After a few forms to fill out and some simple communication between myself and the woman behind the desk, the hard currency was counted out and handed over to me. The largest denomination in the country being the 10,000 Won bill, and that being approximately the equivalent of ten American dollars, the stack of cash grew higher and taller. It seemed, to me at least, that we were giving away a small fortune, and certainly much more than I wished to give. But hand it over to Q I did, and he took it in repayment for the charge that was at that time on his Visa card, and our cash reserves had dwindled in those few minutes to a fraction of what we would have much more comfortably liked to have to live on for the next few months in the country we were about to travel to. Little did we know how much more was in store, and how much water and of what turbid character it would be, that was to travel under bridges not yet seen.

And so we were then transported to Inchon International Airport, and flew off to Bangkok. The time there was pleasant in fact; refreshing and enjoyable for some time. Until the funds began to get near the bottom. We were getting short and were considering that we ought to make another cash advance withdrawal, when a minor tragedy struck. Not the kind that harms you physically mind you, but definitely frightens the victim and that was my travel company in this case, and also inconveniences and troubles the recipients that being the both of us. Janvieive was robbed.

Now under normal circumstances it wouldn't have mattered as much. But it was because of our unique and delicate situation that we were particularly alarmed. It was a clear cut pick pocketing case on a crowded street so the damsel was not damaged in any way, other than the distress. I was not with her at the time so was not able to do anything. In the moments after the crime was committed Jan quickly determined the losses: the cash she had on her person was gone, the approximate equivalent of 100 Euros. We weren't too concerned about that; not that we had very much cash, but in the great scheme of things it didn't seem like very much. And then there was her ID cards, and the credit cards. And yes, the very one that we needed to make our precious cash advance withdrawal with. This was the greatest setback.

Of course I had my copy of the same credit card, but when one has a card stolen, there is an implied mutual understanding between thief and unsuspecting victim, that the new possessor of the cards in question would use that card for their own personal and joyful, not to mention free, spending spree!!! And at the card owners expense, which happened to be us! But with quick thinking and fast action, Jan headed for the nearest bank, which there were plenty of in that section of Bangkok, and rightly and wisely called for the immediate cancelation of all cards. This would effectively put a stop to any expensive shopping bonanzas on the tab of yours truly. Only that wouldn't be the only problem we had to face.

Now it is a fairly well known fact that when one loses a credit card, the company belonging to that card, will more or less promptly issue a replacement card to the owner. The only problem in our case was that we were not at the address that we had given them when we first opened the account. We had since moved from it, and were in fact for all impractical purposes, at no fixed address. This resulted in a dilemma for both the credit company, and also for us. But we couldn't very well give that as our location.

After much phone calling back and forth across the world, and that in opposite time zones, so it meant being woken up in the middle of the night on more than one occasion, and much explaining of the unique situation, and also proving of the appropriate information to verify our identities, a decision was made on the situation. A new address had to be registered, and it had to be local. Now this posed another problem. Our mail would be sent to that place thereafter. Well anyway, we managed an address somehow, and they promised to send the new cards. Which was another situation, because they were not actually the real cards because they were what credit companies refer to as temporary cards. And guess what? You cannot make cash withdrawals on them. (Here, the reader should put in their own personal sound, noise, exclamation, preferably, for me, one of exasperation.)

The temporary cards were sent, quite promptly by courier, and received. Relatively promptly anyway, despite the fact that it was on a weekend, and there happened to be a national holiday in between as well. (You'll notice that capitals are being used in this piece at this point, and we all know what capitalization can mean.) The temporary cards were made good use of in the interim period of additional waiting, until the regular cards came with the cash advance feature, which we were intending to fully utilize upon receiving it.

We then moved on to better, meaning free, lodgings, of missionary friends living in the central plain region of Thailand. We would wait it out there until our regular cards were sent to a third address, the home of Kitty and Becky, two single missionary women working among the Nya Kyuur tribe in a little village called Wong Ai Poh.

I couldn't possibly do justice to all that followed in that waiting period. The normal, the commonplace, everyday language falls short of explaining the truth of the things that happened in that *amphur* of central Thailand. But I will do my utmost. Even the best photograph, with just the right caption, couldn't fully express the life experiences that we encountered there.

An *amphur* is the Thai term for county. In specifying a certain place in Thailand, first there is *jangwat* province, then amphur, then *tdambon*, which is a certain smaller area or district. And this particular amphur we were staying in, just happened to be the poorest one in the entire country of 70 plus million people. As one could imagine, because of this fact, and that we were in a somewhat remote area, and in a foreign country, as aliens, and staying with missionaries in the midst of their work as well, it would prove to be a most memorable time, to say the least.

I can't go into every adventure or each situation that we encountered there but will here record but a few that we experienced, all while innocently awaiting our infamous replacement credit card. First there was the drought. Now in this amphur, (which could very well be why it's the poorest), the water shortage is an ongoing problem. This means going down to the pond and hauling water at times, which is just what Becky and Kitty would do from time to time, along with all the other good villagers there. Then there was the *ohngs*, the ubiquitous huge concrete containers that surrounded their wooden Thai house in order to catch and store rain, when it came. Water was a precious commodity and was used, and reused, carefully and wisely.

Then there were the sounds. Normally it was quiet there, but now and then the good villagers had in their often mundane, usually idyllic lifestyle there, a celebration, or perform some custom according to their national religion. But these events were very noisy affairs, and often lasted for long hours, and went late into the night, or even all night. Live and let live I always say. But when it comes to my sleep, sometimes that little rule can infringe on one's personal needs. However, what were we to say as visitors in a foreign land, and guests of our friends there in the secluded little village of Wong Ai Poh.

I knew we were in trouble when they began setting up a wall of speakers and amplifiers directly across the road from our house, faced in our direction. A young man had just entered the monkhood and they were going to celebrate this rite right, with food and drink, and friends and family; and music. Very, very LOUD music. We couldn't help but join in on the festivities for a time, and you've got to admire them for their love of merriment. But it became a little too much for us Westerners, and we attempted at least a temporary escape. This actually didn't turn out very well, and we were reluctantly forced to return to the neighborhood party. The fun lasted late into the night and we slept as best we could. And the neighbor became a monk and all's well that ends well.

There were other things that our friends introduced us to, well known to that area. There was the Ga-jeo flowers, which bloomed by the thousands on the sides of the mountains, and only at that time of year. They were purplish-pink and they were beautiful. Then there was a foggy, misty cliff that many tourists come to visit, and it was known as Suut Pan Din Loke, which when translated into English means The End of the Earth.

Our neighbors were friendly and hospitable, and our hostesses were genuinely warm and sincerely gracious. We couldn't have been treated better in our unpredictable, personal, card situation. There was one neighbor in particular that seemed to like to sing. She, or he, we were never really sure, and according to our friends there, the neighbor was still trying to figure that out. Any way the neighbor sang with great gusto, in the morning, and sometimes in the afternoon or evening. It was a slow, kind of a melancholic song, and according to our friends, who understood the language of the Nya Khooor people, entirely made up by the singer her or him self. They were simple lyrics of everyday things like collecting wood, or picking rice, or just going to buy food. And so we were serenaded day by day as we stayed there. The neighbor's window by the way, was very close to the guest bedroom window. We heard the singing often and only when the neighbor went away did the music stop.

The mail was dealt with quite some distance from the village, and it was mail that we were waiting for, so this required trips into town. They had an old used vehicle that had been passed on from a former missionary and it ran. Back and forth down those dusty roads, driven by faithful Becky.

Then there was the final phone calls to seal the deal. And then there was the walk out in the country to find a place where the hand phone that we had at that time could function. It was a long walk, and the tropical sun was hot. This is where even pictures can't properly describe all that is in a scene. One cannot hear the sounds, smell the odors, feel the temperatures, experience all that is there. Although we walked to the top of a hill, even to the point of climbing a tree, but still the signal on the hand phone was not strong enough. There was though, one spot that you could possibly get a connection and make a call, but unfortunately it was in the middle of the main highway, and even with that it kept fading out and disconnecting, which was quite frustrating to say the least. It was only a two lane highway, and although it wasn't that busy it was still the main artery for that area. There were trucks, and buses, and tractors which intermittently passed by, so we thought it was just too dangerous.

Now there was also our friend's personal hand phone at their wooden house. But we didn't really want to ask them because we had picked up on a Thai trait called *grengjai*. There is no English translation for this word, but it is something like polite, but more like tact. There isn't really a word for it because Westerners don't usually have this, at least in excess. We didn't really have much choice since it was either ask them or climb the hill, and up the tree!, or stand in the middle of the main highway. We did use their phone, and it turned out that the call was somehow free and didn't cost them a dime. Even though it wasn't a collect call nor a toll free number. And some people say there is no God.

We were getting close to the end now, and finally on one of the journeys to the post office or PO as the Americans referred to it in those parts, there was our forwarded package. It was the cards! We were all ecstatic. Then back to the village to make the phone call to activate the cards. But we didn't need to go up the tree or in the middle of the highway this time to do it. We used Kitty's phone, and called the credit card company to activate our new cards. Well it turned out that that wasn't too difficult but the PIN was going to be a problem. The Personal Identification Number was needed in order to use it at an ATM. Now this wasn't going to cause any trouble, as long as you could find a bank where they had the service that you could make a cash advance from inside the bank. And those it seemed, weren't that common in the somewhat remote amphur we were staying in. So off we went in the old car, with Becky at the helm, in search of a bank with cash advance on foreign credit cards service inside the bank.

An aside note on the ATM and using the PIN option before I reach the story's climax. The customer service representative of the credit card company regretfully was unable to issue us a PIN over the phone due to the constraints of company policy, otherwise we could have simply gone to any ATM (with international service, and in English) and withdrawn cash. But even then it would have to have been one that would accept that particular card, which wouldn't have been too difficult. But the credit card representative was able to graciously mail us a new PIN for our new cards which we had just received. It would take two to three weeks, depending on local mail delivery in the particular foreign country. It could be mailed directly to the PO nearest to the village we were staying in. Little did it matter, because we were about to hit paydirt in the neighboring town of Lumnarai, the nearest thing to what we might consider civilization, that is by our standards.

We made the final trip, the last lap, the longest mile, in old Betsy, with Becky again as Chief and Capitaine of the worthy vessel. We were on our way to the small city of Lumnarai, about a 45 minute journey through the rice and tapioca fields of that part of the land. The bank was open thankfully enough, and in we went to claim our prize, that pot of gold at the end of our vibrant, somewhat rocky, multi-colored rainbow. We approached the special desk, this time in a different country and a much different situation, but for basically the same transaction that we had reluctantly made with Q in Seoul about two months before. I filled out all the proper forms, and gave them all the right documentation, and I waited. And as I sat there across from the polite Thai bank representative I thought, we've certainly been through a lot. And also isn't it amazing that we're able to get cash like this simply from a piece of plastic, in a far away country, and even in their own local currency. Isn't it amazing?

Then the woman politely informed me that the card wasn't working, and she asked if we could use a different one. No. This couldn't be happening. I asked her to wait a moment. I went to Jan and Becky who could tell something was wrong and dreading the worst. But I took cell phone in hand, and made one last call. I can't remember if our phone actually functioned in the bank that day, or if we used Kitty's, but call I did, and it was cleared up in a matter of minutes. Back to the special transactions desk, and one more try with same card. She swiped it…and it worked.

The cash, in Thai Baht, was handed over in the form of ten crisp 1000 Baht bills, and I accepted them on behalf of Jan and I, and thanks to Kitty and Becky, the Nyaa Khyuur tribe, Wong Ai Poh, the PO people, the young monk across the road, the singing neighbor, the End of the Earth and the little mountain flowers called Ga-jeo.

Editor's note on currencies: The 10,000 Baht would go a lot further than the 10,000 Won (US$10.00). The Baht we received in the bank that day in Lumnarai, was equivalent to one to two months salary in Thailand. And that money would go a long long way. And so Dalee and Janvieve had a happy time in various parts of the country, enjoying the beaches the shopping and the delicious Thai food, before they set off on their next journey after those funds ran out. Then it was on to Papua New Guinea to teach English for a year. Another country, another journey. And so ends the Legend of the Replacement Credit Card, to be passed on again and again. Until…another adventure came along.

Dalee put the pages down, and lay back on the sofa he had been sitting on. He rubbed his eyes, and then stretched. He reminisced a little, staring straight ahead at the ceiling. His mind was full of memories, his eyes looking back in time. In his eyes at that moment one could see distant lands, the experiences, the fears, the challenge, the memory of another time, another place. He got up slowly and, in a sort-of trance, ascended the stairs. He changed into his bedclothes and lay down beside his wife. He lay there a few moments, tired from the day, but still remembering. Then after some time, he thought he heard the faint sound of distant bells. He was drowsy and he couldn't think of what they reminded him of. It was a pleasant sound. Were they wedding bells? Were they Christmas bells? Or maybe it was another sound; of the tolling bells. And he did not want them to be for him. But then he heard them louder. The clear ringing of bells on the morning breezes, the peal of bells in a beautiful song of crystal clear music. It was his dream.

And he knew it was the sound of the Bells of Paradise. The paradise he had visited so many times before in his dreams. The bells were ringing in the dawning of a new day, a new beginning; a place where there was no time or schedules or deadlines. Where life was simple and there were no troubles. A new world where skin color didn't matter and everyone was your brother or sister no matter what they looked like or how much money they had. Where there was no hatred or prejudices or crime or fear. And there would be kindness and love and consideration for other people.

And there was no need for credit cards or money, and

everyone had enough. There would be no more war or murder or killing. The hopes of the suffering would be realized. The world would be a pleasant place with clean air, and pure water. Pollution was just a fading memory. People could drink from streams and rivers. And the oceans would be clean too, with no toxic wastes. Just the blue blue waters for miles and miles, clear and clean. And the sky would be blue too, blue skies with the sun shining in all its brilliance. Yellow and golden, warm and beautiful. This was why the bells were ringing. Ringing to announce the beginning. Ringing to call all those who yearn for this land of peace and health, of prosperity and safety. Calling the old and the young, the rich and the poor, the sick and the dying, the lost and the lonely. Calling them to come, and join the new place, a land far away from all troubles and fears. To come to live in the paradise. And Dalee dreamt on.

✦ ✦ ✦

23

This was the beginning, the beginning for planet Earth, but also the beginning for Mr Joseph Cazara, the founder, visionary, and CEO of the whole new system. And for those who managed it. All his rulers and ministers, and all the aides and assistants that go with them. All the office staff that it takes to operate this conglomerate, this mega corporation, this epicenter of the international government, the main center that would rule over the vast domain of the whole world. In the near prophetic words of Mr Cazara himself, "Never before has this been legitimately attempted, and never before has there been the opportunity, the possibility." Never before had this been achieved. And now they had finally accomplished it. It was established. Everything was in place, from the first Region to the last, from North America to Australia. From Communications to Commerce, from Cazara to Sverge. Everything and everyone was in their place.

The world had taken its place in the new order, and the world for all practical purposes was in order. All the people from all the parts from every place were registered. Now by that, it is meant they were sealed, they were imprinted with their personal number in the form of a very small barcode affixed to their bodies. And all the information that they would ever need was in that code. Of course it wasn't literally in it, but was only a reference to be scanned and then the needed information could then be accessed from files which were stored in various parts of the world in the appropriate hard drives of computers. Yes, computers. Possibly man's single greatest achievement in modern times. Or perhaps, throughout all of time. One could argue that it was the wheel. But the wheel just wouldn't carry the weight that the computer does in such a comparison. With the computer man can communicate, transport, educate, eradicate, assimilate, and simulate. The possibilities are virtually limitless. With the computer, the internet, and with this new system, we have united the forces of good in the world, the great minds of the world, all the best of every nation, into one great pool of knowledge and power and potential. And now that it had been made, it could not be unmade. One cannot go back, the technology and the progress can not be undone. The future was here.

Mr JS Cazara and Co. had decided to set up office in Jerusalem after all. It was the most sensible, the most practical, and, now that the wars had ceased, the most peaceful place on Earth. It was also the most central. It was almost as if the land and the people, in such huge relief, were experiencing as much peace as there was strife, and war, and hatred, and enmity for so long before the treaty. It was the opposite and equal reaction from the force of good, as much as it was from the force of evil formerly. War, and then peace, equally. There was an atmosphere of friendliness, of brotherly kindness. There was a camaraderie that they'd never known before. Jews and Muslims working together, living in communities side by side together. There was apprehension and hesitation at first, but then there was a neighborliness and a comfortable coexistence like they had never imagined possible. The level that they were mingling together at, in communities, villages, at borders, were the civilians. To them, their neighbors weren't Palestinians, or Israelis, they were just people. Human beings. At the military level, the men, and women, and children were a little more cautious. It would take some time for them to trust their Jewish brothers, or their Islamic sisters. After such a long period of tactics and counter attacks, and strategies of warfare, they were still tense, their muscles taut, their minds ready for battle. They were, after all, soldiers. It would take time. But how long, no one knew. Time would tell.

The main USE headquarters was in Jerusalem. But it was more than just that. It would be their White House, their Kremlin. The address was simply, Green Peace Place, Jerusalem, Earth. It was a colossal and ornate structure. They had taken a former palace and made some changes and renovations. It was also part of an elaborate temple as well. Together, these two parts, with the new additions, formed the huge compound that was to house offices for the Executive Director of USE, all of his Council members' offices, and then an office for each of the Regional Rulers, of which there would be eight. Then there would also be an Audience Room, a Map Room, the War Council Room, various libraries, a Diplomatic Conference Room, the Multi-Cultural Room, the JC Dining Hall, the Art Room, and several other specialty rooms, lavishly furnished and exquisitely decorated. No expense was spared in the creation of this unique and singularly great architectural masterpiece.

There would be other branches in other cities, but not

nearly as elaborate. In fact, the USE would eventually have branch offices in five other major cities throughout the world. While GPP was in the final stages of completion, construction was going on for offices in various continents. The USE would continue to use Cazara's building in London in the UK during the transition period. There would also be a branch in Chicago, USA. Then also in São Paulo, Brazil, and another in Shanghai, China. And finally one more in Sydney, Australia. The London office would handle any pertinent affairs for Europe, and because of its proximity to the African continent, the GPP would have any business for that region, directed to Jerusalem. That office would also handle the Mid-East and Eurasia. Shanghai would take care of the rest of Asia, and also Russia. Of course the GPP in effect handled all matters ultimately, but with such a massive volume of work, the other branch offices would assist them in the work of the world. The business of running the planet.

As Cazara was moving in and setting up shop at 1 Green Peace Place, the first order of business came to his desk. There was a problem in the Middle-East. This was to be expected. But he didn't think it would be this soon after the peace deal. As it turned out after a briefing with Chairman Lee, there had been many rallies in support of a certain Muslim cleric as a candidate for the co-leader for the Asian Region, but he had just been assassinated. The Mid-East, and some Central Asian nations had strongly protested the appointment of a Chinese ruler over them and had demanded that they have their own ruler from their own people. And the selection process had been progressing well, until this happened. Cazara discussed it with Chung Wang Lee and other advisers, then called his speech writer. He was intending to give an address to that area within the next 3 hours. He also contacted Supreme Commander Draik and instructed him to show a little force in that region at selected strategic targets.

The speech was to target those insurgents and rebels who opposed the Asian Region's order, and the Global community's peace as well. He would use shame and foster loyalty. This problem had to be dealt with quickly and firmly as an example to any others wishing a similar show of rebellion. He and the USE would make it known that they saw these types of high handed actions of rebellion as opposition to the international order, and not just of their own locality. They were part of the bigger picture now and not alone. The speech writer wrote prolifically, and Executive Director Cazara would deliver it eloquently. And the words, in the climate of a new and advancing society and with the backdrop of the recent Mid-East peace treaty, those words would hit their mark in the hearts of the loyal and ready citizens of the United Society of Earth.

The following day a new search had begun for the Regional Ruler for the Middle East. The Regions would remain the same, and there would be seven areas, and portions of the Earth sectored off for administrative purposes, but for the Asia Region there would be two Rulers, Mr Lee and a yet to be appointed second ruler for the Mid-East portion of Asia. In fact there were already several possibilities, due to the earlier screening process, but no one from the camp responsible for the assassination. The party guilty of the crime was captured and the organization he belonged to was held accountable, and the nation that harbored them remained nameless. No candidates from that place were accepted under any circumstances.

The selection process was underway and one Ta Dar Somola was the front runner and most likely to win the seat. He came highly recommended and was very popular with the whole region. The only problem lay with himself. He was the typical reluctant hero. He felt that he was not worthy of such a high ranking position, over so many nations, even though it would in fact be the smallest sub-region within a much larger area. His supporters, however, had every confidence in him. Mr Dar Somala was in the process of simultaneously being fitted for a possible position as Ruler in the Mid-East, and being persuaded that he was the best for the job, when a faction on another front occurred.

In the African Region a rival Ruler had appeared and was in competition with the existing one, Mr Dalugani Tsabi. Although the present one was popular and well-liked, the new one was more aggressive and more powerful. He had rallied many supporters and had a huge following. Some of the USE Council, along with the African Regional Ruler, and Mr Cazara himself entered into talks over this dilemma. After some days at the negotiation table they came to a consensus. In lieu of the recent unification of the nations, and for the sake of peace, they seemed to have no other recourse but to let that region have two rulers as well. The people were divided over the two possible leaders. The two figures would end up having a kind of dual-governance kind of system. It wouldn't be so much in terms of geography, but rather in regard to responsibility. Mr Tsabi would deal with administrative, environmental, educational, entertainment, and health matters. And the other ruler, Hadar Toologa was his name, would handle finance, military, transportation and communications, technology, and some additional responsibilities yet to be disclosed.

This was now approximately two weeks into the time that the USE had moved into the GPP headquarters. The registering of the world's global citizens had taken six, so the autumn season was about to begin by the time planet Earth's rulers and council members had finally ironed the final wrinkles out of the system. There would, as it turned out, be a total of nine Rulers for the seven World Regions: North and South America, Africa, Europe, Asia, Russia, and Australia. The USE's Council had not changed however and remained stable. They also had set up their offices at the GPP compound, in addition to arranging their local offices in each of their respective Regions. Certain ones however didn't have as much time as the others due to the matters related to the divisions in two of the regions. The Supreme Commander of Military Affairs, for one, had been preoccupied.

Cazara was back at his office one day in September when one of his personal aides approached him.

"Mr Cazara, Sir," and bowing slightly to show respect, then asked for permission to enter. Upon receiving it, he began again. "The GNCN media corporation has requested that we do an interview with them."

Thinking a moment, he responded that that was an excellent idea, but they would have to work out the best timing of it. They looked over the schedule for the next few weeks. Travel, business, and certain functions prevented it for that month. They decided that October would be best, and they discovered a date that would be perfect. It was the one year anniversary of the attack in Rome, Italy. This would be the celebration of triumph over the violence, the rejoicing in the peace that the United Society had established in the Middle East and on Earth. It would be the antithesis of that event showing the ultimate good in all that they had achieved, beginning with the Peace Treaty of all times, and ending with the establishment of the new world order. Yes, he would accept the offer. It would take place on October the 27th. And Mr Dalee Delliv himself would be officiating.

Things were going as planned. The new system was set up and it was accepted or was being accepted, across the board. They were setting up their headquarters in the now Capital of the World, Jerusalem, much to the astonishment of all who had doubted them. All ministers were in place at the Council, as well as the nine Kings of the seven Regions. It was almost a year since the final major terrorist attack; which had been in direct opposition to Cazara himself and his colleagues, and their cause. Now they had turned that around, and the world upside down to create a safer world to live in. As well, the Khoda world currency system had been set up, every human being on Earth had been registered, and they were up and running. They were online. Billions and trillions of monetary transactions were completed every day. Billions more still of record keeping from the whole spectrum of administrative tasks. It was working. And now an interview with the largest broadcasting organization was arranging a meeting, an interview which would be the crowning jewel of all these events. The world would hear from the great Cazara himself, and about his success on the world's stage. The Society had been born and he wanted the world to know it.

✦ ✦ ✦

24

At 428 Estevare Road, the Washington office of Global Network, or just Global Net as GNCN was sometimes called, was in full swing on a Saturday. They always operated on weekends, but usually only with a skeleton crew. This time it was fully staffed, and the supervisors and cleaners, and managers and even Mr Executive Producer himself was there, Dalee Delliv. He liked to have his weekends off, but made an exception this one time to oversee a particularly important story.

Now he was a firm believer in rewarding those who stepped up and gave up their time, going beyond the line of duty. Or those who stayed later than necessary going that extra mile. On this particular Saturday, it was nearing lunchtime so he took the liberty of ordering Thai food for all the workers and having it catered in. He called his favorite Thai restaurant and spoke with Tassanee, in his limited language ability he had achieved so long ago during their extended stay there. He ordered *pad thai* for 5, *tom yum goong* for 6, 15 servings of *penang guy*, 30 portions of *khao soy*, and 30 portions of *Gaeng gai gai*, along with the best rice, the jasmine kind, enough for the whole staff and then some, and the delicious sweet milky orange-colored ice tea, or *cha yen* as they called it, for all to drink with their meal. He also threw in about 10 more plates of *khanom jeen*, just in case someone was still hungry.

He didn't tell them what they were getting. He just told them he was getting lunch for them. So when Tassanee herself arrived, along with her helpers, and the feast, the staff were delighted. They got set up in the lunch room and dined on the exotic and quixotically provided for food. Somehow or another Dalee got placed by the infamous talker Mr Gift-of-Gab himself, Cecil Carter. So there Dalee was, enjoying his delicious Thai food, with Cecil on his right and one of the cleaners on his left. That's what he got for buying lunch for the Saturday staff of Global Network. The cleaner it turned out was more well mannered than Cecil. Her name was Deco.

She had worked there long before Dalee had arrived and was actually nearing her retirement time. Deco thanked Dalee sincerely for such a nice lunch. He was impressed by her genuineness and her graciousness. At his right elbow however sat the talker. And talk he did, before the lunch, during the lunch, and for sometime after the lunch as well. It was his characteristic high-pitched slightly raspy voice, but it was the unusual whistling sound that got to Dalee. He could probably take the ongoing monologues and stories, which he seemed to have an endless supply of, but that unusual voice of his...Dalee stared ahead and periodically turned and gave appropriate responses when Cecil would pause to breathe or try to remember some person's name, or the brand of toothpaste someone had used, or a particular address, which all had tremendous bearing on his story. The Producer considered that his radio persona was made distinct by his style of presentation, his stamina, but it probably was mostly due to his strange voice, with its funny whistling sound when he spoke. Dalee pondered this as he stared ahead, with a long tale being spun at his right ear.

"Two hundred thousand dollars!" he was saying. "Can you believe it? And that was the last I saw of them." He had been explaining about a house he had up for sale in New Jersey, some years before. Dalee wasn't aware of the story line at that point though, so had to ask him to repeat the question. The exclamation had jolted him and made him realize he wasn't listening. He then decided to ask him how the Devron story from the week before went.

"Oh, it was just fabulous, Mr Delliv. The story went out just like we said we'd do it. The advertising worked like a charm. And the calls that came in..." and here he whistled. Dalee thought it sounded just like his other whistling when he talked, but this was just more controlled, and made with his mouth instead of originating in the radio man's throat.

He began to think of the peculiarity of the sound, and Carter's successes. And how this type of thing happened with others in the media and other businesses. Rod Stewart's voice was unique. But he was also a talented singer. Then there was Wolfman Jack. Then there was that crocodile guy, he'd seen on clips from long ago. It was his enthusiasm and love of the environment and the animal kingdom that made him. What about in business? There was Trevor Dantalade, who made Danaco what it was today because of a single distinctive: Be the best, beat the rest. And he had some funny thing about him too, what was it? Dalee had always noticed it when he saw him on TV. When he talked to someone during interviews, sometimes he would kind of squint, or wince, almost as if the question was a blow, and he was bracing himself against it. He wondered if anyone else noticed that, and considered asking Cecil but he was saved by the bell and everyone, himself included, needed to get back to work.

He approved the spending for the next week, changed water companies for the second time; then went over the programming schedule for the next day, Sunday, which was the reason they were there that day. After he had finished his necessary responsibilities, he took a look at some new projects he was working on and worked on those for a while.

Dalee Delliv. He had come so far from his early beginnings in West Virginia. His parents emigrated out of Pakistan so many years before. They themselves had been moved so many times, in an attempt to find greener pastures and to better themselves. Not that they had done too badly for themselves in their own lands, but they just weren't able to achieve the level of success they were aiming for. They were severely impeded by their own countries' poverty and international standing. They knew of people who had succeeded and broken out of the vicious circle of saving some funds only to lose it or have it taken away. There was always a war, some disaster, corruption of the government, or some other unknown worse factor that came into play. They thought, if others could do it, then so could they. So, like so many others who had gone before them, they moved to America in search of the realization of their dreams.

It was a struggle, even for years in the beginning, but hard work and perseverance prevailed. And also being good to people, even those who were against them. It wasn't easy with the unpleasant prejudices of ignorant people against them, and sometimes even aggressively, and with deliberation. But goodness prevailed, and evil assailed as it will always do. The

Delhi's succeeded and their small business grew to a small empire. And that's what Dalee's life was built on, their small fortune, which had accumulated by the time he was in his late teens.

Their name was changed to Delliv; that is Dalee and Janvieve. And then later on his parents assumed the name also. At the time when Dalee was about to leave home and start out on his own, there had been a controversy associated with the city of New Delhi in India. Wanting to disassociate themselves from the stigma attached with the same name they decided on altering it just a little. They tried many variations, but the father was involved in this process; and he didn't like any of them. In fact he was dead set against any change of his family name at all. Mr Delliv senior felt that there was honor in his good name and to lose it would mean in essence to lose his identity, and somehow disrupt his family's long history, of which he was fiercely proud of. He wouldn't exactly put it in those words, but had made it clear to his son and new daughter-in-law on no uncertain terms, that was his name and he would not change it.

However, Dalee and his wife privately worked on an appropriate substitute. They considered several options some of which sounded good at the time but then were later scrapped when they were about to present them to the family. They were then at the stage that they figured that they would only be able to get a mild approval from his father, of simply allowing him to tolerate the newlyweds using a new name. Some of their choices were Dellhigh, Delheed, and Delheme. They thought they had almost gotten it right when they came up with, Dellee, but he didn't like the way it sounded with his number one son's first name. They also tried a number of other combinations with various additions like, Delcort, Delcomb, Deligh, and Delees. But none of those would do. Then they came upon a few where *they* really thought they had something, that is from their perspective.

Just plain Dell was one, they both really liked that one. And then there was Delux. That one might've even had a nice sound if it was pronounced with a French accent, and he had, after all, married a mademoiselle. But Dalee's favorite was Delta. It sounded good to him, and he liked its link with the Greek alphabet. However neither father, nor wife would consent. He couldn't even get his own mother to side with him on that one, and they vetoed him on the delta name.

Finally one day when they had near given up, a delivery man came to the door with a package, the receipt was signed, and he left. But someone clicked in and had the idea of something to do with the word delivery. They played around with it for almost an hour, and couldn't seem to agree on anything. Then Janvieve took to writing her name with a few variations of the word. Finally on one try she penned *Janvieve Deliv* and then spoke it out loud. Everyone liked it. They tried it out with Dalee's name. They talked it over. Mr Delliv was willing to accept it, but only for the younger couple. And it would have to have two Ls. They would keep one that belonged to the original name Delhi, and one would be taken from the word deliver. So it was then *Delliv*. Dalee particularly liked the reference with the word deliver, or deliverer, in the more ancient use of the term when it meant, 'to rescue; also to save, or to set free from something'. To set free, as in the meaning: 'to liberate'. He liked that part almost as much as Delta, so he was satisfied. It also carried the meaning to send something, which was also a good concept.

For his new bride, she liked the rhythmical sound, the way she pronounced it in a French accent, Janvieve Delliv. It seemed everyone could accept this new formation for their family name. But it wasn't until much later that the parents would take it as their own and change their names to be like their son's and daughter-in-law's. For them it would take time, time to watch, time to observe its use in America, and time that would be needed for their other relatives to accept it. And in time they did.

Dalee himself started out in West Virginia, and then was educated in D.C. itself. He later went from college directly into an internship at the State Department. His exceptional intellect and extraordinary motivation soon earned his way into varying degrees of successes and climbing up the rungs of the political ladder. However, feeling dissatisfied he took some leave without pay and traveled. He said he missed out on what other people had, when he went straight from graduation to internship in Washington. Said he needed to see the world, sample other areas of life and work, and also learn about other cultures which always seemed to hold a fascination for him. On one of his tours, he landed a good job in the field of journalism, which was another of his passions. This led to a full five years away from his initial career. He did however return to Washington after that. But then he went back to the journalism field in the end, but with some connections remaining in the nation's capital.

He checked his email, collected all his things, and locked up his office for his short weekend. It would only be Sunday this time. He walked through the main area on his floor, said goodbye to those still working, and headed for the elevator. 'Done for the week', he thought, staring up at the blinking red numbers as they sequenced from 11 to 10 to 9 to 8. When he reached the ground floor, he wrapped his wool scarf around his neck to get ready for the cold of an autumn evening. The temperatures had been unusually low for that time of year. He found his car, and got in to drive home. He wouldn't turn the radio on this time for fear of getting some more of Mr Carter. He popped in a CD of selected instrumental piano pieces by Hayden, with some string accompaniment. The stars were shining above him.

✦ ✦ ✦

25

The new Executive Director of the newly established USE, had agreed to the interview by Global Network, but on his terms. It would be at one Green Peace Place in Jerusalem, at 10.15 on the morning of October the 27th, 2050. He had graciously allowed the audience room as their interview venue, which was normally reserved for royalty, heads of state, and diplomats. But since they had sent such an esteemed personage to conduct the interview they made an exception. Mr Dalee Delliv of GNCN, the Executive Producer, and Supervising Director of their Productions Division, the former Acting Secretary of State for the United States, and currently Washington's emeritus resource person for international affairs, was holding the interview with Mr Cazara.

The terms of Director Cazara were that there would be no photographers, and no video or any kind of recording, other than the interviewer's notes which he would make from questions that he could ask. Mr Cazara would have his personal aide with him, but Mr Delliv must enter the Audience Hall unattended. He may have his assistants with him up to that point.

Dalee had many pre-arranged questions which him and his team had discussed and developed and perfected in the days before the actual interview. His initial ones centerd around the United Society and its present state of affairs. Then he was to ask positions on several different issues. He was also pressured by *his* superiors to ask some pointed, and as far as Dalee was concerned, even malicious questions. He personally, didn't like some of the questions that the media had taken to asking in these times. He actually had a few of his own, apart from the ones that he had down on paper with him.

He entered the Audience Room, leaving his assistant at the door. He was immediately approached by one of Cazara's top aides, who supervised the careful and complete scanning of their guest with a hand-held device. The security was meticulous when it came to the Society, so Dalee discovered on this trip, and in the course of time. Mr Cazara greeted him warmly, but with a cool professionalism that seemed to warn Dalee to keep the interview strictly up to specs. He didn't see what the trouble could be. He and his associates made sure that every requirement was followed to the T. Cazara even was to check the pre-published interview himself for words taken out of context, or anything that might be considered slanderous, before it went out. He took his seat.

After about 15 minutes, at 10.30 a.m., Dalee asked what his views on Capitalism were.

"Capitalism is useful, as far as it can be harnessed and utilized to the benefit of the people."

"The United States was built on capitalism, as were many other postmodern nations."

"Yes, of course. No doubt Mr Delliv. You should know that, more than anyone." His tone light, his manner disarming. "No one is denying that. I'm simply saying that it has its limits."

"In what way."

"Not that I have anything against certain nations' use of that particular ideology, but I simply believe that it has its limits. It, as with all things, reaches its peak, its limit, and then it will decline, as it has in the past. So anyone can see." Dalee didn't like the implied connection. "For years, centuries, it has been used, in your own country for instance, and all benefited from it. But as can be seen by the mega monopolies recently emerging, their control of certain markets, and the effect that it has on the society and the general economy, as I said, it has limitations. Not to mention its squashing of the little guy. Who's going to look out for him? Certainly not Mr Clibberd, of Tell-Tale Corporation."

"Then what do you propose to do?"

"I'm pleased that you asked that question Mr Delliv." Dalee was sure Cazara was. He felt a bit like the fly that just walked into the spider's web. "There must be balance; that is the key. This isn't the whole picture, you must understand, but an important part of it. In a global economy one must be careful to make use of many systems, several models which work in their cultures, and will work well in conjunction with other cultures as well. This is very important." Dalee was making a note on the last point, and then started a new page.

"There is in fact no right system when it comes to commerce. Or rather should I say, 'correct'. As I said, capitalism is good, insofar as it works in a society. But when people suffer as a result of its extreme use…"

"…But what about those chairmen, founders, and CEOs who give so generously and benefit others. Would you not say that this is keeping that balance you talked about?"

"Yes, but who exactly do they benefit. And perhaps a few are generous. However, there are many who do not share their wealth quite as magnanimously as the benevolent philanthropists you speak of Mr Delliv. I do consent though, that there are some who spread a small portion of their vast wealth to aid in causes which the particular tycoon may deem worthy of his funding. As a tax write-off, I might add," Cazara added lightly with a smile and in a humorous way, as an attempt of breaking any ice which may have accumulated as a result of their mild bantering.

Dalee looked up from his notes and resumed his questioning. "Mr Cazara, do you think democracy is the ideal system for our world today?" Dalee knew it was a loaded question, but he asked it anyway. Without missing a beat, Cazara began again. "Democratic thinking is, I believe, what established your, and other societies. It is the power of the people. Which is always good. When we try and take our brand of democracy, and force it into other people's cultures, it will either grow and adapt, it may mutate, or it will be rejected entirely. Mr Delliv, we need an entirely new political ideology. Something that the world has never seen." Here Dalee thought, "And of course you have it," but he thought it better not to verbalize it at that time. Cazara went on, "Our world is made up of so many kinds of different peoples, as I know you have personally discovered in your work, Mr Delliv. We must not allow ourselves to think that we can rule or dominate the world with any one type of system. If anything, it must be a composite of several of the traditional, and something, as I have stated, entirely new. With a new system, a truly global community can not only function, but it will thrive. It will flourish. And under the direction of the USE, we will, my friend. We will."

Dalee was unphased by his theatrics. "Your leadership, or domination as you put it, will *it* be the sole power that we earthly citizens are to answer to, Mr Cazara?"

Smiling, but only a little, and with eyes of clarity and vision, he spoke with authority, "We are the rulers of this Earth." He accentuated each individual word. Then coming back to earth, "By we, it is meant the other Chairmen and I, and the nine Rulers of the seven Regions."

"Weren't these Rulers also referred to as Kings once?"

"Ye-es, they could be considered Kings just as easily as rulers."

"And since there are nine…"

Chuckling at Dalee's reference he added, "And I suppose you expect to see me wearing a golden ring. I do in fact wear one, though not for the reason you presume." He lifted his hand to display a plain golden band on his right hand, but on his index finger. Dalee glanced at it. Still chuckling, but a little louder, Cazara pressed, "Mr Delliv, do not take works of fiction so seriously." Then with less laughter, and more of a questioning, convincing tone, "Come now. What do you think this is? Some kind of Tolkienian fantasy?" Dalee simply absorbed his interviewee's comments without affect, then looked down and scribbled a few more notes on the legal pad in front of him. "Our Rulership is reality, not fantasy, or fictional I assure you, Mr Delliv. And it will endure. The power which one man will wield, is in fact shared with the nine. So your reference, even in jest, is inaccurate." He spoke with a slight condescension, and not without distaste in his words.

Dalee changed the subject. "How is the Khoda system

working out?"

Cool but calculated, he replied, "It is the most ingenious system yet known to man, and it is not surprising, since a genius is responsible for its genesis."

"Did you yourself receive the ID imprint?"

"Yes of course. The same as everyone else."

"Do you have any regrets of how the meeting which was held in Rome one year ago turned out?" This was one of those questions Dalee's superiors insisted he use. He didn't like the association of blame and the laying of guilt on Cazara personally for the loss of those lives of the people at his meeting there. This included his colleague, Sam Delainie. And that's just what this question did. But they were his bosses and he was required to use certain focal questions that they considered essential for the success of the interview. Dalee however did change one part. The original said, '...the meeting which you held in Rome' and he changed it to which was held in Rome. He didn't particularly like Cazara, but he didn't see it as essential to go for the jugular, necessarily.

Cazara didn't miss a beat. "The criminals, as you yourself know Mr Delliv, and the organization which they belong to, have since been justly dealt with. The outcome, as you have asked me about, couldn't be more glorious, wouldn't you say, Mr Delliv?" He paused, but didn't expect an answer. "Look around the world today. Read the newspapers; you above all should know. Better than anyone. Why, you are the one that produces the stories. Your finger in on the pulse of current events, as soon as they occur, am I not right, Mr Delliv?" The tone and inflection of the question was paternal. Then lighter, and with more enthusiasm, "The terror issue has been eliminated. It has become a non-issue. Who would have thought it possible? The Mid-East now has peace. One year ago you or anyone would have said that was a false statement and an impossibility. And yet it is true. Middle Eastern peace. It was once an oxymoron," he said laughing lightly. "I'll say it again, because I want the world to hear it and it is music to everyone's ears. There is peace in the Middle East." Dalee was filling another yellow page.

"The merging of all the banks, and then the use of one currency for another example of the impossible becoming a reality. One currency for the whole world. Who would have ever imagined a completely perfect, cashless society. Achieved. Period. Not only did the Council achieve this, but in addition, an entire new system of identification was implemented. For the whole world! Also achieved. All within the timeframe of the initiation of the USE on July first of this very memorable and historic year."

He had finished his mini-speech segment and Dalee was considering his next question. He only had a few left, and the time was running out anyway. He had one on religion, and one on freedom of speech. And if there was time, the culture question. He'd start with the second one. "Will people have the rights they enjoyed in their own countries, as a part of your new society?"

"Human rights have been abused and misused. Human beings have been mistreated, from women to tribal groups of various nations, or because of their skin color or their social standing, all throughout time. So it is no surprise that we still have this problem today. You earlier asked about capitalism. And we said that it has some merit. Well now let's bring in the merits of other ideologies, such as pure communism, socialism, or as in certain nations, monarchies. These all can, and do work, but must be held in the delicate balance of their culture and the treatment of the citizens as human beings. There is nothing more important than the rights of our fellow man. That is why the rights they enjoyed before, will certainly continue and overlap into the new Society. Inasmuch as it does not infringe on the rights of other human beings, whether in that individual's country, or in another. Now most of the time this balance is not disturbed, and we all go on living in the cultures we were born into, as many choose to do, or that we have moved into. If and when this balance has been tipped, and the scales are teetering, then we have top people monitoring these matters on a global level. Now when I tell you, top people, Mr Delliv, rest assured that they are indeed the best there presently is on the face of this planet. Our system though perfect, is continually being perfected, if it could be put in those terms. What I'm saying is, it is still in its early stages, and it can only become better and better."

"And what about freedom of speech?"

"This also can in fact be taken so far, that others will suffer from the apparent freedom of others. One must always have restrictions in any society, Mr Delliv."

"And you will decide those restrictions?"

"My team of course. All of us, collectively. It is not good in the present, nor has been historically, for one man to wield such power alone, as you have so literarily and deftly pointed out to me in your allusion earlier in this interview," Cazara remembered with a slight smile.

"You handled the Muslim and Jewish religions well in this

country. What can you do about other religious prejudices in other parts of the world?"

"I'm also pleased you asked this question. We have a new department within our Council which is in the process of being formed. It will be the Ministry of Religious Affairs. This department and its chairman, will be responsible for all matters pertaining to religion and faith, in all countries. When we have more to report, you, I'm sure will be the first to know."

"I see my time is running out, do you have time for one more question?" He observed that the Executive Director's pause and expression allowed it, so the interviewer offered his final question. "What will the world culture for citizens of USE be in say, 25 years from now?"

"Your guess is as good as mine. Who knows the future? But I can tell you this: it will certainly be better; and each nation will still be unique."

"Thank you for your time Executive Director Cazara."

"Thank you, Mr Delliv. It has been my pleasure I assure you."

The two men shook hands, and Dalee was escorted by the aide to the door. In fact the aide took him to a debriefing room in a nearby wing of the palatial structure where he was asked to hand over his notes. Two assistants carefully checked the pages. Dalee asked if his writing met their approval. When they were satisfied, he was shown out of the building. Then he got the next flight out. Back to DC. Back home.

✦ ✦ ✦

26

At the airport, while waiting for his flight, he checked his email. He saw various familiar ones but then another he was vaguely familiar with, but wasn't sure. The name was in another script, not English. Looking closer at it he saw it was Hebrew. He also saw the 'dabra' with the net added on in the address. *Dabra*, it struck him. As in *ca*-dabra. Altogether it was *abra ca-dabra*. Right! He felt a small satisfaction from his discovery. It was from the rabbi.

> From: <elzoe@dabranet.is>
> Date: October 27, 2050
> To: Dalee Delliv <dalidelhi@world.com>
> Subject: Hello Dalee
> *Dear Dalee:*
>
> *Greetings in the Great and Glorious Name of the God of the Universe and all that is in it.*

Must have been in a hurry, Dalee thought. He didn't use the Tetragrammaton this time. Dalee also wondered for a moment about the abra ca-dabra part. Why does a Jewish holy man use a magic word in his email address? He thought that a bit strange. But he read on.

How does life unfold for you these days? I hope in-the-Lord that you are well.

I hadn't heard from you since my last message and it had been some time. I wondered if you received it. Did you get it? It was in answer to your questions regarding my book. And also some other questions related to my sources. Would you like me to resend it? I still have it. I keep all of my messages religiously.

Dalee paused and wondered: Was that a joke, or was it a misuse of the word. He wasn't sure, but it was pretty lame, he thought, either way.

How are your family, and your wife....?

It went on to tell a little of his own life, and then closed. Dalee clicked the reply button instinctively and began to write a response.

From: Mr D Delliv <dalidelhi@world.com>
Date: Thursday, October 27, 2050
To: Dr David Ben-zoheth <elzoe@dabranet.is>
Subject:

Dr Ben-zoheth,

How are you? Just a quick note to tell you that I did indeed receive your last email message. And I do thank you for your reply. It was both informative and enlightening. I was surprised at some of your sources, and yet intrigued. Never heard of the 'Book of Job' before. And had no idea of even the pronunciation of the author's name. Thank you for your rabbinical guidance.

My flight is in another hour so I have some time here. I just completed an interview with the incomparable himself, Joseph Cazara. I will be piecing together a story from my notes over the next 24 hours. You can look for it on our web site, www.gncn.com. Or wait for the old paper version in the morning.

Is your synagogue doing well? Did you hear about the new Minister of Religious Affairs that USE will be selecting. Well, you can read about it in the news coming up shortly. By the way I did have a couple more questions for you, doctor.

Why do you have abra-cadabra in your email address? and what is your take on what has happened in Israel? All the changes. What does it mean for you personally?

He looked up and was considering a *Subject* for the message. Sometimes he just put the airport code for the city he happened to be in, such as LAX, or YYZ, or CNX. He was checking a nearby monitor when it dawned on him that he was in Tel Aviv. He found the code and put it in anyway. TLV. Then he debated whether or not to send it. He figured he would just phone the doctor instead since it was a local call. He decided he would do both. He checked over his message, then signed it, and clicked the send button. Everything was on the screen these days. Nothing was real anymore. What was real, anyway?

The travel system certainly was a lot more efficient since the inception of the Khoda system, as it was being referred to. The term was used for both the currency, as well as the entire identification referencing network. Now when Dalee traveled he need only have his stamp code scanned upon checking in, and then that was it. No boarding pass, no passports, in fact no ticket at all. Once inside the travelers' area, he was in the system. No one else could enter, nor could he leave either. Unless he needed to, and then he would just have to recheck-in. And then the whole x-ray the carry-on baggage set up was completely streamlined as well. One just simply walked through a screening tunnel, with carry-ons, purses, laptops, wallets, fanny packs, even baby carriages. And your shoes and belts could be worn! No more removing everything, and then recollecting at the end of the big-boxed machine and the conveyor belt. It was all taken care of with a simple stroll through a tunnel. You hardly would know you were going through it. The technology had been so developed that the scanners could hone in only on what security was looking for. And it did not interfere with any electronic devices on someone's person, like pacemaker, hearing aids, etc. If there was any problem, the security officer would politely ask you a few questions.

Even immigration had become simplified. And upgraded!, if that could be thought possible. With a scan of the hand, the officer could determine everything he ever wanted to know about Traveler X. The rude questions and unnecessarily impolite scowls were reserved for genuine criminals and would-be terrorists. In fact, when it was determined that it was a traveler returning to his or her country, or even home city, a Greeter would meet them immediately after the immigration check. This designated individual would have a few words of welcome for the returning native, and depending on the length of absence, small to large token gifts were imparted on the, usually weary but grateful traveler. Set gifts were given for 1, 2, 5, and up to 10 years leave from a person's home country. After 10 years there was another special gift, and particularly if the traveler was a senior citizen. In that case it would depend on the length of time the senior had been away. Also, for visitors of a country, and tourists, there were other kinds of Greeters arranged especially for their situation. And at this point it was completely commercial free. There were no sales pitches, or push for any particular hotel. It was just a warm welcome. For example, in India the Greeter would put their hands together in the praying position for the customary greeting, and wish the visitor a pleasant stay in the country.

After sending the email, he thought, now how am I going to get his phone number. The phone book…probably in Hebrew. His card?… no, he didn't have it with him. His email…sometimes people put signature tags on their emails with contact info. He pulled up the doctor's last email message. Sure enough there it was.

Dr D. Ben-zoheth,
Bethelzoe Synagogue
Jerusalem
Home: +972-564-2253
Office: +972-554-7854
HP: +972-3434-8957

Dalee chose the hand phone and wrote it down on a notebook he had with him. He closed his computer, picked up his bag, and looked around him for the nearest telephone station. After finding one, he walked to it, picked up the receiver and began to dial. A Jewish greeting on the other end, and then asked who it was also in that language. Dalee not understanding a word, simply said hello and asked in English for Dr David Ben-zoheth. Still puzzled, the rabbi asked in English who it was. When he discovered the identity of the caller he was delighted. And when he found out where he was, he insisted on Dalee meeting him somewhere, but he regretfully had to decline. His flight was about to board. He just wanted to say hello since he was in Israel.

Dalee asked him if he had seen his email message, to which he replied he had not. The good doctor was in his car, and it was good that he had called the mobile phone number. They couldn't really have a proper conversation under the circumstances but the rabbi promised to view his email, and that he would reply first chance he got. Dalee bade him farewell, and the Jewish man gave him a Hebrew blessing for travel and the conversation was over.

Dalee heard his flight number over the loudspeaker and looked at the counter at his gate. They had begun to board. He walked over to his flight's line of passengers and they slowly began edging their way to the doorway to the jet way. As the line slowly moved forward, he wondered what the rabbi thought of what was happening in the new Israel. Someone in front of him hadn't bathed that day. There were some things that technology couldn't fix. He looked back at the terminal he was just leaving. A group of Japanese tourists were tightly gathered around their leader. Then he saw a sheikh with a long poofy beard and the thick, puffy white handlebars of his moustaches drooping down the sides of his face, and then curling upward. A small child ran from his Indian mother, who was wearing a unique bright green sari, but she wasn't wearing a veil and he wondered what state she was from. An unmistakably African-American woman had a very large back-pack mounted on her, with everything from pots to skates hanging from strings on the sides.

He entered the long hallway, then down the corridor, and into the metal hull of the aircraft with the other passengers. Then the preflight rituals, the taxi, and ascent into the great blue beyond. Up, up, and away, they soared into no man's land. Into the sky of endless space, where they rested; on automatic pilot, suspended in space, over the expanse of the Atlantic. The waves were so far below now, but the sky seemed like he could touch it. Was he closer to Heaven there? Was there any Heaven?

The travel companions brought the complimentary refreshments. One smiled at Dalee and he thought she looked a little Venezuelan, but it was so hard to tell these days. Where was anyone from? Indeed, he didn't even know where he himself was from. He recalled when the doctor asked him if he wanted to return to his people. And he had asked him the question, "Where are my people?" He thought about this question as he watched the screen in front of him with a map indicating the aircraft's position, first in relation to their point of origin. Then as it related to their destination. The little blinking airplane symbol slowly inched its way across the screen, across the sky. He thought his people must be the Americans, since that was all he'd known. In West Virginia, in DC. But that was only his origin.

He thought he had another origin, or he had other origins. India, and Pakistan, where his parents immigrated from.

Those were his origins in that sense. But he also came from his mother's womb, and his father's bloodline. His immediate family was his origin. And he loved them, and was grateful to them. One's loyalties lie with their family. This was true. But one's family is not a nation. "So where are my people in the sense of that question?" Dalee asked himself, and settled in for the long haul from East to West.

Dalee Delhi. Who was he? He was indeed a composite, a compilation of many parts and places, and not just one place. The sum of the parts made the whole of what he presently was. But it was changing, therefore he was dynamic. He liked that; he was: Dalee the dynamic. He was compiled of all the parts that pieced him together. From DC to Virginia, from Pakistan to all his travels, even to France through the influences of Janvieve. Also there was his formal education, and his work, and his friends, even his dreams. He was a complicated interwoven connection of all of these, and more. The lights went dim and many were resting in the cabin.

He was definitely not a machine, he knew that. He was made up of organic materials definable by organic chemical compounds. What about his people? Were they chemicals too? Or protozoa and paramecium? He didn't think so. No, his people were the people he knew and loved. That's who they were. The one's he'd seen and known throughout the long journey of his life. The path he had taken. The road in the yellow wood. The screen re-blinked to life, and the in-flight movie came on. He watched the previews first. And then the main feature came on. It was 'Dumb and Dumber', with Jim Carrey and Jeff Daniels. This kind of thinking was too deep, he thought. Someone must have requested an oldie. But it was a goody. So he put on his headset and put the seat back.

And Dalee was smiling.

✦ ✦ ✦

27

He was walking calmly in the forest behind their home in the suburbs of the capital of the United States. It was autumn and the air smelled of the sweet delicious aroma of the wet dead leaves. How could something decaying smell so good. He walked a calm walk through the paths with the last of the leaves falling all around him. Not the hurried, harried gait that one must keep up while catching the next train. Or while getting across a busy intersection in the downtown core. He was serene.

He was thinking about words. What was the big attraction for Dalee anyway? With words one could communicate, express precisely what one wanted to say. It can be spoken, or written. Many have used other mediums. Painting, instrumental music, sculpture, photography, theatre, film and the cinema. But Dalee's fascination, perhaps preoccupation… Obsession? (he thought not)…was with words. Language is communicated through words. Thoughts are expressed through words.

His language was English. But it just as easily could have been any other. Telugu, Farsi. French German Spanish. Chinese Thai Korean Japanese. They all could express themselves in their tongues, with words. So the language was not the key. In fact the language was arbitrary, insignificant, immaterial. But for him it was English, therefore the vehicle of expression, the portal out of which his thoughts and ideas could flow. His use of three or more different possible words in English to express the importance of language when one would do, indicated his ability to utilize the language to the fullest.

Others could use photography, or film as expression of their message. Or music. But Mr Dalliv's preference was: words.

"The Brothers Gibb knew what they were talking about," he sang and spoke into the forest air as he walked along a simple path that wound its way through the trees. He sang the chorus of the Bee Gees song *Words*. "That's all we have. It's all anyone has, when it comes right down to it. Imagine if we didn't have language. Sure, you could use all those other things. But there would never be the precision, the exactness of the thought expressed, as with words.

Picasso had his cubist period, and he painted the trio of musicians. We got the message. But there have been so many many interpretations. Van Gogh and his Starry Night. What was he saying? With his pale and acrid colors. With the stars and the swirling sky. What about David… The sculpture of a youth. His gaze fixed on his enemy. Did Michelangelo capture the original thought? And Ludwig van Beethoven. What of his Symphony No. 9 (Scherzo)? The strings, the drums, the notes, the melody, the crescendo. Magnificent! In-comparable. He expressed a feeling. A mood. A tone. The time period was captured. An era encapsulated in a musical piece. No words.

Shakespeare said it through his creation Hamlet. His friend asks him what he is reading. To which he replies a simplistic line, a repetition which stands alone in all literature – 'Words, words, words.' What did William Shakespeare mean three hundred years before? Did he mean that they were nothing more than words? Or was it that he was enraptured with what he was reading? This famous playwright knew exactly what he was doing. He was the best that time knew. It is in fact one of the only remaining written forms of plays of that time period.

And what of the poets. Of Byron and Wordsworth, of Yeats and Eliot, and Thomas and Dylan. Ah yes, Mr Zimmerman. The poet from Minnesota. Where did he get his inspiration? From the hills and rivers? From the lakes and the trees, or the little towns in that part of the United States? Why was he so gifted with the expression of words?

Dalee began to sing the words to *Blowin in the Wind*. The silence after his song was peaceful. The words echoed in his ears, even though he only sang it softly. He looked around him at the wooded patch of trees he was in. A few birds were singing. The temperature was cool but pleasant. The smell was fragrant. Autumn. He paused, then began again. He sang much of the words to Dylan's *I Shall Be Free No. 10*. Laughing while he sang.

Was it his combinations of words, because there wasn't anything life changing in that. But his Wind song was deeper. We all must die. All must develop and achieve and reach one's zenith. And he seemed to think the answer was out there somewhere. To Dylan it was somehow…in the wind? Nature maybe? God?" He wasn't sure. But Dalee pressed on. And what about faith. Where does that come into play? This is an endless unlimited source.

Is faith part of the equation? Where does faith end and responsibility begin? We can change things, I know that. History has been progressing along, and then someone comes along and changes history. Take the invention of flight for example. The two brothers achieved it, Wilber and Orville Wright. But then it wasn't until later that Howard Hughes, in spite of all his oddities, pushed the limits of flight, until he made it better, faster, and the aircraft itself, much stronger. If it wasn't for him and his propensity for the highest and the most extreme, we would still be flying in paper airplanes. Or taking weeks, or months traveling by ship. With, quite possibly loss of life and/or limb.

And what about Mr Gutenberg himself. Why, with his invention alone he changed how we humans communicate, and skyrocketed the literacy rate world wide. Not to mention, using Luther's words with his technology, he uprooted the church and caused a reformation that would alter the world's major religion of the time. I don't know of any quotes by him, and yet he single-handedly caused all of this. He was one who indirectly used words. He had a machine that revolutionized the civilized world. That got the word out. That put into the hands of every human being, the printed page; in all its shapes and forms. Books, being only one. The words changed them. And Gutenberg was the initiator.

Then Mr Timothy Berners-Lee came along. What did he do for words? And images; and sound; and music; and film. Not to mention banking, and business, and travel, and so on and so on and so on and so on. Every library in the world is available to every country in the world. Every book store in the world is accessible to every person in the world. Every newspaper, and e-zine, and radio and TV station, are all there for any one, any where, any time. Just get online and start soaring. Up, up and away, through fiber optics, on satellite waves, on radio waves, over oceans, through the skies, and over the mountains. Without leaving your seat. He never knew the breadth, the vastness of the extent of the influences of the Net.

How could he have known? How can anyone realize at the time what they are doing, and the full extent of its influences. We cannot know. Otherwise we may never do it. Look at Einstein. Did he know about Hiroshima when he was playing with physics formulas in his lab some years before? Could Leif Erickson have any idea what would become of North America when he set foot on it some 1000 years before Columbus arrived. Or Bill Gates when he developed his Windows and DOS in the latter part of the 20th Century. Edison, da Vinci, Marconi, and Clibbard. They all had no idea what the ramifications of their discoveries would be, and the full extent of their influences nor of the developments of these in the future.

What about today? What is this Khoda System and where is it going? It has made life so much easier, so much more efficient, simplified, and organized. We thought the twentieth century with electricity and the automobile, had brought us so far from the Dark Ages that we couldn't get any better. But then with the computer, and the internet; and now this! It's almost as if, it seems as if, nothing is impossible. Where do the limits end? Space travel. Telepathy. Teleportation. Time travel. Can we conquer death?

Who is Joseph Cazara? What does he want, and what is he after? Does he know what he is doing? Does he understand the depth and the breadth of what he is doing? Of all that he is changing? And how his influences are going to change our history, our future?

He was quiet for a while and the forest seemed quieter,

almost silent. Nothing was wrong, he had just stopped walking, and the day was almost over. The shadows were becoming longer. It was that time of day between daylight and evening. Dusk. In the twilight the smells of the woods didn't change. The air just became a little cooler. He looked around him. Then he thought of the article he had just supervised and published based on the notes from his interview with Cazara.

He gave the notes to the writers, but he had told them that he would work with them on it. Once it was drafted, edited, rechecked, and perfected, it was, as part of the agreement, to be approved by Cazara's people. They made a few minor changes. There wasn't much to change. Dalee knew what they were looking for. Did he have freedom of speech? Did it even exist anymore? The article was met mainly with praise and acceptance of the new world leader. But it was not completely without opposition. There seemed to be a small resistance movement in reaction to the new United Society. They didn't really have an identity, or a name, but Dalee had received information from his sources, which were good, that they were becoming organized. He would like to see how this would pan out. And he wanted to see the USE reaction.

He returned home by a different path than the one he had come by. He came out into the clearing and saw the soft glow of the lights of their home. Home. It was where he belonged. He had a place in this world. A place to call his own. Safety, freedom, convenience, and prosperity. It was all he'd ever known. Many didn't enjoy those things and he was very aware of that. Apparently Mr Cazara was even then attempting to eradicate poverty, oppression, major diseases, and his favorite enemy: war. Dalee was right back to his initial questions of

Where are we headed, and Where is this taking us? He didn't know. But they were going there now. And fast. Without much say in the matter, he felt as if he, and everyone else he knew, were on a conveyor belt of time and progress.

✦ ✦ ✦

28

Outside the GPP compound the guards, heavily armed, stood at attention as the Ministers, the Chairmen, and other office personnel steadily streamed into their workplace. All the members of the Council, and all the Rulers of the seven Regions had offices there, but the entire company was almost never present at the same time. The Rulers all had their own regions to govern and had their local offices to run on their own continents. The South American Ruler was not in the line of limousines that morning. In São Paulo, Chairman Cecamante was in the moments before his alarm would awaken him and when his day would begin there in Brazil. Chairman Lee was there though, and now getting out of his vehicle, the door held by a crisply fully uniformed chauffer who would then close the door and wait for further instructions from his supervisor. The temperatures were extremely high there in Jerusalem, but the governing management of USE required full uniforms during hours of duty.

The Minister of Commerce was there, his vehicle then passing through the gate. He stared straight ahead from the back seat with its tinted, bulletproof glass just to his left. The guard he passed also stood looking straight, but outwards, away from the compound. He would only see this Minister out of his peripheral vision. Any other regarding of the Council Member would be disobeying a direct order from his commanding officer. Minister Cromwell had important business there that day. All the Ministers were usually there at the compound. This was their main work place, and the central hub of the Council's activities; though they did travel to other Regions, as was necessary. His driver pulled into his reserved, name-plated parking space, and assisted his exit of the limousine. To the left, two reserved parking spaces over from his, was an empty place which no one would use that day. It was for the new Minister of Religious Affairs.

Inside the building was the usual morning buzz of activity. Coffee or teas were served by attendants who knew just how their bosses liked them. Messages were collected and delivered to the appropriate desks. Faxes, little colored slips of paper with telephone messages on them, the very few pieces of traditional correspondence that still circulated in the world those days, and any pertinent notes to be brought to the immediate attention of the Chairman or Minister of that office.

Executive Director Cazara was sitting and sipping his coffee while reviewing that morning's memos. There he sat, alert and ready for the world's needs; established in his position, and successful at the setting up of the Council and the Regions. At this point he wasn't taking much notice of these things, but simply carrying out his responsibilities, and preparing for the duties of that particular day. It was Tuesday, November the 2nd, the year 2050. His plan had worked, and his efforts succeeded. The new United Society was completely in place. There were still a few other additions to make but they would be taken care of. For the time being, the office of the president of the world, was set up.

The entire office of Mr Cazara, as well as the offices of the Chairmen of the Council were quite pleased with how the interview turned out and its article which followed shortly thereafter. Of course they were happy; it gave a glowing report on the doings and the developments of the world's latest and the greatest, the US of E. Dalee had attempted to do all he could to ward off the influences of other great powers' control, but he felt that unfortunately, he was being used as a vehicle in another's propaganda agenda. The article itself was well done, and he felt satisfied with its delivery, presentation, and the writing itself. It was just that he didn't want GNCN to end up being pulled along by invisible strings held by some other powers, regardless of greatness or smallness. And while the world sang the praises of Cazara and his USE, it left a bad taste in his mouth. But he didn't have much choice; it was either print it with their approval, or not at all.

Mr Cazara did also meet with his new Regional Ruler (really a kind of sub-ruler) for the Mid-East, and that was in the mid-afternoon. He was very careful to never give that impression to him though, that it was ever considered a lesser position than the other regional rulers so as not to injure his, or their, pride in any way. They were granted this request, however, because of the continual unrest in that area, and the Executive Director was not about to have anything to do with even the slightest hindrance which could cause or instigate any unnecessary escalations. The new ruler, with the kind of background and personality which he had, as far as Cazara and his council were concerned did not pose a threat or problem in any way at all. So their meeting was fruitful. He would continue to meet with Chairman dar Somola even on a weekly basis, until full stability was accomplished in that region which had historically been characterized by its political and social unrest. In fact dar Somola had alluded to a possible resurgence in Israel. But he was vague and distant about it. He gave no hard facts, so Cazara kept this in mind, but didn't take it any further. Although after their session he put some of his best espionage agents on it.

In the late afternoon he recapped some of their successes with a few of his advisors. They went over their established regional offices in Chicago and Sydney. These were fully staffed and operational, equipped to handle any situation which might arise. As well as the everyday duties which they were responsible for; generally speaking: the maintaining of order in the Regions of North America, and Australia, respectively. Charles E. Dargon, the North American Regional Ruler had an office there in Chicago, as well as one in the Jerusalem headquarters. He daily dealt with the multitude of needs and developments for Canada, the United States, and also Mexico. The Australian Ruler managed that continent-country, along with New Zealand, and the islands up to a set boundary which had been decided upon by the Council itself just a few months prior.

The advisors with Mr Cazara that afternoon also went to great lengths pointing out the success of the Khoda System, the great and widespread use of it, and the prospects which were in store in the near future. The reports of the economies in country after country being on an upswing, and several had formerly been in a recession or worse. The praise for the elimination of currency exchange was across the board. No longer were companies having to make calculations for goods and services for international trading. No longer did stock brokers need to consider exchange rates in Zurich and Hong Kong, when trading out of London. Tokyo, New York, Mexico City, Melbourne, Mumbai, Moscow, Frankfurt. All on the same page. Not to mention what it did for the individual, and for the traveler. For one thing, the money exchange division of all banks had now become extinct. Much to the dismay of those working in exchange booths in the multitude tourist hot spots from Rio to Bangkok.

There was one currency, and it was the Khoda. And it would buy hamburgers in Ohio, to dim sum in Szechwan, or baguette in Nice, and vegemite in Adelaide. You could pay for a concert ticket or a new car with it, a roll of black thread or a box of finishing nails. A renovation on your house or a repair on your DVD player. They were all paid for in Khoda. There was no more under the table money, there could be no more black market financial deals. No more counterfeit bills.

And another great leap was made, simultaneously. It was a completely cashless society. With one scan of the hand, or in some cases the forehead, the appropriate identity and information was called up, and *ding* the transaction is done. There were no more bills, no more denominations. And what was more, no more coins. For all those who used to have to use coins, for buses, for subways, for laundry machines, and vending machines, this also was completely changed. The ID code printed on each individual's hand or head, was all that was needed. All machines had successfully been modified to accept the code, and exclusively and only accepted Khoda. At a Coke machine, one simply waved one's code in front of the infra red scan, and push the selection of their liking. The product delivered, the appropriate amount deducted, and everybody wins. As well, there would be no more coin rolls either, which indirectly cut down on annual sales of aspirin, which was an unforeseen side effect on the pain reliever industry.

The ID code was administered at birth, so no one was without it. Without it no one could make any transactions, financial or otherwise. All information was referenced from that one code. The police records and checks, credit checks as well. All library information, driver's license data, all health records, including general and specific histories, operations, all tests, and medications and allergies. All memberships to clubs, grocery stores, institutions, and schools. All affiliations with religious organizations, or societies, and also insurance policies, other legal documents, such as wills, divorce papers, etc. These and other sensitive materials however required additional access codes, and various other security measures. One of the manual tasks but most gratifying to shoppers which greatly improved with the initiation of Khoda, was buying large quantities of groceries. If one cart, or possibly two or three, or even more carts were filled with food and various other items, it was no longer necessary to remove them and put them into bags. In fact they could be put right into the bags in the cart, while shopping. Then when it came time to pay for the purchases, one simply would do a walk through at the checkout counter. Everything in the carts would be read, and a total was given. Nothing would be missed, nothing would be added that wasn't intended to be bought by that shopper. The person would be presented with the total, for example 83.4 K, that is 83 Khoda, and simply 4 tenths of a Khoda. There was no other additional name for the amount after the decimal point. Also, it was decided that there would be no more one hundredth parts of the new currency. There was from then on only one decimal place.

The advisors gave the review to Mr Cazara and he was very proud of all that they, and he, had accomplished. They further went over his health reforms and his plans of massive campaigns against major and widespread diseases. He was working with the World Health Organization, and its director. He was also working with the UN and their efforts to diminish poverty to a manageable level in third, and second world countries. He, and the teams that the UN had furnished him with, were vigorously working on the sources of nations' poverty problems, and how to solve those problems. Then there was his latest project related to the religions of the world. He was developing a proposition and a model that was based on his achievements at the Summit of Peaceful Nations the year before. But there would be other days, and other challenges to conquer, and he and his staff had used up another productive day at One Green Peace Place. They would shut down the operation, lock up their offices, and call it a day.

✦ ✦ ✦

29

The final department, the final Ministry, of the USE was like the finishing touch or the last stroke of the brush for the artiste. The coup de grâce. The Ministry of Religious Affairs was to oversee all matters of religion, faith, or anything related to the spiritual needs for the people of planet Earth. What was more, Cazara had a plan to somehow unify them, to amalgamate them, and make them into a single faith. This had of course been attempted before from within a particular religion; but never before combining all the faiths of the world. But then again, this was Joseph Cazara's forte, this was his style.

He again arranged for a special council, not of war, or even peace, but a consortium of sorts, a merger of clerics, a meeting of the minds: representatives and/or the leaders of the world's major religions. There would be at the meeting, a show of support from, and an indication for participation in the amalgamation, for the following faiths: Buddhism, Islam, Christianity, Hinduism, and Judaism. One of Buddhism's highly venerated monks Talli Tesendares, as well as the present Dalai Lama himself would attend. There were several other Buddhist priests from the various different sects of Buddhism from other parts of the world. Then for the Muslim religion a Mosque ruler from Mecca, Allad Mustapha Molladad.

Accompanying him would be Mr Khadahar, of the Arab League. Other rulers of other prominent Mosques would also be present. For the Christian faith Mr Stanley Panteen, the Director of the World Council of Churches; and insisting on attending this historic event, the ruler of the Holy See and the Catholic Empire, the Pope himself, David Paul Delluca would attend. From Hinduism almost 80 leaders from India alone, and then an additional 26 from around the world were planning to attend. Finally the Jewish faith would send five of their most respected Rabbis from Israel, and another seven from various other countries. It would be the largest gathering ever, of all the religions at one time.

The day arrived, and those attending flew in to Jerusalem. That is, all except those rabbis who were already there, and of course the hosting chairman himself. The attendees were welcomed and then taken to their accommodations at the best hotels in the City. Due to cost however, the Hindu representatives were asked to narrow down their numbers to a mere fifty Hindu leaders, which they managed to somehow pull off just hours before the meetings were to commence. But commence they did, and right on schedule.

At 9.00 a.m. sharp Mr Cazara was there standing in front of his ornate podium made just for that occasion, smartly and sharply dressed, and he very warmly and congenially greeted his guests. He told them how much he appreciated their coming, and their willingness to cooperate, and assured them that he, along with them, would work toward the elimination of religious prejudice. He also, right at the outset of the meeting, made promises of the great things he had in store for them, and for those they would be serving back in their home countries.

He then quickly proceeded to honor his most distinguished guests. First, Pope David Paul I. And with great fanfare he not only mentioned him, but gave a long list of his achievements, and his most admirable and respectable qualities. There were also short video clips which were quickly flashed on the screen above the Chairman of the meeting, of the Pope's and the Catholic Church's influences in recent years. He also honored other great leaders of the Christian church in the present day and spoke highly of their acts of benevolence in times of great need in the world.

Then he welcomed the Dalai Lama and gave similar words of honor and respect for the great religious figure. Then he paid homage to some of the great leaders of Buddhism, spoke of their superior intellects and many meritorious acts, while showing images of certain elaborate Buddhist temples and shrines throughout the world, with vividly colored photographs of groups of chanting monks with robes ranging from bright orange to subdued greys. He went on to pay respect to Mr Allad Molladad, dwelling chiefly on his contributions to the Islamic world but including other good things he had done to benefit thousands of others. And then he selected three of the most influential of the Hindu leaders, boasting of their divine powers to heal and to help their loyal devotees, and indeed anyone who wished to become a believer. Finally, some of the Jewish rabbis were given credit for their contributions to Judaism, their steadfastness in keeping the ancient traditions of the Hebrew faith, and their great respect for their god Jehovah.

The meetings were planned to last two days at the most, and each session was carefully arranged and prepared for maximum productivity, and benefit to the attendees. The first session would allow selected representatives of each of the five world religions to lay out for their listeners the basic tenants of their particular faith. Before executing this segment, some of Cazara's top aides and advisors were quite skeptical of pulling this off. Their criticism of it, was that to give some of these religious leaders a chance like this, might cause them to give the others of different faiths, a good dosage was how they put it, and a very long one at that, of their own beliefs and doctrines. But miraculously each kept to the allotted time, and none overstepped the bounds of what was acceptable to the others. There was also the (now) standard security, in which guards, heavily armed, were standing backstage, and just offstage on the floor to the left and to the right. In addition, there were several teams posted on rooftops, at the gates, and patrolling all borders of the fenced-in building.

Islam was allowed to go first. Five presenters mounted their podiums and one by one each gave one of the pillars of the Muslim faith. It helped, the previous critics commented, that, number one, there was a timekeeper on the stage with them to ensure that the speakers did not go in excess of the allotted timeframe; and number two, they were speaking in a language completely foreign to their listeners. There were translators, but with the delay it gave the time distance that was needed, and the preachers were well on to the next point, before the hearers had heard and were digesting the previous one. After the Muslims came the Hindus. They gave a kind of collage of ideas and a listing of some of their deities. It was here that the timekeepers were put to good use, for the names of the Hindu gods alone took at least half an hour. And they only mentioned a small fraction of the most prominent ones. They also explained their powers, and gave eyewitness accounts of their miraculous doings in heaven and on Earth, as well as some of their great gods and goddesses in human form. They ended their portion with some chanting of mantra from some twenty or thirty monks, priests, and other holy men and women. It was after a good ten minutes that Cazara gave the order to politely ask them to make way for the next group, since the attendants on the stage were reluctant to stop a religious experience in the process. But the Hindu believers conceded and took their leave.

Next were the Christians and a slick computer generated presentation was projected on the screen behind the two speakers, a man and a woman. Both were finely dressed, but the man was from America with a mid-western accent, and the woman was European, probably Dutch but her accent sounded more like German. They spoke in English. The man outlined a statement of faith explaining plainly and clearly the basic beliefs of the Christian faith. Then the woman gave a general current worldwide missions report, highlighting it with excerpts from missionaries themselves in three selected nations. And finally the Pope ascended the stage and gave a short benediction in Italian. He was in full regalia and had many assistants, cardinals, priests, and bishops with him, in spite of the brevity of his speech. The Christian's spot was the most concise and lasted only a total of thirty-five minutes, not including the benediction.

Then the Dalai Lama himself approached the stage. He gave an in depth explanation of firstly the different branches of Buddhist belief, where they are practiced, and the unifying thread which gave all of the different types their common bond. He gave a short history of the life of Guatama Buddha, his death, and enlightenment. There was no chanting, and no computers used. No props were necessary, save the scroll and parchments in his simple earth-tone carry bag, and his robe of the same color. When he was quite finished, he humbly and softly, without shoes, descended the staircase and made way for the final speakers of the segment. It was the Jewish rabbis who gave the last explanation to represent their religion. Three leaders, all clad in black, with the traditional flat black hat atop each of their grey heads, orderly filed onto the stage and then took their respective places. They each gave one third of the whole presentation. The basics of their religion, which was interwoven with their long cultural, political, and military history. Then they each sang one part of a prayer, very loud with great passion and feeling.

When the last rabbi was finished the last note of his song-prayer, they walked arm in arm off the stage. The room was still resonating with the minor-key, distinctively Jewish music which had just ceased. Then after a brief pause, the Chairman again resumed the stage and the podium. After thanking each religious group represented he proceeded to the next order of business. He himself outlined just how similar the religions of the world really were, and he outlined some of the basic points in which they overlapped.

First he explained that, all of them represented there in that auditorium, all the religions of man, were trying to do good. And they were succeeding very well at it. He then congratulated each one in turn. He also praised them for what they were doing, for each of their peoples, in each of their parts of the world. He also assured them that he was not there that day to change their religions, or to ask them to give them up in any way. This was a great relief to all because a rumor had spread that Cazara was planning to start an entirely new religion that would in effect obliterate all the former religions, and that everyone would have to convert to that new one. He discredited the rumor as false and gave them his word that he would do nothing of the sort. He then went on to explain that we all have a faith in something, or someone, that we call god. And he thought this was good. But the problem arises when god is called by a different name. In addition there are different names for different faiths. And then they all have different practices of course, depending on the culture and the part of the world.

"Therefore," he went on, "what I am proposing to you today, is, not that we change the names of your gods, but merely that when we are communicating between faiths, that we refer to god in the general sense, and simply use the word god. This will make the world of difference and unify the religions of the world in ways you could never imagine. Of course we will still have different practices and rituals depending on the Region, and each culture, but we're going to respect that of one another, won't we. In fact we, that is the use Council, in conjunction with the Rulers of each of your Regions, are going to mandate this just as soon as we can. That is, anyone caught using another name besides god during direct interfaith communications, will be penalized." There were pauses in his speech to allow for translation.

"Now this is all just an introduction to the main event of our meetings this weekend. I have a very special expert in the field to introduce you to. He will explain further on all of this, since it is his area of research, practice, and lifelong devotion." Cazara went on to list the special guest's impressive credentials and long history of active service to god in many cultures and languages. In fact he spoke nineteen languages, not including dialects of those nineteen, and also had participated in some of the rituals and traditions of all five of the main religions. Then, with great anticipation and pride in his voice, he announced, "Ladies and Gentlemen of the great faiths…esteemed and honored guests," he added, nodding to the Pope and to the Dalai Lama, "I now present to you, our newest member of the Council of the United Society of Earth, our Minister of Religious Affairs…" and here even a soft drum roll was given, (with brushes, not sticks), "…Mr Deseronta Shalee!"

There was applause from the small contingency of spiritual devotees from around the world, as a distinguished man approached the stage. His movements were slow but deliberate, his eyes set before him as he walked toward Mr Cazara. The two men shook hands and exchanged a few words of greeting out of the hearing of the audience. Cazara appeared very pleased with his new guest, and the two spoke for a brief moment as if they knew each other for some time. Again he spoke into the microphone which had been temporarily and intentionally disconnected. Then, holding up Mr Shalee's right hand with his own left, as they both faced the audience, he announced, "I give you, the very Reverend Deseronta Shalee." The crowd was applauding, but more as a courtesy, and in response to the Chairman's whole-hearted and enthusiastic endorsement of this new member of the council. But they were also watching him very carefully to determine what kind of a man he was.

Once the introductions were over, Cazara relinquished the spotlight to Reverend Shalee, who appeared to have no inhibitions or reservations at all about assuming this new and rather daunting role. This immediately served to put the onlookers at ease, and they were so disarmed. He began by saying there was no further need to tell any more about himself since the USE Executive Director had so generously done so for the last ten minutes. And again he thanked his gracious host, and now boss, adding a few compliments of his own for Joseph Cazara.

He started off with a heartwarming little story, one in which a small child was having trouble sleeping because of a thunderstorm, and a loving parent told her a story to take the child's mind off of the flashes of lightening and loud rain and thunder. He went on to say that God is like that parent, always comforting us and helping us whenever we find ourselves afraid of the storms of life. And God gives us strength to battle through those difficulties and enables us to survive. He then went on to expound how God had given all of us, of every race and creed, and color and country, an intelligent mind to solve life's problems. And then at the same time we must show respect to God by saying ritual prayers and personal prayers, and being kind to our brothers. "Not only of our own faiths," he added seriously, and speaking slowly as he looked straight at each religious group, "but also the brothers in all the religions in our global society today." He spoke the last part lighter and with a slow benevolent smile.

The Buddhists liked him because of his mention of the intellect, and he appeared to be of Asian descent somehow, but they couldn't quite figure out where because of his way of speaking. The Muslims approved of him because he spoke of the attention to daily prayers, and he had even said it should preferably be five times a day. The prayer part was one of the unifying links that he used, and continued to expertly do so, throughout the rest of the meetings. He was put in charge from the time the Chairman introduced him. The Arabs also warmed to him simply because his skin was a little dark. The fact was, it was difficult to tell his origin because of his unique style of dress, his mannerisms, and his accent. He was actually a Native American Indian though after he was born his family traveled and he was educated in the UK. The Christians appreciated his birthplace and education. He'd also spent much time in the country of India, which he often referred to as the cradle of religion, which satisfied the Hindus. And especially so, when he in mid-sentence, searching for the right word, switched to Hindi. The Jews liked his approach, and his theology seemed to be correct from what they had heard, but there was something about him. Of course he was a Gentile, but they were willing to accept that since he appeared to be God fearing. They were the only ones who seemed to have some reservations.

For Cazara things were going splendidly. The small problem with the Jews could be worked out, whether sooner, or later, it made no difference to him. In the meantime his newest council member was succeeding, and therefore his latest plan. Unify the world's religions, get them all under one umbrella, make sure they were all on the same page. It would simply be called One World Religion, or OWR. It would be pronounced our though, and so people could call it, Our Religion, or our faith, or simply, the faith. He would leave the details of religion to the Minister of that department. Cazara would then be free to get on with the business that was his: to govern his world. This was what he had set out to do, and that's what he wanted to get back to. This, religious sidetrack for him was just that, simply a means to an end. He would assist Mr Shalee in whatever administrative ways necessary, but beyond that, religion would be his business.

The meetings were concluded the next day, and when the attendees and devotees exited the building, the media was there to meet them. They had been like vultures circling high overhead, waiting in anticipation for the meeting to die. And then at the close of the final segment, and the religious leaders and reps gathered up their scrolls, and scriptures, their prayer beads and calendars, their laptops, and all their belongings, the media members would swoop down upon them and pick at their brains with questions. And there would be the flash of photographs, and the stream of video footage to their Internet sites and television stations, all live from that moment.

Dalee sat in his Producer's chair at his office in DC, and watched. And he wondered at what he saw.

✦ ✦ ✦

30

There was in fact a growing resistance to this new world society. It was first among a small group of dissatisfied citizens. They themselves would never consider themselves the citizens of the USE, but many were forced to put the ID code on their hands and their foreheads, and so they were registered within the system. But others somehow escaped the process, and they lived off of the grid. These people were, in its initial stages, the holdouts, the anti-globalism protestors, and the die-hard anarchists, from all over the globe. They began small, but their numbers grew. And then they needed a leader. His name was Tadd Karnik.

They all rallied under his underground leadership, and the more militant of his group insisted that they combine all their military know-how, and every able-bodied man, woman, and child who could hold a weapon, in a last chance, all-out final assault on Cazrara and his cohorts. They would plan an attack at night, and at the main headquarters at One Green Peace Place, Jerusalem, Earth. They intended to not capture, but kill Cazara, as many of the Council as possible, whatever Regional Rulers that may be there at the time, and completely level the whole compound.

Many former terrorists had joined with them, but

Karnik was having trouble keeping peace with them, since they considered him and some of his anarchist lieutenants, 'infidels'. It was difficult keeping order with such a variety of different peoples, especially when there was no translator. Small misunderstandings could turn ugly quickly, cause serious injury, or sometimes result in the death of one of their own number. This couldn't exactly be called friendly fire since it was intentional, so he just wrote off the times that it did happen as causalities of war. He didn't actually mind that much. Their mission was simply to get in, kill and destroy whatever was in their path. A suicide mission really. Karnik had little real military training, but he was very determined, and he just wanted to knock out Cazara and as many of his group as he could.

They collected as much weaponry as they could get their hands on. It was amazing how easy it was, he thought during the process. But then again, they were working with former terrorists. They weren't exactly former, because they were very much in business during this current operation. They collectively decided that night was the best time to make the attack. They figured they would have both cover of darkness, and the element of surprise on their side. And they needed all the help they could get. They had friends of friends who worked in the compound at a menial level, and so the security layout was acquired. This told them both how many guards there were, and where they were posted. This would give them the advantage at least of knowing their enemy's position at the time of attack. They also received a tip as to when Cazara would be working late.

They traveled from a secret location about 2 hours outside

of Jerusalem, arriving at 01.16 Israel time. There were just over one thousand soldiers by Karnik's assistant's estimation. Soldiers, in these desperate times, meant anyone who was willing, anyone who could fire a weapon. There were few who hadn't received the barcode tattoo, and even fewer who were willing to risk their lives like this. Karnik considered himself lucky to have even this many. But his rag-tag outfit still seemed so small to launch such an attack against USE and all their combined and auxiliary forces. Karnik didn't care. He had but one purpose for his unit. That was to strike the serpent, and right in the head. Whatever happened after that was insignificant. Oh, he knew they would strike back all right, he just didn't know exactly what their retaliation might be; or what the outcome would be. Who knows, he thought, in a best case scenario they might even see this as a kind if coup d'état. Without a leader, they might even look to the victor of this little battle as their new Director. The tables could be turned and suddenly he would be the world leader.

But if anything like that was ever to happen, Tadd Karnik would be different. He would never oppress or dominate anyone. He would immediately initiate a Free Society. It wouldn't be a USE, as his group distastefully called it. They even had a chant: "Don't be used by USE; USE is USING us." And they repeated this at their house meetings over and over. But never too loud, and they'd never use it in public for fear of being discovered. He didn't really think they would want him to be the world leader, but he was just thinking about it, just in case.

When they arrived they kept out of sight, and got into their positions as rehearsed in their training. The heaviest weaponry was being set up, the soldiers were getting into position, the lieutenants were giving their final orders for the attack... when suddenly all the outdoor lights turned on at the GPP compound. Someone was exiting the front doors and had a megaphone shouting: "Hold your fire, men! Hold your fire!" Karnik and his followers suddenly realized they had walked into a trap!

It was Joseph Cazara himself, and he was now boldly walking into the front yard of his building. The truth was, Cazara's secret sources had long before discovered the existence of this resistance, and even determined the details of their plan of attack on him and his administration. When the resistance realized what was happening, some opened fire directly on Cazara himself. But by then it was too late. Four guards, from behind glass were carrying a large bulletproof shield surrounding their leader in front, on both sides, and at the top. The other guards had by this time taken their cover positions.

Cazara had handed the megaphone to a soldier and apparently was speaking into a mike connected to the compound's outdoor security communications system. And he was actually smiling. He spoke. "Mr Karnik and your band of rebels, good evening." They stood dumbfounded where they were, just looking at him, each other, and the situation. "But I'm afraid it is not likely to be a very good evening for you. Unless you surrender." The last sentence was spoken with authority.

Karnik changed his look from bewilderment, to one of grim determination. "Never," he hoarsely whispered out loud, the muscles in his face and neck taunt. Then louder, "NEVER!!!

NEVER!!!…" Slowly, rhythmically, and then the call was taken up by his soldiers, and soon the air was filled with their chants. Then they switched to their slogan chant, "Don't be used by USE!!! USE is USING us!!! Don't be used by USE! USE is USING us!!! Don't be used by USE! USE is USING us!!!" They brought out signs and boards that a few had brought along and displayed them for the security guards and all at the compound to see. But they weren't the only ones watching.

From a safe distance, cameras were rolling, photos were snapped, and digital records were made of the scene. The whole world was watching. The USE had made sure that the media, all the media, was tipped off of this event. And they were there in full force. They had been screened of course by GPP security, and also only a limited number were permitted to participate. GNCN, and Global Network were there. Also several other major national TV stations and Internet sites from selected and significant countries. And when he heard of this, Dalee wanted a team there, and he also wanted to be there himself personally. So the media was there capturing all of this drama on record, and so, the world could also look on, in shock and morbid anticipation.

Cazara, during the chanting and commotion in Karnik's camp, had been talking with his aides of the next step. A general handed a communication device to his superior and informed him that Supreme Commander Draik was ready to speak with him. When he took the military phone, he told him that he had something else in mind, and that his services wouldn't be required this time. Surprised, he double checked to make sure that he'd heard him right. When he did, the channel was disconnected and Cazara turned to his aide again. He spoke to him and then he left on apparently the business which his boss had just sent him.

Karnik was watching closely, and so were his lieutenants, for some opportunity to make a last effort attack. But they didn't want to be foolhardy, but to advance strategically, and cautiously, when they could see some tactical advantage. And he sensed something was happening. Perhaps to their advantage. Someone else was escorted out of the building and brought inside the shield next to Cazara. He was oddly dressed for military personnel, thought Karnik, or even for an official at USE. Cazara began talking with his new Religious Affairs Minister, Reverend Shalee. They discussed something for a few moments, then Shalee put his hands on Cazara's shoulders from behind, as his leader faced forward. Cazara was staring, looking a little upwards, with, perceptible even at that distance, an unusual look on his face. The media later described it as, 'otherworldly'.

Shalee finished with his peculiar ritual, and then the top portion of the shield protecting the men inside was detached, and lifted off! This was what Karnik had been waiting for. He felt it was an act of God. It was his big chance; his only chance, and he knew it. He looked over at one of his lieutenants who was already speaking to a man who was aiming a rocket launcher, carefully, steadily at the one point of weakness. Cazara by this time was staring even farther upwards and raising his right hand into the air with power and great strength, and he spoke loudly and clearly. The soldier with the just aimed weapon of destruction had become disoriented, because just then, huge flames of fire engulfed them, shooting down from directly above the resistance rebels. They screamed in surprise and fright, and then pain. Running every which way in panic and chaos they scrambled to escape. The first blast was over. Cazara raised his arm again and repeated the same motions. Fire poured down from the sky again, straight down, directly, and only, onto the band of rebels in front of the compound and to the sides.

The light lit up the night for at least ten minutes, just in the second blast alone. Still Cazara stood there with his arm upraised, and his hand formed into a fist. With the bright orange-red flames mirrored in his eyes, he victoriously gazed on his defeated enemies. The soldiers were burning, every one. Their bodies on fire, from the blaze that seemed to come out of nowhere. In shock and horror they fled the seemingly unlimited source of fire that seemed to keep burning and burning. In vain they ran, because it kept coming, unquenchable, unstoppable. Their ammunition supplies started to go off. Their vehicles began to explode. But by then it mattered little anyway. They were all dead, or dying.

The fire from the skies stopped after a few more minutes. Cazara continued staring upwards a moment. Then lowered his gaze to look at the carnage. The blackened and smoldering remains, some fires still burning. The charred corpses scattered throughout the battlefield. No sounds came from their camp now, only the hissing; the snapping of the final burnings, as it consumed anything else that remained.

And Dalee stared on from the sidelines. If he hadn't seen it with his own eyes, and wasn't present there at the moment that it happened, live, he would never have believed it. His mind still insisted it was some kind of trick, and he, and many others in fact, would investigate thoroughly the unusual phenomenon.

In the meantime, stories had to be delivered, reports had to be made. The world was waiting.

✦ ✦ ✦

31

Dalee sat and watched it on GNCN, NBC, ABC, BBC, MSN again and again, and again. He had been watching the coverage, and the reports and the commentaries, and the speculations for half the day already. Genvieve needed to go out somewhere, so there he sat in his living room in front of his TV as it sat on the entertainment center, viewing almost the same scene, over and over again. For a change he'd switch to an interview or something else on a different channel, but they would always at some point take the viewers back to the same event. Different ones would show slightly different angles, however they were all basically the same. Cazara somehow had caused fire to come down from out of the sky, and destroyed a group of people rebelling against the new world order.

He himself was there. He knew it was true, exactly the way it was displayed before him now. But he just couldn't get over it. He was still in shock and disbelief, but the clips he had been watching just kept confirming continuously that it really did happen that way. Investigations were complete and some were still going on, and they were thorough. Dalee knew. And they kept coming up with the same thing. Cazara had no mechanical, chemical, or any kind of external help whatsoever, from any other source, other than what they all had witnessed that night at the GPP compound. It was on record that he spoke to his Commander in charge of his military operations, General Draik. The entire conversation was produced in its transcript form. Clearly he denied his repeated, insistent requests for the use of their military force to stop the enemy intruders posing a safety threat to the USE administration. And Cazara's response was not just a deferment; he plainly declined even the Supreme Commander's second offer. Now, it all could have been staged to make the fire blast look even more miraculous. The conversation with his military chief could have been prearranged for the benefit of the watching world. They very well could have pulled a stunt like that. Dalee recalled that he was tipped off of the event, and that by USE personnel.

But then how did he do it? There would have been some evidence of a source of heat or fire from above the compound area. And yet nothing at all was discovered, not above, not below, or anywhere near the area within a hundred kilometers. Thorough investigations had come up with a blank page. Yes there was fire, yes the people died, but nothing was uncovered that would point to the source of that fire. The only thing that they could determine was that it was clean, meaning it didn't come from any kind of fuel that was mixed or formed in any way by man. It came from a source that hadn't been refined at all the way oil and gasoline are. It was in fact not like anything the investigating chemists had ever seen before. Normally forensic scientists on a case like this could find some clue as to what was behind it, but they came up empty.

In a long-shot effort, some officials in the investigation sought out and found David Copperfield, one of the world's greatest illusionists. Though he was long into retirement, and at that time in his nineties, he was willing to cooperate with authorities in an attempt to unmask any hidden method Cazara may have used. He searched all his techniques, everything he thought humanly, and otherwise, possible. He concluded that it was definitely not an illusion, and therefore the act must have been carried out by some power that the man himself possessed.

What did this mean? Could it be true that this Joseph Cazara had magical or some supernatural power to make fire come down out of nowhere? And destroy people?! And if he could do this, what else could he do? Dalee was alarmed. What was happening? What was all this? This was bigger than he realized. He reached for the remote and switched off the TV.

He picked up a newspaper and checked one of the articles, to see something in black and white. It was explaining about the part where Cazara raised his right hand up over his head and was about to begin. It read:

"Mr Joseph Cazara, the Executive Director of the newly established USE, then began to stare upwards towards the night sky of Jerusalem. Nearby witnesses reported that his gaze at that point was somehow looking beyond, as if in a trance. The microphone he was wearing, at that time was switched off. Those who were closest in proximity to Mr Cazara were the only ones who heard his words. In several interviews the surprised witnesses all confirmed the same report that the words he spoke were, 'Fire from heaven, I command you, come down.' The same thing was repeated three times, with little variation, approximately ten minutes apart. The time that the blaze commenced was 2.04 a.m. Jerusalem time."

It was true. It was really true. This new leader was much more than what he appeared to be. Dalee got himself cleaned up and got ready to leave. Janvieve arrived as he was leaving. They spoke briefly in the front yard. He explained he had to go in to work to do a few things. She also was surprised about the strange events and asked if anyone had come up with any explanations. He could only reply that he wasn't sure yet, and that he had to check on some things. They said goodbye and he left.

Driving to the office building, he had more time to think. Okay, this much he knew: the new leader of the new government which had recently taken over the whole world, apparently had some kind of ability that went beyond what humans could normally do. He was not an ordinary man. Did other leaders have supernatural powers in the past? He searched but he couldn't think of any. Maybe Buddha. He achieved enlightenment. Also, Caesar in Rome, they considered him a god. Some royalty, even in the present day and age were considered god-like. This was crazy, he thought. Those people didn't actually do anything miraculous, did they? And what about Jesus Christ. He was supposed to have healed people. Or maybe even make them come back to life after they were dead. Mohammed was supposed to have performed certain miracles, wasn't he? What if something like that was happening now?

He still thought it was crazy. He pulled into the parking lot and put his car into the assigned space. Everything seemed normal there. He got out and locked up his vehicle. Security was in place inside the building. He stopped at the elevator and while waiting, breathed out a sigh. Seeing everything in its place somehow made things back to normal. The office on his floor was buzzing with activity. "Good day, Mr Delliv," was the repeated greeting as he walked through the corridors. He unlocked his personal office, flicked on the light and took of his coat. Sitting down at the desk, he began some research on the net. Finishing that, he did a little of the work he had gotten behind on in the midst of this latest big story that seemed to put everything else on hold. After completing those, he put it aside and looked up.

Checking the calendar on the wall he looked at that day's date. 2050 was almost over. They had only just begun this new era with the United Society, and now this bizarre turn of events had taken place. Some of the leaders of countries, including himself, at that Globalization conference in Holland wanted to see how things would go having Cazara in charge. Now look what had happened. It wasn't all that bad of a situation, really. Wouldn't it be good to have a ruler like that who could destroy his enemies? But then, one certainly would not want to become his enemy in a case like this.

So he had powers. That was alright with Dalee. How would world leaders respond to this? Other than this one display of aggression, he seemed to be doing an excellent job of governing the entire globe, amazingly enough. This was the only show of force that had been necessary. Things had been progressing quite smoothly up to that time when the opposition at the headquarters took place. He checked the web site again. Ah, there it was. Dalee had been waiting to see the responses of certain heads of state. Statements were issued as to the reaction to the events that took place approximately 24 hours before.

The German Chancellor's statement was one of praise for 'swiftly and efficiently eradicating the insurgents'. Strangely there wasn't much mention of the method Cazara had used. The President of India however, made very much of it. He declared that God had descended to Earth in human form, and that Mr Cazara was the reincarnation of several deities, which he listed in the statement. The Prime Minister of that same country also made reference to Cazara as having supernatural powers and without a doubt, that he must have received them from a god. He read several others, and they were all exclamations of praise, and declaration of support. The Japanese PM also congratulated Executive Director Cazara in his triumph over his enemies, and wished him continued success and prosperity for many more years to come.

So, the world was endorsing this super leader. He seemed to be becoming more and more popular with each day that he was in this unique role. What would come next? What kinds of things were in store in the many more years to come? Dalee sat at his desk and reviewed the statements again. Where was Cazara's? He checked around, then in the most obvious place, at use.com, he found it.

My beloved citizens of the United Society of Earth. By now you will be fully aware of the occurrences which took place 24 hours ago at the Green Peace Place headquarters in Jerusalem. I do not want anyone to be alarmed or concerned in any way. An aggressive attack was attempted against your faithful servants, the leaders of our new world order, but of course was foiled. A final chance of surrender was offered to the insurgents; they however were defiant, and unmoving. It became necessary to use force, and so we did, destroying their entire unit.

Now many may be wondering as to the method of defence that was used in this case. I can assure you that this was no trick or deception in any way whatsoever. But what you and billions of others have witnessed was a display of my unique reserve of supernatural powers. With the assistance of one of my right hand men, the Highest Reverend Deseronta Shalee, I was able to channel the powers of good, against the side of evil. This was what you saw when the fire consumed our enemies. In the future, we will not only defeat enemies like them, but we will conquer every problem that comes in the path of mankind, and of the ruler of this glorious world in which we all share and love.

You have my solemn promise, that together we will work, relentlessly, diligently, until all people have a quality of life never achieved before in all of history. We will overcome disease and poverty, put an end to war, and famines. We will stop prejudice and all religions will be one, as we have now achieved. All will have enough to live comfortably, and peacefully, in every country on the whole Earth. Not just in the first world, but in those developing nations, and in the least developed countries.

My citizens, these are my pledges to you, that in the months and years to come, we will make a better world, for each and every single one of you. Peace and prosperity to you all.

Director Joseph Cazara,
United Society of Earth, Jerusalem"

✦ ✦ ✦

32

Icy sleet was blowing across the fields of a farm in Iowa in the central United States. Rain was falling on the West coast of Canada, on the island of Vancouver. Drifts of powdery snow blew across frozen mud roads in Northeastern China. It was the coldest part of winter in 2051. And yet the temperatures were strangely low in many parts of the world. Still, in Jerusalem the Middle Eastern sun burned brightly and high, over the Mediterranean sea, as mid-day passed and she began to sink into the western sky. A few clouds dotted the deep blue expanse above the place where the minds and mouths of the rulers of Earth, where the eyes and the ears of the new powers that be wielded their authority, made policies and wrote and rewrote their international laws, and governed the peoples from East to West, in every city, and in every home.

The way was clearer now, as clear as the waters over the great sea just off their shores, 50 kilometers away. The resistance which threatened to stop their progress, and which stood in the way of the advancement of the human race, was now put aside. And the Council, and the nine Kings of the Earth could carry on with their business. The business of making the world a safer place, a peaceful place, a more prosperous place for all. Their one head and leader was the highest. He governed over all of their affairs, and over all the affairs of the nations of the whole world. He was indeed at the uppermost level, for there was no one higher. His power was now the ultimate, and his authority supreme. Mr Joseph Sargan Cazara.

Afternoon was now passing and there was work to do. Continuing the set up of the satellite offices in various major cities. Managing the new financial system and transforming the old one to adapt to the Khoda System. Rearranging a seemingly endless supply of files on every human being alive, and in fact the storage system for the data related to those deceased. The Ministry of Science and Technology did have gargantuan storage capacities, but they decided on a cut off of one hundred years previous. With so much information, the line had to be drawn somewhere. Then there was the colossal task of keeping political stability…in every single country in the world. This was no small task.

The Slorc in Myanmar had to be pacified, as well as the Tamil Rebels in Sri Lanka. There were uprisings in Southwestern Russia, at the same time that FARC in South America made demands on Mr Dalingeste Cecamante and his administration there. The IRA was lobbying Northern Ireland's government's newest bill of religious freedom. Executive Director Cazara was briefed on all of these issues weekly at a meeting he had with the Rulers on Tuesdays precisely at 9.45 a.m. He would listen and advise them, and keep aware of new developments. Decisions had to be made, sometimes hard choices that would have a rippling effect on, not just one group, but neighboring countries and even overseas. But this was all in the demands of the position, the duties that fell on the men whose responsibility it was to see to it that order was kept in their areas, as well as their neighbors'.

But this was only one role of the great leader Joseph Cazara. And he had other matters, even more pressing to tend to. His programme on disease control was in the making. It would involve several organizations which would assist him. It would bring the director of the World Health Organization, for one, and the president of the Center for Disease Control, for another, to Jerusalem.

Both of these leading experts in the field would meet with Mr Cazara on the same day. They arrived and were kept in a receiving room and entertained by some of Cazara's staff. They had chosen the Diplomatic Conference Room as their venue for the session that afternoon. They were first received, then brought into the conference room and briefed on the subject matter of their meeting with the Director, and then they waited again.

Another 12 minutes passed after the final briefing before Cazara and his assistants entered the room briskly. They apologized and explained that something had come up and required Executive Director Cazara's immediate attention. They accepted and waited to proceed.

"Mr Durkham and Dr Croller, thank you for agreeing to see me today."

"Quite all right, I assure you. The pleasure is mine," the first man replied.

"It is an honor to meet you Director Cazara," the doctor added, echoing his colleague's sentiments.

"Yes, well let's get right down to business. Please, sit down." And with that he and the others took their seats.

Cazara's assistant laid a map on the table that showed

regions where epidemics and outbreaks of certain diseases had taken place in the last ten years. These health experts were acutely aware of the situation and very familiar with these problems. Cazara stated that he knew that, but for reasons of clarity, and by way of introduction he chose to begin with this. He then went on to explain a plan to clean up those affected areas. He had the funds now, and wished to channel them, in this first phase, to the previously outlined areas which needed it the most. This massive sanitization was his first step in creating a world free of major diseases, and it had to begin with the hardest hit portions of the Earth first.

"We're putting our focus, gentlemen, on the elimination of these diseases which have plagued us repeatedly for so many years. Our new system of commerce is finally permitting us to do so. I'm sure you have enjoyed many of its benefits, but this is one I'm sure many have overlooked. Millions are being saved, millions of Khoda that is, and now one of our first priorities since other issues have been settled, and as I have said the funds are available, I wish to put our efforts in, so-to-speak, in your gentlemen's direction."

Very pleased, they were more than willing to accept this generous offer. But it didn't end with the monetary assistance. Cazara wished to offer his facilities, and his faculty in the Department of Health, to work together on this project with them.

He further outlined his plan to provide training of acceptable hygiene practices and, in addition, the improvement of conditions of certain zones of certain nations. This would actually be his Phase 2 and 3, respectively, of this strategy against disease. There would in fact be some overlap between the two, since part 3 would need to be carried out at the same time as 2, if not in some cases, in some countries, before.

They were discussing the latest outbreak of the H7N7 and H3N8 viruses in the country of Kazakhstan when an attendant entered the room. He went directly to the Director and spoke quietly to him. Apparently something, perhaps the same issue as before, required his involvement. He excused himself and the two health officials were left alone at the conference table with four assistants. They exchanged small talk for three or four minutes and then one of Cazara's aides came through the doorway and approached the table. He spoke without sitting and informed the guests that Mr Cazara would be busy for some time. And that if they wished to stay they may but it was uncertain just how long this current affair might take.

They remained in the Diplomatic Conference Room for approximately thirty minutes, discussing the first three of the plan's phases, which countries they were going to target, and some other additional strategies. They checked the time and saw that it was getting late. Another aide came in and asked them if they might be more comfortable in the Reception Room and so they relocated. They were in that room some ten or fifteen minutes when Cazara himself returned and asked if they needed anything. They replied that they regretted that they had another engagement and they must be leaving. He thanked them for coming and asked if they could resume their meetings in the morning. They agreed on a time and the two were escorted out of the building.

The matter which had arisen was one of some significance and weight, since it involved the whole of Region 5, that is Russia and its annexed areas as well. Cazara had received intelligence pointing to a clandestine movement which was in competition with his own Ruler, Ryzard Lazniek. He had begun reviewing the information they had collected on the subject and was discussing with his advisors, and had conversations with Lazniek himself on a secure telephone line. This was what had taken him from his Health meetings. His best people were on it, and were attempting to determine who was leading the movement.

The next morning the three reconvened, but this time in one of Mr Cazara's personal, more private chambers. They discussed the remainder of the plan, worked out a time frame, and began listing those they were going to enlist for each sub-segment of each Phase. They had decided on an 18 month timeline, hoping to finish by August of '52 at the earliest, and giving themselves a window of error of two months, October of that year at the latest. They had to factor in human error, natural disaster, and further outbreak at the time of carrying out a particular Phase, and possibly dealing with that disease on the spot.

They were near complete this time, when they were interrupted for the second time. Cazara told his aide to leave them and he would be with him as soon as he could. He apologized to the officials, which they graciously accepted. He concluded the meetings by giving his guests a copy of the proposed plan on a small computer storage device, a handy drive, and assured them they would be able to access it from any terminal. They took it and reassured him that they would work with him in this effort, and that they would recruit the necessary manpower that was going to see it done.

Cazara then shook hands with the two health experts and

disappeared through another door. That was the last time they met with the Executive Director face to face, though they saw him on a screen a few times between then and the end of the second Phase the following year. They were satisfied with this new, sometimes unusual and surprising leader. He had in mind the concerns of the world. He wanted to do something about her problems, and he put his money where his mouth was. They would carry out this project. And they would do it with great fervor, and all the workers and volunteers they could muster.

✦ ✦ ✦

33

It was like the feeling of the pull of a magnet toward metal, when you hold a small magnet in your hand. That's what it felt like when he was just falling asleep. Between being awake and unconsciousness. The sleep pulls like the metal pulls the magnet, and the mind is drawn into the magnetic field…and snap, you're on the other side. This time there was fire. The land was burning. Hectares and hectares. Trees and buildings and brush. The telephone poles, the grasses, and all the plants. Everything, burning. And overhead he saw them, circling. Black and ominous. Circling, closer now; waiting. They were very patient, these creatures. Just out of danger of the fires that were burning. They were vultures.

Dalee awoke suddenly, and opened his eyes. He lay there in the semi-darkness, wide-eyed, startled. He'd never had that dream before. What could it mean? He lay there going over it in his mind, replaying the scenes, and trying to figure them out. His wife lay beside him, breathing softly. It took him over an hour to get back to sleep. But finally he did.

This time there were trees, huge trees. And they were not burning, but standing tall, towering overhead. Were they redwoods; or something else? He couldn't tell. The wind was blowing on them…softly; and the light was reflecting off their leaves. Shimmering...shimmering. Rustling. Softly rustling. He could hear them. He could hear them because there were no other sounds. All was quiet except for the trees, and their leaves. And the breeze.

In the background there was nothing. There was nothing at all. He tried to look above the trees, but all he could see was sky. Blue, no, it was more white sky above. No clouds, just whitish blue sky. He couldn't see a thing directly ahead for the forest was too thick. He looked all around and it was the same. Nothing but the trees. And the sky. He listened for a time, to the sound of the wind. It was pleasant, he thought. And soothing. Soothing to his soul. He liked that sound and he wanted to stay there. So he did.

Then after some time, he heard another sound. Faintly at first, but then a little louder. It sounded like a bump, or a bang. But it was so far away and so faint at the beginning that it was difficult to determine just exactly what it was. After a while he realized that it was rhythmical, like a pulse. A beat. It was a drum. It continued on a steady, spaced tempo, just how it started. He listened again. It was just a single beat, repeated, spaced about four seconds apart.

He was in a different place now. It seemed to him he was high on a mountain, maybe Mt. Everest. He looked around. But it couldn't be. There was no snow. It was certainly high elevation, he could tell that much somehow. There was grass, and a few plants. It was very rocky. He tried to walk near an edge to see the area below. It was a sort of plateau. His movements were slow for some reason, his steps impeded. It was as if he was under water, yet there was none. He made it to the edge of the top of the mountain, for that was what it was, and looked over the edge.

It was high. Many kilometers high. How many, he didn't know. And it didn't matter anymore, because the view was beautiful. He could see cliffs and valleys far down below. He could see other mountains, but all lower than the one he was on. He could see small villages on the sides, and at the summit of the mountain. What color was it? It was grey but bluish-black. But more violet, but darker. Was it purple? Mountains are purple, he remembered thinking. He'd always wondered how stone or rocks could be that color but there it was in front of him. It was truly breathtaking.

Then he looked, and he could see farther. Somehow he could see the cities nearby. Established communities, organized civilizations; and people walking, traveling, getting around their town. Then he looked further and he saw the desert. Barren and dry, scorched and uninhabited. On and on it went, with just a few desert plants dotting its landscape. The wind was blowing there, howling. The sands were moving, shifting. Changing. It blew and drifted like snow, but it was cleaner, and it didn't melt. The wind was crying, a slow mournful song. He could hear it. And he listened.

He thought he may have heard words. He listened harder, straining his ears from where he was perched high atop the mountain, so far, far away. But still he only heard the rushing, faint whistling sound of the wind, blowing through the desolate plains of the desert. Wait. There was a word. Was it a word? Whispered on the wings of the wind? "…deeees…" What was it? He listened even harder. "…eeessss…" He could barely hear it, and he could only hear snatches of it, through the sound of the wind itself. "…ineeee…" And then it trailed off.

What was it? What did it mean? He didn't have time because the scene changed, and then he found himself over the ocean.

Speeding across the surface of the waters, fairly close, he could see. Nothing but water as far as the eye could see. Going fairly quickly he looked ahead. It was like the movement of traveling over water in a helicopter. Only the sound wasn't there. The chopping sound of the blades. In fact there was no sound at all. It was silent.

When he looked ahead it was just the sea in front of him. And looking to the sides it was the same. With effort, he surveyed the rear, but only found the same. Nothing. He felt as if he were in the middle of the ocean, moving forward. It was blue. It too went on, seemingly forever. But not the same as the desert. This was even larger. No matter how long, or how far, he went, it didn't cease. And it was fresh. He could feel the spray, faintly in his face. It quenched his parched skin. It moistened his dry throat. But it was salty. And the ocean was alive. Beneath her waves was life. Where there was water, there was bountiful life. The sea was teeming with it.

There were swimming fish of every kind, and rainbows of color. Somehow he could see them now. Dolphins and sharks, barracudas and swordfish, tropical fish of blues and yellows and greens and pinks. And there were clams and shellfish of every kind, shrimps by the thousands, and lobsters and crabs. Red and silver, and brown and purple, a symphony of colors flowing beneath the surface of the waters. Then there were coral of every color swaying to the movements of the currents and the tides. And sea flora that swirled with the movements of the ocean, drifting and swaying. And larger animals that found their home in the seas. Blue whales, and humpbacks, and grey whales, who sailed the waters, finding their nourishment there, their home.

He was on the mountain again, and from his vantage point, he could see the cities. And it was night. He could see the bright lights, the skyline, the towering office buildings. It could have been any metropolis really. He saw the major arteries streaming with the white and red lights of vehicles. Moving, slowly. From his perspective they seemed to be crawling along. But having been there, he knew those little spots of light could have been traveling anywhere from 80 to 220 kilometers per hour.

Then he saw another city glowing within the black void of darkness. He viewed it from quite a distance at first. But then drew closer. He could see that it was Kuala Lumpur, with the twin peaks of the Petronas Towers. He saw its skyline, and its skyscrapers, and its freeways. Then another city. It was Hong Kong, with all its lights along the harbor. Busy and bustling, as the day was about to begin, and the dawn was breaking. Then he saw Shanghai, with its award winning architecture, Seoul with its snow covered mountain peaks. Farther and farther he went. St. Petersburg with its beautiful churches and golden domes, and then London and its castles and palaces, also Paris and its Eiffel Tower and the Seine winding its way through the city. The cities were there for him to see somehow, one after another. They seemed to pass quickly, and yet he could see their distinctive characteristics when they came into view.

Rome and the Coliseum and Vatican City, then on to other cities. Athens and Beirut, Jerusalem and Cairo, Johannesburg, Mumbai, and Bombay. Bangkok, Brisbane, Melbourne... Then onto Mexico City, Bogotá, São Paulo, and then Kingston. Miami, Washington, New York and Toronto and then up. He could see all of these places and he knew what they were. He knew their identities and what country they were in. And it all happened so quickly, yet he could still recognize them.

When the last city was finished he then could see the cold; frozen regions, with ice and seas stretching out in all directions. It seemed like the northernmost part of the world. There were enormous icebergs, and mountains and cliffs, and the wind was blowing. He couldn't tell if it was day or night, but there was a strange light, unlike what he was familiar with. He even felt cold. They say that the snow is old there. That it doesn't melt for years and years. And it was blowing, across the plains, across the waters, the snow was blowing, and drifting; and shifting.

He heard the wind again, and it was crying. It was calling. The wind had a voice, but he couldn't make out the words. What was it? What is it? Howling, blowing, past frozen wasteland, through icebergs, over the ocean, on top of icy mountains. I can't hear it, he thought. The words, what was it? "What is it?!!!" he suddenly spoke out loud into his dark bedroom. His wife, startled, was awoken.

"What is it?" she asked taking his arm. And then he repeated his question, still not quite awake yet.

"What is it?" she was then asking again, so that they were both shouting the same question to each other, confounded.

Finally he realized it was a dream, and told her so.

Rubbing his eyes he said, "The words...I couldn't hear the words."

"What words?"

"Nothing. It was a dream. I'll tell you about it tomorrow."

"Are you alright?"

"Ya, I'm ok," he breathed out as he lay back down. "Goodnight."

The next time he woke up the sun was shining through the window, and it was to the sound of the telephone. It was Gávrá Tuldiá, Cazara's personal secretary.

"I apologize if I inconvenienced you, Mr Delliv, with the time difference, this was the only time I was able to call."

"It's alright. What can I do for you?"

"The first interview which you conducted with Executive Director Cazara was very successful. We thought it was time we arranged another one."

Oh, do you? Thought Dalee. "That's fine. We can set up a date…"

"We've decided on February 16th, if that is convenient for you. We'll hear from you if it is otherwise?"

"That's fine," responded Dalee, a little gruffer than he had intended. The two hung up and then Dalee sat up. He looked out the window at the cloudy February sky. He thought of his dream again. He could still hear the wind in his mind. He stood up and pulled the curtains back a little further. The snow was blowing outside. He'd have to shovel the drive a bit to get out. He thought he should get going. He had work to do.

✦ ✦ ✦

34

The conditions at DC's airport were less than perfect and Dalee didn't know if they would let the plane take off at all. So he waited. There wasn't much there in the lounge for the gate where his plane was about to take off. An excellent LG HDX LVI TV was there, the latest and the best. With the volume turned down of course; and no visible controls to alter that. He looked around and saw an unattended Washington Post, so he walked over and picked it up.

The news seemed different to him these days. It seemed so packaged. So predictable. Maybe it was just his imagination. He had always done surveys of the products of the other media companies. He enjoyed observing the competition, watching how they presented what, and their timing; scrutinizing their reports, even down to the wording and phrasing of sentences in their articles. Not that he disagreed or disliked them. He simply used them as a reference point, a gauge by which he could compare his work to.

He looked up at the nearest monitor, finding the line that pertained to him. 'UA 331 JERUSLM GATE 14 DELAYED 09:48' The delayed sign was still flashing, and according to the clock in a top corner of the same screen, there was still 53 minutes to go. He calculated, that with boarding time, that should mean some activity at just before 9.30. That was, what…a half hour, 35 minutes till boarding time. Maybe less. This was what they call optimism. We're dealing with the weather here, he told himself. And the weather is one tricky customer.

It turned out that the snow and the storm began to subside, sooner, rather than later, and they lifted off the ground more or less at the time that they had expected. The landing gear was tucked away, the seatbelt lights blinked off, and the travel companions distributed their initial offerings with almost as much warmth as the weather. Then, after a few more presentations in the form of a hot meal, a new in-flight movie, and later, drinks on the house, they were descending in one of the formerly most dangerous airports in the world. This time, after he got through immigration and customs, with the amazingly smooth new and improved airport system, there was someone there waiting for him at the passenger exiting point. She was holding up a white sign with a black border of curving and curling designs. But the center portion was clear so to be able to read the words in large lettering: 'Mr Dalee Delliv', in plain bold type.

His contact person was in her late twenties, he surmised, with thick and healthy pulled-back, beyond shoulder-length hair; light brown, streaked, so to give it a golden color mixed with the natural chestnut. She had a careful walk. But not cautious. It was the stride of the proud, of those who knew their position in life, where they came from, and were going to, steady, unhurried. Deseree, her name pin stated. She was professional and courteous, efficient, but not curt. She escorted Dalee to the limousine waiting in front of the airport automated sliding doors.

He sat opposite her in the rear of the vehicle and she exchanged small talk with him. He observed her quiet confidence and noticed that she bore the mark of the USE training, as well as having the qualities which she must have possessed that would have caused them to choose her over hundreds, perhaps thousands of others, all vying for the same job. This liaison was certainly the result of the careful grooming of Cazara's staff at his headquarters. And yet she was a feminine expression of such fine manners and regal speech.

They arrived at the center and the hub of USE activities. Dalee recognized the architecture and the fountains at the front of the building, but it looked a little different at night. The many lights of varying colors and brightness arranged as spotlights along the borders of the largest fountain gave a very pleasing effect to all who approached Mr Cazara's front doors. He had arranged to do the interview at the late hour that it was, for scheduling reasons. Miss Deseree delivered Mr Delliv to the reception desk, beyond the foyer of the main building, and she was gone. The arrangement was to be almost the same as the set up of the previous interview, in that the interviewer was to be alone with Director Cazara, the security check before entering the interview room, and afterward Cazara's staff would review, and alter if necessary, all of Dalee's notes and recordings during the session. There were also no cameras of any kind permitted. This time, the interview was held in the reception room just outside of Mr Cazara's personal office. Dalee should have felt honored, had there not been one other stipulation during this second interview. He would be given certain prearranged questions, which of course were written by

Cazara's own staff. Dalee didn't particularly like this condition, but he still had his own questions, and in the end, he was the one who published the final product, so he consented.

He passed the security check, was conducted down a wide tastefully decorated passageway, and into a large comfortable room with several couches and tables with lamps on them, arranged in various places. Mr Cazara was seated examining some documents in a leather bound file holder. Upon Dalee's arrival he set aside his work, stood and shook his guest's hand firmly. He then asked him to be seated. The aide who let him in, then retired to a desk in a not-too-far-away part of the same room, and occupied himself with some of his own duties. Dalee could see a little further away in the other direction, where a door stood open. This must have been Cazara's office, and he could see little else but a security official standing near the doorway. Cazara noticed the direction of his gaze and assured him it was standard procedure. In fact he called to the aide and asked him to close the door.

"There's no sense in making Mr Delliv nervous during our interview is there?" he articulated to no one in particular. "Now then let's get right down to business. You've got some questions, and I've got the answers."

"For the most part," Dalee began.

"You always were witty, Mr Delliv," Cazara laughed. "I know you are aware that some of the topics were prearranged, but that was in order to best address the relevant issues. I'm sure you'll understand once we are well into it. Let's get started then." he ended, gesturing to Dalee's notes.

Dalee skillfully guided the questioning through the opening segment regarding some basic points which would update the public from the last personal interview. Then he began on some new subjects which would certainly peak the interests of the world wide audience which would soon read these words yet to be edited and refined.

"What is you aim with this new project with your Ministry of Health?"

"My Ministry of Health, alongside of the WHO, and several other very necessary and professional organizations, are setting out to change how we all view the treatment of disease, and how to prevent it. Together we can, and will eradicate these terrible plagues which have affected millions for so many years. We will succeed, I assure you."

"And how do you propose to do that? Can you give me specifics?"

"Certainly," he replied, and then went on to outline, as briefly as possible, the several Phases in his Disease Cleanup Plan, and then Disease Prevention Programme. He also explained that this would take some time, and laid out when they should be finished which stage, and which parts of the world would be given assistance first, and who would be next. And then finally when the whole program would be completed.

Dalee had filled almost an entire page just on the health issue alone. When he resumed his questioning, he began with, "Why is your government spending so much money on this project? And where are the funds coming from?"

Cazara then went on to explain the surplus which the Ministry of Science and Technology, and each of the nine Regional Rulers had received as one of the benefits of the United Society's new and superior, and extremely efficient system. The funds couldn't be used for a more important, more pressing issue which troubles the human race. "And disease is only one form of suffering," Cazara explained. "We should all be concerned for the millions that have been affected by this one problem, and in so many different parts of our world. And we will achieve this, with the help of so many willing and excellent workers. By our collective efforts, we will beat this I assure you. But as I have said it is only one form of suffering. But one must choose some place to begin to alleviate the sufferings of the people, and we have chosen this one. When we have finished with this, we will continue to work for the benefit of all, and proceed to yet another. Even now we have teams and the great minds of the world working on which will be the next, and the next, and how it should be executed, and who and where and when. Mr Delliv," and he continued more seriously, "We are in this government for the long term. It is what we live for. This is why we are here." He ended his point with a fixed gaze ahead, and with a clenched fist.

Which reminded Dalee of his next question. "How do you explain what happened here at this compound a few weeks ago, in the exchange that took place between Mr Tadd Karnik and his followers, and, well…yourself." Cazara changed the fist into an open hand, gesturing gently, in an offering position. "I say yourself," the interviewer added somewhat nervously, "because the altercation was between the attackers and only you. Neither the army, nor the security was brought in at all, isn't that correct?"

"That is correct," Mr Cazara began in a gracious and affable tone. Pausing, waiting until Dalee was finished with his notes, he then explained about his powers over nature, and that at times of extreme need, he was able to call upon a

"Higher Power" he called it, which enabled him to carry out such feats as his listener, and the rest of the world witnessed that night. He also included in his explanation Rev. Shalee's role in all of this, when Dalee inquired about it. He revealed that Shalee and himself had some history together over the past ten years, and that they had worked together before. They had met in Africa when Cazara was carrying out a campaign there, and later they worked together again, by choice, in Asia. Rev. Shalee apparently being a religious man, had some role in these powers he spoke of. He attempted explaining this but it seemed a little vague to Dalee. When he pressed Cazara about it, he simply referred to the Reverend as his "assistant in spiritual matters." Not getting anywhere with this, he moved on to another subject.

They then discussed the economic situation in certain countries, the status of the Peace Treaty between Israel and Palestine, and the new Ruler for the Middle East. They also talked about terrorism and its absence in the world overall since the Conference and the multi-nation agreement at The Hague in '49. Dalee also mentioned terrorism on a smaller scale, to which the director replied that he was taking care of the big fish, and it was the responsibility of the local governments to manage micro-terrorism, or 'the little fish'. Then the interview was concluded with a tour of Director Cazara's office.

He had large photographs of well known world leaders, even entertainers. There were a few very expensive famous paintings as well; originals of course. A large mahogany desk, sofas, and some beautiful tropical, and other exotic plants. There was also a large picture window which overlooked the GPP compound. At night it was all lit up, and there were fountains in the inner areas as well. It was quite a spectacle. Dalee wasn't expecting this personal tour, and so thanked him, then explained he must be on his way. Miss Deseree was called upon and she escorted him, first to the debriefing room, and then outside to the waiting limousine.

Dalee intended to fly right back after the interview and give the materials personally to his staff there at his office. He would sleep on the plane. The story needed to be published. The world didn't sleep. He bade his guide farewell, got through airport security and immigration in no time at all, and was seated comfortably in his seat on the plane idling on the runway in Jerusalem, Israel. He couldn't give the rabbi a call this time. Not at this hour, he thought. And he closed his eyes. "I'll send him an email when I get back...after the story..." And he fell into a deep sleep.

✦ ✦ ✦

35

In the far north, in the east, all was quiet, looking from the outside in. Northern Siberia's mild temperatures could reach the deep sub-zero levels. That day the thermometer read –53°C. The only light was in a small window at the back of the thickly walled, heavily insulated small structure where the underground was meeting. The yellow light was a warm contrast to the thick frost on the window, the deep snow on the slanted rooftop, and the blowing and drifting piles of snow in the surrounding yard, and fields beyond the building.

A small station 200 kilometers north, Northeast of Yakutsk was the only location where they could go undetected. Inside the outpost, the ancient oil furnace blazed and raged with all its power and might, simply to keep the blistering freezing cold, just outside their walls, at bay. Even as the inhabitants sat around their shabby table in the stark room, they were vigorously rubbing their hands together, constantly shifting and moving, in an effort to keep warm. And they also wore thick fur and animal skin coats to further ward off the fierce and relentless bitter temperatures of the north.

But in spite of the surroundings, there was a light in their eyes. A light that signified hope for their movement, and a desire to see their leader have a voice in this new and "forced" regime of the new Society. Askatov Novoskor was the one who lead these free people. He had lead them during the communist up-surgence, and through the revolution, and then in later years when it seemed to everyone that freedom was coming. But then they again returned to a new form of communism. A repackaged, renamed, however still basically the same, form of communist government.

He had already had his following when Cazara arrived on the scene. And then when he appointed this Ryzard Lazniek, he and his followers thought that all was lost. But they kept on, in spite of the new and powerful regime. The local one they would now have in Russia with Lazniek, and the much larger one which backed him from Jerusalem. It was large, and it was powerful, with much support, and also many allies world wide, but they had stood against such formidable opposition before, they had endured powerful, monumental foes in the past, and they had survived. They endured! And came out afterward, still pursuing freedom, still chasing their dream. It had been kept alive this long, and one man was not going to stop them. Even if it meant having their meetings at the end of the Earth. Even if it meant working undercover, in secret meetings, always changing, always moving, using codes and covert operations and agents, keeping their core dream alive, the belief that every Russian person, rich or poor, young or old, regardless of status, deserves to be free and to dictate the affairs of their own lives, not living at the mercy of the communists, living in fear, every day, every hour.

In Jerusalem, Mr Cazara and his staff were working on further additions to their legal policies when they were interrupted by a messenger. New intel was obtained on the

Russian underground developments. He excused himself and went with the message bearer and met with agents in one of the lesser known rooms within the compound. Only those authorized with 6th Level clearance were permitted in this wing.

Cazara was briefed, and they went straight to the strategic maneuvers table. He discussed with his advisors and agents what could be done. They worked it over and around, considering the different possibilities. Cazara didn't like it this time that it was moving toward a diplomatic agreement, again, similar to the ones in the Middle East and in Africa. They had split their leadership into two rulers for each region, and now it was looking as if this may happen a third time. His opposition to this idea, stemmed from a fear that their government may appear weak, giving in to every division or schism that came along.

They continued to discuss their options for some time, and went back and forth again and again, sometimes for hours at a time, without break. Finally they all, in frustration and exhaustion decided in agreement to permit the rival Russian leader a secondary role. He would be allowed a leadership position but it would be in subordination to their Ruler, Lazniek. If he and his people didn't like it, there would be no other recourse for their movement. This was the only offer they would give them. They would have no other choice but to take it. Cazara didn't seem to have much choice in this case either. If he squashed Novoskor it might possibly cause a small riot. Or then it could be a large scale revolution. His following was underground, but it was large. The Director of USE could not afford this imbalance in the Russian Region.

Brushing aside weariness, and disregarding the lateness of the hour, Cazara ordered his aides to get this Novoskor on the line so that he could speak with him personally, and immediately. They talked for at least half an hour, quite harshly at first, but then when negotiations begun they spoke more civilly, and the two leaders came to terms they could both agree on. A diplomatic expert was handed the phone, and within fifteen minutes, a deal was brokered.

And so, this was how the Russian Region came to be shared between the two leaders, Lazniek and Novoskor. Although the first had more than his share of the authority, the second man always made sure that he kept him in check. So the balance of power was achieved and the delicate equality which existed between the Russians and their new government(s) was accomplished. The underground Freedom Movement became the Freedom for the People Party, and no longer was it necessary for them to meet secretly in the northern spaces of the outer limits of Siberia. In dark corners, where no one could detect them. Communicating in codes and special languages to prevent anyone from finding them out. No longer did they need to live in fear and hopelessness, and under strict dictatorship where freedom was merely a dream, a word which existed, but had no meaning in Russia.

Now Mr Novoskor had a title, and his staff had positions of influence. Now they had their own offices at the Regional Office nearest, which was in Shanghai. Now he would also have a place in the center of the world government in Jerusalem as well. But these, as grand as they were, meant little to him, in comparison with other more practical benefits which he and his followers valued the most. He and his staff had power to make changes, to alter the way the former governments did things. They had the say in the laws and the many conditions by which they and all of the Russian people had to live by. Novoskor was not against Cazara. In fact he agreed with, even liked many of his ideas. Now that he was a part of his umbrella organization, he would work with his Council, and their administration there in Jerusalem. He liked their views, and their political policies. They were good for his people, his country.

Of course locally they would still have their own set up of their government. They would still have the Kremlin, they would still have their president, and their national government did not suddenly cease to exist. But like all the other nations of this new system, this new Society of Earth, their government would be under the direction of the Regional Ruler for that continent. And of course the directorship of the Council and their Executive Director.

It would all work together, just like a finely tuned machine. Like a natural and organic system, helping one another in a symbiotic relationship, working together in harmony, all towards one purpose: the smooth maintaining of world order, and peace for all in the United Society of Earth.

✢ ✢ ✢

36

The winter was lessening there in Washington; it was day by day becoming a little less cold. But it still wasn't nearly warm enough for Dalee. He liked the summer; even the hottest times. But then again at the worst of times during that season he was almost 100 percent of the time surrounded by air conditioning. At that time, he was in his car on the way to work, and he had the heat on full blast, at his feet, on the dash board, and through every vent that his vehicle was equipped with. He felt relieved that day because that big story was completed and out; the one on the interview he was asked to go to with Cazara in Jerusalem. He remembered when he pulled into the icy but sanded parking lot at 428 Estevare Road that he owed Dr Ben-zoheth an email, so he thought he had better tend to that before he forgot.

Locking up, and then entering the building, he found things much as they usually were, except that someone finally decided to take down the Christmas decorations. They actually gave the place a little more color than usual, a change in the routine. Maybe they should put more paintings in the hallways or the reception rooms, he thought as he passed the workers' stations. 'Good Morning Mr Delliv'. He returned the greeting and continued through the corridor to his office. He stopped at the door and found his key. 'Dalee Delliv', it read on the door. With, 'Executive Producer', just below it, all in straight black lettering.

Inside he hung up his coat, took a look out his window for a moment, then finding his email program and the right spot to send a message, began to write. He had written a few lines when it became necessary to check back to the last message which his rabbi friend had earlier sent him. After the headings and the greetings, Ben-zoheth had answered Dalee's questions.

My synagogue is doing well. I have been teaching in the Book of Isaiah. Perhaps you have heard of him. He is the prophet who once saw a vision of God that resembled a gyroscope long before it was invented. That's what makes him a prophet, you know. He saw things before they were in existence. The word prophet means, one who foretells future events. Not quite in the same way that the fortune tellers do it, but I think you will get the idea. Those individuals tell a person's fortune, whereas a prophet tells simply the future, and it was usually for all Israel or even several nations at once, and often in its context with social, and political happenings at that time. They did also tell an individual's future at times. For example the Prophet Daniel fortold of King Belshazzar's demise. Well, he didn't exactly come up with it himself, but he interpreted what a hand that appeared on the palace's wall which wrote an unusual inscription. But that's a whole other story for some other time. Incidently, that's where the saying: 'The handwriting is on the wall', came from.

We are also making preparations for the Passover holiday coming up soon. This is a very important Holy Day for the Jewish people. It represents the time when the nation of Israel was under cruel bondage in Egypt, and our God... YHWH...came to our rescue and delivered us. We have many celebrations and we always want to remember what God has donc, and to never forget. This tradition is very important to us and I am responsible for my people to carry it on.

Speaking of fortune telling, you also seemed to have deciphered my email address. Yes it is as you say, ca-dabra, as in abracadabra. This word is actually of unknown origin, though tradition says it is a compilation of the initials of the Hebrew words, well the first portion anyway: 'Ab' Father, 'Ben' Son, as in my name, and Ruach Acadsch – the Holy Spirit, RA. So you see it does have some roots in my heritage after all, if only by tradition.

You had many questions in your last message and I do wish we could have talked when you telephoned me. It would have been even better if we could have met, but your circumstances didn't permit it. However, I will answer your final question here.

The rabbi then concluded his message with an explanation of his views on the dividing up of Israel with the Palestinians in recent months, and his view of what Cazara had done there. He told him in his own words how Israel's land had been given to them by God himself, and that interfering with that divine distribution of land was to meddle with God's own affairs. He also said that while he understood the Palestinian's dilemma, he also recognized their history and wished them to move on to another country. He was concerned, and stated so in his writing, that Mr Cazara had overstepped his bounds in this matter, which did not concern him. David also wrote that he was aware that his message that he had written could be considered subversive, but that was how he felt. He finally told him that he had enjoyed Dalee's article on the interview with Mr Cazara, and found it enlightening.

Dalee sat up straighter and then stretched. After thinking a moment, he leaned back in and began to write the rest of his message.

While I realize that I hadn't responded to your previous message, before your latest one, doctor, it doesn't mean that I didn't appreciate the things you wrote. That last email that I sent you from the Tel Aviv airport was rather hurried, and then when we spoke on our hand phones, you remember, we weren't able to have a proper conversation. I also have been rather busy as I'm sure you yourself can appreciate. But enough of apologies, I'll get to my response.

The Book of Job was intriguing to me in that, if a true account, the individual did indeed have a greater appreciation of who you call God, in the end. He also described, and used words and language of a very lofty type. But then I suppose when one is referring to such a Super or Supreme Power rather, one really must use elevated, somewhat Superior, or even Supra-language.

I also wondered what you thought of this supernatural power that Cazara has exhibited recently. Or should I call it a supranatural power instead. Perhaps that would be more appropriate in his case, don't you think?

And, how do you feel about this new Ministry of Religious

Affairs which has emerged from the USE's Council?

Respectfully Yours,

Dalee

The response from the rabbi, which although did take some time, is recorded here in its entirety.

From: <elzoe@dabranet.is>
Date: March 18, 2051
To: Dalee Delliv <dalidelhi@world.com>
Subject: Answers to Questions

Dear Dalee,

Greetings in the Great and Wonderful Name of the God of the Universe:

How are you and your wife, and your families? I pray that you are well.

As you may know we have been in the midst of Passover celebrations in Israel, so you will have to forgive me, as I have had very little time to tend to my computer-related responsibilities.

Yes, I am very aware of this Ministry of Religion you mentioned and its leader, the so called 'Reverend'. The religion they refer to as OWR religion was agreed upon by a few, what I would consider rather liberal Jewish religious leaders. Not that I myself am as conservative as many here, but I think that those rabbis at that meeting with Rev. Shalee and Mr Cazara were too liberal for my views. I feel it was not given enough time to develop and not enough observation was made of the man and this new concept of what some call our religion. Those are my views on that.

Now as to Mr Cazara's own personal powers, I cannot really comment on that at this time. I only know that it occurred. Of this we can be sure. There is no denying this fact. You yourself were there you tell me. What more is there to say?

I cannot write long here today for I must go now. But I must also inform you that I have some new responsibilities which are taking me to America. It will be on the west coast, in California in fact. My life has become even more busy I'm afraid. But let us keep in touch. And perhaps we will see each other again one day Master Delliv.

In the gracious Name of God I commit you,

Shalom,

David.

✦ ✦ ✦

37

Al-Admahar picked up the solid gold rook in his right hand and moved it to his desired position. Three spaces to the right, and two spaces back. He carefully counted them, and placed his chess piece down in that square. He had thought through five moves in advance and this was the first of the five. He looked over his opponent, General Gohnd, and watched. The Muslim stared down his opposition, and the general lifted his hand to make his move. Al-Admahar was expecting several possibilities, but they could only play out into the trap which he had laid for his opponent. The next few moves would clench the victory for him. There was no escape. When the gold was in the general's hand, he felt its weight, and he let it fall into his palm, enjoying its heaviness which only this precious metal could possess.

In front of the medium-sized screen was Dalee with a pen and pad in his lap. It was his personal pen which he had designed to suit his specifications. Gold, variegated texture, and shiny bits of mirrors on the bottom portion near the tip. He was previewing a new film a friend of his had just completed, and he wanted Dalee to critique it for him before he showed it to the review board. Berac had sent him word that he would fly him, and his wife, to Hollywood for the weekend. They left Friday after Dalee finished up work, early. It was now Saturday, and he sat alone in the dark room with just the light of the small circular hole in the wall behind him, illuminating the screen before him.

A door opened and light flooded the room for a second, then all was dark again, save for the screen with the two characters engaged in their battle of the minds. It looked as if Al-Admahar was retreating with his last move, but Dalee knew the game, and the man. He would win. Besides, he had read the screenplay. Janvieve came and took a seat beside her lover. He could smell her. Perfume, fresh air, and her scent. He didn't need to see her.

Leaning in towards him, he breathed her in even more. She whispered slowly, enunciating delicately, and yet as if she were shouting, "Let's go to lunch."

"Just a few more minutes." She sat and watched with him as the scene then changed.

When the screen went black, he stood up and felt for the lights at the door. He opened it and told a nearby worker to tell Berac that he was finished. A few seconds later a scruffy 34 year old film producer made his entrance into the viewing room. He looked at Dalee with wide eyes and asked a question with one word, "Well…" With no visible response fast enough, he repeated, "Well?…" Dalee rubbed his neck and looked at him, then over at Janvieve who was getting up and heading for the door.

"It was good."

"Good, what do you mean good? That's good that you liked it, but I need details, Dalee my friend. I need feedback." He spoke rapidly like someone awaiting news of a lost loved one after an accident.

Knowing his friend, he assured him he will give more details. He looked at Jan and then back. "I need to go to lunch and then I'll get right back to you. I need some time to hash it over a bit in my mind, Mr Producer. To digest it… And my lunch," he added, rubbing his stomach. Berac smiled stretching the shape of his patchy beard a little, into a different formation.

"Okay, okay." He looked at his watch. "I'll see you at one. No…one thirty. Okay, one thirty, back here. Gotta go." He spoke while walking away and pointing a finger at his reviewer. And then disappeared.

They walked outside into the afternoon sun and discussed the possibilities. He didn't feel like driving. She had seen a little Greek restaurant within walking distance. As they walked they watched the cars, looked at the unfamiliar buildings, and appreciated the palm trees.

She had a delicious salad, filled with olives and anchovies. And he had the gyro, with baklava for two for dessert. And a nice, hot cup of tea to wash it all down. They talked of California and its climate, and the film producer and his latest project. Their waiter returned with the check and a device to scan the customer's ID code. The total came to 27.9 K.

They had another round of tea since it wasn't necessary to get back yet.

"This is too much like work, thinking I have to hurry back. Let's stay a bit."

"Okay. Do you know what you think of the movie yet?"

"Ya, it was fine. Just a little controversial that's all. You know Berac." She did indeed. "Always trying to push some controversy. But he's going to have to be careful. There's a new board now, and it's not the same as the old kind. Unless he has forgotten, he's under the Ministry of Entertainment now. This is a global operation, not just American. He's gonna have to play by some rules."

"How's it going with those dreams of yours?"

"Oh, I did find that book. I just haven't had a chance to read it yet." They talked until someone looked at the clock and realized the nearness to one-thirty. They got back to the studio and found his friend busy. Once he was free they sat in his office and Dalee gave him his review. He took it like he always did, with a pinch of salt. They finished up there and Dalee rejoined Jan in the lobby. They had the rest of the weekend. So they hopped into their rented aqua convertible, and with the warm sunshine, the wind in their hair, and prospects of the beach on their mind, they lit out.

It was good to get a break. His job could be so serious and demanding. He was glad to be away. He thought these things as they sped along Sunset Blvd. And not a cloud was in the sky that day.

✦ ✦ ✦

38

In Israel however, it was a different story. Lifelong hatreds were brewing. Disagreements which lasted over generations were resurfacing.

In the beginning, in those initial months and then the first few years after the Treaty between the two peoples, there was peace. But then gradually, ever so subtly, the cracks began to form in the walls. The walls of this place of peace housed within the borders of this nation which was then known as the New Israel. In the third year, it began covertly in the form of mild dissatisfaction of certain nationals at some of the bordering towns where a boundary line was shared between Palestinians and Israelis. Nothing was spoken, no threats were made, it was just the religious, the national differences that began to be observed, and then some disapproved. They knew that they were not supposed to have ill feelings toward their neighbors; they knew that there would be consequences for any action taken, or even words spoken, but they felt these dislikes all the same.

"How could they not?" they questioned. "Look at the way they teach their children. Mohammed isn't even mentioned in their schools. And what about prayers? Some of them don't even pray one time a day properly, let alone five, which Allah commands us to. They might go to their synagogues once a week to pray if they did that. That is what it is, a sin-agogue, because they are all sinners, not respecting God's name Allah, and Allah's prophet Mohammed." These were the thoughts of some of the Palestinians as they lived side by side with their new neighbors, and watched them day after day. And then the days turned into months, and months into years.

"Why don't they celebrate the Passover, one of the most significant Holy Days for God's people. They just ignore it, neglect it altogether. And Hanukah, they don't recognize this either. And what about bar-mitzvahs; they do it all wrong. And their children, they sometimes leave them uncircumcised for years before they finally perform this sacred ritual. Ridiculous. Unrighteous." So the Jews would think of their neighbors.

And when the Muslims would leave on their pilgrimage to celebrate the Hajj, they would look back in disgust upon the Israelites and wonder, 'Why don't they go?' But the Jews would stay where they were, and quietly carry on their own religious and cultural traditions, oblivious of the what the other side thought, and heedless of what may come.

But then one day, the words began. Just a few words exchanged between two merchants, or a couple of farmers selling, or buying. Verbal disagreements didn't amount to much, at the beginning. But eventually there was a point at which the words were replaced with blows, and someone was injured. Now under the new system, any kind of exchange such as this was punishable, and was not looked upon favorably. Strict laws were in place, and offenders paid hefty fines, and/or spent moderate terms in prison. The new overseeing government hit them where it hurt; in their wallets. And the time in jail, usually served by a man, who was also a father, and a husband, also put the strain on a family financially during the sentence.

So the Regional Ruler, backed by the USE, kept a tight lid on whatever violence that would surface in Israel. At first. At the start of these minor disturbances, they were able to monitor, and even control them. Then the bombs started. It was in the sixth year, 2055 that is, that suicide bombing came back. They were minor incidents, because at that time the materials to create them were simply gasoline and a spark. Anything more couldn't be obtained without authorization. And they were infrequent. Only one in a month. And that was nationally. But that was only at the onset of this phase. Then it became worse.

The frequency increased, regardless of the intervention of the military, or whatever penalty that the local government or the international one could impose, they would continue on this escalation of violence, killing innocent civilians in bombings on a weekly basis. It was becoming what it once was in the past. Before the Treaty. And there wasn't a damn thing anybody could do about it.

By 2056 there was all out war once again in Israel. Somehow heavy artillery, hand guns, rifles, ammunition and bombs of varying sizes and types were successfully smuggled in. People who had friends and relatives working in high places asked for favors. Bribes were given to officials. Ambushes were set. The instigators of the violence didn't care who was sacrificed, or what the cost was. And the soldiers didn't mind their price they had to pay, even if it meant death. Because this would save them a seat in the one way trip to Eternity, where their God would congratulate them on a job well done.

Not all of the Jews and the Arabs felt this way, however. But these were the ones who made the news. The ones who led the way in God's holy war were the zealots, the extremists. And they made the choices that caused the unrest to resurface. It was they who pulled the triggers, who trained the young and the innocent, and it was those people who strategically planned an attack, even on holy sites, where unsuspecting victims had their lives extinguished in a moment. And their families grieved and missed them. They mourned their senseless loss. And then vowed swift and vicious revenge, in the holy battle, for God.

Midway through '56 both sides of the warring factions were taking heavy losses. The two leaders hadn't spoken in over a year, Israel's Prime Minister, and the new Chairman of the PLO. Both vowed they would see justice done on their enemy. And both had the true God on their sides. Talks had been attempted, but they got nowhere. The USE's military was brought in at one point and an attempt was made to put an end to the violence using force. But the end result would have been worse than the current situation, and the last thing that the world government needed was the total destruction and demolishing of an entire country on their record. There didn't seem to be any way to do it without enormous devastation on a national level.

The Regional Ruler for the Mid-East, Mr Dar Somola, wasn't being of much assistance in this matter either. He held his position with the other Rulers at the USE headquarters, and he would represent his people at their meetings. But then when he went back to deal with the problem on the field, he would sympathize with the needs of those directly involved in the war. He did well in not siding with one or the other, but because he would not take a stance against either side, the war was permitted to continue. He allowed the violence to continue, and so could not be a part of the solution.

Jerusalem itself was secure however, since the Society's main office was there. Nothing would or could penetrate the security arranged not only around the GPP compound, but also the immediate vicinity. In addition multiple posts were set up along the periphery of the whole city. And at all times the entire border was patrolled by soldiers watching and guarding, to ensure the safety of their leaders. Their military technology and manpower were second to none. Nothing or no one entered the city without top authorization, and without their knowledge. But regardless of these measures, Green Peace Place was in a war zone by the end of that year.

The moment the bombs and the violence began in the area, Supreme Commander Draik ordered the immediate deployment of troops in that area. Many were killed at that time, at the start, but Cazara intervened and put a stop to the offensive attack against both Jew and Muslim. He ordered the lockdown of the city of Jerusalem, but called off the attack. It is here that we resume our story.

✦ ✦ ✦

39

Director Cazara was meeting with the now ten Rulers of the seven regions of the Earth in Davos, Switzerland. It simply wasn't safe enough to meet together in Jerusalem then. With all the action going on so nearby, it was declared a war zone. The distinguished delegates were housed in the best accommodations that the Swiss had to offer. After all these were the upper echelons, in fact the highest level on Earth. Above them there wasn't anything else, only Cazara himself. Europe's leader was there, Donald Carleighs. And Ta dar Somola of the Middle Eastern division. He would need to give a first hand perspective as to the state of the situation, and offer insights that none of the others could give. Technically it was Chairman Lee's territory being in Asia, but now that the eastern area was portioned off and given its own leader, Lee's say in their matters were more a formality. The newest member was there, Russia's second-in-command, Mr Novoskor. All had congratulated him on his new appointment. He was happy to be there, but not for that reason. This was a secondary function to him. His first duty was to the Russian people, and the ensuring at all times that their freedom was preserved and maintained.

All of the Rulers of the United Society of Earth were present that day by mandate. Chairman Cazara had summoned them there as a first step in determining the fate, of one nation, and two peoples. They met in the GV Conference Center, only Davos' best for their highest-level guests from the four corners of the Earth. There was the usual introductions and announcing of the new Kings of the Earth, and much was made of their willingness to participate in this matter of international security. Once the preliminaries were over, they met in the Council Chamber, especially designed just for Cazara and his regional administration.

They permitted Mr Dar Somola to speak first giving a solemn account of the grave and troubling situation in Israel. He spoke with regret that neither they, nor himself, nor the world government could resolve this problem. He passionately spoke of the Peace Treaty and how good it was when it had worked, and how they had indeed achieved peace for so long. That was, until the present year, when the violence began again, and they were then right back to where they started.

"No disrespect Mr Chairman please, but where has it gotten us? Nowhere! What has it accomplished? Israel has returned to its former state of political turmoil, and now the battle rages on in her streets, just the same if not worse than before! My fellow Rulers, Mr Lee, what can we do?"

Next Mr Chung Wang Lee followed with his knowledge of the situation at hand, it being his Region, and then he gave his and his staff's prospected possible solutions. They proceeded with a discussion as to other possible ways to resolve this age old problem. Many legitimate possibilities were presented. All were focussed on this problem since it affected the stability of the region, and this in turn affected the economy of the rest of the world. In fact some even went so far as to say that the economy in some respects hinged on, not Israel alone but definitely the Mid-East, due to the oil industry. Cazara himself said little. There was a moderator present who kept the meeting in order, so he simply listened. He absorbed all of their concerns, but the solutions he paid little or no attention at all to.

He had called this meeting more for ceremonial reasons than functional. He had been considering some different options himself. And one stood out in his mind more than the others. But for the sake of appearances he had the meeting of the Regional Rulers in Davos. There he would listen, or appear to. And there he would discuss the different possibilities. And it was there, that the Rulers of the Regions of the Earth's United Society would decide what to do with the Israel problem.

Late in the afternoon of that same day, when all the Regions had finished all of their possibles and probables, that was when Cazara began. He began with sympathy for the two warring parties. And for the region. He also verbalized his concern for the international community, the economy, and expressed his distaste for this kind of black mark on the USE's perfect record. His Rulers up to this point gave grunts or murmurs of wholehearted approval.

"Time is marching on, gentlemen." He looked at his audience sympathetically, paternally, wisely. "And we must do something about this subject, and take care of it once and for all. This is not an isolated incident. And I don't think this problem is going to go away." Up to this point, all ten representatives were in agreement. "But my fellow rulers it is time to take action. Decisive action. And measures that will end this dilemma, once, and for all." His last few words accentuated by pounding his fist on the conference table, first on once, and then again on all. More alert now, the rulers paid more attention to what was next.

He then asked them to consider a world without war, a society without racial and religious prejudice. He also asked them to think of their own present world, but without its present problem. They all seemed to agree that it was the sole trouble that they had had to deal with over the past year or so. "Although it may seem simplistic in its approach, 'Eliminate the problem' has worked in the past, so I ask you: Why can't it work now, for this?" Some were trying to anticipate what he meant by this, and some were feeling a little uncomfortable.

"It comes down to this: the Muslims, and the Jews. The former group being quite large, and represented in various nations throughout the Earth. The latter being but a small people, concentrated mainly in one nation. Now I put the question to you. If one ought to be eliminated, then which would you choose?" There were murmurs, but this time not of approval. There were questioning faces, but at the same time, some knowing and approving looks around the room.

They further discussed the details of what Cazara was proposing and discovered that, though superficially, his plan seemed inhumane, it did have some merit, in that there were times when a sacrifice had to be made for the greater good. Some of the ten who disagreed were coming over to the Chairman's side so that there was a majority in the end who agreed with him. There were others who opposed, but it meant little to him. He could proceed without their approval. The one who did pose a minor threat was dar Somola. But he would deal with him. He planned to keep him occupied until the whole mess was completely over and done with. By occupied, this meant exiled, and under the highest security.

The meeting was wrapped up, each went his separate way, but Cazara would go to meet with his military leader, Halloway Draik. He would go over his plan with him again, and finalize the details. They would meet the very next day at an undisclosed location and settle this problem for good. There was no press allowed at the Davos meeting, and there were few who even knew about it. This whole issue had become a T4 Level issue, and that meant only top personnel were involved, and no one else.

The next day Joseph Cazara and Halloway Draik sat across from one another, making the final decisions and fine tuning the plan to effectively and in one blow, stop the violence in the Mid-East forever. In spite of minor opposition from certain leaders, the plan went forward, and those opposed were either pacified, or silenced in one way or another. The location was remote, and very few other than the two men present knew about it. Only those who it was absolutely imperative to include, knew. There was little else in the room but the table, chairs, an overhead lamp, and the few necessities in front of the men to conduct their business effectively. Cazara had his laptop, and the General, a few rolled up maps of Israel and the surrounding area.

Their plan was to destroy the Jewish population within the borders of the nation of Israel. Every last person. They had discussed various other strategic possibilities. The Muslims were too numerous and spread out over too many countries.

What was more, they had terrorist connections that the Jews had nothing to do with. If they had to destroy one, if one had to be eliminated, sacrificed was the word they preferred, it would have to be the Jews. There was just no other way. They had been over it, and over it. But that was not the purpose of this meeting. This meeting was to prepare to strike.

The USE headquarters residing in the capital of Israel posed a problem. This definitely ruled out a nuclear strike. And to have any kind of attack, the Palestinians were going to be needed to be evacuated before the action was taken. This also posed a problem. It could be done, but it would need to be planned out carefully. So they devised a plan, with the use of highly advanced biological weapons. The Palestinians would indeed be evacuated, quickly, and during the night. The GPP would also be absent for some reason or other at that time. The biological missiles would be dropped, and effectively eliminate, and sacrifice the Jewish peoples, for the greater good of all mankind. The Palestinians would be returned unharmed to their new country, after the clean-up of course. There would no longer be any violence in the newly named nation of 'Palestine' and the whole region would be a safer place as well. The GPP compound would not be harmed or destroyed in any way, and business could resume once the whole unpleasant incident was completely over and done with. In addition, the USE would not only be free of any bad press, but would be congratulated on a job well done. After all, who could oppose them? They ruled the world.

And so it was done. It was carried out just as the Rulers had decided, and just how Supreme Commander Draik had ordered it using his troops and his jets. The missiles were dropped, the millions were killed, and it all happened so smoothly, so efficiently, that as time went on, the memories began to fade. There were a few minor incidents such as the so-called twinkle effect but the overall objective was achieved. And in late December of '56 the problem was settled, the Muslims took over what was formerly known as Israel, and peace finally reigned. Peace rose out of the ashes, and from the graves of those deceased. It grew from the soil like a new plant evolving out of a single dead seed. And it blossomed in the months that followed, and the fruit of their labors paid off from the devastation, and destruction, and the sacrifice which had to be made.

✦ ✦ ✦

40

Peace did reign, in the weeks and the months after the changeover of Israel to Palestine. The new inhabitants celebrated their victory, and their brothers in their region and from other parts of the world congratulated them and rejoiced with them. Operations resumed in Jerusalem at One Green Peace Place. The world was indeed a better place. There was some backlash in the media, but it was quickly squelched, and the offenders made to restate their views, rewrite their stories, and in fact make a public apology. All was in order again. The problem behind them, they could press on to a new and even better world. One in which there was no war, and prosperity reigned under the command and strong and stable leadership of Director Cazara, the Ruler of the World. And all had to agree that it was truly a wise and necessary deed that was done, in the name of global peace.

That is, all, except one last voice. One last resistance to the USE and its authority. A lone force against the new Society. A single entity remained in opposition to Executive Director Cazara. During the time of the peace treaties and the elimination of terrorism all of the networks were shut down, disbanded. But there was one solitary, small but determined organization that slipped through the cracks. ACTA was still alive. And its members were active, but at a very minimal level. Their membership was low key, and they met infrequently. No one knew of their existence, except a choice few who belonged to their group.

Their mission was to destroy those who prevented people from following extreme conservative Islamic teachings. And Cazara had crossed that line, first when he advocated that the Muslims join with the Jews and allow their religions to coexist. For that alone he deserved death. But then he did later give Palestine their country back, so that was working on his side. But they simply could not tolerate this OWR religious system. It desecrated the name of Allah, and it allowed Muslims and infidels to pray together, and even go to a mosque! It was an outrage, and it had to be stopped.

So for years after the Peace Treaty they had been planning, and waiting, and preparing for a future time, when they could be sure that it would work. They didn't care how long it took, they would wait. And they did wait for several years, but the elimination of Israel took place and this put their plans on hold, for a few months. They waited a little more for the dust to settle, until they could see what they should do next. In the time that they waited they would train. Privately. Secretly. Where no one else could see. Where watching eyes were absent, and listening ears could not hear. And no mouth could tell of what they were preparing for.

There was one student out of them all that showed more promise. His name was Ageez. He was young when he began, only a boy, but they liked to train their men early. He trained in fighting, marksmanship, use of the blade, also survival training, anatomy, and coping with psychological and other types of torment. By the age of fifteen he was a soldier, strong and ready for action, mentally, physically, and spiritually. He was also trained in Islamic extremist teachings. He was small in stature, even for a fifteen year old. But this would later work to his and his fellow brothers of the network's advantage. And he was left handed, which would also turn out to be advantageous in the end.

He was trained those eight long years since he began, to fight and to defend God's army and the people of Islam. But it was in the last two of those eight that his superiors noticed his extraordinary zeal, his small but wiry physique, and his devotion to their view of the faith. He was chosen for a special mission, in fact the most important mission in their history. Perhaps it was, unbeknownst to them, the most significant act which would change the fortunes of men. He was prepared and made ready for the single purpose of assassinating Joseph Cazara.

Planned meticulously months in advance, their plan was to penetrate the security of the GPP compound and carry out their mission from the inside. It would mean almost without a doubt, certain death for the soldier, but that was his calling, it was his reward. He was honored to be the one who would carry out this act for God. It was arranged through one of the members, who had a friend, who had a friend, who had a cousin, who had a friend, who worked on the cleaning crew which went into the GPP compound weekly to do certain duties. It was through this that Ageez was smuggled in. One of the cleaners noticed that there was a small cabinet kept behind Cazara's desk. Memorizing it they were able to make an exact replica of their own. The plan was to bring in the copy, with Ageez inside, switch the old one with their replacement cabinet, and let their soldier do his work.

He would be in the cabinet at the most 6 hours, but he had trained for this type of situation. Also the cabinet would have to pass security checks. But they would disguise it to look like their everyday equipment. Ageez would also need to carry a knife. The knife, however, was one made of a new alloy, designed to not set off detectors. And yet it was sharp as a fine razor. The only problem was the switching of the cabinets in Cazara's personal office. They would have to resolve that part before the day of entry.

The day arrived, the cabinet was safely delivered to One Green Peace Place. Then the cleaner made it through the first security check. But at the second check the guard started poking around in the cleaner's equipment. Acting casual but with nerves on the edge of snapping, he told a crude joke, which for a moment took the guard's mind off the equipment. He laughed, relaxed a little, and then let him pass. Breathing a silent sigh of relief, he wheeled his cart down the hall and began his duties. Finishing the first floor, his partner finished the second. So he went to the third. Finally, it was time to go to the fifth level. This was where Cazara's personal office was.

Whistling as he exited the elevator, but increasingly nervous, he started on the first room of that floor. When it came time to do Cazara's office there was a final security check. He made it through. Acting natural he began to sing, but in a raspy, off key, tinny kind of voice. Cazara looked up and asked if he had some kind of throat trouble, which the cleaner replied that he did. The Director picked up his folder and sat up. The cleaner reduced his singing to humming, but just as badly. Then Cazara walked through the door into the adjoining room. This was the big chance. He quickly and as quietly as possible, exchanged the cabinets. The only difference between them, was that there was no latch on theirs. And its hinges were oiled to perfection. No sound was made when it opened. The cleaner gave the three soft taps on the top of the cabinet to tell Ageez he was in place. With heart pounding the maintenance worker finished his duties, but not too quickly, and then exited the room.

Then Cazara returned to his office. And sat at his desk. And continued with his work. He received a few calls, had one visitor in the form of an aide, and went to a shelf twice in the time that the unnoticed visitor in the room waited. When he was sure, when he was prepared and ready, he would step out of the cabinet.

Finally, it was time. He softly pushed open the swinging door. He saw his unsuspecting target directly in front of him. He stepped onto the carpet silently with his naked feet. He crept silently and directly behind the ruler. When he got near the back of the large black leather chair, it was just like he had rehearsed it again and again during training. He kept his extremities tight, in close to his small body, until the right moment. Then…in one motion his left hand with the blade in it, rose up and around the neck of the victim in front of him. And just under his left ear, severed the carotid artery, causing a sudden flow and pulse of blood from his neck.

Cazara felt the movement as soon as it was too close, and so too late. With blood pulsing from his throat he swung his right arm around to strike his attacker. But he fell and slipped against his chair, tumbling to the floor. Delirious and dizzy he called for help. The youth, finishing his primary task, took out a piece of paper from his pocket, and with the knife stabbed it onto the surface of the wooden desk, pinning it securely in place.

The assassin then jogged out of the room and into a larger corridor. Someone with a pistol drawn called for him to stop and he started shouting in response as he ran down the hall, 'Allah Akhbar! Allah Akhbar!' Not knowing if he was armed or not the guard called for his immediate cooperation to lay down on the floor with his hands behind his head. Not complying, and also his partner shouting from the office of the attack that Cazara was fatally wounded, he shouted once more but the assailant kept running. He began unloading the ammunition in his pistol and the young soldier's body jerked forward with the impact of the bullets, until he crumpled onto the plushly carpeted floor. With many footsteps pounding toward him he breathed out his last few breaths, repeating quietly in his own language, "God is great, God is great," now only in a whisper, with the last of the air escaping from his punctured, bleeding lungs. And he looked toward heaven as he passed from this world into the next, certain that he gave his life for a good purpose.

Those who came to their leader's rescue found him, as would be expected, gasping, trying in vain to put pressure on the wound to stop the bleeding. But the wound was a clean severing of the major artery, it was expertly inflicted, and it did what the killer intended it to do. Paramedics were called but by the time they would arrive it would be too late. The aides and security people did what they could for Mr Cazara, but within nine minutes of the deed, his lifeless body lay on the floor, in the office of the most powerful center in the world.

The note pinned to the desk with the murder weapon, clearly outlined that it was the work of an undetected terrorist network. Once it was translated from Arabic they were able to gather all the information they wanted from it. The name of the network claiming responsibility was ACTA, and they threatened that whoever opposes God will have to deal with them. And that anyone who replaced their dead leader, attempting the same type of religious amalgamation, would receive the same fate.

✦ ✦ ✦

41

The Council wanted to act quickly, both in the apprehension of the connected terrorist organization members, and in the carrying out of the wishes of their late leader. The media, as soon as they had heard about Cazara's assassination, covered it with everything they had. It was the biggest and basically the only story that was published and broadcast that day in the news. It was either the step by step recounting of the actual event, or a write up on the terrorist organization allegedly responsible, or some story related to what had happened. The funeral coverage was going to be just as big, and would be carried with as much if not more focus and attention.

Commander Draik took control of the investigation, and recruited his best people on the case. They would follow the trail, beginning with their clues at the scene of the crime, and also their most recent intelligence on terrorism. They had their assassin and had caught him with his smoking gun. And he had already been brought to swift justice at their own hand. But those evil powers behind him, those twisted leaders who sent him, he would hunt them down until they were wiped out from the face of the Earth. Draik would make certain this time that no form of terrorism would ever resurface again.

According to the instructions of the deceased the service

was to be the very next day after his death. His administration and his fellow Rulers made sure that every detail was followed, and that it was a very public and lavish affair. Only the very highest quality and the very best were good enough for this one ruler of all the Earth. They were expecting visitors from all over the globe. All the leaders were invited, and royalty as well. His body would lie in state at the Green Peace Palace, they had decided to rename it, when the actual funeral service would commence, and thereafter. The Most Reverend Deseronta Shalee himself would officiate.

Because of the masses of people who wished to pay their last respects to their beloved leader, the Council devised a plan. It simply was not possible to accommodate the literally hundreds of millions of mourners who desired to see him one last time. Chairman Rajiv set up a virtual arrangement which appeared to satisfy all. He and his team hooked up 18 different web sites with a view from a live camera on Mr Cazara's body as he lay in state in the Palace. Even with all 18, they still had overloading problems because of the volume of people wishing to view the late Executive Director of USE. At the Palace itself, the in-person viewing was limited to a very small circle. But this also could be watched live on the Internet, or on live TV.

The day for the funeral arrived. There were thousands attending and special arrangements were made to accommodate the seating of the large crowd. Every nation who could attend was there, and if the head of state wasn't able to attend, dignitaries were sent to represent their country. The ten Rulers had special seating up on the platform. The Council Members were all present, and also were on the raised level in a higher position than the rest. The sun even seemed veiled and pale that day, as the world sat and watched, from the audience there in Jerusalem, and from around the world in their homes. That day was declared an international day of mourning. In front of the massive crowd, at center stage stood the ornate elaborate coffin, with the USE blue and white flag draped over the top.

His only living relative, an aging uncle, approached the stage when he was called. He carefully and slowly, with the aid of a cane made his way to the microphone on its stand. He began by telling of the boy he knew and loved and of seeing him grow up. And then how he watched him as that boy turned into a teenager. In his own simple way, he related how he felt about his nephew Joseph.

"I always knew he was different," he was saying. "Not just smarter than the rest, but he had that something extra special. He had a star quality you don't see every day. He knew where he was going to. Yep, he had his work all cut out for him, even when he was a youngster. People tried to sway him off the track, but he just kept on. And there was just no stopping him. That's my Joseph." And he looked over at the coffin, "Goodbye Joseph. We'll miss ye." He wiped a tear from his eye and hobbled back to his seat, attended by one of the ushers.

There were several highest level heads of state who gave their own views of the tragedy of the passing of the world leader. First, the ruler of England, King Edwin gave his testimony of his experience of Mr Cazara. Then the Presidents of Russia, the United States, and then China. Several of the ten Regional Rulers also stood up and said a few words in honor of their Ruler. Finally, three of the USE Council gave their deepest sympathy for the loss of their Chairman and friend.

When all of these were finished, the Rev. Shalee stood, and

with ornate, multicolored robes and a jeweled headpiece, he approached the center stage with great ceremony and began his eulogy.

"Presidents, dignitaries, Kings and Queens, distinguished guests, Rulers of the World, and my fellow Councilmen," he announced nodding appreciatively in the direction of those on the stage, and in the crowd, and in a high and formal voice continued. "We gather here today in the common bond of grief, at the passing of our dear leader and friend, Mr Joseph Sargan Cazara." Silence for a moment. There was only the hissing of the sound system, barely audible. "Joseph Cazara was not just a good leader and a good person...he was a great Ruler. He was in fact the greatest leader the world has ever known." Pausing again, and looking around at his audience. "No one could contest that Joseph Cazara accomplished more in his limited lifetime, than what great leaders of the past had strived to achieve all of their lives. No one can compare..."

In the coffin behind him, the body lay on soft satin cushions. A 4800 Khoda suit was put on him, and the wound on his neck was covered with makeup so that nothing was seen. His arms were laid across his chest with great care. His rings were showing on his fingers. It was dark in that space below the lid of the 1.2 million K elaborate coffin housing this irreplaceable, this unique and great leader of mankind.

And then he opened his eyes.

Unfolding his arms, he began to push on the lid of the burial container. "...a Peace Treaty that changed..." Shalee was saying, when gasps and shocks of horror from the crowd caused him to stop in mid-sentence. Then he turned around just in time to see, the body of Joseph Cazara, sit up in his coffin!

He staggered back a step with a hand over his mouth. And then Cazara turned to Shalee and said, "I'm alive."

Finding his own voice when his leader spoke, he stammered "But, how?…You were…dead?" He almost choked on the words as he forced them out.

He made his way hesitantly, toward the man who was then beckoning him, and managed to help him out of the coffin. Cazara stood, and the crowd was astonished. There was nervous laughter, and tears and shouts of amazement all at once. In the chaos, Mr Cazara, arm in arm with his Minister of Religion, approached the edge of the platform. And raising up his hands he shouted louder now, "I'm alive!" And again, "I'm alive!!!" The crowd was cheering; some of the Rulers had approached from the sidelines and were coming to see him, to touch him. Should they congratulate him? What should they do? What was happening?!

✦ ✦ ✦

42

Dear Dalee,

Greetings in the name of the One and Only God, YHWH.

Thanks be to God that I was spared the evil and wicked deeds of that monster who destroyed my precious people and my nation. I mourned their loss and ask for strength and wisdom to go on. Thank God that I was in the United States the day of the disaster in Israel. So very few were spared, and I was one of the very very fortunate ones. I do not know if I should be glad or full of remorse. Perhaps it would be better for me to have perished with my brothers in Jerusalem.

I have one important find to share with you. Since all of these things have happened I have taken it upon myself to delve deeper and to research into this matter more broadly. In all of my searchings I found one point which is of critical importance. I have some friends here in California, and they have pointed me in the direction of the Book of Revelation.

Now this is highly irregular for a man of my position and faith, but please hear me out. This Book of Revelation is the last book in the Christian Bible, and in the 13th Chapter, in the middle of that chapter it reads:

'…And made the Earth and its inhabitants worship the first beast, whose fatal wound had been healed.'

I wanted to send this to you right away so that you would have the insight that I had when I saw this.

Dear Dalee, please do take care, and I will write you more when I know more. It is all I can say for the time being.

May God protect you and your families,

David

Outside the wind howled. And it called out to him through the bedroom window. He could hear it clearer now. He listened. Had it stopped? He got up, walked over to the window and opened it wide. It was cold, and it was night. But he could hear it now, whispering…"deeeee…stiiiii…." Then the wind again. Then finally, "…neeee." He leaned out further; the snow was swirling and blowing near his face. But this time he caught it… "deeees…sss…tiny." Yes, that was it. *Destiny.*

✦ ✦ ✦

'Et stetit super harenam maris...'

'And the beast stood on the shore of the sea...'